Us in the 21st Century

Annie Leigh

*Bibliografische Information der Deutschen Nationalbibliothek: Die Deut-
sche Nationalbibliothek verzeichnet diese Publikation in der Deutschen
Nationalbibliografie; detaillierte bibliografische Daten sind im Internet
über dnb.dnb.de abrufbar.*

*Die automatisierte Analyse des Werkes, um daraus Informationen insbe-
sondere über Muster, Trends und Korrelationen gemäß §44b UrhG („Text
und Data Mining") zu gewinnen, ist untersagt.*

Verlag: BoD · Books on Demand GmbH, Überseering 33, 22297 Hamburg,
bod@bod.de

Druck: Libri Plureos GmbH, Friedensallee 273, 22763 Hamburg

ISBN: 978-3-8192-2868-1

Thank you for picking up this book.

It's an honour for me.

— Chapter 1 —

The twenty-first century was said to be a place of boundless wonder.

People were exhilarated about it. A new millennium.

They called it a new start—a book full of unwritten pages and new hopes.

Nao had always wondered whether he would make it that far, if he could see the promised land everyone had been dreaming about. Maybe one day, his life would just magically flip around like a page on a calendar, opening up a new, clean sheet without the smudges of a hopeless past defiling it.

Although at this very moment, it seemed like he didn't have to worry about the *woulds* and *ifs*. He might just die altogether before he could even catch a glimpse of it.

The boys from his class surrounded him. Two squared up in front of him, while two others stood behind his chair where he was sitting, trying to eat his lunch. Right now, it looked like that choice had been taken from him as well.

He dropped the spoon into his soup and looked up. They sneered at him.

It had been two weeks since his transfer to this school. And he had already seen those grinning grimaces more than enough.

An arm was wrapped around his shoulders—it was Sho. "Miyamoto, my friend," he whispered beside his ear. "Your lunch looks great. The boys and I are starving. How about you buy us some snacks from the vending machine?"

Nao stared at the table and brushed the arm off. "I don't want to."

"You don't want to? But you are the newbie here," Sho lamented, slinging his arm around Nao once again. "You can't let your seniors buy their own food."

Sho was so close that Nao could smell his deodorant. He could feel his breath fanning his cheek. The warm air was spiked with the scent of cigarettes. Nao felt nauseous.

"I told you, I don't want to," he said.

Sho huffed. He clenched his jaw and looked around to make sure no teachers were watching them. "You are messing with the wrong people, my friend." For a second, they glared at each other.

Then, Nao shrugged. "Are you finished? I want to eat the soup before it gets col—"

But he couldn't finish his sentence. His face was pushed into the bowl in front of him. Soup spilled over the edges as Nao's face was dunked into the hot liquid. He struggled to escape the grip on his neck. He kicked and punched aimlessly around, and as the hand on his head finally loosened, the bowl tumbled over the edge of the table. With an ear-deafening crash of metal on tiles, the bowl hit the floor. Rolling down the aisle of tables, it dragged a trail of soup behind it.

Nao gasped for air. He wiped his face with his sleeves when he heard the roar of laughter. The boys threw their heads back in joy, their ugly grimaces etching deeper and deeper into their faces.

"People like you should be careful," Sho warned. "Let's try to get along better next time, okay?" He smiled, patted Nao on the back, and left with his friends. Their laughter still ringing across the hall.

Nao's heart was pounding. He looked around, but the few students watching them had already turned their attention back to their meals.

It didn't surprise Nao. This wasn't like his previous school. Or like most educational institutions. After all, this was a school for problem children. Who cared if a student's head was dunked into his lunch? As long as it wasn't their own.

Nao despised that school. Just like the one he had attended before. He was tired of students positioning themselves above others, of stupid hierarchies and frail dominance. But what he despised even more was leaving school and going home.

He had spent the rest of the break picking noodles and vegetables out of his hair. It was quite possible that there were still bits left in his black strands, but he didn't bother. He doubted his parents would be surprised.

The way home was arduously long from his new school. In the past, there had been a car picking him up and dropping him off from classes every day. Even though his old school had merely been a twenty-minute walk away from the building he lived in. But now that he had been shoved off to the outskirts of the city, there was no one coming for him.

Nao plugged in his discman, put on earphones and walked down the street. In his ears played another vapid song on another meaningless day.

The elevator brought him up to the thirtieth floor. It wasn't the penthouse, but it was close to it. The white marble tiling with the golden embellishments all over the floor and walls was quick to tell you in what kind of world you had fallen into.

Nao slid off his shoes and shoved them next to the entrance. The apartment smelled of mild detergent and fresh flowers—their housekeeper Mrs. Takahashi must have bought them today.

It was his mother's quirk to always have fresh flowers on display in every room. Sometimes she would shoo away Mrs. Takahashi in the early hours of Sunday morning to buy a whole new bouquet if she found even one petal amiss.

Nao tried to sneak into his room before anyone could spot him, yet failed. "Nao." A deep voice resounded from the living room. He stopped in his tracks. It was his father's voice.

He was perched in an armchair, reading a news magazine. Just like his voice, his father was the epitome of masculinity. Tsuyoshi Miyamoto was tall and broad-shouldered. He had dense black hair, a protruding jaw and pervasive, dark eyes. His forehead was speckled with wrinkles, which seemed to have only grown deeper in the last few months.

"I wanted to inform you that we'll be meeting your grandparents for dinner."

Nao's face dropped before he could control himself. He tried to put back on a neutral expression, but it was already too late.

"No discussion! Your grandfather asked for it. And after everything you've ruined, it's your duty to shoulder the consequences! Man up and try for once not to embarrass our family. Your brother manages it as well."

Nao clenched his fists. "Yes," he said and turned around to leave.

"And Nao," his father added. "No word about…that topic, understand?"

He nodded. "Of course."

Nao peeled himself out of his school uniform, which had brown stains around the collar and a sharp stench of broth. He threw it into the laundry basket and pulled out a white dress shirt and black pants from his wardrobe. He didn't like them. They were too tight, had too many buttons, and reminded him of his school uniform. But his parents always insisted on dressing formally when meeting with their grandparents.

Though Nao doubted that dressing up would change his grandfather's opinion about him.

They were supposed to meet their grandparents in a restaurant nestled inside the heart of the city. A chauffeur drove Nao with his parents and brother to the building it was located in.

An elevator took them up to the thirty-second floor, where a waitress led them to a private room their grandparents had booked in advance. They were already waiting for them inside.

The entire east side of the room was made out of glass. Behind it rested the glowing city. Hundreds of lights illuminated the depths of the night. It was so bright that there were surely no stars to be seen in the sky.

"Father!" Nao's own father said joyfully as they entered the room.

His grandfather smiled widely. "I'm glad you could make it so quickly, Tsuyoshi." They shook hands and sat down. The rest of them followed.

Although shrunken in size over the decades, Nao's grandfather was still surprisingly tall. It was a trait his own father had clearly inherited from him. Nao and his brother had not.

"I'm delighted to finally see you again. Especially my grandchild Toyo. I heard he got first place in the school exams yet again."

Toyo, his little brother, blushed beside Nao.

"Yes, we are very proud of him. If everything goes as planned, he might get an offer for a scholarship from the Eastern University soon."

"And this at his young age!" His grandfather shook his head in awe. "Though I'd love to see him in the Western University too since it's the university I attended." He grinned at his grandchild.

Toyo just shook his head in embarrassment.

Their grandfather was right in one thing: Nao's little brother was still pretty young. With only fourteen years, he had achieved so much more than Nao ever had. He was top of his year, the classroom president as well as the vice president of the student council. He had participated in a number of school contests and won several of them. His future shone twice as much as Nao's ever had.

Although if one looked at Toyo without knowing him, they'd be surprised. He looked much younger than fourteen and appeared almost childlike with his thin frame and small stature.

Nao was still sometimes surprised by how eerily alike his brother and mother looked. Physically, there seemed to be no drop of their father's blood in him. Their mother and Toyo both had the same feathery black hair, round, innocent eyes, and dainty features. From afar, they looked so much alike it was almost scary.

Nao, on the other hand, took after none of his parents. He was neither broad nor thin, neither bulky nor dainty. Sometimes he wondered how he could be related to them.

"If there's anything you want, you can tell us. Great achievements deserve to be rewarded," their grandmother said with a smile on her thin, red-painted lips.

"Thank you." Toyo smiled. "But you should also praise Nao. He got fifth place in the last exam season." Toyo rested a hand on Nao's shoulder. "Right?"

The smiles of the adults dropped. It was like lightning had struck the table. Nao could almost hear the tension crackling in the sudden silence.

"Yes, but that was in his old school," his father responded after a long pause of stifling stillness, which loomed above them like the calm before a storm.

His grandfather cleared his throat. "I heard that your brother has been transferred to a school for…*difficult children.*"

"Y-yes, father. That was unfortunate. But our eldest son is trying his best to improve his grades and get accepted into a respectable university next year. Isn't that right?"

Nao was taken aback by the sudden wave of attention. He caught his father's stern gaze and nodded silently.

"It is truly unfortunate. But I have to admit that I'm not thoroughly surprised." His grandfather's eyes grabbed Nao's attention. They were the same unfathomable, pervasive eyes his father possessed. Nao's heartbeat immediately doubled.

"From the day of his birth, I could tell he would bring nothing but trouble to the Miyamoto family. It was written all over his face. I have a good eye for things like that. If you ask me, he shouldn't spend too much time with Toyo. One bad apple with a worm inside can contaminate the whole basket."

"Yes. I will take that into consideration, father."

His grandfather stared directly at Nao. "I will think about your academic future, Nao. But you should at least have enough commitment to your family to marry a decent woman and keep the family line alive, shouldn't you?"

Nao could feel his father's eyes piercing him from the side. He didn't have to look to know what demand was hidden inside them. Nao knew better than to ignore them.

"Yes," he said.

His grandfather nodded slowly.

"Don't worry. We will make sure Nao won't bring any more shame to the family name," his father assured him with a strained smile.

"Good. Now that that's out of the way, we should start dining and raise a toast to my beloved grandchild Toyo's achievements."

— Chapter 2 —

Nao wasn't exactly a top student, but he wasn't a total failure either. As Toyo had said a few days prior, he had received fifth place in his old school's exams.

Maybe it had been just luck, but Nao was actually a fast learner. He could memorise things easily and understand connections fast; he just didn't have the motivation to study. Contrary to his parents, he had never valued academic success.

He didn't know where this dislike came from—whether it was a natural disposition or stemmed from his family's early pressure. As the eldest son, all of his family's wishes and expectations had been cast upon him.

He was but a child—young and malleable, but also naive and breakable. He couldn't possibly carry the weight of their aspirations on his narrow shoulders. And he definitely couldn't grow with it pressing him into the ground. His whole life there was never the question of what Nao wanted but only the demand to fulfil his family's duties.

Maybe that was why he had turned out like this. Standoffish and aloof. Immune to ambition and success alike.

Either way, even if he'd liked to study, it would have been impossible in these circumstances. He might have been transferred to a school for problematic children, but it was also an all-boys school, which meant the classroom turned into a zoo once the teachers left.

Screams and shouts, laughter and chatter filled the already way too thick air. Nao tried to concentrate and finish his homework for the next class, but the volume was draining the energy out of him, like water beneath the scorching sun.

He sat alone at his desk. The other students had met up in small groups. They were chatting loudly, laughing and playing games together on their handheld consoles. It was an onslaught of noises Nao tried to block out, though it was as easy as ignoring a mosquito buzzing around one's head.

He focused on writing down numbers on a sheet of paper when something hit him squarely in the back. With a thump, the object bounced off him and rolled to his feet.

Nao turned around. At the back of the room stood a group of boys, waving at him awkwardly. "Sorry!" one of them called out. "We tried practicing our pitch. Can you throw it back?"

Nao gazed at them for a second and then turned around to continue working on his exercise.

The boys started to mumble. "Hey, newbie! Throw it back."

Nao didn't listen. He concentrated solely on his homework.

The mumbling grew louder. Nao blocked it out, just as he did with the rest of the noises, when suddenly there was a shadow emerging before him. A boy bent down and picked up the baseball.

"You could just throw it back instead of making me walk here," he said. "It's not that hard. Look." He tossed it to Nao, who instinctively dropped his pen and caught the ball in his hands.

"And now throw it back," the boy said.

Nao glared up at him. He was ready to see the ugly grin of his classmates sneering down at him, but to his surprise, the boy looked at him with an amicable smile.

Nao threw the ball back, harder than was appropriate.

"Thanks," the boy replied. "But no need to try to assassinate me with it." He gave Nao a crooked smile. It was peculiar, though. His voice was as light and joyous as the rippling of a stream, his eyes sparkled like the refracting sunlight curling on the surface of its water. It was almost like the semblance of an oasis in this barren wasteland.

To others it might look lighthearted and amicable, but to Nao it just seemed idiotic.

The boy turned around and walked back to his friends while throwing the baseball up and down in his right hand.

The boys in the back were still whispering. "No wonder that loser is always alone," one of them muttered loud enough for Nao to hear.

He pretended he didn't notice them and picked up his pen again.

The food in the canteen was even worse than in his old school. Nao filled his tray with the watery rice and mushy curry, the only appetising thing being the small cookie served with it as dessert. It was Nao's favourite, thus he sneaked two on his plate.

He tried to wind through the groups of students playfully pushing and pulling each other in the line when someone squared up in front of him and blocked his way.

It was Sho and his three lackeys. Of course.

"Nao!" Sho said excitedly. "Long time no see."

Nao tried to walk over to the side, but one of the boys blocked him.

Sho took a step forward and slung his arm around Nao's shoulder, consciously making him bend down a little. "We didn't have a good start last time and I'm sorry about that. But now is a good time to try and get along." The arm around his shoulders was crushing him. His clavicle seemed to break beneath the pressure.

"You don't want to buy us food. That's okay. Just pay us with your lunch from now on."

Nao broke free from his grip. "Leave me alone."

Sho huffed.

"I'm asking you *nicely*."

"I do too," Nao responded. "Leave me alone."

They glared at each other.

Nao didn't like confrontation. He preferred his seclusion and the calmness that followed it. This was what he had learned to become comfortable with. But in this very moment, he didn't avert his eyes. And he could see that it made Sho furious.

Before he could react, his tray got thrown to the floor. The curry and rice splattered all over the ground, leaving splashes of brown and white on Nao's shoes.

"Wipe that arrogant look off your face, homo," Sho whispered between closed teeth. "I will make you regret this."

He took a deep breath and pushed Nao out of the way, heading toward the exit of the canteen.

Sho promised him payback, and surprisingly, he was a man of his word.

It happened merely a few days later.

It had been a long school day. The longest of the week to be exact.

Nao shouldered his backpack and put on his earphones. As every day, he listened to music on his discman while walking home.

Though it was late spring, the weather was still cold. The digits on the thermometers stagnated and there seemed to be no rise of temperature in sight.

The weather was unusual—colder, longer, and greyer than last year.

Nao was a bit chilly, yet he hadn't brought a jacket with him.

He walked out of the school gate, music playing in his ears, gravel crunching beneath his feet.

Since the school was nestled in the outskirts of the city, the area was fairly unpopulated. Low and aged buildings formed the sparse neighbourhood. Behind the frayed curtains was barely any movement. The only testimony to the presence of humans were the potted flowers on the windowsills. The purple and blue blossoms grew beautifully in the otherwise bleak environment.

Nao was walking along the narrow streets when Sho suddenly stepped out of an alley in front of him. With his hands in his pockets, he sneered at Nao, immediately causing goosebumps to trickle down the latter's spine.

Sho just pointed with his head at the alley he had come out from. He didn't say anything, and he didn't have to. Nao knew exactly what he wanted. For a moment, he thought about just retreating and ignoring him, but in the end, he knew Sho would never let him go that easily. So, he tensed his jaw and followed after him.

While walking, he took off his backpack and earphones. He wrapped the cable around the discman and put it in his bag, closing the zipper.

As he had expected, the three classmates always hanging around Sho were waiting for him in the alleyway. They stood between the dumpsters, which had been pushed against the walls. They were Yamamoto, Takamoto, and Kitamura, if Nao remembered their names correctly.

Sho stopped in front of him; his hands were still inside his pockets, posture slightly bent forward. His spiky black hair was shorter in the front and a bit longer in the back, giving him a distinct look of carelessness and rebellion. His thin lips curled up into a smile.

"I told you we'd see each other again," he said. "We still have a few things to discuss, after all."

Sho took a step forward and sighed dramatically. "You know, Nao, there is one thing I really hate; and that is disrespect. It bothers me when people don't know where their place is.

"I gave you so many chances to learn yours, and yet you still dare stare at me with that stupid face of yours. What's so hard to understand?" Sho jabbed his finger into Nao's chest. "*You* are the newbie. *I am* the senior. *You* are beneath me."

Nao stared squarely into Sho's eyes. "What do you want?"

Sho glared back. "I want you to kneel down and apologise."

He took a step back. A grin sprouting across his face. "Kneel down and apologise. And I might forget about everything."

Nao clenched his jaw. His hands twisted into fists. With furrowed brows, he looked at Sho, growling, "I would rather die."

Sho's mouth twitched. It took less than a second.

In the blink of an eye, Sho's fist was in the air and ready to strike, but Nao had expected it. He dodged the punch and landed his own fist in Sho's face. His punch was so strong and unexpected that his opponent stumbled backward against the wall.

After this, the world seemed to have been put on mute. Nao stared at Sho, surprised by his own action, while the latter touched his mouth, staining his fingers with blood.

Suddenly, Sho started laughing loudly. "You fucking bastard. I didn't know a homosexual could punch that hard." He wiped his mouth and looked over to his lackeys, who immediately understood.

Nao knew that this was his moment to run away. Still, they reacted faster than he could.

They grabbed him by his arms and flung him against the dumpster. From that moment onward, Nao didn't have the slightest chance. It was four against one, and though he tried his best to counter their attacks, he was only a human with two arms and two legs. Not enough to stand against four people and their longing for blood.

They punched him in his stomach, causing him to double over. They kicked and tore at him like he was paper—made to be crumpled and torn apart. Here and there, Nao managed to dodge an attack and counter with his own, but he ultimately couldn't win against them.

Eventually, Sho gave the sign to stop when he slumped to the ground. The metallic taste of dust and blood mixing in his mouth.

Sho looked down at Nao from above. "This is your place. Right there on the ground."

He crouched down next to his opponent, digging a hand into his hair, and pressed his head into the dirt. "We can repeat this lesson as often as you want, Nao. Until you finally understand that there are people in this world you should not mess with."

Sho smiled and rose again. He took a last excited, savouring glance at his victim before turning to his mates. "Let's go." He gestured and they strode out of the alley, leaving Nao alone between the dumpsters.

His body ached. He could feel his face swelling up. It'd been a long time since he'd been beaten up like this. He thought he had forgotten this pain—yet, as it turned out, one would never forget the aching of their body after being overpowered. The stinging of fresh wounds and dull pounding of bruised skin; it was always the same sensation, and therefore anchored painfully in Nao's consciousness.

For an indefinite while, Nao stayed on the ground. He stared at the clouds passing by in the distant sky until he found the strength to get up.

Nao knew he should feel angry and furious, ready to take revenge on Sho and his mates, but he was tired. Somehow he couldn't find the energy to get angry. His body was too exhausted and his head hurt too much.

He opened his backpack and took out his discman. He unwound the cable and put on his earphones. Listening to the same songs as always, he continued his way home.

It was already evening when he arrived. The sun had set and the night was slowly creeping in.

The street lights had turned on and glowed dimly in the half-dark. Nao knew he was far too late. When he entered the apartment, he could hear the clinking of cutlery and plates from the dining room. Carefully, he slid off his shoes and put his backpack on the ground. He then walked slowly to the dining area where his parents and Toyo were already eating.

Silently, he sat on the chair beside his little brother.

Nao knew what he looked like. There was a cut on his left cheek, which had doubled in size as it had swollen profusely. His lip was bloody and his knuckles bruised. Drops of blood stained the white collar of his school uniform.

He stared down at his empty plate, feeling his father's gaze on him.

Their housekeeper Mrs. Takahashi came out of the kitchen to fill Nao's plate, but his father waved her off. Quietly, she left the room.

"I see, you are the weak link in your class," his father said serenely while cutting a piece of steak.

"Did they find out about your little secret?" He skewered the meat with his fork, looking directly at his son.

Nao wanted to say something but he didn't know what, so he just stared at his lap, digging his fingers into the fabric of his pants.

"I have never had high expectations for you, Nao. You know that. But when you told us you are interested in men, I lost all hope in you." He brought the fork to his lips. He took the piece with his mouth, and for a moment, the only sound in the otherwise dead silent room was the meat being torn between his father's teeth.

After an excruciating while, he eventually broke the silence with a sigh. "Go to your room," he spoke, his voice was tough and bloody like the steak he had just consumed.

Nao stood up. Before he left, he turned around to look at his mother and brother, but, as always, they stayed silent. They had never spoken up for him. Not once. This was another of the many points those two had in common.

Nao left. He lay down in his bed, curled up, and eventually fell into a restless slumber.

— Chapter 3 —

After telling his parents, Nao had never made a big secret of his sexuality again.

He had never gone around and told people specifically about it, but he also didn't try to keep it a secret anymore.

He'd been absolutely terrified to tell his parents, although when he finally did, he had felt as light as a feather. It was the moment the burden of his best kept secret had finally been lifted off his shoulders. Yet that feeling had lasted merely a few seconds before his father's fist had landed in his face.

It was like Icarus falling from the heavens.

Nao remembered slumping to the ground. He'd felt his cheek stinging and his heart hammering against his ribs as the reality of his parents' reaction broke over him.

It was the angriest Nao had ever seen his father. And he understood why.

Getting bad grades, refusing to study, bad manners; all of those could be fixed. They were flaws able to be changed and improved to his father's liking. But feeling attracted to the same gender…

Even his father knew that this was a mortal flaw he could never fix—a shame he had to live with.

They'd never told his grandparents. Even without talking about it, Nao was aware that he could never tell them. In his father's mind, this was a secret he should keep to his death.

It probably would have been smarter to have never told the truth at all, but Nao had decided to do it anyway.

He had always been prone to making bad decisions, so he had just committed to another one.

And even though he was gay, there was little chance of his sexuality actually being lived out. After all, his heart was an ugly place. Devoid of anything special.

Who would ever want to get close to him anyway?

Poets loved to describe one's heart as filled with passions and feelings, loaded with the facets of human experiences and emotions. But Nao's heart was none of that. No, it wasn't some kind of flowery poem. It was simply filled with blood vessels and tissues. Tendons and nerves. It beat because that was its only purpose; not because it was stuffed to the brim with something special. His heart was not special and it certainly was not poetry material.

There was nothing to see. So how could someone possibly ever like him? When they'd try to enter his heart, only to see the sobering truth about him.

His heart could fear, it could ache and clench. It could make his chest feel like it was about to explode. He had forcibly learned to become familiar with those sensations. But to experience it fluttering or jumping, skipping in joy or singing in anticipation—he had not yet felt something like that. And he strongly doubted that he ever could.

There was nothing worth seeing in it. Even if someone could ever come close to his heart, they would only be disappointed by the numbing reality of how unsensational it was, and would hence realise that he was not worth loving.

Most of the time, he felt like he was not worthy of being loved either. Be it because of his boring appearance, aloof personality, or dull heart.

He was, in every aspect, unlovable. So much, in fact, that not even his own family could do so.

And if they couldn't, then who else would take the time to do it?

His heart wasn't an inviting shelter. It was blood and flesh, simply keeping him alive, allowing him to realise just how unwanted he was in this world.

And this was once again apparent in the way his classmates treated him.

The people from his school knew about it too. His sexuality surely was one of the reasons Sho liked to torment him, but Nao knew that it wasn't the only one.

He was sure that even if they hadn't known about it, they still would have picked on him. That's who Nao was—a person people liked to bully around.

He felt all of this anew when he returned to school after the weekend.

The marks of his fight with Sho were still visible on his face. His cheek had taken on a purplish-blue colour. It still stung when he touched it by accident, but at least it wasn't swollen anymore.

Nao's classmates started whispering about him as soon as he entered the classroom. They didn't seem to care whether they were loud enough for him to hear.

Nao tried to ignore them, nonetheless. He sat down at his desk while they gossiped right behind him. "Looks like he got beaten up bad." "That's to be expected when he messes with Sho." "But Sho seems to have been beaten as well. He has a bruise on his lip, didn't you see?" "Yes, but surely not from this weakling." They snickered.

"What are you talking about?" A new voice entered the conversation. "Who fought with whom?"

"That newbie with Sho."

A pencil case hit Nao's back. "Hey, newbie! Is it true? Did you punch Sho in the face?"

Nao turned around. Behind him sat four boys around a desk. Next to them stood the boy who had collected the baseball from beneath his desk last week. He must be the one who had just joined the discussion.

"Yes. Why?"

The four boys snickered again. "If you really did, then you'll be dead by tomorrow," one of them said. "Sho doesn't go lightly on people who fight back."

"But don't worry, we'll bring flowers to your grave."

Nao looked them straight in the eyes. "I'm not afraid of Sho."

The boys started roaring with laughter. They rocked back and forth while laughing boisterously.

"Good one! What do you prefer, newbie, white roses or lilies?"

Nao was on his way to the canteen. The corridors were empty. The time for the mob of students pushing through the narrow halls like madmen had already passed.

Nao had deliberately waited after the chime of the bell until his classmates had left the classroom.

After their mumbles and glances throughout the morning, he wanted nothing more than to avoid them. Their gossiping annoyed him and he didn't want to hear their curious whispers behind his back anymore.

He walked along the empty corridor when suddenly the sound of running footsteps resonated behind him. The person appeared next to him before he had time to turn around.

"Are you okay?"

Nao stopped. Surprised, he stared at the boy who had just emerged on his right.

It was the boy with the baseball, the one who had joined the conversation in the classroom earlier that morning. He looked at Nao curiously and pointed at his cheek when the latter didn't respond. "Your bruise," he said. "Are you okay?"

Taken aback, Nao nodded. "…Yes."

The boy smiled. "Good. Sho has a really hard punch, so I just wanted to make sure. Next time, you should kick that asshole in his balls." He grinned. "Well, then, see you." With these words, he gave Nao a quick wave and retreated in the direction he'd come from.

Dumbfounded, Nao turned around to watch the boy walk down the corridor. He disappeared around the corner, leaving Nao with the question of why that guy even cared.

He clenched his fists. Most likely because he found it funny that Nao had become a punching bag for the notorious Sho and was glad that it wasn't him; just like everyone else…

School felt awfully long that day. Nao was glad when he could finally leave the building.

With the chime of the bell, the crowd of boys stormed the exit. They swarmed out of the school like a herd of wild bulls, yielding to the call of freedom. Nao waited in the back until the crowd had slowly dispersed and only a remnant trickle of students crossed the courtyard.

As always, he walked slowly to prolong the time before he arrived home.

It was still a cold, early summer. This time, Nao had brought a jacket to shield himself from the everlasting coldness. He looked up at the cover of clouds, which seemed to have become a constant state this year. Strangely enough, Nao wished for sun that summer. He normally didn't like the unbearable heat and stiflingly hot air that followed suit, but this year, he felt bizarrely cold. Even with his jacket on, he could feel the cold breeze gnawing at his skin.

The little hairs on his nape rose, and at first, he thought it was because of the wind. But then he felt chills running down his spine. An instinct like an animal feeling its predator's eyes upon it kicked in—yet it came too late.

A force like a car ramming into him threw him to the ground. He could barely process what happened. Trying his best to stand up while pain and confusion clouded his mind, he felt four strong arms grabbing him and pulling him up. Hands like vices tightened around his arms. Confused, Nao tried to escape the sudden confinement, but they held him firmly in place.

He craned his neck to peer at his attackers' faces and was not surprised to be confronted with the mugs of Kitamura and Takamoto.

"Hi." Sho appeared in front of him and waved happily. A wide grin spread across his face. "How have you been? Was your weekend relaxing? Your face must have hurt, mustn't it?"

Nao glared at him. "What do you want? Didn't you have enough fun last time?"

Sho grinned. "Oh, I did. Seeing your pathetic, battered face was really delightful." He snickered. "But unfortunately, there are petty rumours saying you put up a good fight." He pointed at his lip where the cut from Nao's punch was still visible. "I have a reputation, just like you. Now I gotta show everyone that you're just the small, weak bug, and I am the sole squishing you into the ground. Don't take it personally." He took a step toward Nao. "…Or, on second thought, maybe do." He lunged out and hit Nao in the face.

It was a punch that would have had everyone go down on their knees. But due to the strong arms holding Nao up, only his head was thrown back before snapping forward again.

"Wow!" Sho exclaimed joyously. He shook out his hand. "That was a great punch!"

Nao felt a trickle of blood flowing out of his nostril. He could feel the immediate swelling of his nose bridge. Colourful specks floated in front of his eyes, and he had to blink a few times before his vision normalised again.

Suddenly, Sho stepped forward and grabbed Nao's chin. Nao tried to move away, but Sho just dug his fingers deeper into his skin. "Hmm… I don't think that's enough damage yet. What do you think?" He looked at the lackeys on either side of Nao.

"I'm sure he can take a few more blows before losing consciousness," Kitamura said.

"People should see what happens when someone dares to mess with us," Takamoto agreed.

Sho smiled. "I think so too." He took a step back, rolling his shoulders to warm up for the next punch. "Think positively, Nao. You're surrounded by men touching you, that's how you get off, isn't it?"

Nao clenched his teeth. The pain in his nose made it nearly impossible for him to think clearly, but the anger burning inside of him managed to overshadow almost all of the anguish he felt in that moment.

He couldn't move his arms; but his legs were free.

Thus, he used all of the strength he could muster, lunged out, and kicked between Sho's legs. The intended target felt surprisingly small.

An anguished scream echoed throughout the neighbourhood. Almost immediately, Sho sank to his knees, whimpering and cursing. It'd been a perfect hit.

The grip around Nao's arms loosened as Kitamura and Takamoto stared in shock at their sunken leader. This was Nao's chance.

He broke free and tried to run away. He charged toward the end of the alley as he was yanked back by his backpack. Frantically, he tried to escape the force pulling him back—when it suddenly vanished. Whoever had been holding on to his bag let go and Nao hurled forward onto the ground. Behind him, he heard the sound of shuffling feet and grunting. Dazed, Nao turned around to see what the heck was going on; there he gazed at something that almost made him believe he was imagining things.

Between him and his attackers stood a fourth person.

A boy in their school uniform faced Sho and his group head-on. In his shadow sat Kitamura, clutching his bloody nose.

"That's enough, Sho," the boy exclaimed. "Three against one? That's pretty unfair, even for you. Let's stop this now."

The student turned around to Nao, who gaped at his saviour in disbelief.

The boy with the baseball stood in front of him. He held out his hand to Nao, who didn't take it, and instead rose on his own, staggering to his feet.

"Of course it's you, Takeo," Sho said after he had managed to stand up as well, though his stance was a little crooked.

Takeo shrugged, unbothered. "I haven't missed you either, Sho. Now piss off. Your little show is over."

Sho huffed. His eyes flickered between Takeo, Nao, and his mates. He clenched his jaw and tightened his fists while glancing back and forth. The gears in his mind seemed to be working non-stop. Veins bulged on the back of his hand and his eyes darted restlessly from one nuisance to the next. Ultimately, he gritted his teeth so hard it felt like they could break apart and turned around to his mates.

"Let's go," he forced out, his voice strangely strained.

"But Sho…we can…"

"Let's go," Sho said again, a bit more decisively this time. "We'll make that bastard pay next time."

Uncertain, Kitamura and Takamoto looked at Sho, but followed him regardless as the latter strode toward the end of the alley.

"I can't wait for it," Takeo called after them with a nonchalant smile, waving goodbye. The three didn't turn around as they disappeared around the corner.

Takeo turned to Nao. His gaze flickered briefly over his disheveled classmate.

"Your nose. It's bleeding," he then stated concisely. "Wait." He pulled a tissue from his pocket and held it out to Nao, who ignored it. Instead, he wiped his bloody nose with the sleeve of his jacket.

"What are you doing here?" Nao asked curtly.

"I figured that Sho might try something funny after the gossip at school, so I walked around the neighbourhood to look for him till I heard a scream."

"You shouldn't have come. This is none of your business."

"They would have beaten you to a pulp if I hadn't come."

"I can take care of myself."

Takeo stared with wide eyes at Nao, evidently taken aback by the other's coldness.

"Are you not even gonna say thank you?"

"I didn't ask you to help me."

With those words, Nao grabbed his backpack and turned around, leaving the alley with the boy behind. He could hear the shuffling of feet behind him, as though Takeo was thinking of walking after him, but he didn't, and so Nao went home, mentally preparing for the condescending looks of his parents when he arrived with yet another bruise on his face.

The next day, the gossiping and whispering behind his back had surprisingly stopped. Here and there, Nao still received some looks for his swollen nose, but they didn't talk about him or Sho anymore. He was sure that Sho had found a way to shut them up after what had happened the day before. Who would want everyone to know that they lost a fight because of a kick between the legs and had to retreat in silence? Nao kind of understood it.

Though he knew that this truce was only for a brief period until Sho found a way to get back at him, he was glad to have some of his silence and invisibility back. Even the pain of his bruises was manageable after their housekeeper Mrs. Takahashi had given him some pain medication upon seeing his bruises that morning.

It had been three weeks since his transfer to this school and today seemed to be the first calm day since his arrival. At least, that was what Nao wanted to believe until Takeo suddenly showed up next to him as he was leaving the building.

He appeared beside Nao with a smile. "Hi. How are you?"

Nao ignored him and just kept on walking. Takeo followed him, unperturbed.

"I thought a lot about yesterday, and you're right. You shouldn't have to thank me," he said while strolling alongside Nao. "So instead, I thought about treating you to a meal."

Nao stopped in his tracks. Surprised, he looked at his classmate. "Why would you do that?"

Takeo also stopped and looked at Nao with a smile, happy to have earned the other's attention.

"You are not afraid to stand your ground against Sho. He hates you, and everyone who's an enemy to him is a friend to me," Takeo said. "You even kicked him in the balls like I told you to. So I want to treat you to a meal."

Nao gazed at Takeo with knitted brows. Sho was an asshole and all, but what kind of disdain must this person harbour to even treat strangers to a meal for simply defending themselves?

Takeo must have read the question on Nao's face because, with half a smile, he said, "Sho is the reason I got transferred to this hellhole of a school."

He shrugged nonchalantly. "Let's go eat something. I'm dying of hunger."

— Chapter 4 —

Takeo navigated them through the neighbourhood. More or less voluntarily, Nao followed him.

They walked side by side, mostly in silence. Sometimes Takeo would pipe up to talk about the small shops they passed by. He would tell Nao about the ramen or fish cakes they sold, and whether the owners granted a free refill if you were nice to them. But Nao had deliberately turned deaf on that ear and didn't really pay attention to what he said.

Instead, he took the opportunity to actually look at his classmate for the first time.

Takeo was a few centimeters taller than him. He was broad-shouldered and had an athletic frame. His hair was neatly trimmed with a side-part to the left, though he didn't really seem to care about styling it as it was rather messily tussled by the wind. Black fly-aways danced in the breeze and framed his handsome features.

On the left side of his face, Nao noticed a thin, pink scar running from the corner of his eye to his ear. It didn't seem to be very old yet, the edges were still clear and protruded slightly, as though it was still settling into the skin.

"Here we are!" Takeo suddenly announced, and Nao looked up to see a rundown convenience store before them. The windows were so dirty one could barely see through them into the store. Dead plants decorated the windowsills and the LED sign displaying the name of the store above the entrance was broken. Weather and bird excrement had washed out the colour of the facade almost entirely. It was an almost pitiful sight.

"Don't be fooled by the exterior," Takeo said. "They have the best food in the neighbourhood." He opened the door. "Come inside."

The interior wasn't much better, but Nao didn't feel like pointing that out.

They went to the refrigerated section, which, like the dim lights above, was buzzing abnormally loudly.

Takeo crouched down and reached into the back of the refrigerator. "I'm a little short on money, so I hope you like tuna." He pulled out two packaged onigiris. On the front were large orange stickers, marking them as reduced in price due to the expired best-before date.

He grabbed two cans of mango soda as well, then proceeded to the checkout. Nao watched Takeo from behind as he paid the cashier. He pulled out a few coins from one pocket, searched the other, which seemed to be empty, and then rummaged through his backpack until he found a few more. He put the money on the counter, grabbed the food, and walked out. Nao followed him outside to a rusty white camping table and a couple of chairs that stood in front of the store.

Takeo let himself fall into one of the plastic chairs and gestured toward the other one across from him. "Bon appetite." He smiled proudly.

With a sigh, Nao slid off his backpack and sat down. He took the onigiri, and while he was still busy peeling off the wrapper, Takeo was already busy gulping his down. He opened the can and took a large mouthful of soda. With a refreshed sigh, Takeo thrust the drink back onto the table. "Nothing is better than mango soda after a long day of school," he exclaimed, taking another bite out of his rice ball.

Nao had finally removed the wrapper. Wordlessly, he took a bite.

"Try it with the soda!" Takeo suddenly chipped in. Lightheartedly, he leaned forward, grabbed Nao's drink, and opened it for him. A fizzing sound reverberated out of the thin aluminium can. "It's the perfect mix!" he said. "Try it."

Nao looked at Takeo. He believed the latter would eventually see the lack of interest in his eyes and leave him alone; yet Takeo gazed at him with big eyes, his face full of expectation.

Thus, Nao asked himself whether that guy didn't get the clue or was simply choosing to ignore it. Whatever... He grabbed the can and took a sip. Maybe then he would leave him alone.

The flavour of sugary sweet mango spread on his tongue and finished with a slight tart taste. It was, most surprisingly, very tasty.

"You like it!" Takeo said, his lips blossomed into a smile. "I can see it on your face. For a second that brooding, dark expression of yours lifted." He beamed. "I guess no one can resist sweet drinks. Ha ha."

Nao put the can back down and leaned back. "You talk a lot," he commented.

Takeo shrugged. "That's one of my best traits." He took a sip of his own drink.

Quietly, he leaned against the back of the chair, the excitement in his eyes fading a bit as they flickered across Nao's face. "Does it hurt a lot?" Takeo suddenly asked, pointing at the other's nose.

"No," Nao said.

"You know, I get the slight feeling you're not telling the truth."

Takeo sighed. "You should be more careful around Sho. Do you know why everyone at school is so scared of him? Not just because of his lunatic tendencies. They are actually much more afraid of his older brother Katsu."

"Why?"

41

"Because he's the head of a gang."

"A gang?" Nao asked, his interest suddenly piqued.

Takeo nodded. "It's a relatively small gang, and they are only active here and in the surrounding cities, but they should nevertheless not be underestimated. Their main occupation is dealing with laced drugs, but they are also known for their tendency to use violence and blackmail to get what they want. Sho acts almighty and bratty because he knows they got his back."

"It sounds like you're familiar with them."

Absentmindedly, Takeo stared at the can of soda in his hand. "I told you Sho is the reason I got transferred to this school... We still have an outstanding score to settle."

Nao scrutinised Takeo's face. There was a bitterness in his eyes he hadn't seen yet. A darkness hidden behind his otherwise cheerful face. It was surprising, and also a bit unsettling—almost like watching a cat devour a mouse. One was so used to seeing the lovely pet that it was quite frightening to remember they were also carnivores, tearing and ripping their prey apart.

This was how Nao felt a little upon watching Takeo's face change so unexpectedly. He had been so blinded by those cheery smiles that he'd almost forgotten how startled Sho had been when he saw Takeo as his opponent.

Silently, Nao ate the rest of his onigiri and rose to his feet. "I'll go now."

Takeo looked at him, surprised, and also a little dejected. "Already?"

Nao grabbed his bag. "Thanks for the meal," he simply said and turned around.

On the way home, Takeo's words reiterated in his head. Sho's arrogance and the deeply ingrained fear of the students; it all made sense to Nao now. No wonder the other students called him as good as dead, even though Sho himself wasn't all that powerful. A bigger threat lurked in Sho's shadow, ready to strike if he wanted.

Nao felt even more disgust for that boy growing inside of him, as if he were witnessing a parasite leeching off a beast rather than a human being.

He'd been so deep in thought that he barely registered his arrival home.

The elevator carried him up to the thirtieth floor. He shoved off his shoes and slid into a pair of slippers. As usual, he tiptoed down the hallway, trying to become as incorporeal as he possibly could. Yet, today, he failed.

"Nao. Come here," his father's voice resonated from the living room.

He sucked in a deep breath as he yielded to his father's command. His hands and feet began prickling with agitation. "Yes?" he said quietly upon entering the living room.

Tsuyoshi Miyamoto sat in his armchair; a pile of documents and a telephone were laid out on the table in front of him. "I had a call with your grandfather just now, regarding your educational path."

His father took off his glasses and leaned against the back of the chair with a heavy sigh, as though just seeing his eldest son was enough to sour his spirit.

Nao could instantly feel the sweat breaking out in his palms.

"Your grandfather has decided to give you another chance. If you can prove your worth to him, he might be benevolent enough to consider transferring you to a better school."

"…What?"

"If you achieve good grades and behave accordingly, he will consider helping you and getting you out of that school for failures. Which means, pull yourself together and stay out of trouble. Your future's looking rather bleak as of now, so take this seriously."

Nao nodded.

"I dare you to embarrass our family again! And get that thing with your face under control. Those bruises make you look weak. Do you understand?"

Nao nodded.

"Do you understand!?"

"Yes!" Nao forced out.

"Good. Now go to your room."

— Chapter 5 —

The following week passed by like the wind; swift and airy. For the first time in a long while, Nao tried to actually improve his grades.

He listened attentively to the lessons, worked hard on his homework, and studied at his desk at night.

The bruises on his face had also begun to slowly heal. They had morphed from shining blue and purple into faint patches of green and yellow.

On this lengthy Wednesday, the classroom was particularly quiet. Due to a meeting between the sports clubs, the students who were part of them were absent that morning, including Takeo, who was a member of the baseball club.

A good third of the class was missing that morning, and Nao used the uncommon quiet to revise his notes for the next lesson.

In concentrated silence, he flicked his pen across the paper, writing down annotations and comments. He was so deep in thought, he didn't even register the classroom door opening or the frightened gasps of his classmates. He only noticed something was amiss as he was grabbed by his collar and pulled upward.

Someone threw him onto his desk, two arms pressing him back-first against the wooden surface.

It happened so abruptly that Nao had barely any time to comprehend what was going on. Realisation only dawned on him once a familiar face rose over him.

"This time I won't let you get away!"

Sho's livid eyes stared down at him—a contorted face full of rage above his.

His hands closed around Nao's neck, pressing down on his windpipe. Nao immediately tried to throw Sho off. *W-what is this maniac doing!?*

He dug his fingers into Sho's hands, trying to pry them off, but they didn't move a single millimeter. He grabbed Sho's wrists and his arms, doing the most to tear them off, but his fingers just cut deeper and deeper into Nao's skin—like a snake burrowing its fangs deep into its victim's flesh.

He tried to throw himself to the side, to stand up or kick Sho off, but the latter was in the stronger position. Wholly unaffected, he squeezed Nao's neck, watching him struggle beneath his hands.

What does he think he's doing? Is he really trying to kill me in front of the whole class? Nao's thoughts whirled through his shaking mind like snowflakes in a storm. He relentlessly tried to throw Sho off, but it was pointless.

More and more, Nao started to feel the lack of air. He tried to inhale, to get any oxygen inside his aching lungs, but it was nearly impossible. He started feeling fuzzy, the edges of his vision blurring, the tips of his fingers going numb.

He would soon lose consciousness. Someone had to help him!

Frantically, his eyes darted around, trying to find *anyone* willing to stop him from being strangled to death, yet no one came.

"Are you searching for someone to rescue you? Your saviour Takeo isn't here to help you! See how weak you suddenly are!?" Sho spit the words in his face, a crazed smile flying across his lips.

Nao gasped for air. His windpipe ached unbearably beneath the force crushing it. His lungs burned like fire.

Weakly, he hit Sho's arms. "S-s-to...p. S-t...o...p."

But Sho did not listen. His hands kept twisting his neck. Veins started popping out on his forehead. Unable to free himself, Nao stared at that gruesome face above his. Gritted teeth, popped out veins, eyes sparking with bloodlust. He didn't want this to be the last thing he saw.

Again, he tried to pull himself out of Sho's grip one last time, but it failed. His consciousness slipped away, he lost control of his body and his vision dwindled…

—when suddenly his throat opened up again.

He barely felt the fall to the ground—only registered his lungs filling with oxygen.

Nao took gulps of air, coughing and gasping as he could finally breathe again. Through watery eyes, he looked up and saw Sho standing above him. Their classmates had formed a large circle around them. They stood with their backs pressed against the windows and walls, staring at them with pure horror in their eyes.

"Look closely! This is what happens to anyone who dares to anger me!" Sho shouted at them. "This time it was just a warning! But next time I will kill this mutt!"

Their classmates twitched nervously, their gazes flickering back and forth between Sho and Nao.

"Relay a message to Takeo! Tell him there are some old friends waiting to meet him! And tell him as soon as you see him, understand!?"

The boys stared at their feet, trying to avoid Sho's eyes.

"Understand!?"

"Y-yes," a few of them responded, frightened.

Sho nodded contentedly. His eyes fell back upon Nao, who was still on the ground, holding his neck.

For a second, they glared at each other. Nao didn't think he had ever accumulated this much hate for another person in his life before. He could feel it bubbling in his chest, churning in his stomach, and he was sure the other could also read it on his face.

But for now, Sho just stared back at him with the glint of victory in his eyes.

Eventually, he broke eye contact with a sneer and left the classroom. The students jumped left and right to make space for him, forming an aisle like peasants would in front of a king.

Nao watched him leave. His heart pounding in his chest like crazy.

He tried to stand up. But his legs were shaking. He had to hold on to a desk to pull himself upward.

His classmates just watched him do so, mumbling and whispering nervously amongst themselves. Nao managed to sit back at his desk. He grabbed his pen and tried to finish his notes, but only then did he notice how much his hands were shaking.

He placed the pen back down on the table.

He closed his eyes and took a deep breath, trying to recompose himself.

Like the merciless ruler he was, Sho had given an example of what would happen if anyone dared to defy him. He had wanted to prove to everyone just how superior he was, and he had succeeded.

The story of Sho nearly killing a student made it around school fast. Not only did the staring behind Nao's back start again, they also tried to avoid him out of fear that Sho could target them as well. The peasant Nao Miyamoto had dared to get on the king's bad side and thus became a criminal ready for execution. Anyone raising their voice in his favour was just another corpse speaking. Although there was one additional person who didn't fear Sho's reign: a knight in broken armour, but with courage bigger than that of anyone else.

Sho hadn't just promised his revenge to Nao, but to Takeo as well. Nao didn't know what he had meant by old friends waiting to meet Takeo. He could only assume that it was about whatever had happened between Sho and him in the past.

Those suspicions hardened the day two men showed up in front of the school. Both of them were in their early twenties. One had an undercut with the remaining hair tied into a messy bun at the top, the other one had thin, shoulder-length hair and patchy beard stubbles around the rough base of his chin. They hung around in front of the gates, smoking and watching the students passing by.

The two men held their stance over the next few days. Every afternoon after classes had ended, they waited and preyed on the people exiting the gate as though searching for someone. Now and then, when they seemed bored, they'd flick their cigarette butts at students, shouting obscene things at them.

Like most people, Nao blissfully ignored them. They were annoying, but whatever these two were waiting for, it was none of his business.

Nao passed them on the way to the sports hall, though he didn't spare them a second glance.

He got dressed for the PE lesson. In addition to their sports uniform, Nao had also brought a track jacket. He zipped it all the way up to his chin.

Considering that Nao was bad at studying, one could assume that he might excel in other fields, like PE or arts, for example—but this was not the case. Just like with every other subject, he was merely mediocre. Neither in the front nor the back. Always in the midfield.

They started the lesson by warming up. The sports hall smelled strongly of wooden floor, chalk, and the rubber of basketballs. The bright LEDs drenched the room in a cold blue light, reminiscent of the sky on a chilly clouded day.

They jogged in circles around the hall for ten minutes. On other days, it would have been easy for Nao, but today he tired out faster than usual.

Relieved once the warm-up was over, he let himself fall on one of the mats. A fine sheen of sweat clung to his skin and he rolled up the sleeves of his jacket, relishing in the cool air grazing his arms.

"Everyone gather around the mats," the teacher exclaimed. He stood at the head of the hall, hands on his hips. Watching the students assemble, he announced, "Next up we'll do sit-ups. Find yourself a partner to practice with. I'll give you two minutes to pair up."

The boys started mingling in small groups. Nao watched them run up to each other and spread in duos across the mats.

Nao, though, stayed put on the ground. There was no reason for him to get up. The last person failing to find a partner had to pair up with him anyway. That was how it had always been.

At last, a group of three boys approached him. They were arguing, throwing brief glances at Nao in between.

"You go partner with him."

"No, I already had to pair up with him the last time, now it's your turn."

"I don't want to! Didn't you see what Sho did to him!? I don't want him to think we could be friends or something!"

"Then let's play rock paper scissor. The loser pairs up with him."

"That's unfair! I always lose at that game—HEY!"

The boys were pushed out of the way and Takeo crouched down in front of Nao. With one eyebrow cocked and a glint in his eyes that could be described as unconcealed annoyance, he turned around. "Get away," Takeo said dismissively, pointing with his chin to the other side of the mat.

Dumbfounded, the boys stared at each other. For a moment, they were scandalised. One of them opened his mouth, ready to spew an insult at the newcomer for pushing him so rudely, but he was quickly stopped by his friends. They squeezed his arm, and suddenly the boy seemed to realise that he had been given the salvation to his problem. He swiftly closed his mouth and the group scrambled away, relieved.

Takeo turned to Nao with an apologetic smile. "Are you ready?"

Baffled, Nao gazed at the other. He didn't know what to say or how to react, after all, he wasn't sure what he had just witnessed. But his struggle was quickly resolved when their teacher blew the whistle, immediately gathering everyone's attention in the hall.

"Everyone found a partner? Good, then you'll have one minute to do as many sit-ups as you can. After the minute you switch and repeat. Understand? Let's go." The trill of the whistle rang through the hall.

Nao lay back on the hard mat, his arms behind his head, while Takeo pushed his feet to the ground.

In silence, they carried out their task. Nao finished his set, and after a moment of catching his breath, they switched places. Takeo rested on the mat while Nao sat before him, pushing down his feet. The teacher gave the signal to start.

Nao watched Takeo curiously as the latter moved up and down.

He absentmindedly gnawed on the inside of his cheek, thoughts swirling in his mind like a hurricane. There was a question that had been swarming on his mind for the past few days. He hadn't asked Takeo about it yet, but now that he was right in front of him, he couldn't hold it back anymore.

"Those men…in front of the school. They are here for you, aren't they?" he said.

Takeo glanced up at him. "Those two morons? Yeah, they are waiting for me."

"Are they the two friends Sho has been talking about?"

Takeo nodded. "Do you remember what I told you about that gang? The one Sho's brother is the head of? Those two are his subordinates. I guess he sent them here to scare me."

So, Nao was right. Sho's and Takeo's dispute was somehow tied to that ominous men.

The whistle rang again. Takeo sat back up, a thin layer of sweat glistening across his forehead.

"Are you scared?" Nao asked bluntly.

The semblance of a smile flew across Takeo's face before he shook his head. "No. Like you, I'm not scared of Sho and his games. I've tried to avoid them until now because I have no motivation to deal with them." He ran a hand through his ruffled black hair. "Man, Sho really is a nuisance. He was pissed off that I interrupted his little power trip in that alley and ran straight to his older brother to get revenge on me. I hoped I'd never have to deal with those assholes again." He sighed.

He opened his mouth to add something, but then his eyes dropped down to Nao's neck.

Confused, Nao peered down as well and noticed that the zipper of his jacket had loosened. The collar opened and beneath appeared the remains of Sho's hands on his throat.

Nao wanted to zip it up when Takeo suddenly reached out. He touched the collar and pulled it gently to the side, revealing pink marks which stretched around his neck like a noose. This simple movement rendered Nao completely speechless. His body frozen in surprise.

Flabbergasted, Nao stared at Takeo as his eyes flickered across the bruised skin. Like a shadow, his gaze hovered over the wounds, observing every imprint of the fingers and nails Sho had left there. It made Nao squirm with discomfort. He couldn't read his expression, but he knew it wasn't anything good. Takeo's face had become a stiff mask, a surface-level poker face, seemingly devoid of any emotions that could hint at what he was thinking. Yet beneath the edges of that mask loomed a dark shadow.

After a few seconds of tense silence, he let go of the collar. Still, with the same blank face, he stood up and walked off.

Stunned, Nao's gaze followed him. *What was that?* He zipped the jacket back up.

Nao rose and joined the rest of the class for the next exercise, but weirdly enough, Takeo didn't talk to him again that day.

Nao only got to meet Takeo again the day after.

He walked out of the school building right after classes had ended. It was a mild day.

Although not particularly sunny, a lukewarm breeze blew through the city. And besides the usual scents of asphalt and cigarettes, the air also carried a hint of grass and warmth. It was the first time that year that summer felt like merely a grasp away.

Nao passed the school gates. As expected, he could see the two men hanging around the exit. He didn't even have to give them a glance to confirm their presence. They had already become a staple in his peripheral vision. But that day, something unusual caught his attention. A shift so out of place it struck Nao like lightning.

He turned around, and his gaze abruptly fell upon a third person.

At first, Nao didn't think much of it, yet after a second glance, he realised the reason of said unusual shift. The third person... It was Takeo.

Nao stopped dead in his tracks.

Takeo stood in front of the two men, seemingly engaged in a calm conversation. Nao was too far away to grasp what they were saying, but he could very well see the disgusting smiles on the faces of the two men as they spoke.

Nao didn't understand what was happening, though, before he could think of any logical explanation, the three of them started moving.

They walked east: an area Nao wasn't familiar with. He didn't understand why Takeo would suddenly talk to them after having declared the day before that he was trying to avoid them. And why would he follow them now, knowing they were sent by his biggest enemy? No matter how much he turned this in his mind, it made no sense!

In the end, however, it was none of Nao's business.

Whatever the deal with Takeo and those men was, it had nothing to do with him. He already had his own pile of shit to share with Sho, and for the sake of himself, Nao should stay out of trouble and act like he saw nothing.

But still... Nao stood there as if petrified and watched the three vanish into the distance. He couldn't explain it, but something was feeling horribly wrong in his stomach. It was an uneasy foreboding twinging at his gut.

For a few more seconds, he stood and stared. It was neither his business nor his problem.

He could just leave, with no consequences.

This was none of his business.

He could leave...

Yet, before he could do the most rational thing and turn around and go, Nao felt his legs moving on their own, following the three men around the corner.

— Chapter 6 —

Nao trailed them like a shadow. He kept a safe distance from the three, hoping they wouldn't spot him just yet.

The two men led Takeo through a jumble of streets. The farther they went, the less Nao was familiar with the area. Eventually, they stopped at an empty construction site. A scaffold was standing next to an old building. Piles of gravel and wooden planks were scattered across the ground, and yet the construction site was as empty as a ghost town. Only a blue plastic tarp, tied to the scaffold, swayed leisurely in the soft wind, rustling quietly in the otherwise dead silent atmosphere.

Takeo stopped and turned around to face the two men. With his hands in the pockets of his grey sweater jacket, he glanced at both of them with raised brows and a mocking sneer. "Is this far enough for you?" he asked leisurely.

"Don't get cocky," the man with the bun said. "We're here to give ya a good old-fashioned beating."

Takeo huffed. "And I'm here to tell you to keep your greedy hands to yourself. Tell Sho that he has to stop hurting people who have nothing to do with this. This is a thing between *him* and *me*, get it?"

"I see, your arrogance hasn't changed since then. You still think you're in the position to argue with us." The man with the long hair licked his lips. He rubbed the knuckles of his fist with a taunting grin. "Brats like you really make me want to beat them even more—first spouting nonsense, then blood. Though, if you comply nicely, we might make it quick for you."

"From my experience, idiots like you are the most rewarding to bash. They puff themselves up like gorillas—only to weep the hardest once they've been beaten," Takeo said and let the

55

backpack slide off his shoulders, throwing it next to a few empty buckets. The men's brows twitched indignantly.

Nao hid behind a brick wall. He stood with his back pressed against the cold stone, watching the three around the corner.

The two men had Takeo cornered against a wall. For a moment, they glared at each other like predators observing one another, finding the other's weak points and calculating the best spot to tear their claws into. It was hair-raising, the atmosphere unbearably thick with the tension of boiling blood and cold sweat. Finally, they launched their attacks.

The man with the long hair lunged first. He threw a punch at Takeo, who easily dodged it. The second man joined in, but miraculously Takeo managed to evade his fists too.

Nao didn't know what to do. He watched from behind the corner, his heart hammering against his ribs.

For a brief second, it looked like Takeo could end this fight easily and fast, but it was only for that moment. One of his opponents managed to sling an arm around his neck, pulling him against his body and squeezing his throat. Takeo choked. He dug his fingers into his attacker's arm, trying to tear it off and failed. Takeo was a good fighter, no question. But it was still two against one, and such imbalance of manpower was the factor turning the tides.

Nao watched with wide eyes as the man with the bun reached into his pants pocket and pulled out a clasp knife. With a broad grin on his face, he raised the knife into the air, the afternoon sun twinkling in the silver blade. "Sho said we could have some fun with you." He snickered, excited. "Where do you want me to start? Neck? Face? Maybe that loud mouth of yours?"

Fuck it. Nao gritted his teeth. He had already defied all logic and sense of security by following those three here. Now he couldn't just sit idly by while someone was getting sliced up like a mackerel ready for dinner, could he? Ah, how much he despised himself when his legs started moving yet again, and in the split of a second, he acted without thought or plan.

He threw off his backpack, clutched one of the wooden planks at his feet, and whacked it against the man's head. The hollow sound of wood on bone echoed throughout the ghostly construction site. Instantly, the knife tumbled out of the man's hand and he tried to turn around, but Nao just hit him again. Strong and ruthless.

The second time, he collapsed onto the ground—unconscious.

In momentary shock from this sneaky new attacker, the other two seemed to have gone silent as well, but then Nao heard the sound of a heavy object hitting the ground. He turned around and saw Takeo standing above the other man, breathing exhaustedly.

He looked at the two unconscious men in the dirt, and then his gaze wandered up to Nao. Takeo's eyes were wild, his hair disheveled and all over the place. In utter disbelief, he gaped at the person in front of him as though they might be an apparition.

"What…are you doing here?" he asked, puzzled.

Honestly, Nao didn't know it either.

Takeo sighed and closed his eyes, sinking to the ground.

"Whatever you're doing here…" He took a deep breath. "Thank you." He opened his eyes again and gazed at Nao. "Thanks for helping me, even though you shouldn't have done that."

Nao threw the piece of wood to the ground—a dull ache lingered in the bones and flesh of his hands after the brute force of the impact. "What do you mean?"

Takeo glanced at the men, his eyebrows furrowing. "It was a dumb decision. Now they'll come for you too."

Nao shrugged dismissively. "I don't think I can get any more hated in Sho's eyes."

Takeo huffed out a laugh and smiled. "Yeah, that might be true." He stretched out his hand to Nao, who eyed it skeptically. "Mind helping me up?"

Nao blatantly ignored this request and instead walked around the corner to pick up the backpack he had left there. Behind him, he could hear Takeo's exhausted grunts as he struggled to stand up.

If it were up to him, Nao would have already left and gone home, leaving all of today's surprises behind. But since he wasn't familiar with the area, and would probably have gotten lost after the first ten steps, he had no choice but to rely on Takeo to navigate them through the neighbourhood.

During their walk, Takeo told him once again that those men would tell Katsu and Sho about him and that his interference would bring consequences, but Nao didn't feel scared. On the contrary, he felt anger. Nao couldn't explain it himself; he wasn't brave or anything like that. But something about Sho and his actions—his arrogance as well as his recklessness—made him feel furious. He could hardly swallow it down.

The two of them entered a broad street. A few cars drove leisurely past them. They crossed beneath an overpass when suddenly the sound of something ripping cut through the air. At once, his backpack felt significantly lighter, and Nao turned around to see the contents of his bag strewn all over the ground.

He took it off and spotted the broken zipper. It must have broken when he had thrown it off during the fight.

With a sigh, he stared at his books and papers tumbling in the dirt. *Of course it had to happen to* him...

"Ah, shoot," Takeo said and crouched down to pick up the pens rolling across the asphalt.

Nao followed suit and together they collected his belongings.

He threw his pens back in his pencil case when he noticed Takeo's gaze skimming over a piece of paper out of the corner of his eye. He didn't have to take a closer look to know it was his math homework from last week. The teacher's red scribbles marking all of his mistakes were evident all over the paper and stuck out like blood on snow.

His breath hitched, and he hastily snatched the paper out of Takeo's hands.

The latter stared at him in surprise. "Sorry, I just picked it up..."

With a deep frown, Nao grabbed the rest of his belongings and rose to his feet. His arms full of books and papers, he quickly left and walked homeward without uttering a word of goodbye.

When Nao arrived at school the next day, he had half expected to see the gang waiting for him in front of the gates, ready to beat him up. But in reality, everything seemed to be the same as always. Except for the empty space where the two men had been hanging around for the past week.

Nao entered the classroom without being immediately jumped at by either Sho or his lackeys on the way there, and he subconsciously let out a sigh of relief.

But Nao's day didn't go well even without them interrupting it. It all started going downhill during math class.

Nao wasn't good at math. He never had been and probably never would be. But due to his grandfather's proposal to get him out of that school if he proved himself, he'd tried really hard to study. He really did! Yet all the hours spent sitting at his desk hunched over books, eyes heavy and bleary, seemed to have gone down the drain as the teacher handed out their tests from a few days prior.

Twenty-seven out of fifty points. It was better than the last one, but still, inevitably, a failure.

He stared apprehensively at the red digits in front of him, his chest bubbling with frustration. *Again.* He had failed *again.*

His chest started tightening up, his throat swelling shut. Tunnel-eyed, he stared at the twenty-seven before him, could hear its taunting voice, its condescending sneer. The red ink of the pen—the blood his failure was written in—grew in front of his eyes. His vision was completely covered in red. *Red* as in his failure. *Red* as in his churning frustration. *Red* as in his father's angered face and shaking fists once he saw those two digits…

Nao was so taken up by those boiling feelings he almost didn't notice the person appearing at his side.

"I can help you if you want," the person said and laid his test on Nao's desk.

Forty-eight out of fifty points.

Nao looked up at Takeo, who gazed at him with an amicable smile. "As a thank you for saving me yesterday," he said. "I owe you."

Nao blinked at him briefly, but then quickly lowered his eyes and stuffed the test into his backpack. "I don't want your help," he choked out.

"Are you sure? I used to help out friends all the time at my old school."

"I don't need your help! I can do it on my own."

Takeo's smile faded. "Okay, then," he acquiesced and returned to his seat.

Nao took a deep breath and tried to unclench his jaw. Even when trying his best, he was still failing. Those had been his father's words over the course of the past years.

Although they had become much more than just words to him. Slowly but surely, they had turned into a prediction, a glimpse of the future he could not change. They had become a part of his life, ingrained in everything he did.

Nao had accepted those words a long time ago. But them being proven true to him again and again still felt horrible.

His day continued to go downhill even more steeply when he arrived home. Today, the apartment was filled with busy clamour as the living room was tidied up and decorated for the esteemed guests visiting that evening.

It was an event dedicated to his little brother's academic future. Representatives from the university would come to their home, and if his family was lucky, Toyo would receive early admission to their scholarship. Well, that wasn't completely true—it wasn't about luck. Luck was only for the weak and dumb, as his grandfather liked to say. Solely with sacrifice and determination, one could achieve something in life.

Still, Nao didn't really understand why he had to participate in such an event. Maybe it was to show support for his brother. Maybe it was simply to humiliate him.

He had to once again dress up in the black pants and white dress shirt he didn't like. As the early dusk broke in, the guests were welcomed into their home.

The apartment was brimming with people that night. Besides the representatives and his grandparents, a catering service also attended the festivities and diligently prepared aperitif and dinner.

They were served expensive filet and fish. Nao sat silently at the table, chewing on a piece of tender meat. He didn't pay attention to the conversation of the adults since it didn't concern him. And fortunately, no one seemed to be interested in him anyway. Instead, they talked about Toyo and his outstanding achievements. His grandfather didn't leave out a single chance of praising his grandchild and calling him a leading person for the country's future. Toyo just laughed awkwardly, politely denying his grandfather's praising words, though his ears turned bright red.

Glad to get a chance to escape, Nao helped clean the table after dinner was over. He brought a stash of dirty plates into the kitchen and helped Mrs. Takahashi scrub them clean in the sink.

She praised his cleaning skills and Nao's mood seemed to lift a little when suddenly a voice rang out behind them. "I agree. This might be the job you'll have to pursue if your grades stay like that."

Nao turned around to look into the steely face of his grandfather. He stood in the doorway, his broad stature nearly filling out the frame.

"Can we have a talk, Nao?" It wasn't a question, though; it was a command wrapped in the pretence of one.

Reluctantly, Nao nodded and dried off his hands on a towel before following his grandfather into the hallway.

"You didn't forget my promise, did you?" he asked, staring straight into his grandchild's face.

Nao shook his head. "No, I'm studying hard to improve my grades."

"I hope so, Nao. You shouldn't be the first Miyamoto to fail to go to university." His grandfather wrapped his strong arm around Nao's shoulders, holding him in a firm grip; although this was not what it felt like. The feeling was much more akin to a bunny trapped in a snare. The rope tightening around its ankle with every attempt to escape.

His little bunny heart leapt.

"Do you see that?" his grandfather asked and pointed at the festivities in the living room across from them. "This could be for you. Not for a renowned university like the eastern one, of course, but I'm sure for a smaller, less eminent university. You still have the chance to prove your worth to us. Do you understand me?"

Nao nodded silently and his grandfather smiled. "Good. I hope you know I only have the best intentions for our family in mind. And if I see someone threatening to mess up that garden of Eden I've been planting my whole life, you must understand that I just can't look past that. My father, I, and your father, we have all dedicated our lives to picking the weeds out of that garden. So, if I see a particularly stubborn one that always keeps growing back, no matter how many times I pluck it out or try to turn it into a flower, you hopefully understand how frustrating that is for me. After all, a garden of Eden is only a paradise because of its immaculacy. I can't let it go to waste because of some small, little piece of weed. I've been trying to trim that sprout for a long time, but it can only develop nicely if it wants to change itself. If you were that weed, Nao, what would you do?"

Nao gulped heavily. His legs felt numb, and he was only held afloat by his grandfather's arm gripping him. "I'm… I'm…" he stammered, trying to clear his shaking mind. "If…if I… were that weed… I guess I would change…"

"Is that so?" His grandfather smiled intently. His eyes formed into crescents, but it looked rather unnatural. "Well, I hope the weed will soon realise this as well. A gardener has only so much patience."

He let go of his shoulder, and only then did Nao notice how much his muscles were hurting from tensing them up for so long. His grandfather, however, smiled as if they'd just had a nice little chat between grandpa and grandson, not a hunt between hound and bunny. "I think they are going to serve the cake now," he suddenly chimed. "I've been waiting for this all evening. It's raspberry marzipan flavour. I've commissioned it myself." He smiled joyfully, heading with feathery steps toward the living room.

Nao was left alone with his heart thumping aggressively against his ribs. He took a shaky breath, feeling his hands trembling from where they were digging into the fabric of his pants.

Numbly, he watched from afar as a cake with sparklers was carried inside the living room. He was vast dimensions apart from them as he observed everyone gathering around the cake to watch the candles burn down in spectacular sparks and glints. The crowd clapped and smiled brightly.

His grandfather had said that something like this could be arranged for him as well.

Nao looked at his parents, who stood beside Toyo. They were both smiling. A view that was unfathomably rare.

Nao watched the crinkles on his mother's delicate nose, the fine upward curve of her mouth. He observed his father's curled up lips and the small wrinkles around the corners of his eyes. His hand patted Toyo's back gently.

Nao asked himself, what if he were like his brother—a spectacular flower in said garden, a good student with good grades and outstanding achievements, a future full of success ahead of him. Would they look at him the same way as they did with his brother? Would they look at him with smiles on their faces instead of scorn?

Nao would really like to know.

So much, in fact, that he approached Takeo at school the next day.

Takeo looked at him with big eyes when Nao caught up with him on his way to the classroom. He gazed at him in all seriousness and asked,

"Do you still want to teach me?"

— Chapter 7 —

Over the course of the next two days, Nao and Takeo met up to study. After classes had ended, they would meet in the study room on the third floor. Normally, one would have to book the room beforehand, but it was always empty anyway since no students actually used it to study. That was to be expected from a school full of pubescent, troublesome teenage boys.

The small room was filled with shelves stacked to the brim with books and binders, which appeared to have not been touched in a very long time. In the center stood a rectangular table along with three spare chairs. Thin rays of light slanted through the small window on the west side of the room, which offered a view onto the running tracks outside.

The room was old and abandoned, and it showed in the chunks of dust that floated in the grey streaks of daylight. Even though they had opened the window to lessen the smell of old carpet and damp wallpaper, Nao's nose still itched from the dust flakes every time he set foot inside.

Takeo and Nao tried to make themselves comfortable in the cramped room. They sat next to each other, a math book propped up in front of them while Takeo explained the exercises step by step.

Nao was positively surprised by him. At first, he had been skeptical whether it was a good idea to ask Takeo to teach him, but he turned out to be an exceptional tutor.

He was patient and considerate. He explained the process of solving the questions simply and slowly. If Nao got stuck on a task or didn't understand what he was talking about, he'd help him out with serene patience.

Nao's head was spinning from so many formulas and numbers, but Takeo was a great help in bringing order to the chaos.

The second day of their teaching spree, Nao was hunched over an exercise while Takeo sat next to him, sipping on a can of mango soda.

A sliver of sun peeked out from behind the clouds and threw specks of sunlight through the canopy of the trees. The hue of the light told them that it was already getting late, as instead of the feeble grey daylight, the rays had turned into a cozy orange.

"Don't forget to change the algebraic sign here." Takeo pointed at one of the many numbers. "Maybe write that down since you seem to forget it a lot."

Nao nodded. He scrubbed the paper with an eraser, scribbling over his mistake.

Takeo nodded contentedly and looked at him with a cheerful smile. "You're doing good. You learn really fast."

Nao shrugged. "You're a good teacher, I guess."

Takeo's smile deepened. "I'm glad to hear that. I want to become a teacher." Nao couldn't see it properly in the evening light, but there seemed to be a slight blush blooming on Takeo's cheeks.

"A teacher?" he asked, and Takeo nodded.

"Yeah, that's always been my dream. It's fun teaching other people."

Nao was a bit dumbfounded by his words. They were filled with so much honest excitement and almost child-like innocence.

During their first meetings, Nao would have never guessed that there was a dream like this fluttering its wings beneath the surface. Yes, Takeo was amicable and cheerful, almost bubbly, to the point Nao found it nearly too much at times. Those qualities in themselves were probably already good foundations for a teacher, but now that Nao had spent the last two afternoons with

Takeo—being taught and guided by his soft voice and gentle words—he truly began to realise his potential.

There was something calm and encouraging in his soft-spokenness when he corrected a mistake, and the way his eyes shimmered brightly as he explained a task. Priorly, Nao had been confused as to why Takeo had volunteered to help him out, thinking the other might do it out of pity or boredom, but he came to the understanding that Takeo was just genuinely enjoying it.

Nao didn't notice at first, but it seemed that he had been staring at Takeo the whole time. The latter cocked his head to the side with a curious smile. "Everything okay?"

"Yeah!" Nao stammered quickly and averted his eyes. "I… I just think it's surprising that you already know what you want to do in the future."

His smile widened. "It's just a profession I've been admiring for a long time. Do you already know what you want to do?"

Nao shook his head. How could he know? He was a mutt in a kennel. It had never been asked or even allowed for him to think about his own wants. In the end, there had always been only one destination for him, one road his feet were allowed to walk—and they were branded with his family's name.

Takeo shrugged nonchalantly. "Well, there's still a lot of time ahead. So there's no need to stress about it already, right?"

Nao almost laughed out loud. Was he really that good-hearted or just a bit idiotic?

Nao believed it wasn't as easy as Takeo made it out to be, but the moment he looked into his bright face with the encouraging smile, he nodded nevertheless.

"Now, let's get back to math. Where did we stop?" Takeo scanned the paper Nao had previously scribbled on when suddenly the sound of a phone ringing cut through the air.

He turned around to pull a cellphone out of his bag. Nao fleetingly read the name *Mamoru* on the display. Takeo's face blanched as soon as he saw the caller ID. It was only a fleeting moment, like a leaf being swept away by the wind, but Nao caught it nonetheless.

Takeo turned to him with a shallow smile. "Can you start the next exercise without me? I'll be back in a minute—I just have to take this call."

Nao nodded, and Takeo headed out of the room, closing the door behind him. He settled onto the next question, ready to try his luck once more, when the muffled voice of a man reverberated through the thin door.

"TAKEO! WHERE ARE YOU!?" Nao flinched involuntarily.

"I'm at school." He heard Takeo mutter in response to the angry man.

"Did you give her money!? Did you give her money again!?" the man shouted.

"No...no! I swear, I didn't."

"Do you know what I have to deal with right now!? Come home! Come home right now!"

"B-but I..."

"Don't give me any of your bullshit! You come home right now!"

Takeo wanted to start a new sentence, but the connection was cut off, like a guillotine falling. Then there was silence.

It was thick and stuffy. Nao tried to act normal when the door opened again and Takeo walked in as white as a sheet. If it weren't for the fact that his face had been drained of all colour, one wouldn't have suspected that anything had happened at all. Takeo smiled as usual and walked over to grab his bag. "That was my brother," he said calmly. "There is some trouble at home, so I have to go. I'm sorry but I need to end this lesson early."

"No problem," Nao said and Takeo smiled gratefully. "Thank you. I'll see you tomorrow, then?"

Nao nodded and his classmate rushed out the door.

Nao hadn't given any thought to the call between Takeo and his brother after he had gone home. It was none of his business, after all. As much as he disliked people stuffing their noses into his privacy, he also despised doing the same to them. But when Takeo arrived at school the next day with a scrape on his left cheek, he was still surprised. His initial thoughts went directly to Sho, though he quickly realised that his bruises would have been much more severe in that case. It must have been somehow tied to the trouble at home the other had mentioned.

Nao and Takeo usually didn't talk to each other during classes, yet when they met up in the study room, Takeo was strangely quiet as well.

He was still tutoring him patiently, but for the first time since they had met, Takeo's smiles looked forced.

For a split second, Nao thought about asking him what had happened, but he dismissed the thought as quickly as it had popped up. Nao would've *hated* it if anyone asked him a question like that, so he didn't want to bother anyone either. But still, there was this uneasy feeling stuck to Takeo, as if his head wasn't entirely there.

"You forgot to solve question five." Takeo pointed at the paper.

"You told me to skip it."

"Did I?" He looked at Nao with wide eyes. "Oh, yeah, sorry… I guess I forgot that."

They ended that day's lesson slowly and sluggishly. It was already turning dark when they finally exited the school building.

Even though the sky was totally clear, the air was still cool. Nao's nose tip turned cold as soon as they stepped outside.

Gravel crunched beneath their feet as they walked down the pathway.

"I'm sorry if I've been a bit distracted today. I'll be fully present next time. I promise," Takeo said and his lips distorted into another half-sincere smile.

Nao would have liked to tell him to stop forcing smiles if he didn't feel like it, but instead he just nodded his head. "Then, until next time."

"Yeah, see you."

They turned in different directions, each heading homeward. Nao managed to take three steps before he stopped again. Behind him, he could hear the crunching of Takeo's footsteps.

For a second, he was unsure, but then he turned around to say "Hey, Take—" when suddenly a bag was pulled over his head and he was blind.

— Chapter 8 —

Nao was blind. He was disoriented and confused.

Someone was pinning his arms against his back, another person, or maybe two, had grabbed his legs and carried him. He tried to kick his attackers, wrestle his way out of their grasps, but they held him so tightly that he would for sure have bruises on his arms and legs the next day.

He was too scared and overwhelmed to scream. His voice seemed to have disappeared the moment they had pulled the bag over his head. All he could do was wriggle helplessly in the attackers' arms.

Through the fabric clasped over his ears, he could hear the muffled sounds of hurried footsteps. There must have been six, seven, or maybe eight people. Nao had lost all sense of time, but eventually, he was thrown on top of something firm. He heard a grunt as he collided with said thing. Nao then picked up heavy breathing next to him and realised that it was Takeo they had thrown him onto.

Panicking, he ripped the bag off his head and squinted into the light of a single street lamp. He quickly tried to get a grasp of the situation.

They were in some kind of alley. High walls rose to their left and right, reaching into the dark sky. He and Takeo sat on the ground. In front of and behind them stood two groups of men. He counted nine.

"Welcome to the day of your last judgement!" a man before them shouted rapturously.

He appeared to be in his early twenties. The sides of his head were shaved while the rest was dyed bright red, glowing almost as vividly as fire in the dim light. His ears were adorned with countless rings and studs. A large, silver ring protruded from the center of his nose.

Nao let his gaze wander and caught sight of a disgustingly familiar face in the crowd.

Sho! He stood in the twilight and grinned at them with a taunting smile. Suddenly, all pieces fell into place.

"You bastard!" Nao could hear Takeo growl next to him.

He rose, both of his hands clenched into fists. "Are you serious, Sho!? All of this!? You gathered all of these people from your brother's gang just because you lost a fight? You coward!"

Sho stepped forward and crossed his arms. His chest puffed up like that of a boxer. "I don't care what it takes to see you get beaten up. You strut about like you're so much better than everyone—like you don't know fear! But I will show you where you stand! You'll learn how to fear *me*! Yield to your superiors, once and for all, Takeo!"

Takeo clenched his jaw, veins crawling up the sides of his neck. "If you want to beat me so badly, then why do you have to pull other people into it!?" He stepped in front of Nao, stretching out an arm in an attempt to shield him. "If you want me, then just take me."

Sho laughed coldly. "Exactly, this is one of the reasons I want to crush you so bad. That glorious, obnoxious hero complex of yours is one of your biggest problems. It's seriously pissing me off. Whether you want it or not, you and the mutt will be crushed."

Nao slowly woke up from his shock. He stood up and pushed Takeo's arm out of the way. "I can fight for myself."

Sho laughed again. "See! Not even the people you're trying to protect want you! You should learn how to keep your hands out of other people's business." He looked over at the man with red hair. "Kubo and the others are here because you managed to piss off not only me but also my brother, whose subordinates you've beaten up. And blood calls for blood. Especially if it's such dirty blood like yours."

Nao could see Takeo's eyes flickering around. He was searching for an escape route, but there was none! They were caught in a human cage. Four people in the back. Five in the front. Two mice in a circle of cats.

Sho nodded at Kubo, and the men started closing in.

Nao knew that there was basically no chance for him and Takeo to win. It was two versus eight.

Takeo wasn't a bad fighter, and Nao would claim he wasn't terrible either, even though he wasn't the strongest. But still, what were the chances of them actually winning? He gritted his teeth. *Fucking shit! So be it!* Nao would never go down without a fight.

He readied himself when the first men came dangerously close. They looked at him with bloodlust in their eyes. For a second, he asked himself if those were even humans and not just shells filled with the animalistic urge to hunt. It would be a lie to say Nao wasn't scared of being subjected to those cruel yet excited gazes, but he did not falter. He dodged the first punches that were thrown at him—though, as expected, he was quickly overpowered. One of the first hits was right in his face.

Nao was thrown back, a searing pain shot through his nerve tracts.

It was only the prelude, though. A taste of what was yet to come.

He was punched in his face, his chest, and his stomach. He tried to stay on his feet, swaying from one side to the other. Here and there, he managed to land a hit of his own, feeling the dense skin of another person caving in beneath his knuckles. These hits sent surges of pain down his arm. The ache of the rebound shot up his shoulder, and it felt like it was about to get dislocated by the brute force. He clenched his jaw, rolling his shoulders slightly before setting up for another attack. But he was inferior to them. In number, limbs, and strength. Quickly, they struck him at his vital points. A punch in the stomach, a knee in the back, and a kick in the back of his knees. Like paper, he crumpled to the ground.

His head hit the stone and the world started spinning.

Nao lay in the dirt, adamantly holding his arms above his head while his attackers kicked him like they had grown hundreds of legs. Nao breathed in the dust that was stirred up by his opponents' feet. It scratched in his throat and he had trouble breathing. Cautiously, he opened his shield of arms to try to inhale fresh air, and thus caught a glimpse of Sho, who stood at the sidelines of the fight and puffed a cigarette in morbid serenity. He leaned against the wall of the neighbouring building as though taking a long-deserved break. With a content smile on his face and the cigarette between his lips, he tranquilly watched the scene unfolding in front of him.

Nao's blood started to boil. He wanted to get up and slam Sho's head against the wall, giving him the same treatment he was receiving right now, but his attackers held him captive on the ground.

Nao had no idea how long all of this went on. He didn't know whether they beat him for ten minutes or an hour. On top of that, he had no clue what had happened to Takeo. With legs and bodies obscuring his view and jeering laughter drowning out everything else, Nao couldn't tell where the other was. Had he also been knocked down like Nao?

Finally, his attackers stopped thrashing him as he was on the brink of losing consciousness.

The faces above him were flowing together incessantly, their laughs and footsteps sounding strangely disconnected from reality.

Nao stared at the dark sky above, specks of colour floated in front of his eyes, when a familiar face loomed over him.

Sho stood above him, his feet planted on either side of his shoulders, taking a last long pull from his cigarette. He stared at him with a wide grin and flicked the stub next to Nao's head.

He stomped out the ember with his foot, and Nao could feel the scorching heat of the cigarette beside his ear. The crunch of the shoe scratching against the dirt resonated so loudly in his ears that it was painful.

Oh, how Nao would have loved to jump up and grab that bastard by his neck, to turn that self-pleased smile upside down! But he could barely keep his gaze focused. His brain was twitching. Between all the things in front of him, flowing and melting together in nauseating swirls, he clearly recognised the wide grin on Sho's face as he stared at his victim's immobile state. In the distortion of his vision, the grin contorted even further, the edges of his mouth tugged unnaturally high, making him look almost like a Cheshire Cat sneering at him from above.

Sho blew a final cloud of nicotine through his nose before walking over to Takeo, who lay only a few meters to Nao's left.

With a broad smile cracking across his face, he strolled over to him and stepped with one foot on Takeo's chest, causing the other to groan.

Sho leaned over him, put more pressure on his ribcage, and spit in his face.

Takeo flinched as the substance landed on his cheek, and Sho snickered, delighted. "This reminds one of old times, doesn't it?"

Takeo breathed heavily. "Don't…get too full of yourself. I won't let it end like last time… You can bet on that."

Sho laughed heartily. "If you try, I promise you, you'll end up worse than back then. You should learn when it's time to stop."

"The same goes for you, Sho."

He huffed and stepped off Takeo. With his hands in his pockets, he turned to the gang members. "Good work, guys. Let's get out of here quickly. It reeks of lowlife." He laughed. "Dinner's on me tonight."

The men cheered, and snickering and laughing, they left Nao and Takeo behind. Nao could hear their footsteps fading into the distance.

It seemed he had lost consciousness right after that, because when he opened his eyes again, he was gazing up at the night sky, where the stars had fully blossomed.

Constellations had shifted, and the night sky was darker and the stars even brighter than before he had closed his eyes.

For a moment, he was confused and disoriented as to where he was, but then the memories flooded back to him, just like the pain.

Nao's body felt heavy. His head was pulsating. His eyeballs and tongue felt too big for his skull and pressed against the insides of his bones. He tried to breathe but there was a sharp pain piercing his chest every time he inhaled.

He felt like losing consciousness all over again.

Nao stared at the constellations above him when he heard a sound to his left. Despite the pain, he tilted his head to the side. "Takeo," he asked, his voice croaky. "Are you okay?"

It took a while, but eventually he could hear a quiet voice answering him. "Yeah. I think so."

Very slowly, Takeo sat up. He held his stomach with both hands. "How about you?"

Nao followed his lead and tried to raise his torso slowly and cautiously. He groaned, feeling like every pair of his ribs had been used as drumsticks. "Alive…I guess," he muttered.

He glanced over at Takeo and immediately felt sick looking at his face. What had once been normal, tanned skin was now bloody and swollen. He could have come straight out of a horror movie with all that blood staining his face. His left eye was swollen shut. The puffed skin glistened morbidly in the light of the street lamp.

And Nao realised that he must look the exact same as Takeo. He might have thrown up if his body hadn't been so exhausted.

Groaning, Takeo stood up. He limped toward a nearby flight of stairs, setting himself down very slowly. After a moment, Nao followed and sat next to him.

They sat in the mouth of an alley. Across from them stood the empty shell of a closed restaurant. The glass doors were locked with a pair of chains and above the entrance hung a big LED sign in the shape of a noodle bowl. It illuminated the night with its bright red gleam, the fluorescent tubes flickered like a nervous heartbeat.

It was a desolate area. They hadn't seen a single soul since they'd been dragged here. But it wasn't anything novel. After all, it was a slow-dying city they lived in. More and more, the inhabitants moved away like rats leaving a sinking ship. Slowly but surely, the city was turning into a ghost ship, drifting aimlessly across the country's landscape.

People like Nao and Takeo, who had no option of leaving the cruise, were bound to watch it sink and disappear until it was fully engulfed by the depths of complete namelessness.

Nao suppressed a groan as he leaned back on both arms, lifting his head to look at the night sky above them.

"How funny," Takeo suddenly spoke into the silence.

Nao turned his head to him, but Takeo was staring straight forward, his face unusually stern. The blood on his face reflected the cold light of the street lamp, giving it a metallic sheen. It made him look almost alien.

Takeo's lips curled into a bitter smile. "Do you sometimes think about what you must have done in your past lives to deserve this?" He gazed at Nao. "I sometimes think I must have been a murderer or something like that in my past life. And in this life, I'm paying for my sins."

Nao was taken aback by his words and didn't know how to respond at first. They were surprisingly dark and he needed a moment to swallow them. Could something like that even happen? Being a murderer in your past life and paying for it in the next life? Nao didn't know whether he believed in past lives in the first place, but as he pondered it for quite some time, he thought that it could make sense. After all, the universe had always had a morbid sense of humour—his own life was the best example of that.

"If you put it that way…I think this might be the case for me too," he said after a while.

Who knew, maybe all of this was some kind of strange punishment. It would at least explain why things always turned out for him like this.

Takeo turned around and looked at Nao, his expression unreadable and yet bittersweet. He huffed. "Then I guess there was no way this could have ended happily."

Suddenly, Takeo burst out laughing. It was unnervingly loud and rang in Nao's ears. It sounded hollow and almost maniacal. Eerily, this laughter haunted the empty street like a resentful ghost.

Nao was startled. He stared at the other with wide eyes. "Why are you laughing?"

Takeo doubled over, holding his stomach. The laughter was obviously causing his body pain, but it didn't seem like he could willingly stop. "I don't know," he said, wiping the blood out of his eyes. "I guess all of this is just so fucked up that it's hilarious. I try and try but still end up like this. Is it because I'm not allowed to live easily? Is this a punishment for my previous life? Will I live pathetically until the day I die?"

Nao scowled. "You must have gotten too many hits on the head."

Takeo's body, on the other hand, was still shaking from laughter. "I don't know why I thought about it now, but…I just wish I could have been there when you kicked Sho in his balls. That must have been so hilarious!"

Takeo's sudden words took Nao by surprise, and he huffed. He must have lost his mind, Nao thought. Or maybe he really had gotten too many hits on the head. Could someone turn stupid from a beating? But as Nao reminisced about that incident, it caused him to unconsciously break into a faint smile. "…Yeah, it was funny."

Takeo looked at him, his eyes filled with tears of laughter and agony. "It even made you smile!"

Nao huffed again, but he couldn't stop his lips from curling up. He didn't know whether it was because of the stress, the pain, or because of Takeo, but he kept smiling at the absurdity of everything.

Maybe he had gotten too many hits on the head as well. He figured someone could really go stupid from it.

"It was funny," Nao repeated.

Takeo nodded. "Yes, it was."

For a while, they sat on the stairs. Too tired and in too much pain, they rested. It was cold and dark, but the stars, which were in full bloom, cast a little bit of light.

— Chapter 9 —

Nao's face stung as Mrs. Takahashi dabbed a disinfectant-soaked cotton ball across his many wounds.

Mrs. Takahashi nearly had a heart attack the moment she saw Nao coming out of his room that morning. He had been so tired and exhausted the night before that when he came home, he didn't even bother to wash off the blood and just went straight to bed. Now his face was crusted and swollen. His cheeks and chin were puffy, the skin green and purple, and a big gash stretched across his forehead.

The housekeeper had forced him to sit at the kitchen table and tried to tend to his wounds. She had wiped the dried blood off his face and disinfected his bruises. It hurt every time she dabbed the cotton ball on his raw skin, but Nao tried to swallow it down.

"I can't believe you got into a fight like this," Mrs. Takahashi said. Her face was contorted into a deep frown. A single vein popped out on her forehead. "I know you young boys are competitive and like to show off your strength, but this goes too far!" In her exasperation, she pressed the cotton ball a little too hard onto his bruises and Nao flinched.

"Excuse me," she mumbled and immediately softened her grip.

She placed the cotton ball, which had taken the colour of dirty crimson, on the table and sighed resignedly. Taking a few bandage strips, she began taping the wound across his forehead.

"You really should have gone to a hospital," she said, but Nao stubbornly shook his head, just as he did every time she mentioned it.

The housekeeper sighed again, and with a slight disapproving shake of her head, continued taping his forehead. Her gaze was full of concentration. Her fingers moved carefully and quickly across his face. And even through his swollen skin, he could feel the warmth and softness of the fingertips seeping in.

They were nearly finished when Nao's mother entered the kitchen. She was dressed in full work attire: a grey blazer and long pencil skirt, ready to leave for her job at the law firm. Her black hair was tied back in a neat bun, red lipstick adorned her full lips. Not a hair was out of place, not a single eyelash askew. She truly was a beautiful woman. Dignified and elegant in appearance, yet cold and distant, like ice and frost. In a hurry, she grabbed her leather briefcase from the table where her son and housekeeper were sitting.

Her eyes flickered briefly over the two of them, then to the table, which was littered with bandages and bloody cotton balls. Her mouth twitched, displeased. "Clean the table. You know I hate it when there's filth," was all she said before exiting the room.

Mrs. Takahashi grumbled quietly and finished treating Nao's wound. Nao couldn't be too sure, but he thought he saw something like anger flare up in her eyes—something he rarely witnessed on her motherly face.

"So…all finished," Mrs. Takahashi finally said as she cleaned her hands with a tissue. "I don't think it will leave a scar, but still—promise me you'll stay out of trouble." She gave Nao a serious look and he nodded.

"I mean it," she said. "It's not good for your reputation in this house if you always come home like this."

"I will try," Nao said and stood up. "I have to go now." He was about to head out when Mrs. Takahashi suddenly stopped him. "Wait." She reached into her pocket and pulled out a blister of pain medication. "The pain shouldn't keep you from concentrating in class." She shoved the blister into Nao's hands.

He nodded gratefully and headed out to get ready for school.

Subconsciously, Nao started looking around for Takeo as soon as he arrived, but the latter was nowhere to be found. It seemed like he had ditched school that day, and Nao could understand why. Normally, they would have met for their math lesson after class, but he assumed this was a telltale sign that their meeting was cancelled for today.

Nao sat through the classes, already used to the stares of his classmates by now. They still didn't dare to approach him. He guessed he had become some kind of bad omen for them—like a black cat one would rather not cross.

Too scared to draw Sho's attention to themselves, they just watched him be his favourite punching bag. There was only one person who wasn't afraid of being near him.

Nao carried his books in his arms as he switched rooms from history to chemistry. The whole class headed down the hallways, the pace slow and dragging as multiple classes appeared to be changing rooms at the same time.

Nao wordlessly followed his fellow students when he was pushed to the side, his shoulder and elbow bumping against the wall with a dull *thud*. He looked up to see the ugly mugs of Sho and his lackeys passing by. Wide grins were etched into their faces.

"Lookin' good, Miyamoto," Sho shouted, and the students behind him snickered maliciously. "The look of a victim suits you."

Nao dug his fingers into his books. He wanted to punch that idiot in his face so bad! He gritted his teeth, chest heaving and falling heavily. His blood boiled, as it had the night he was beaten up—yet, somehow, he managed to ignore Sho's savage provocations, keeping his head down and putting one foot in front of the other to get away as quickly as he could. The cruel laughter still followed him, just like the nervous glances of his classmates when he caught up to them.

Nao slowed down his steps again and fell behind them, so they could stop gaping at him. Whether this was more beneficial to Nao, because he escaped their piercing stares that way, or to his classmates who got rid of the curse that would bring nothing but bad luck to anyone getting too close to it, was unclear.

Nao's stomach was still heavy when he exited the school that afternoon. Matching his feelings, the weather had once again become grey. What had been a few summer-like days over the past week had again turned into the grey, cold soup it had been since the beginning of the year.

Nao was so absorbed in his thoughts, he nearly didn't notice the person waving at him from the other side of the street.

Huh? He had to look twice before he recognised Takeo, who was standing across from him on a blue bicycle and waved at him with a big, cheeky smile.

Nao furrowed his brows in surprise. He looked behind him, then left and right in case there was another person he could be waving at. But Nao was the only one around.

Hesitantly, he crossed the street.

"What are you doing here?" he asked, confused.

"I'm here to pick you up." Takeo grinned. His face still looked heavily distorted. His left eye was swollen shut and had taken on a nasty black colour. The cuts on his cheeks and chin were still partly open, and Nao figured there was no one to take care of his wounds like Mrs. Takahashi had for him.

"I know we are supposed to be studying today, but I think we've practiced so hard the past week that today we deserve a break." He put one foot on the pedal. "Hop on. I'll drive us."

"Where?"

"The sea," Takeo said as if it were the most obvious thing in the world. "If we go fast, we'll be there in about twenty minutes."

Nao looked around, strongly suspecting there might be a hidden camera reveal about to happen, but to his bafflement, there seemed to be no camera around. He gazed back at Takeo. "You are crazy," he then concluded with a skeptical glance. "You can't even cycle with only one eye."

"I made it all the way here, didn't I?" Takeo shrugged nonchalantly. "And I promise you—I'm the safest cyclist out there. Now hop on."

Nao turned around and tried to leave, but Takeo rolled after him, insistent as always.

"Come on. It won't kill you," he persisted.

Nao stopped and turned around. Takeo gazed at him with a wide eye and that dangerously innocent smile. It thawed his icy refusal like spring thawed winter.

Nao sighed deeply. "Okay," he finally acquiesced, defeated.

"Super! Get on!"

Nao pulled his backpack tighter and swung his leg over the back of the bicycle, settling behind Takeo.

"Hold on tight, okay? I'll go fast." He pushed down on the pedals, and, startled, Nao dug his fingers into Takeo's sides. He tightly gripped the fabric of the shirt between his fingers as they rode down the street. The cold wind pelted his face.

Safest cyclist, my foot! Nao thought as soon as they started. *Forget that!* Takeo's cycling was fast and reckless. They jolted over sidewalks and potholes. Nao had to hold on tightly to the other in order not to be thrown off.

The only advantage of this wild ride was that they quickly arrived at the sea. Even from hundreds of meters afar, Nao could spot the grey giant in the distance.

Soon they arrived at a path leading down to the beach. Takeo leaned the bicycle against a fence, and together they walked down the sandy trail.

Nao was still a bit shaky and nauseous from the ride, to be honest. His stomach greatly rioted against the unorthodox way Takeo handled a bike. But that feeling soon faded as he was greeted with the sensations of the sea. It overcame him like a spring tide.

Nao's feet sank into the milky sand. The saltiness of the air spread on his tongue like water, and the shrieking of seagulls echoing from the skies filled the shells of his ears.

He took a deep breath, expanding his lungs with the crisp, ripe ocean breeze, savouring the sweet scent of seaweed and foam.

Nao had never been a fan of the sea. He had visited it in the past with his parents when he had still been a young child, but, even then, the sheer vastness of the ocean and its unpredictability had always scared him.

Now that he was back for the first time after so many years, he felt nothing but amazement.

Wide-eyed, he stared at the turbulent water. It stretched out to the far horizon where it melted into one with the sky. Stormy clouds and grey water became one confusing chaos.

"It's really beautiful here, isn't it?" Takeo commented. "I come here quite often. It's one of my favourite spots."

He took a deep breath of the fresh air and sat down on the sand. Hesitant, Nao followed him.

He felt his body sink into the cold sand. "And what are we supposed to do now?" he asked.

Takeo shrugged. "Sit, enjoy the view, talk… Whatever we want to do."

Nao wrapped his arms around his legs and gazed across the sea. "That's not very precise."

Takeo huffed a laugh.

"Then...let me ask you something." Nao decided to speak, after all, and turned around to face the other. His chest was burning with that one question that had been restlessly stirring inside him since their first interactions. "I don't know why you're doing it, but...you're always laughing so carelessly. I can't tell if you really don't mind or if you're just a bit dense...but how are you able to be so cheerful even after what happened yesterday?"

Takeo looked at him in surprise. Then, he shrugged lightly. "I'm neither careless nor dense; I just think it's better to laugh it off instead of brooding about it. Crying doesn't change anything, so I'd rather just laugh about it."

"But laughing doesn't change anything either! Those assholes are still getting away with everything they do."

"Yeah, it may not change anything that's happening, but I don't want to spend my time full of anger because of them. I want to use my free time better than torturing myself with problems I can't solve in that moment anyway."

"Still, I don't understand how you can just brush it off so easily. What is there even to laugh about? Those assholes are winning...and nothing changes."

Takeo looked intently at Nao. His head was crooked to the side. "I can understand you. I really do. I'm also angry. Very much! But I don't want to give up any more of my happiness because of them. When I'm here by the sea and watch the water and the sky, I try to only think about that and enjoy this moment. It's not always easy, but I try."

Nao drew his legs closer to his chest, resting his chin on top of his knees. He gazed across the grey water. "Don't take it personally, but I honestly still don't fully understand it. What does it matter whether I'm in the moment if sooner or later all of the crap I'm trying not to think about will happen anyway? I don't get how I could possibly enjoy the moment if it will inevitably turn into the very thing I'm avoiding. What's even the point of that?"

Takeo pursed his lips. "Well, that's how you stay sane."

He shrugged. "At least I do. Sometimes I just have to think about something different than this fucked up shit. Distract myself with something that makes me happy."

Nao sighed. Takeo could always talk so easily. In Nao's world, there was nothing that could take his mind off things. Wherever he went, school or home, it was always the same. As if he were running in an endless circle—a spiral that only descended deeper.

Takeo watched him attentively from the side for a moment, and then suddenly rose. "Okay, then let's try and take your mind off those thoughts."

Surprised, Nao looked up. "What do you mean?"

"Let's try to shout out all of our anger. It'll free your mind."

Nao furrowed his brows harshly. "That sounds like something you'd read in a cheap self-help book."

Takeo grinned. "Come on, let's try it. I promise you'll feel better."

"I don't want to."

With a gentle smile, Takeo extended his hand to Nao, who turned away with an exasperated huff. "Forget it," he said, pulling his legs closer to his chest.

But Takeo wasn't the type to give up easily. He grabbed Nao's arm and simply pulled him to his feet. Nao glared at him with a deep scowl which was met with a warm smile. "Watch me," Takeo said, taking a step toward the sea. He looked up at the sky, sucked in a deep breath, and then let out a long and loud scream.

Startled, Nao flinched and glanced frantically around. "Are you crazy!?" he whispered between closed teeth.

Takeo just laughed. "Now you try."

"No! Forget it."

"There's no one around to hear us. And even if there were, no one cares. So give it a try."

"No, you are crazy!"

Still grinning, Takeo turned to face the sea. He cupped both of his hands around his mouth and shouted, "I HATE SHO AND THAT GANG OF ASSHOLES! THEY CAN GO FUCK THEMSELVES!"

His voice reverberated across the vast ocean and was swallowed between the sounds of the crashing waves.

He looked over at Nao. "Come on. Try it one time."

Nao pursed his lips. "Will you finally leave me alone if I do it?"

Takeo nodded and Nao sighed.

Eventually, he faced the water as well, took a deep breath and shouted with all his might, "I CAN'T BELIEVE I'M DOING THIS! THIS IS DUMB!" Just like Takeo's scream, his voice was carried across the sea by the salty winds and enveloped by waves and the shrieking of seagulls. Almost as if they were trying to carry his sorrows far away.

Nao took another deep breath, cupping his mouth with his hands. "SINCE THIS GUY WON'T LET ME GO UNTIL I SHOUT, I'LL JUST DO IT!

"I HATE THIS SCHOOL! AND I HATE SHO!" He exhaled and inhaled again. "I HATE MY FAMILY! AND MY GRAND-PARENTS! ALL OF THEM CAN GO AND PISS OFF!"

"I HATE MY PARENTS TOO! AND THIS SCHOOL AND CITY!" Takeo suddenly joined in.

Nao glanced over to him for a second before turning back to the sea. "I HATE BEING BORN INTO THAT FAMILY! I HATE LIVING THIS LIFE!"

"ME TOO! I HATE THIS FUCKING LIFE TOO!"

Nao let his arms fall down. His heart was pumping. His throat felt hoarse. Adrenaline filled his veins up to the very tips of his fingers and he could hear the blood rushing inside his ears. It felt...*enlivening.*

"Do you feel better?" Takeo asked.

Nao looked at him. "...I think so."

Takeo smiled proudly. "I promised you, didn't I?"

— Chapter 10 —

Their battle scars slowly began to heal over the course of the following week. The swelling of Nao's face went down and the gash across his forehead closed up. Takeo's bruises had become a soft yellow and he could finally open his eye again.

They hadn't had much time to study together since Takeo was fairly busy. The baseball team was preparing for a match against a neighbouring school at the end of the month, so they often met for practice.

Nearly a week had passed since the incident with the gang before Nao and Takeo found the time to study again.

Nao's head was fuming from all the equations, but Takeo told him that he was slowly getting the gist of it. Nao wasn't so sure about that, though he appreciated the other's words nonetheless.

Finally, the lesson came to an end, and with a sigh, Nao started packing up. He shoved the papers in his bag when Takeo suddenly piped up. "Do you have time tomorrow?"

Confused, he looked up. Tomorrow was Saturday. A weird day to meet for a study session, he thought—but Nao nodded anyway.

"Good, some people from the baseball team and I are going out tomorrow. Do you want to tag along?"

"Huh?" Nao gazed at Takeo, dumbfounded. Unsure, he pointed at himself. "You want me to come with your friends?"

"'Friends' is a bit of a strong term. We are just teammates, but sometimes we go hang out at karaoke bars or arcades. It'd be fun if you joined us." Takeo's lips lifted into a gentle smile.

Nao stared at him, still puzzled. "I don't know. It'd be a little weird if I just joined in."

Takeo shook his head reassuringly. "No, not at all. Just come with us tomorrow. I told you: distraction is a good method to forget about all the crappy things and stay sane."

"I don't know…"

"Okay, it's settled. Tomorrow, at eight, at the convenience store near the big intersection. Don't leave me hanging! See you!" Before Nao had a chance to voice his objections, Takeo had already grabbed his backpack and fled out of the room, leaving him behind.

At a loss for words, Nao stared at the door the other had just rushed through and then let his head fall onto the table with a resigned sigh. Right now, the only thing endangering his sanity was that guy.

In all honesty, Nao would have rather gone to bed than to get dressed for wherever they were about to go. He only decided to come because of Takeo. He was the one giving him math lessons for free, so this felt like something Nao should do for him in return.

Although, as he stood in front of his wardrobe, he seriously contemplated that.

Why should he even go there? No other person there would want him to join them anyway. They'd only be aggrieved to drag him along.

Nao sighed deeply. *Such a stupid thing…* he thought. Angrily, he stared into his wardrobe, considering just staying in, but when he thought of Takeo's disappointed face, he picked out a hoodie from it, nonetheless, and got dressed.

He took a black cap and pulled it over his hair.

The air was mild and the sun close to setting as he stepped outside. Since it was Saturday, the streets were fairly crowded. The shops were brimming with people, and Nao wondered where the baseball team was planning to hang out tonight.

Leisurely, he walked to the convenience store Takeo wanted to meet at. Even from a hundred meters away, Nao could spot the all-too-familiar frame beneath the blue-green LED sign. The moment Takeo saw him too, he broke into a wide grin.

"You came." He beamed.

"You wanted me to come," Nao deflected.

Takeo glanced at his wristwatch. "And we should be right on time. Let's go," he said joyously and set off. Nao followed him wordlessly.

He was two steps beside Takeo and couldn't help but peek over at him.

Takeo was still wearing those ugly purple shoelaces that Nao had seen him wear all the time. He wasn't sure whether he had bought the shoes like that or put them on himself. Either way, Nao thought it was a weird choice. Today they appeared even more prominent because of the loose, sky-blue button-up shirt Takeo was wearing.

As with a lot of things, they were on different sides of the spectrum. While Nao was dressed in dark clothes, with his hair and face hidden beneath a cap, Takeo was basically glowing in his bright clothes. It was almost comical. Like the picture of a Shiba Inu and a black cat strolling along the streets.

"Where are we going anyway?" Nao asked after they had turned into another street.

"The arcade," Takeo said. "Have you been there before?"

"Yes, but it's been some years."

They continued their leisurely stroll through the crowd until they finally arrived at a two-story building. A group of six teenagers was lounging in front of the store already. Takeo waved at them.

"Hey, have you been waiting for long? You could have already gone inside," he chattered.

The boys didn't answer and instead looked skeptically over to Nao. Their eyes were filled with equal parts of surprise and dismissal. Nao was all too familiar with such gazes.

"What's the newbie doing here?" one of them asked, eyeing him with barely concealed dislike as his lips curled downward like he was swallowing something bitter.

Takeo smiled at them, totally unbothered by their reaction, and gently wrapped his arm around Nao's shoulders. "You mean Nao? He's a friend of mine. I asked him to join."

"A friend?" another boy asked in disbelief, and Nao couldn't even blame him for it. He was just as surprised to be called that.

"Yeah." Takeo nodded confidently. "Then, can we go inside? It's getting cold."

After exchanging a few critical glances, the boys let up on the surprise guest and moved inside.

Takeo's arm was still wrapped around his shoulders and Nao stood rooted to the spot.

"Let's go." Takeo glanced at him with a soft smile and let go of him to join his teammates. Slowly, Nao freed himself from his petrification and followed suit.

The arcade was just like in his early memories—filled with dancing lights, bright colours, and wildly blinking devices of all sorts and shapes. The air, brimming with the smell of cheap plastic and greasy food, trodden-down carpets and sweat, filled Nao's nose and scratched at long-forgotten parts of his brain, cooing memories to the front that had been believed to have vanished a long time ago. Children from middle to high school roamed the space and the atmosphere vibrated with elated voices and cheerful music. It was as scarily overwhelming as it was exciting.

Taken aback, Nao followed the group of boys across the hall.

"Where do you want to go first?"

"I don't know. But the racing game was fun last time."

"I wanna try the zombie shooter game. I've been getting quite good at it."

"But there's a huge queue in front of it."

"Then let's go over there. I haven't tried that yet."

Nao walked behind the group, clueless. He had been here a few times in his early middle school days. Back then, he had used the little pocket money he had gotten from New Year's and Christmas to play some games by himself. He barely remembered what he had played, and even less how those games were played. So, he just silently tagged along with the others.

Ultimately, they split into two groups. One went to the racing simulator while the other participated in a one-on-one combat game.

Nao watched two of the boys, Akira and Ichiro, compete against each other in a virtual duel. Shouting and yelling, they hammered the buttons as if they were piñatas at a birthday party. Takeo and another boy named Yoshi cheered them on while their characters threshed each other mercilessly.

After a few rounds and Ichiro winning, they moved on to the dance machine. Nao would never in a hundred years go on such a monstrosity, but Takeo was one of the first to volunteer.

He and Yoshi stepped onto the dance mat. Excited, they picked one of the songs and started battling. Both of them were *really* bad at the game, and Nao was overcome with second-hand embarrassment. In the end, he was just glad that no one asked him to try it.

Takeo lost the battle by a few points and asked for a rematch, but Yoshi wanted to keep his victory and declined. After bickering about what they were going to do next, they eventually decided to rejoin the other group.

Fortunately, it wasn't as hard to find them inside the over-crowded hall as it had seemed at first. One of the boys was cursing so loudly at one of the games that they could quickly make out the source of it. Kenzo sat in front of a solo player shooting game and yelled angrily at the machine. "This stupid thing!" he raged. "This can't be possible! This machine is broken!"

The boys next to him giggled mischievously.

"Are you losing?" Akira asked, amused.

"No. This thing must be rigged or something like that..." Kenzo muttered, irritated.

"Maybe you just suck! Let me try," Akira said and pushed Kenzo off the chair. Thrilled, the other boys watched as Akira tried to take down the boss.

All of a sudden, a lightbulb flashed to life in Nao's brain, enlightening an old memory. The graphic, the characters, it all seemed strangely familiar. Nao believed he remembered that this was one of the games he'd played back when he'd visited the arcade as a child.

Takeo seemed to have taken notice of the change in Nao's expression and scooted slowly closer. "Do you know this game?" he asked.

Nao nodded. "I think so."

Angrily, Akira kicked the machine. "Piece of junk," he cursed as the words *Game Over* slid across the screen.

"Who sucks now?" Kenzo asked condescendingly, and Akira shot him an almost fatal glare.

As the others debated who should try the impossible quest next, Takeo shoved Nao into the center without hesitation whatsoever.

"Nao wants to try," he said confidently, and the other was struck speechless.

"W-what?" he stuttered and gazed back at Takeo, who just looked at him with an encouraging smile. *You can do it*, he mouthed, and Nao swore that he'd break his neck later!

He didn't want to move, but as the others scooted aside to make space for him, Nao had no choice but to hesitantly sit down.

He could feel the eyes of the seven boys glued to him. He felt their stares running down the back of his head, prickling in the tips of his fingers. Nao could barely press the start button.

For a horrible second, he forgot how to play. He couldn't defend himself or move during the first few hits, losing HP, but then the game slowly started feeling familiar. His fingers began moving, and so did the character. The longer he played, the more his middle school self seemed to awake, and after a few minutes, it felt like he had never left the arcade.

His fingers flew across the buttons just like his character dodged the attacks. He managed to dodge and attack and fly over his opponent's punches as if it were nothing. And suddenly, he had won.

The boys behind him started cheering. Their shouts of excitement and admiration rang through the air and Nao could feel them slap him approvingly on the back.

"How did you do that?" "That was amazing!" "Did you secretly practice before coming here?"

Nao just nodded politely, overwhelmed with all of the positive feedback. He let his eyes slip over to Takeo, who beamed at him with a bright smile. Tentatively, Nao smiled back at him.

After his win, they decided to try out some more games. Nao participated in a few but let the others take on most of them. Then, eventually, after having spent a few hours at the arcade, the group decided to end the evening with dinner in the adjacent restaurant.

They ordered pizza, ramen, and hotdogs. Nao nipped at a cup of ice-cold lemonade and Takeo had somehow gotten his hands on a can of his favourite mango soda.

At some point, all of the boys started chatting about their baseball practice, and since Nao had no idea what they were talking about, he just spaced out. He was only pulled back into the conversation once its center of interest shifted to Takeo.

"But our Takeo has been really lenient with practice lately," Kenzo noted off-handedly.

The boy in question just shrugged it off. "I had a lot to do," he deflected passively.

"That's right. I heard you've had a lot of trouble with Sho Nishimura lately," Akira pressed, and the others nodded. "Are you picking up your business from middle school again?"

Nao was confused. He looked over at Takeo, whose body had become as rigid as a board. His fingers around the can tightened and little dents appeared in the soft aluminium.

Yoshi snickered. "Surely. A junkie doesn't supply themselves."

"Speaking of which, how's your mother—"

The bang of Takeo thrusting the soda can onto the table shook the room. A few of the boys flinched, and the smiles fell abruptly off their faces.

In shocked silence, they stared at Takeo, who glared at them with a scarily blank expression. "We're not here to talk about old stuff, are we? I thought we wanted to discuss the upcoming game," he said slowly, and a few boys gulped nervously.

"Then, how's your pitching going, Ichiro?" Takeo shifted the focus. He had put on a smile, though it could not be called that— rather it seemed like a distortion of his features. As if the face beneath the smile hid a graveness that could hardly be concealed by the forced lift of one's lips. "I've heard from our coach you had some trouble with that."

Startled, Ichiro looked up, but then nodded slowly. "Y-yeah, the coach has been thinking about giving me extra lessons."

Hesitantly, the conversation picked itself up again. The tension gradually died down and the ripples eased again. The topic had circled back to baseball practice, and the boys talked passionately about how to improve one's pitching technique, yet Nao was only looking at Takeo. The latter seemed calm, but his eyes were directed at the plate in front of him. His shoulders were slumped forward and the corners of his mouth drooped down. He looked exhausted, Nao thought.

Not too long after the incident, the dinner came to an end. The group said goodbye and split into smaller fragments. Ultimately, Nao and Takeo were left by themselves.

They stood in front of the shop. The wind had turned colder with the deepening night, Nao shivered lightly.

The atmosphere had been kind of awkward since the incident. Nao had no idea what the boys had meant, but he also didn't know how far he could ask or if he should ask at all.

All he knew was that Takeo had been abnormally quiet since it had happened. So, he mustered his courage and asked, "Is everything okay?"

Dumb question. He immediately regretted it and wished to punch himself.

Nao would have *hated* it if someone asked him that, but fortunately, Takeo didn't seem to mind.

"Yeah, of course. They can just be idiots sometimes who can't keep their mouths shut." He shrugged, seemingly unbothered. "But more importantly, how was it for you? Did you have fun at the arcade?"

Takeo had shut himself off. He obviously didn't want to talk about it, and Nao accepted that. He didn't dig any further.

"I think so, yes," he said. "It was better than I thought."

"Good." Takeo smiled. It was a genuine smile. "You were really good, especially at that combat game."

"That was just luck."

"No! It was not. You were really good!" Takeo insisted strongly, his brows furrowing in conviction.

"Well, I was at least better than you playing that dance machine game."

"Huh, what do you mean? I was really good. I nearly won."

Nao shook his head. "No, you were horrible."

"I think I was pretty good."

"No. You were *really* bad."

Takeo looked at Nao with wide eyes and then suddenly burst into laughter. He bent over laughing, holding a hand in front of his lips. "You really have no filter, do you?"

Nao frowned. "Don't get me wrong," Takeo quickly said. "I like that. It's good."

He wiped his eyes. "Next time, I want to see *you* dance on that machine."

Nao instantly shook his head. "Never," he denied immediately, and Takeo grinned. "I'll get you on that thing one day."

Sighing resignedly, Nao ran a hand through his hair and accidentally knocked the cap off his head. It fell down to his feet. Before he could move, Takeo had already bent down and picked it up. "Careful," he said and leaned forward to put it back on Nao's head.

Takeo acted so briskly that there was no time for Nao to react. He only felt the other move closer. One hand at the back and the other at the front of the cap, he pulled it over Nao's head. Nao could feel Takeo's hand grazing his hair in the back. He could sense the warmth of his palm radiating against his face. And suddenly, Nao felt his heart skip a beat.

Startled, he took a step back.

Takeo looked at him with wide eyes. "Are you okay?" he asked, confused.

Nao stared at the ground. His heart beat loudly in his chest. "Y-yeah... I-i just... You pulled my hair," he stuttered, shocked.

"Sorry, my bad." Takeo grinned apologetically. "It's getting cold. Shall we go, then? I can walk you home if you like."

"No, no," Nao quickly denied. "I can go by myself. B-bye!"

He turned on the spot and walked away. He didn't even know whether it was the right direction. He just hoped to get as far away as possible and for his heart to stop beating so abnormally.

— Chapter 11 —

Nao woke up and stared at the ceiling. His eyes were still heavy with sleep.

With the sun already risen, the light of a new day flooded his small bedroom.

Drowsily, he sat up and rubbed his eyes. Last night still felt like a dream to him.

He couldn't remember the last time he had hung out with people in a casual, easy way like that, or if he ever had at all.

Nao hadn't been sure what to expect from it since he wasn't even really invited, but, to his surprise, it had been better than he'd initially thought. It was actually…fun.

He rubbed his face. Well, he had solely shown up in the first place because Takeo had pestered him to go, but…

He froze.

Takeo.

The memories of them alone in front of the restaurant flashed back into his head like a mighty wave. He was crushed by its weight and drowned pathetically in the memories of said moment. Still in shock, Nao looked over to his desk where the black cap from last night lay. He stared at it with big eyes.

He remembered it. The cap falling off his head and Takeo gently putting it back on.

Nao remembered it too clearly. Takeo's face suddenly so close to his own. His hand grazing the tips of his hair. The texture of his skin in the dim light, the yellow and green bruises lying beneath its surface. He could see the mole on his left cheek and the scar running from the corner of his eye to his ear.

Nao shook his head. *Idiot!* he told himself. Why did he think about that? He hit the sides of his head, now fully awake. *Absolute moron!* he scolded himself and stood up.

Decisively, he grabbed the cap off the desk and threw it back into his wardrobe. He hoped it would rot there until he forgot about it!

A few minutes later, Nao sat with his family at the table and ate breakfast. Mrs. Takahashi had prepared rice, miso soup, pickled radish, and salmon.

As with most of their meals, it was dead silent at the table. Only the sound of chewing and clanking chopsticks filled the room.

This was the proper etiquette in his parents' opinion. Nao was just glad that they barely had to talk.

Quietly, he chewed on his rice and radish. To his left sat his younger brother Toyo, whom Nao saw gleefully munching his salmon from the corner of his eye.

"You've been staying out late recently, I've noticed," his father suddenly broke the silence.

Surprised, Nao gulped down the lump of rice. It got stuck in his throat. "Yes," he forced out.

"I thought you wanted to study hard. What is the reason for your sudden behaviour?"

Nao tried to swallow the chunk stuck in his throat. He coughed while trying to withstand his father's pervasive eyes. "A-a classmate has been giving me extra lessons," he eventually croaked out. "We have been studying together after classes."

Nao tried to hold his father's gaze, and, ever so slightly, he could see his eyes widening. It wasn't a big movement, nor was it long, but his father didn't bother to follow up with another question after that. And Nao was greatly surprised because this was the most positive feedback he had ever received from him.

Silently, he went back to eating, feeling a little bit lighter in his chest because, for once, he had done something that wasn't frowned upon.

Sluggishly, Monday arrived, and Nao returned to school. He had spent the rest of his Sunday solving the math exercises Takeo had assigned to him. They had an upcoming exam soon and Nao still had a lot to study for it.

After class, he gave his notes to Takeo, so the latter could grade them and talk about it in more detail tomorrow.

Nao felt dumb for the uncanny agitation tickling in his spine and fingers when he stood in front of Takeo. He couldn't even exactly pinpoint why he felt that way, but he was filled with great relief at the realisation that his heart beat normally this time.

Thanking him, Takeo took the sheets and slid them in his bag.

They packed up and sauntered outside.

"I'll look over it later, but seeing how you've improved over the past weeks, I don't think there'll be much to correct," Takeo said easily as they headed toward the school gates.

It was a cloudy day. The thick, hazy clouds hung low above the city, and the air smelled of mellow petrichor.

"You'll ace the exam for sure!"

As always caught off-guard by Takeo's unshaken optimism, Nao scoffed. "Let's wait till we take it."

"It'll be good, I promise," he stated confidently and laughed. "I'll see you tomorrow, then." He lifted his hand to wave good-bye when suddenly—

"*Takeo,*" an unfamiliar voice resounded.

Nao didn't recognise the person speaking, but by the way Takeo tensed up and his eyes widened in pure horror, it seemed that he did. Slowly, Takeo turned around.

Behind him appeared a petite woman. She seemed to be in her forties or fifties. Her frame was thin and almost scraggy. The worn-out clothes, with loose threads and stains all over them, clung to her like a shirt on a hanger. Her hair was long and unkempt. The frizzy, black strands fell over her chest.

Nao was struck speechless by the haggard woman. His heart stuttered instinctively at her ghostly appearance. At first glance, he believed she might be one of the homeless people who liked to stroll through this part of the town and beg for money, but nothing could have prepared him for the words Takeo muttered upon that woman's emergence. "*Mom,*" he breathed.

She gawked at him with vapid eyes. Her skin looked grey and sickish beneath the daylight, like old paper, crinkled and dried out. Dark eye bags lay sunken into her face as if they were already deeply ingrained there.

When she saw the face of her son, her thin lips lifted into a smile, which caused her to look even more unsettling. "I have found you," she said, her voice sounded hoarse. "I have come here to see you. I need money. Do you have money?"

For the first time since Nao had met him, Takeo looked truly scared. With widened eyes and ash-grey skin, he glanced around.

A few students, who had come out of the school, stopped to look at the strange woman. Shocked, they eyed her and then turned to each other, whispering immediately.

Takeo became paler by the second. "What…what are you doing here?" seemed to be the only words he could get out.

"I need money. Your brother said I couldn't have any more. But I know you have some, have you not?" Her words sounded weird. They were ever so slightly slurred at the end, a weird lilt lying beneath every vowel. She spoke like she was under some kind of influence—her words and intentions born from an unclear mind.

Takeo grabbed her by the scraggy arms. His face was contorted in fearful shock—pale and despaired. "We have to go," he choked out. "Come."

"I don't want to!" his mother suddenly cried out, and even more people turned their heads. "Give me...give me my money!" Takeo grabbed her more tightly, desperate. "O-okay...I will... But now, please come with me! Please."

He tried to pull her away, and reluctantly, she followed him.

As Takeo dragged her along with him, he turned around and met Nao's eyes. Nao had been frozen in shock until now. But as he read Takeo's eyes, he could understand the silent plea written inside them. *Please, let me explain later.*

Then he turned around and tried to pull his mother far away from the gawking eyes of the people.

Nao watched them disappear around the corner, but the whispering didn't stop. If anything, it grew even bolder.

"Is that the guy? Takeo Iwasaki?" "What do you mean?" "You know who I mean! Takeo Iwasaki, the guy who had a drug empire in middle school. He used to beat people up and blackmail them. That's why he was transferred here."

"Ahh, I think I've heard about that... And that woman...that was his junkie mother?"

"Looks like it. I guess the drugs run in the family." The boys giggled quietly.

Frozen, Nao stared at them as they walked past him, still whispering and snickering.

Takeo Iwasaki and a drug ring? Takeo Iwasaki who beat up and blackmailed others?

Nao thought back to Takeo that evening at the arcade. He remembered the vivid smiles and warm laughter, the gentle touches and encouraging words.

No, something wasn't right. This couldn't be the same Takeo as in those stories!

— Chapter 12 —

A day later, Nao and Takeo sat in the study room.

The air was heavy with the events of the prior day. Although not spoken aloud, both of them could feel the unvoiced questions filling the small space like a creeping tsunami. The tension ebbed away, only to surge back with an intensity multiplied by a thousand.

Takeo sat on the chair with his arms crossed in front of his chest. Brooding, he stared at the ground. They had originally met up to study, as always, but Nao already knew that today they wouldn't get any math done.

After quite some time, Takeo broke the stifling silence. The first wave hitting the shore. "You…must have heard all kinds of things about me." He slowly lifted his head to look at Nao. "From Sho, in the restaurant, and I'm sure people ran their mouths about me yesterday as well."

Nao gazed back at Takeo, though the latter's eyes were impossible to read. Hesitantly, he nodded.

"It must have been confusing hearing all those things about me… Why have you never asked about it?"

Nao shrugged. "It's not my place to dig into people's private matters. If someone wants to tell me, they do. If not, they don't."

Nao meant what he said, but, of course, he had still been curious about the background of Takeo's and Sho's relationship. What was the deal between them? Why would each of them go to such lengths to destroy the other? And what was the history between Takeo and that godforsaken gang?

He was definitely curious, yet Nao would never ask directly about it.

He had known for quite some time that there was more to Takeo than what he had shown him in the past weeks. Nao had foreseen it when he'd talked about Sho, in the alley after they'd been beaten up, as well as yesterday, when he'd come face to face with his mother.

Nao had the feeling that both of them were quite similar in that case. They had neither home nor shelter they could seek. All they did was run from one problem at school to the other at home. From one disappointment to the next.

The sole difference between them was that Takeo closed off all of his problems behind a smile, while Nao closed himself off. It was almost ironic how two people could be so similar yet so different—like day and night, sea and land, spring and winter.

Takeo ultimately let out a deep sigh. "Okay, then…let me tell you about it. I'm used to people making up their own stories about me…but I want you to know what the truth is. You've been dragged into this whole thing because of me. I owe you an explanation."

Intently, Nao listened to Takeo as the latter took a deep breath and began his story.

"Sho Nishimura and I went to the same middle school. Even back then, he was already an obnoxious and wretched asshole.

"He beat up and tortured the younger kids with his lackeys while taking all their money—not that different from the Sho of today, actually. He'd prey on the students after school to beat them up or force them to hit each other. One day, he tried the same on me and my friends, but well, we fought back and instead Sho was the one to receive some punches. I could tell that psycho wanted to kill us for that—but he was also scared, because for once there was someone who not only refused to kneel in front of him but also forced him to yield in return.

"Then our last year of middle school began, and that's when it all went downhill. It started when Sho's older brother Katsu began meddling in his business. Back then, his gang was in the first steps of creation. They wanted to become successful fast and etch their name into people's consciousness, so they needed quite a handful of subordinates to do their bidding. Well, what do you do if you need a bunch of people to commit crimes for you quickly? You just blackmail them. And who do you blackmail? Those who are most defenseless, of course. The younger and weaker, the better.

"So, Katsu came to our school and started forcing the students Sho tormented to follow him. He and his gang members would beat them up, stalk them relentlessly, and threaten to kill them if they didn't comply. There was even a rumour going around that they cut off a kid's ear because he tried to report them to the police. I don't know whether that's true, but I can certainly imagine it.

"In the span of a few months, Katsu built himself a small empire on the backs of children, whom he forced to transfer his low-quality stuff for him.

"Sho became king of the school since everyone was terrified of his brother's regime. And you know Sho, he squeezed every little bit of sweet juice out of that power.

"I know it would have been the smartest to act like I didn't see what was happening. To be a bystander, glad to have not been picked as one of Katsu's pawns…but when I saw Sho's people torturing and humiliating children in the alleys behind the school—I couldn't just walk by. So, being the middle schooler I was, I just butted in headfirst and punched back.

"My friends and I did that every time we witnessed someone being assaulted, because that's what humans do, right? They try to help each other out during hard times… But as we could have expected, our interference didn't go unnoticed for long.

"One day, one of Katsu's subordinates showed up in front of my house. He dunked my head in the toilet and told me it was now my turn to work for Katsu. If not, he'd come back and drown me in the toilet bowl. Thus, involuntarily, my friends and I had to start playing his pawns.

"He made us transfer his goods for him. And since Katsu held us by our necks, Sho had a feast. He could finally get back at us and torment us to his heart's content; though he went for me the most. Whether it was because I was always the first one to butt into his fights or simply because he just hated my face the most, I don't know. Even so, we knew we had to get out of there.

"It was Hana's idea. She was part of the photography and videography club at school. She proposed that we film the beatings, the drug exchanges, take testimonies of fellow classmates, and bring it to the police. It doesn't sound like a bad plan, right? We were scared and desperate, so we gave it a try.

"Finding people ready to give a testimony was the hardest part. Most students we thought of as trustworthy were simply too scared to say anything against Katsu. And I honestly can't blame them for that. Although, at last, we managed to find a few classmates ready to state what they had experienced in front of the camera. With all of that footage, we were sure that we could finally bring Katsu and his gang down, we believed their madness would finally stop. We were so sure of that…but well, not everyone we thought was trustworthy actually turned out to be.

"One of the students we had asked to make a statement snitched on us. Too scared of the consequences if Katsu ever found out that he knew about our mission to take him down, he sought them out first and revealed our plan.

"How did *we* find out about that? Well, the gang dragged all of us together, smashed the camera and the film in front of us, and then punished us by breaking each of us a bone. They crushed Hana's thumbs, Kento's foot, a few of Minori's ribs, and my wrist. In retrospect, I should've been glad if that had been all— if a broken bone had been the worst of it. But reality wasn't that merciful. Katsu is a vindictive man. Strike him with a knife and he will pierce you with thousands.

"He wanted to end us once and for all. So they framed us for the drug deals and the injured classmates. They left false traces and forced the students to testify against us.

"That's how we all got kicked out of school. Our families were fined, we got probation, and an entry in our criminal records. I was sent to this school for 'difficult-to-handle children', and the others moved far away with their families after the incident. Only a year after I had been transferred, Sho was also sent to this school. They caught him smoking behind the school building where he accidentally set a curtain on fire. After all that's happened, a really dumb reason to get kicked out of school for, if you ask me." Takeo smiled weakly.

"Well, that's how I ended up here and why everyone thinks I was some drug lord in middle school.

"To be honest with you, I still think our plan could've succeeded. I know they destroyed the evidence in front of us, but they didn't know Hana. She would've always double-saved the videos. She was always extremely careful and thorough with her materials. Especially when it concerned such a crucial matter.

"After the dust had settled, I asked her where she kept the copies of the footage, but she told me she never made any. I'm sure she was lying, though. It would've been very unlike her to only keep one copy. But back then… Let's say…the lingering terror had fully swallowed her.

"Hana was always the brave type. But that incident really disturbed her. So, whether she had a copy or not didn't matter because I knew she'd never dare to go up against them again. The fear just sat too deep."

Takeo sighed.

"Well, and that's it. That's the full story."

Takeo smiled awkwardly, but Nao could just stare back at him. He felt a complicated range of emotions after hearing the story, but one was the strongest of them all. *Anger.*

If he could, he'd go to Sho straight away and crush every single bone in his body.

Nao looked at Takeo. "That's…a complex story."

The other's eyebrows rose. "You believe me?" he asked.

"Of course," Nao said. The story sounded very much like Sho. And, of course, a lot like Takeo too. Endangering himself to save his classmates was very much like him. One of the things Nao had learned about him in their brief time together was that Takeo was a hero caged in the body of a weak high school student. A storm trapped in a bottle.

The latter shrugged. "It's all in the past now anyway. There's nothing I can change about it, and there's no reason to cry over spilled water. This time, I just want us to get out of this situation safely. A better outcome for this story. That's my wish."

"I will never submit that easily to Sho."

"I know." Takeo laughed. "And that's what I like about you. You are extremely brave."

Normally, Nao wouldn't have believed such words, but out of Takeo's mouth, they sounded so honest and pure that Nao's face turned warm.

Dumbfounded, he touched it. Had his cheeks flushed?

If Takeo had noticed anything, he didn't give it away. Relieved about getting the story off his chest, he smiled.

"I'm glad you believe me," he said earnestly. "But I don't think we'll get any more exercises done today, to be honest. Let's look over them tomorrow."

Nao nodded. "Okay."

When Takeo walked home that afternoon, he felt strangely at ease. It felt great to finally have those words lifted off his shoulders. Not many people had listened to his story with the intent to believe him.

And Takeo was glad that he got to tell Nao. As much as he appreciated the other's interest, he was also relieved that he didn't ask any further questions. Especially in regard to his family or mother. Takeo knew that the incident with her must have been somewhat disturbing, and the other was probably itching with questions. But somehow Nao seemed to notice that Takeo would only reluctantly talk about her.

When meeting Nao for the first time, one wouldn't expect it, but he was actually a very sensitive person. He could easily sense if Takeo felt uncomfortable about a topic and never pressed him to talk about it. He appreciated that tender sentiment of his a lot.

When Takeo arrived home that day and looked in the mirror, his eyes wandered subconsciously to the scar on his left side. Carefully, he let his fingers run across the pink stripe stretching from the corner of his eye to his ear. The surface felt soft and bumpy.

He sighed in relief that Nao had never asked about the origin of this mark. Because this scar was the daunting reminder of the night he got kicked out of school.

It was the evening after his punishment had been decided. Takeo arrived home, long after the sun had set.

He had tried to avoid going back there as long as he could. For hours, Takeo had sat at the beach and watched the fierce waves crashing onto the shore. He had wanted to hide from the stern eyes of his brother, his face full of disappointment and anger. Even though he knew he had to eventually face him. Takeo couldn't hide forever, but his fear and shame were too great. He stayed by the beach as long as possible, although soon it was getting bitterly cold. He lost the feeling in his fingers and toes, and so, slowly and dejectedly, he dragged himself back home.

Shaken with cold and chaos, he entered their small one-story house. It was an old building. The walls were thin and the roof crooked.

His brother had avoided talking to him since the police investigation, but now that the decision was final and he was expelled, he knew that they couldn't postpone the confrontation any longer. Still, there was a little bit of hope left as he entered the house that maybe his brother had decided to go to bed early that night. But, of course, he wasn't that lucky.

Mamoru sat at the table in the kitchen with a bunch of documents in his hands, staring at them with a bleak expression. Nervously, Takeo fumbled with the cast around his left hand as he stepped into the lion's den.

Mamoru was older than him by eight years. He had finished his bachelor's degree last year and was now working full-time at a tech company. Takeo knew he hated that job, yet it was the only source of income they had.

Holding the documents from the police investigation in both hands, Mamoru looked up. His thin, fox-like eyes focused on Takeo.

Since they were brothers, they naturally shared a lot of similarities in their appearances. Both of them had been blessed with the same straight and pointy nose—which they had allegedly inherited from their father—the same oval face shape, as well as a pair of sharp eyebrows. Even their body frames were somewhat similar. Both were of average height with broad shoulders and an athletic build. But where Takeo was thinner and lankier, Mamoru was broader and buffer. He could look very intimidating if he wanted to, and right now he did.

Icily, he gazed at his little brother. "Why did you do this?" were the only words passing his lips.

Takeo felt his heart tumble. His chest aching. "It wasn't me," he said, trying to suppress the quiver in his voice. "I never did any of those things, I swear. I'm innocent."

Mamoru clutched the piece of paper in his hand. It crumpled beneath his grip. "Do you know what you did to us?" he forced out between closed teeth. "Do you know...what you did...?"

"I never hurt those students or sold drugs! I was just trying to help! They framed us for it. I'm innocent, believe me, I'm innocent!"

"Because of you we have to pay money we don't have, Takeo. You got kicked out of school. You got a criminal record. You ruined everything I have done for you."

"Mamoru... It wasn't me. I'm innocent. Please—"

"I DON'T CARE!" Mamoru bellowed, his voice roaring like thunder in the dark sky. "I DON'T CARE whether you are innocent or not! It doesn't matter! Do you understand what you have done!? Do you understand what you have ruined!?"

Scared, Takeo closed his mouth.

"Ever since our father ran away, I've had to carry this family! I've worked my ass off to provide food and a roof for us. I have been working multiple jobs since high school, so we could keep

this house. I tried getting our mother clean so you wouldn't have to see her in that vegetating state. I took out a loan during university so you could attend that fucking school, Takeo! I did all of this because I wanted you to live a better life than me. I wanted at least you to have a future! And what did you do? You threw it all away! You ruined everything I sacrificed for you! And for what did you do it!? For a bunch of strangers! Why did you have to do it, Takeo!? WHY!? Why did you have to help out some strangers when you should have thought of us first! Of what this would mean for your family! For yourself!"

Takeo looked at his brother, his eyes brimming with tears. His chest felt heavy with anxiety and between the stinging beneath his ribs and the lump blocking his throat, he could only mutter two feeble words, "I'm sorry..."

"Shove the apologies up your ass. I have no idea how we can clean up all of the shit you've produced. If all of us starve to death or end up on the streets, it's your fault. I want you to know that, Takeo. It's all your fault."

Mamoru grabbed some of the documents and started tidying them up with shaking hands. "Now leave. I can't bear seeing your face again today."

With his eyes watering, mouth quivering, and hands trembling, Takeo turned around. His heart was aching. It felt so painful he wanted to rip it out.

Barely able to walk, he dragged himself toward the door when he noticed their mother out of the corner of his eye. She sat on the old couch in the living room, staring blankly at a comedy show playing on the TV. The flashing images reflected in her large, beady eyes.

Takeo didn't know what he expected. For most of his memories, his mother was an empty shell of the woman she had once been. She had never been able to be a real mother for him. But now he was desperate. All he wanted was a parent to comfort him. At least once, he wanted to experience it. He needed it.

So, in his weakest state, Takeo walked over to her. He kneeled down beside her while she continued to gaze at the show on the TV as though hypnotised.

"Mom," Takeo whimpered, desperately trying to grasp her attention. "Mom, you know I'm innocent, don't you? You know I only ever wanted to help."

She didn't react to him.

Carefully, Takeo reached out to grab her hand. "You believe me, do you not? I'm your son, you believe me, right?" He touched her cold skin, intertwining his hand with her bony fingers.

She turned his head to him slowly. Her big eyes foggily focused on him. Hopeful, Takeo smiled at her, but she yanked her hand out of his and suddenly started shrieking.

"LEAVE ME!" she screeched. "DON'T TOUCH ME!"

Startled, Takeo stood up. "Mom, please, calm down." He tried to hold her arms, but that made her freak out even more. Like a fury, she started thrashing about, screaming things Takeo didn't understand. He tried to desperately calm her down. "It's okay, everything's okay. I'm your son." He tried to hold her, but she was surprisingly strong despite her frail body.

"LEAVE ME! LEAVE ME!" she shrieked, kicking and hitting the air. And then it happened. She grabbed the thing closest to her. An empty glass bottle. And in her delusions, she swung the glass with all her might against Takeo's head.

It was an ugly sound. The glass shattering against his skull.

Before Takeo had time to realise what was happening, he collapsed onto the ground. A horrible searing pain stinging in his head.

The world was spinning and he hardly felt the blood gushing out of his head, flowing down his face and neck. Somewhere far away he could still hear his mother screaming.

All of a sudden, the face of his brother appeared above him. His eyes bulging in shock. "Takeo! Takeo!" He could hear his voice resonating.

Mamoru cupped his head, trying to rouse his brother's attention, but Takeo was slowly flowing away.

Only faintly did he register his brother grabbing the telephone and dialling a number with bloody fingers.

"Hello!?" Mamoru screamed into the device. "I need an ambulance! My brother had an accident!"

Takeo had woken up in the hospital hours later. He'd gotten away with twelve stitches and a concussion.

Mamoru began acting a lot softer toward him after the incident. But even to the present day, Takeo could still sometimes feel his older brother's resentment permeating through his gaze—like a wound that never fully healed.

After being transferred to the new school, the tension straining their relationship slowly eased up, although it never quite turned back to what they'd once had. The school Takeo now attended wasn't even as bad as he had initially thought. He had joined the baseball team and built good connections with his teammates and classmates alike. However, barely a year after his enrolment, Sho had suddenly shown up, and it had all started anew.

He gathered a group of students dumb enough to follow him and then toyed with the weaker ones. The only difference was that Takeo no longer interfered with him.

Scarred from the past, like a deer that had once stepped into a hunter's trap, he avoided Sho and his business like the plague.

For once, he acted like a bystander—ignoring the students who were beaten up and tormented by the other.

He became what he had once despised. But the feeling of the trap tightening around his neck was still fresh and still hurt.

He pretended not to see it, not to hear it—until the day a new student was transferred to the school.

A loner who didn't talk to anyone, and therefore no one talked to him either. That anti-social boy with his gloomy face and no one to care about him was the perfect toy for Sho Nishimura.

Takeo watched as Nao Miyamoto got picked on in the hallways and the classroom. He noticed the bruises on his face as he came to school one day and heard the students snicker at him behind his back. Takeo pretended not to see—not to think.

But the thin surface of that attitude broke when he heard Nao mutter the words, "I'm not afraid of Sho."

And it had felt like a punch to his face.

That boy, battered and with no one to care for him, fully exposed to Sho and his cruelties, said in the most nonchalant way that he was not afraid of him. For most people, admitting to having no fear in the face of inevitable danger would have sounded dumb, but to Takeo, it was just brave.

It felt like there was a mirror being held in front of his face, showing him his own cowardliness.

That was when he had decided to swallow his own fear and go after Sho in that alley back then. Takeo never wanted to feel weak again, and he started right there, by helping out the boy he had begun to admire.

Over time, he'd gotten a few glimpses of the person Nao was. It wasn't easy since he was someone who naturally kept very close to himself. When you think you had him figured out, you were actually still far away from doing so. It was like tripping through a maze with no map or orientation to guide you. But

Takeo was sure there was something worth looking for in the middle of it.

Even from the corners, far away, he could see it dazzling so brightly behind all those walls.

To Takeo, Nao had become more than someone he just admired. He was a person he wanted to get to know, someone he wanted to understand. Even if it meant having to wander through every inch of said maze. He would patiently do so.

— Chapter 13 —

Exam season was getting really close. Meaning that in less than a week, Nao would have to face his greatest hurdle: the math exam. Nao and Takeo had only one more study session scheduled before it. Unfortunately, their last tutoring date started with them being kicked out of the study room.

In the afternoon, they had met up in front of the room as usual, but today, they were actually greeted by the faces of two students when they opened the door.

Contrary to Nao and Takeo, they had actually booked the room beforehand, as students were supposed to do, and so the two of them had no choice but to retreat.

With their bags and books in their arms, Nao and Takeo stood in the corridor and looked at each other, dumbfounded.

"What are we going to do now?" Takeo asked, and Nao shrugged.

The classrooms might be free and quiet around this time of day, but neither of them wanted to run into Sho nor his lackeys, and the possibility of that happening was far too high at any other place in school. They could have also called their study session off for that day, but it was the last meeting they had before the exam, and Nao had really started to appreciate Takeo's way of teaching. He would only reluctantly give up on their last session. Thus, it was even harder for him when Takeo proposed the idea of studying at Nao's place.

The latter stared at him with wide eyes. For a moment, he thought about asking why they couldn't just go to Takeo's place instead, but then he remembered that this would probably be the more inappropriate request.

"We don't have to if you don't want to. I just thought it would be quieter than going to a public place like a café."

From a normal person's point of view, it was a valid proposal, but to Nao, it was like someone asking to see him naked. It was a scary thought—fully exposed, with barely any way to cover what should have stayed hidden. Nao wanted to keep everything that had not to be exposed concealed. No one had to see what he desperately tried to cover with his hands and arms.

But if he had to slightly lift his cover…was Takeo the one he'd trust?

Nao sucked in an agitated breath. "O-okay…let's go to my place."

The only reason Nao agreed to take Takeo home with him was because of his parents' fortunate absence that afternoon. Due to meetings and such, they would be out until at least seven. Right now, it was 4pm, so they had about three hours before he had to kick Takeo out.

To say that Nao was nervous would be an understatement. He had never taken anyone to his house before. Well, he'd never had anyone close enough to take with him in the first place, but he also would never have done it because of his situation. Especially not a guy.

Nao could not imagine what would happen if he—as a boy who'd come out—brought another male to his homophobic home. It would have been a different scenario if it had been a girl he brought with him. His parents would probably be over the moon. Maybe their impaired son wasn't as abnormal as he seemed! Maybe there was still hope that he wasn't actually gay! That he was just like other boys!

But Nao was gay, and he brought another boy home with him. Even if it wasn't anything romantic, and completely in a platonic context, it still felt like he was doing something condemnable. As if he committed something so immoral he deserved to be punished for it. If his parents ever found out about this...

"Are you okay?" Takeo yanked Nao out of his train of thought. He hadn't even noticed that he had completely spaced out and needed a second to remind himself that he stood with Takeo in the empty elevator, riding up to his family's apartment.

"Er...yeah," Nao stuttered.

"You look pretty pale. Sure everything's all right?"

"Yeah," Nao waved him off. "Just...tired."

With a *ding*, the doors of the elevator slid apart and revealed the hallway. Curiously, Takeo stepped out and looked around, admiring the white marble tiles fused with golden veins, high arched ceiling, and the shiny polished wooden furniture. He whistled through his teeth. "This is really fancy."

Nao hummed in discomfort.

They slid off their shoes at the entrance and then headed straight to Nao's room. Compared to the rest of the apartment, there wasn't anything special to it. It was a small rectangular room with nothing but a bed, a wardrobe, a desk, and a small shelf for books. Nao wasn't the type to put much worth into material things like souvenirs or photos. So objectively, there wasn't much to look at in his room, but Takeo still glanced around curiously. Nao didn't know whether it should make him nervous or not.

"Sit down," he eventually said and pointed at the chair in front of his desk. "I'll get a second chair."

Takeo nodded and followed his request. He placed his backpack on the desk and started pulling out notes and books.

Nao went outside and grabbed one of the chairs from the dining table. When he came back to his room, pushed open the door and saw Takeo sitting there, it felt too surreal.

His mind still couldn't comprehend that he was really here, in his family's apartment, in his room. Nao had never brought another person to his home before, and suddenly seeing a boy at his desk was like a crinkle in reality. Terribly frightening, to be honest.

Silently, Nao sat next to Takeo, who had already laid out all of the notes on the table. "Where do you want to start?" he asked. Contrary to Nao, he appeared completely calm and collected.

"Let's review integrals."

Takeo nodded and opened the math book. Nao watched quietly as he browsed through the pages. Takeo was here, but what did that mean? Was he supposed to offer him something to drink? Or to eat? Nao wouldn't have known since he had never been in a situation like this.

He was so absorbed in his roiling thoughts that he totally missed Takeo starting to explain and just looked at him with a blank stare for twenty seconds or so.

Takeo cocked his head to the side. "Was I too fast?"

Nao quickly shook his head to push his thoughts aside. "No, no... Do you...need something to drink?"

Takeo's lips lifted into a smile. He gently shook his head. "I still have some water in my bag."

"Okay," Nao muttered and wished to slap himself.

They went back to the confusing world of integrals, and fortunately, despite the unusual surroundings, the session wasn't much different from the others. Nao tried his best to block out the fact that they were at his house, and little by little, he started to wind down. His shoulders slowly drooped, and gradually, his muscles relaxed—when the door to his room was suddenly pushed open.

Nao's heart almost stopped. In raw horror, he fully expected to see the face of his father in the entrance, to witness those terrifying eyes skin him alive; but to Nao's great relief, it was only Toyo who stuck his head through the crack.

"Nao, have you seen my—" He froze when he saw the unknown face beside his brother. With a slack jaw, Toyo gaped at Takeo.

Nao's heart was riding rollercoaster. He jumped up and pushed Toyo out of the door, shutting it behind them.

His little brother seemed just as shocked about the boy in Nao's room as the latter was himself.

"Who is that?" he asked.

"No one," Nao said and immediately noticed how dumb that sounded. "A classmate," he corrected himself. "Next week are exams. What do you want?"

Toyo peeked curiously at the closed door behind his brother's back. "My calculator," he then said. "Have you seen it?"

"I'm using it right now. I'll give it back to you later."

"Okay," Toyo mumbled. He turned around to leave, but not without throwing another glance over his shoulder. Nao waited until he had disappeared back into his room before opening the door again.

His heart was fluttering with relief as the tension, which had rapidly built up inside him and nearly caused his heart to give out right there, slowly unwound. His legs felt suddenly all weak, and heavily he dragged himself back into his room. But just as he wanted to take a deep breath, relieved to have successfully evaded his brother's gaze, he was confronted with another pair of curious eyes observing him.

Takeo had his head crooked to the side, a calm expression on his face. "Was that your brother?" he asked.

Nao let himself fall back onto the chair. "Yeah," he murmured. "He was looking for his calculator."

Intently, Takeo leaned on the desk with one arm, resting his chin in his palm. He eyed Nao with a soft smile. *What is that guy looking at?* Nao thought to himself, trying to resolutely ignore his stare. He grabbed his notes and pen, readying himself for the next exercise, when Takeo's voice rang out next to him, "You know, you and your brother look pretty alike."

Nao spun around, surprised. "What?"

Upon the latter's reaction, Takeo's smile deepened, his eyes twinkling unfathomably. "Yeah, you have the same nose and doe eyes."

D-d-d-doe eyes!? Nao stared at Takeo in utter disbelief. Never in his life had he heard anyone describe him like this!

He gawked at his classmate, expecting him to break out in some kind of laughter, telling him it was a joke, but he just continued to look at him with those awfully soft eyes and gentle smile.

What was this feeling? Nao felt all woozy. His stomach was turning, but not in an about-to-throw-up-way. It was a different kind of sensation. One he hadn't felt yet before.

Flabbergasted, he coughed. "Let's…let's go back to studying. We don't have much time."

"Okay," Takeo complied readily.

Studying felt a lot weirder after that incident. Despite the fear of being interrupted again, Nao seemed to be suddenly much more aware of the presence the boy next to him exuded. He noticed himself flinch internally every time Takeo moved an inch closer to him, feeling like a doe during a hunt. Sticky sweat broke out in his palms as their shoulders brushed against each other on accident, and Nao wanted to shut his eyes and pray that this torture would end soon.

About a quarter to seven, he finally kicked Takeo out. With his heart utterly in disarray and his back drenched in sweat, Nao fell into his bed, burying his head beneath his pillow. What had happened? Was he too nervous because of the exam? He burrowed his nose in the hard mattress and grumbled. Fortunately, however, it was over now.

This had been the last study session before the exam, and soon it was time to see how much their hard work would pay off.

The day of the exam came faster than Nao had anticipated. Early in the morning, he packed his bag and squeezed into his school uniform. Mrs. Takahashi pressed a box of packed lunch into his hands, wishing him good luck. Usually, he would think of it as a desperate need—a necessity to somehow achieve anything in his life. However, as of late, he had more confidence in his skills thanks to his reliable tutor.

The school was filled with rumbling and murmuring right before the test. In the midst of the pre-exam chaos, Nao's and Takeo's eyes met only once. It was brief, but Nao could see the other's encouraging nod through the crowd. For the first time, Nao felt ready to tackle an exam.

Three hours later, his head was fuming. But it didn't feel too bad. In fact, Nao thought that it had been kind of good. It might even be possible that this time it wouldn't happen to be a complete failure.

Out of nowhere, Takeo leaned onto his desk with both arms. "How was it? I don't think the questions were too difficult. Maybe except for questions five and six. Those were pretty tricky in my opinion. Good thing that we studied vectors! What did you think?" he chattered lightheartedly, filled with post-exam adrenaline.

Nao shrugged in response. "I don't know. But I guess it wasn't too bad."

Takeo beamed happily. "That sounds good. I'm relieved." Nao noticed Takeo's hands twitch nervously before he continued to speak. "Since we've now finally finished the exam after weeks of studying, why don't we go celebrate? We could…maybe go to the cinema?"

"You mean with your teammates from the baseball club?"

"No," Takeo said. "Just you and me. Since we've been working so hard lately… You know, as a form of celebration."

Nao looked at the other. Takeo gazed at him with feverish eyes. They seemed much more intense than usual, and Nao could almost feel the tension crackling in the air between them. He knew from experience that he had no chance of tapping out once Takeo had set a goal for himself, since the latter always found a way to convince him anyway. Their trip to the beach, the meeting at the arcade… Somehow, Takeo always dragged him along, so Nao had become smarter—he didn't waste his energy on pointless arguing anymore.

"Okay," Nao said with a sigh, and Takeo smiled brightly.

"Nice! Is there any movie or genre you prefer?"

"Not really."

Takeo pointed at himself. "Then leave it to me."

— Chapter 14 —

Since it was in the middle of the week, there weren't many people present at the cinema.

The few people waiting in front of Nao and Takeo appeared to be mostly couples or parents with their little children.

It'd been quite some time since Nao had last been to a movie theatre, but the smell of the dark velvety carpet, wine-red leather seats, and fresh popcorn were still ingrained deep into his memory.

The countless LEDs shone down on them like hundreds of bright stars, and Nao could feel his shoes sinking into the soft carpet floor. Cinemas always had that otherworldly feeling for him, as though one entered a parallel universe with countless stories and adventures to fathom.

But maybe he only felt that way because Nao was half-certain that this must be some kind of parallel dimension. How else could he be standing here with another boy? The way Takeo had been slowly creeping into his presence and all of the corners of his life was still too surreal for Nao. Takeo was like a wildfire— sneaking up on you, only to engulf you completely before you even had the chance to realise it. At least, Takeo's wildfire was neither hot nor destructive. It was warm and cozy, like a bonfire, filled with playful flames. Nao instinctively knew that they wouldn't dare burn him—he just had to learn to adapt to its unpredictable nature and intrinsic playfulness.

A flame that licked wood, not to hurt or destroy the tree, but to warm the one in the freezing cold. That's who he was.

They bought two tickets at the counter along with two bags of popcorn and drinks. Takeo chose salted popcorn while Nao went for caramel.

Together, they headed into the small cinema hall, searching for their seats in the dark. Once settled in the soft, squashy seats, which gave off a faint scent of velvet and nachos, Nao set his drink into the cup holder and balanced the bag of popcorn on his lap. When everything was taken care of, he turned to the other.

"Which movie did you choose?" he asked, and Takeo shrugged in response. "No idea. I just picked a random one."

"Really?"

"Yes." He nodded. "I also don't have any preferences when it comes to movies. So I thought, why not gamble?"

Nao huffed. "Every time I go out with you, it's like I'm drawing a lottery ticket."

Takeo turned to him with a cheeky grin. "Is that so bad? I think you are always hitting the jackpot, though."

Nao couldn't stop himself from rolling his eyes. "Tsk, you're so shameless. Calling yourself the jackpot."

"But it's the truth, isn't it?"

He decided not to indulge in Takeo's nonsense any longer and shut his mouth. Takeo tried to probe him a few more times, but his endeavours were cut short when the lights dimmed and the white screen at the front faded to black. The light of the projector floated like a stream of starlight over their heads, illuminating the large screen.

Silently, Nao ate his popcorn and sipped his soda while the movie started in front of them. It was an action movie about some kind of robots and cyborgs fighting. And to be honest, it was pretty bad. Even after about forty minutes, Nao could, by his best will, not recap what was happening in the story. After a while, he could hear Takeo whisper next to him, "Man, this is really an eyesore. Do you wanna sneak out?"

Nao turned to Takeo and nodded eagerly.

Hence, they grabbed their cups and popcorn and quietly headed out of the cinema. With the food and drinks in hand, they sat down on one of the red leather benches in the corridor outside the room. They were the only ones around in the half-lit hallway. All of the other visitors were in their respective rooms, fully engulfed in the movies playing on the screens.

"Well, maybe I shouldn't gamble on which movie to watch next time," Takeo said earnestly, leaning back against the wall. He took a sip before turning to Nao. "But what even was that? The robots and the cyborgs? Did the robots come out of space? I didn't really get that part, to be honest. And the special effects were horrible as well. The scene where the guy got his hand cut off, that looked like a rubber hand to me!" He snickered. "But if you view it as a parody, it was actually kinda funny."

Nao munched a piece of popcorn. "Yeah, it was really bad."

"I guess now you can say for sure that robot space movies do not belong to your preferred genre."

"Next time someone asks me to go to the cinema with them, I'll tell them that."

Takeo grinned. "What are we going to do now? The movie isn't worth going back for."

Nao slowly shook the cup of soda in his hand, listening to the ice cubes clanking inside. "I don't know." He looked at his popcorn. "But we still have food to eat."

Takeo nodded. "Then let's eat first."

For a second, there was silence as both of them chewed on the crunchy sweets. It was a little awkward, though. Nao cleared his throat, unsure of what to say, when Takeo piped up all of a sudden. "How much time do you have left before you have to go home?"

"Don't know. My parents don't really care when I come home." *Or if I come home*, Nao added in his mind.

Takeo hummed. "I wish this was my case too. My brother can be really strict about things like curfews. I know he only does it because he cares about me, but it's still annoying. Especially because I turn eighteen next year!"

Nao remembered Takeo's brother. He had never met him face to face, but he had heard his voice before on a phone call with Takeo. Back then, he had shouted so loudly that Nao had heard him through the barrier of a closed door. It seemed like Takeo's brother had taken on the role as his guardian, and, dumbfounded, Nao recalled the encounter with his mother, quickly realising that this was probably the exact case. Takeo's mother didn't seem to be in a state to take care of a child, or even of herself, to be honest.

Out of interest, Nao asked, "Are you close with your brother?"

Takeo pondered that for a second. "Well, I guess so. We're not the typical pair of brothers, but we do care about each other. Mamoru can sometimes be a little harsh, but I know he only acts that way because he genuinely cares about our family. For example, my shoelaces." He lifted his feet off the ground to show the purple shoelaces Nao had noticed him wear all the time. "He got them for me in elementary school. Back then, I was obsessed with the colour purple. I would buy everything in this colour. Including every kind of food I could get my hands on. We didn't have much money, but Mamoru saved up all of his pocket money to buy this pair of purple shoelaces for me as a Christmas gift. I've been wearing them ever since. For every new pair of shoes I get, I replace the new laces with these ones. My brother can sometimes be a little scary, but I know that he loves me. I see it every time I look at my shoes." Takeo smiled. "So yeah, we are close. What about you? What kind of person is your brother?"

Nao shrugged. "I don't know. I don't really know him that well."

Takeo furrowed his eyebrows in confusion.

Nao sighed and leaned back against the wall. He crossed his arms in front of his chest and looked pensively at the ceiling. Should he be honest with Takeo? He barely talked about his family and never about his problems with them. One thing that had been instilled in him very early in his life was that private things like these never belonged to outsiders. Revealing one's problems made you weak and vulnerable. And in a family of politicians and CEOs, this was one of the gravest mistakes one could make. Vulnerability was shameful, weakness one's demise. But…this was Takeo he was talking to.

Nao didn't exactly know how or when it had happened, but he knew he could trust him. With all of the similar hurdles and setbacks he experienced, he could understand him, right? He wasn't the type of person to betray someone. Nao had figured that out.

If he could not trust Takeo, then who else could he trust?

With a sigh, Nao decided to speak, "Toyo…was never my brother. Always a rival or a competitor. For our parents, it was never just a game when we played as children. It was an opportunity to compare us to each other. And when it became clear that my brother was the smarter—the better—of us two, I only became unnecessary baggage. *A failed attempt*, that's what my grandfather called me once. Toyo is everything they have hoped for… I am everything they dislike. I guess that's how we naturally grew apart. A blessed and a cursed child can't see eye to eye."

Nao averted his gaze from the ceiling and looked at his classmate. "That's why I don't know him that well. We're basically only brothers on paper."

Nao didn't know what he had expected Takeo to answer. But it caught him off guard when he blurted out, "Your parents sound like crap."

Surprised by his brutal honesty, Nao burst out laughing. It was loud and a little rough, like an instrument that hadn't been played in a very long time. But in that moment, it resonated clear as day through the cinema's empty corridors.

Takeo stared at him with wide eyes. "Why are you laughing? Did I say something wrong?"

"No," Nao chuckled. It wasn't even that funny, but somehow hearing Takeo talk so bluntly and without any care in the world made him laugh. The latter really had no filter himself! "You just got to the point real quick."

"Well, it just sounds to me like your parents were the reason you never got close."

Nao turned to the other, somehow still a rare smile on his lips. "You're right. They are the problem. It was just funny how you said that."

Takeo shrugged, still confused but also nonchalant. "Whatever. You can laugh at me, it's just nice to see you smile."

"Huh?"

"It looks good. You don't smile often, but you look really pretty when you do." He pointed at his own cheek. "I've just noticed—you even have dimples."

Nao's face turned more and more surprised as the laughter in his throat died down. He wanted to tell himself that Takeo was just joking, but he knew he was not.

Nao didn't know how to react. So he just stared at the other until he coughed awkwardly. Takeo slowly seemed to notice that he might have crossed a line there and spoken a bit too much of his mind. His cheeks flushed pink in embarrassment, and he lowered his eyes in rising shame. "What am I saying?" he muttered awkwardly, scratching his head and laughing. His whole demeanour was the personification of "wanting the ground to swallow one up." But as Takeo was battling with his loose mouth, he completely missed what was really happening inside Nao.

He had tried to push those feelings out of his mind, but right now he could not deny it. His heart was fluttering and his stomach turning. His heartbeat danced excitedly.

Staggering slightly, Nao stood up. "Maybe we should head home now."

Hesitant, Takeo rose as well. "Yeah, it's getting late."

They threw the rest of the popcorn bags and cups into the trash and left the cinema.

They didn't talk on the way home. They just walked alongside each other, dumbstruck.

What was happening right now? Nao didn't dare to put his finger on it.

They arrived at the intersection they had met up at earlier that evening. Both of them stopped and just stood there for a few seconds in stuffy silence before Takeo grasped the opportunity to speak. "See…see you tomorrow, then."

Nao nodded curtly. "Yeah, see you tomorrow."

They still looked at each other. Somehow it felt like there was more to say, yet no words came out of Nao's mouth. So he just turned around and walked away before the silence could become even more numbing.

With his hands in the pockets of his jacket, he hurried into the darkness when he heard Takeo's voice behind him. "Nao!" he exclaimed and Nao spun around.

He was already far away, but he could still see Takeo in the middle of the intersection. His hands were cupped around his mouth like a megaphone, and he took a deep breath. His chest puffed up as he filled it with the crisp night air, and thus, he shouted, "I had fun today! Get home safe!"

Nao was flabbergasted. For a second, he stared at the other, flustered, before eventually finding the power to reply. "O-okay! You too!" he shouted back shyly and ran away.

— Chapter 15 —

Nao wanted to sink into the earth and never emerge again.

What was wrong with him!? Why was he like this? The boy lay in his bed and stared at the ceiling. Wide awake and unable to go to sleep.

It was one in the morning, and like a beetle, he lay paralysed on his back, unable to move on his own.

The air in the room was warm and stuffy, but he couldn't move the blanket off his body or open the window—petrified by worry and self-deprecation, imprisoned in his own little beetle shell.

Drowning in his own head, he stared upward. And he could only ask himself one question: what was happening to him?

Lately, he had been feeling really unfamiliar with himself. Almost as if there were an imposter taking over his mind. He nearly didn't recognise himself anymore. Who was this new person leading his life? Why were they so much more easy-going, pleasant, open, and happier? How was it possible for someone to change so suddenly and unexpectedly? Was he going mad? ...No, he knew what the reason was—or, more accurately, who the reason was.

Ah...that idiot. He really had Nao caught in his clutches, hadn't he? How could Nao be such a simpleton? Letting his heart...letting his heart attach itself to that fool...

He wanted to sink into the depths of the ocean, become seaweed, and never return! Why was he like this? Why...why did he...like Takeo?

Nao rolled around in his bed, letting out a silent scream in the darkness of the night. Even forming such words in his mind brought him inexplicable agony. How could this have happened!? Nao wasn't the type to fall in love. And certainly not the type anyone else would fall in love with either! Why was his stupid teenage heart still acting like one when his reality was so far away from it?

He pressed his face into the cold fabric of the pillow, taking a deep breath.

Nao was horrified. Out of his mind with fear. But deep inside his chest, beneath his fingers, was his stupid, dumb heart, beating with excitement whenever he pictured the other in his mind, reminding him that despite all, he was just a teenage boy.

He cursed his own body.

Nao tossed about in his bed, gazing into the dark. He couldn't ignore the bad feeling churning in the pit of his stomach any longer. As much as romance was glorified in all of those movies he had seen and books he had read, in reality, it wasn't all that beautiful. At least, not his kind of romance.

He had come to a truce with his sexuality a long time ago. It wasn't anything he could change, and there was no benefit in grieving a felled tree. Even though his family knew and despised this side of him, he'd always been certain that it would never escape the confines he had built. It was a prisoner in a dark dungeon, forbidden from ever seeing the light of day. He had been so confident that he'd never worried about it. His heart was a barren land, after all.

But now, suddenly and more terrifyingly than he could have imagined, there were blossoms growing on the naked trees, waiting to unfurl their petals and fill this land of dread. A warm breeze of spring had come, and coaxed the dormant buds slowly back to life, helping them to release blossom after blossom. With the sudden warmth nourishing the land, the trees may soon carry fruit.

Rich and thick fruit might grow on the old branches, overwhelming the tree which had never had to bear such a sweet burden before. And as the fruits, ripe and beautiful, fell from the trees, they might roll through the cracks to the depths of the dungeon, reaching the starved prisoner beneath and giving him a taste of hope and mercy he had never dared to imagine. As beautiful as this idea might sound, it was actually horrifying for the one wanting to keep him locked up. A prisoner who had been defeated by his misery and accepted his eternal punishment was much more obedient than a prisoner elated with hope. The latter being a dormant disaster in the making.

It just felt so unfair. The world had never been kind to Nao, but after realising his sexuality, it had only been crueler. If his heart were now to thaw, he didn't want to imagine how much more difficult it might become.

Why did all of this have to happen to him? Wasn't his life already pitiful enough? Why did the world have to throw this at his face, showing him once again just how pathetic and abnormal he was.

Nao felt like screaming. At last, all of this was going to play out as it always did for him, wasn't it? He would only end up being alone and ostracised by those around him.

Takeo might not abandon you, an annoying voice in his head retorted, and Nao covered his ears. He didn't want to think about it anymore.

As a blessing from the heavens, his and Takeo's paths didn't cross the following week. Math had only been the first of many exams this semester, and all of the students were busy studying for the upcoming tests.

In one week, they were tortured with both the history and the Japanese exams. Nao had barely spoken to Takeo since then, and yes, maybe he was kind of avoiding him. He knew he was a coward! No need to remind him. He just didn't know what else to do.

Though it seemed the universe was finally fed up with his cowardice as well.

On a leisurely Monday, ten days after the math exam, Nao was on his way home, walking past the sports field. On the track stood a handful of guys whom Nao recognised as the baseball club. His eyes automatically darted toward Takeo, who stood among his teammates, wearing a white baseball uniform and holding a pitcher glove in one hand.

As if he had felt the timid gaze sizing him up, Takeo suddenly spun around and met Nao's eyes. His face immediately lit up upon seeing him, and happily, he waved at Nao. After turning around to exchange a few words with his teammates, he headed straight toward him.

Nao tensed up. That was not what he had wanted! His immediate instinct was to run away, but his body didn't want to move. It seemed like his body and mind weren't on par with each other. One wanting to flee while the other yearned to stay.

At last, the second urge turned out to be stronger, overwhelmingly so, and he greeted Takeo with an awkward wave of his hand.

The other was as nonchalant as ever, approaching him with beaming eyes and a bright smile. Cheerfully, he asked, "How are you? How have the exams been?"

"It's been okay," Nao managed to say. "I think I'll pass."

"That's good," Takeo replied. "I haven't seen you much these days. I guess you've been busy studying."

Nao nodded. "History is also a difficult subject for me."

He hummed. "I've also been studying a lot."

For a moment, it went silent between them. Maybe Takeo had picked up on Nao's hesitant behaviour. Maybe he just didn't know what to say.

Awkwardly, they looked at one another.

"Have you—"

"I did—"

Both of them stopped and gazed at each other, surprised, before smiling.

"You first," Takeo said with a bashful grin.

"How have you been?" Nao asked.

"Not too bad, I guess. I've been a bit stressed out because of the exams, but nothing much has happened since we went to the cinema." He laughed awkwardly. "Speaking of which, do you have time this week? If you want, we could hang out again. It's always fun with you."

There it was. Nao had been scared of this. What should he do?

Of course he'd like to hang out with Takeo! But, on the other hand, wasn't it too risky?

He couldn't afford to fall deeper into this situation than he already had. He hated being vulnerable, and right now his heart was lying on the ground, all weak and feeble. He didn't want it to have more footprints on it than it already had.

He looked at Takeo. His face was glazed with a thin layer of sweat from training, tiny dots of sweat clung to his skin like stars in the sky. His black hair was disheveled, ruffled wildly by the mild wind. He looked at the other with a hopeful glance in those dark brown eyes; thus, Nao could feel his heart jump.

"Okay," Nao heard himself say and couldn't believe the words passing his lips without permission. "Let's meet this week."

Takeo's smile widened. "Super! Then let's talk tomorrow. I think I have to get back to training now." He looked over his shoulder at his teammates, who were already glaring holes into the back of his head.

Nao nodded.

Takeo gazed at Nao with a last elated smile before hurrying back onto the field.

The moment he had disappeared, Nao let out a deep sigh. When had he become such an idiot? Now it seemed like he couldn't even trust his own mouth anymore.

He grabbed the straps of his backpack tighter and headed toward the back of the building. He should get out of here as fast as possible before he could say even more stupid stuff! Who knew what he might agree to next!

Nao quickly stalked forward, planning to take the first exit he passed. But it wouldn't be Nao's life if something didn't go terribly wrong.

As he approached the back of the school, a familiar figure suddenly appeared in front of him.

"Whoa, whoa, whoa. Where are you going so fast?" a voice Nao dreaded more than anything else spoke up. "Are you already trying to run away?" Sho snickered happily. His lackeys, who had suddenly emerged behind Nao, joined in on their leader's laughter.

Nao clenched his jaw. "Get out of the way," he demanded.

"What is this? Have you suddenly grown balls now that there's someone protecting you?" Sho mocked him with a sneer. He looked at his mates with an arched brow. "Now that this homo has a boyfriend, he acts all mighty and brave."

Nao glared at the trash in front of him. "I don't need anyone to protect me."

Sho laughed loudly. "What do you think you can do to me? Haven't you already been crushed enough by me? Are you that desperate to be touched by another man?"

Nao clenched his fists as Sho looked at him with a taunting smile. Confident and full of delight, the latter shook his head. "You should think before acting on a stupid whim like that. I don't think my brother would be very happy if I came home with a bruise on my face. You already know what my brother is capable of, right? So don't even think about it."

Nao wanted to cave that bastard's face in. He wanted to watch him bleed out on the floor, but he also knew that he was at a huge disadvantage right now.

Sho was all too aware of it as well, and so his hand snapped forward and grabbed Nao by his jaw. He pressed his fingers into Nao's skin, his fingernails cutting into the flesh.

Nao tried to move away, but Sho had his face in a tight grip. "You seem to have become really close with Takeo lately. You must give damn good blowjobs if someone actually wants to keep you around," Sho sneered threateningly. "Let me see for myself."

With a grin, he lunged out and thrust his knee right in Nao's groin. The latter yelped in pain. He wanted to double over out of instinct, but Sho was still holding him upright by his jaw. "That's for the time you tried the same thing on me." He swung his leg again and this time pierced Nao's stomach. Nao coughed, feeling a wave of vomit surge up his throat.

"And that's because I can."

Sho looked over to his lackeys. "Do you want a bite too?" he asked and Nao could hear them closing in. He was drastically outnumbered. Unable to defend himself. He sucked in a sharp breath. *Ah, shit...*

That was when he heard a new voice. "Hey! Students are not permitted behind the school building!"

Sho quickly let go of him.

"What are you doing here? Aren't your classes already over?"

Nao turned around and spotted the PE teacher at the end of the pathway. He looked at the boys with a deep frown. "And you." He pointed at Nao. "What's wrong? You look sick."

The shock of the knee hitting his stomach sat still deep within him. He wasn't sure yet whether he had to throw up or not, but he could see Sho glaring at him with a menacing stare out of the corner of his eye.

Telling the teacher what had happened wouldn't change anything either. Those idiots only cared about themselves and their reputation. Nao knew from too many experiences that it was no use telling them.

He tried to stand up straight. "I'm okay," he croaked, and the teacher let up on him as expected, turning toward the rest of them.

"Now, all of you get your asses out of here and go home. Classes are over, there is no reason for you lot to still be here," he commanded strictly, and the group slowly started moving.

Nao staggered forward, his groin and stomach aching, when Sho suddenly wrapped an arm around his shoulders and pulled him close. Mouth irritatingly close to his ear, hot breath fanning his auricle, he whispered, *"Never forget, mutt, I will destroy you."* Then he let go of him and smiled innocently at the teacher as they walked past him.

Nao glared at his tormentor. His heart was boiling with a rage he hadn't yet known. Though there was nothing he could do about it at the moment.

Of course, he was always the victim, never the victor. Just as prey would always be prey. Why should the world ever change its laws of nature for him?

Sho left him alone after being interrupted by their teacher. And so, Nao went home and fell right into his bed. The comfort his blanket used to give him didn't work that day. Instead, he felt suffocated and trapped by it. He threw it off and drew his legs close to his chest, harbouring the little body heat he possessed.

Today life seemed to be weighing heavier on his shoulders than usual. It was dragging him deeper and deeper.

He must have managed to fall asleep somehow. It was evening when he woke up. The sun had already vanished, and Nao's body was freezing.

Groggily, he sat up and glanced across the dark room. It was still the same day. He had hoped to at least not wake up until a new one had dawned.

He searched for the lamp on his bedside table. When he had finally found it and turned it on, the room was drenched in a dim orange light. Nao looked at the clock.

It was only eight in the evening.

Powerless, he let his head fall onto his chest. He was still feeling heavy. He was used to feeling this way. But today, it seemed to cling to him even more insistently.

Maybe that was the reason he tried something so unusual to alleviate this pain just a little. Nao wasn't the type to talk about his feelings. First, he wasn't good at expressing them. Second, there had been no one to listen to him either.

But as the heavens played, there was now someone. And that person was actually one of the reasons for his despair, for Takeo was the virus that had infected Nao's heart.

But, in the end, there was no cure for a virus. Especially not if it was such a vicious one as this.

He could only wait for his body to fight it to the death, until either he defeated the intruder wreaking havoc, or the intruder defeated him, building itself a home in his afflicted heart.

It seemed he was already close to losing this battle, though, as he took the telephone from the counter and dialled Takeo's number.

Nao couldn't tell whether he felt more pathetic or selfish for doing it. It was dumb! So dumb, and also so embarrassing.

How could he call this guy, whom he hadn't even known for that long, and ask him to meet, when he's actually part of the problem! It didn't really make sense. And yet, it made sense in Nao's heart. For some reason, he felt a novel sense of ease around Takeo. Even though his heart and mind were in utter disarray, his soul somehow resided in the eye of that storm. It was a place where it could rest without being perturbed by what was happening outside, like the depths of a pond which never took notice of the downpour above.

That was how he ended up waiting for Takeo at an empty playground in the middle of the night.

He fidgeted nervously with his hands while staring into the dark. Nao had rarely felt this idiotic before in his life, but he had brought this upon himself and now he had to live with the consequences. Even if it meant embarrassing himself in front of Takeo.

He had just…he had just felt like seeing him, hearing his voice, and listening to his words. He'd barely seen him in the last two weeks, and this was a huge change from the weeks they had spent studying together almost every day. Nao hadn't even noticed how much he had been getting used to being enwrapped in the other's presence, hearing his stupid jokes and putting up with his silly, lighthearted self, until he was left without it.

Finally, after what had felt like a small infinity to Nao, Takeo's frame emerged from the darkness, cutting through the night like a beam of light.

If he had been angry at Nao for calling him out this late, he didn't show it. With the same amicable smile Nao had learned to miss, he waved at him. "Hey."

Nao's breath hitched. His agitation was almost too great. He tried to force a smile, but it probably ended up as a lopsided grimace. "...Hey," he replied meekly.

They sat down on a nearby bench, silence filling up the space between them. Nao had come this far, but now he was at a loss. Thankfully, Takeo was a born talker.

"What is it? What's bothering you?" he broke the wall of silence.

Nao stared at him in surprise, and Takeo gave him a small smile in return. "I doubt you would've called me this late if it weren't important to you," he explained. "Also, you look pretty down, so I assume there must be something nagging you. So, what happened?"

Feeling bashful, Nao rubbed the back of his neck and stared at the ground. "It really...it really isn't that important, actually. I just...just..." He stopped and took a deep breath before raising his head and gazing directly at the other. "Say, Takeo..." he spoke quietly. "Do you like guys?"

Takeo's eyes widened in surprise, a sound akin to choking left his throat as he gaped at Nao. He opened his mouth and closed it again before finally responding with a crooked smile. "Yes... I do."

Nao clenched his jaw, his traitorous heart taking a leap. "Do you sometimes think it's wrong?"

Pondering for a second, Takeo looked up and leaned backward against the bench. "No, I don't think so," he then answered.

"Then why haven't you told anyone about it? Are you embarrassed?"

His gaze fell back on Nao. "I'm not. I just don't think it's anything that defines me as a person. I also don't go around telling people what I had for breakfast that morning. That's how I feel about it. Why? Are you embarrassed about it?"

Uneasy, Nao fumbled with the fabric of his shirt. "I used to not be," he said. "But lately...I don't know how to feel."

Takeo tensed up ever so slightly. "Do I...do I perhaps make you uncomfortable?"

"No. No," Nao denied quickly. "It's not like that." It was the opposite actually. He felt too comfortable around Takeo! He wasn't familiar with this!

He sighed. "All my life, I've been told that it is wrong. That I'm not supposed to feel like this. But to me...it just felt normal. Since I can remember, I have felt this way. It's like...like you said, what I eat for breakfast in the morning. But no matter how natural it is for me, everyone keeps shunning me for it, like I'm doing something condemnable. I start thinking, what if I really am abnormal? I used to ignore those things, but lately, it has been really hard to do so." He stared at the ground. Nao couldn't possibly tell him that his sprouting heart was the culprit for this predicament.

Takeo had listened to his every word with undivided attention. In his eyes lay an unfathomable glint, and for a second, Nao was scared he had upset him. But when Takeo suddenly spoke up, his voice was strong yet gentle.

"What should be abnormal about you?" He furrowed his brows. "Only because some people keep telling you so? Do you go around shooting spiderwebs out of your hands or move around while levitating off the floor? That would be abnormal. But all you and I do is to fall in love with someone. If you ask me, it's the most normal thing a person could do.

"And even if it were abnormal... heck, who cares!? If I am a sinner so be it. I'm not worse than those people murdering and stabbing others. All I do is give my heart. And who could say that this is a crime worth punishing? ...If there's someone reciprocating my heart, then I'd happily sin every day if it means I get to love and be loved by them. If this is the reason I get punished one day... I don't think I'd have any regrets."

Nao looked at Takeo with wide eyes, struck speechless. He stared silently at Takeo for a few seconds before he could finally say, "You... I guess you do have a point."

"I don't just have a point. I could write you a whole essay about this! Do you want me to?" he asked almost challengingly, obviously fired up after his passionate speech, and Nao could only huff in return. There he was, back with his crazy propositions.

Of course, it had been the right idea to call Takeo. The latter was like the warm spring breeze, rejuvenating the barren land of Nao's heart. He could feel the knot in his chest slowly unraveling, a tension he didn't know had been sitting in his muscles silently loosening.

Takeo's words didn't change the world. In fact, he was still going to get bullied by Sho and his classmates the next day, his parents would still look at him with disdain. But that was not what it was about. Hearing these words out of Takeo's mouth gave him courage he didn't know he had been waiting for. As long as Takeo was around, steadfast like a mountain, Nao could feel a little more confident as well. The blossoms in his heart were flourishing, the branches growing even more pompous.

"I'm sorry I called you this late. I hope I didn't bother you too much."

"You could never bother me," Takeo answered easily. "You can always ask me to come out for a chat. That's what friends are for, isn't it?"

Nao nodded curtly and Takeo smiled. "Don't let it weigh down on you too much, okay?" he said. "To me, you are perfectly fine. Even more than that. I think you are super brave, Nao. You inspired me when I lost my courage. So please don't doubt yourself. You are just right in my eyes."

Nao's heart was riding rollercoaster again. Shyly, he glanced at Takeo, who gazed back at him with a warm smile. And suddenly, Nao's chest started feeling all warm as well. A spring storm ravaged his insides. He could feel the blossoms closing, growing into rich fruit.

Hah... what was he supposed to do? Why did something he had been so afraid of feel so good?

Nao looked at Takeo and felt himself fall only deeper and deeper. He was screwed, wasn't he? But well, he had always been prone to making bad decisions. So maybe, after hundreds of wrong choices, this was the right one. He'd been so scared before meeting Takeo, but he didn't even feel a shred of it now that he was around him.

Hmm... maybe he should just give in. His heart had already conceded anyway, right? What was the benefit in fighting it?

And in said moment, the fruit had ripened. One tumbled from the tree and fell right into the prisoner's cell. In a deep dungeon, where not even light could reach, a full, ripe fruit rolled across the ground. Having been starved for so long, the prisoner picked it up and took a greedy bite.

He had never tasted something so sweet before.

— Chapter 16 —

"What would you like?" Takeo asked, and Nao just shrugged in response. "I don't know. Just take anything."

They stood in front of a shelf filled with countless rows of snacks and more snacks. It wasn't the only one, though. The whole aisle was stacked with shelves overflowing with candy and chips. Takeo looked at the variety of food, pondering it intently as if it were some kind of quantum physical equation he was trying to solve.

Nao watched him do so wordlessly from the side, silently amused by how seriously he took this trivial task. But the other had a talent for regarding everything with the attention of a scientist and yet the excitement of a child.

Nao couldn't care less about what they bought in the end, but he patiently let Takeo analyse the snacks, watching with toneless entertainment as he picked up pack after pack before ultimately putting them back. At last, he concluded his intensive research with a serious "Then I'll the take crab chips." as he grabbed one pack from the shelf. "Do you want to buy anything else?"

Nao shook his head.

They were back at the small convenience store they had visited some weeks ago. Since they had finished the last exam of the semester earlier that day, Takeo had proposed to meet in the afternoon and celebrate the end of exam season with some snacks.

They had grabbed a pack of crab chips and strawberry biscuits. On the way to the counter, Nao picked out two cans of mango soda from the refrigerator and put them next to the other items. The cashier packed them into a plastic bag for them, and with their freshly purchased snacks, they strolled out of the store.

It was a fairly warm day. The temperature was fluctuating somewhere between a cozy twenty and twenty-five degrees Celsius, and for once in a long, grey summer, the sun had decided to peek out between the clouds. Nao had to shield his eyes with the back of his hand as they exited the shadow of the building.

"Where do you want to go?" he asked.

"I've thought of the pond near the park," Takeo said, also holding a hand above his eyes to protect them from the sun. "What do you think?"

"Mm, let's go there," Nao agreed, the white plastic bag dangling around his wrist.

They walked past the round, white camping tables standing in front of the shop and near a group of kids who were sitting on the sidewalk, playing with a handheld game console.

The group consisted of two boys and a girl, all of them barely over the age of seven. Excitedly, they watched as one of the boys hammered onto the buttons of his console.

Nao just absentmindedly passed them, but Takeo slowed down his steps and peeked curiously at the device's display. Suddenly, as if struck by lightning, he stopped dead in his tracks and looked at the kids with wide eyes. "Is this the *Ultimate Yellow Special Star Edition*!?" he asked in disbelief.

The boy looked up and nodded with a wide smile, showing off a cheeky, gap-toothed grin.

"I've been wanting to play this forever!" Takeo exclaimed. Eyes sparkling, he glanced over at Nao. "Do you mind if I take a look at it for a second?"

"Go on."

Takeo smiled appreciatively and sat next to the children on the sidewalk.

"I've been dying to get my hands on it," he said enviously.

"My mommy got it for me on my birthday," the boy exclaimed proudly, puffing up his chest. "I even caught a *Level Three Monster* already."

"Really? Can you show me?"

Swelling with pride, the boy showed the game to Takeo. Nao stood a few steps away, watching the expression of childlike excitement on Takeo's face with growing amusement.

The little girl sitting to the far right pulled a pack of crackers out of her bag and quietly opened them. She handed a salted cracker to Takeo and then looked up at Nao. With a smile, she held up one of the biscuits. "Do you want one too?" she asked.

Nao nodded and gratefully took the cracker out of her small hand. He sat next to her on the ground and peered over the heads of the children at the console while munching on the snack.

The asphalt was warm; its cozy heat seeped through Nao's legs up into his spine. The rays of sun cradled the back of his head as the mild summer heat engulfed him gently.

For some time he just watched the children and Takeo play. He eyed the effortless and happy smile on Takeo's face, feeling his chest light up along with it. Takeo's smile was akin to the sun, warm and bright. And just like the moon shone only because of the sun's light, Nao couldn't suppress the content smile curling his lips.

They had completely lost track of time when the voice of a woman echoed across the street. "Yuta!" she shouted. "Where are the groceries? I told you not to get sidetracked."

Yuta looked up, surprised, and quickly switched off the console. Hastily, he jumped up and grabbed a white plastic bag. "Oh no, I totally forgot! I have to go."

The other children got up as well. They waved Nao and Takeo goodbye before quickly running down the street with their shopping bags swaying in the wind.

Takeo looked over at Nao. "Hah, sorry, that must've been boring for you."

Nao shook his head. "It wasn't." They rose to their feet, dusting off their pants. "I've been trying to save up for that game since last year," Takeo said and sighed. "I hope I'll get it this year!"

Side by side, they continued their stroll down the street. It took only a few minutes before the two of them arrived at the park. The pond covered a large area of the surrounding green field.

They walked up to the knee-high border out of thick black stone encircling the water. In the dark green pond bustled orange and white koi. In a big swarm, they romped about, disappearing in and out of the water like sparks dancing in a bonfire.

Nao crouched down to get a better look at them. At the sight of a human above them, they stuck their mouths out of the water, impatiently opening and closing them in wait for food.

"Do you have something to give them?" Nao asked Takeo, who had also crouched down, but he shook his head.

"Then let's bring something next time."

Takeo smiled and nodded. He leaned over the stone wall and laughed. "They look kinda cute." He hovered his fingers above the surface of the water. Like wet dogs, the koi peeked out from between the ripples and began following the strange novelty. Greedily, they tried to jump up and catch Takeo's fingers with their wide, round mouths. Takeo chuckled upon watching them, and Nao wanted to follow suit.

With both hands, he leaned onto the dark stone. He lifted a hand to touch the soft mirror of the rippling water, wanting to play with them just like Takeo did, but the stone was wet and slippery. His palm slid across the surface before he noticed, and he lost his balance.

Nao fell face-first into the pond—his head broke through the surface of the cold water. He was only saved from fully plunging into the depths thanks to the hand grabbing his arm and yanking him back.

Gasping, Nao landed on his butt, his face and hair soaked.

"Are you okay?" Takeo asked, his hand still wrapped around his arm. Nao rubbed the water out of his eyes and gazed at him, slightly dazed, before realising that their faces were only a few centimeters apart. "Y-yeah," he mumbled, flustered.

Suddenly, Takeo's furrowed brows lifted and he let out a loud laugh. Nao looked at him, utterly dumbfounded. "Sorry," Takeo chuckled. "It just…it looked really funny!"

Nao watched Takeo shake with laughter. His cheeks and nose turned red, dimples formed next to the corners of his mouth, and a hand clutched his stomach. His laugh rang loud and clear, like stones skipping across water. Being blessed both visually and audibly with Takeo's happiness, Nao couldn't contain his own smile.

He rubbed his face with the sleeve of his hoodie. "I can see that," he said.

Takeo wiped a tear from his eye, and then took off his sweater jacket, handing it to Nao. "Take this to dry yourself."

Nao grabbed the soft, grey fabric and used the sleeve to wipe his face.

"Now all the koi have swum away," Takeo said and started chuckling again. "I guess they got scared by the weird fish suddenly falling from the sky."

"Watch what you say or there will be an even bigger fish joining them," Nao responded, wiping a wet strand of hair out of his face.

"Try pushing me in, then," Takeo challenged with a grin.

Nao huffed. "As if," he said and stood up. He extended his hand toward Takeo, who took it happily, allowing himself to be pulled up. But before he could fully stand on his own, Nao suddenly let go of him, and Takeo fell back.

He barely managed to regain his balance by clinging to Nao's arm with both hands—the water of the pond was mere centimeters below him. He gawked at Nao with wide eyes, while the latter grinned mischievously back at him. "I'd never do something as low as trying to push you into the water," he proclaimed innocently. "I promise."

After a few seconds of lingering shock had passed, Takeo's lips rose into a smile. His eyes twinkled with excitement. "I see," he said. "So you can play dirty too. I'll have to watch my back from now on."

Both of them chuckled merrily.

They settled on a bench next to the pond. Nao held Takeo's crumpled jacket in his lap. His hair was still wet and he felt the warm breeze grazing it ever so gently.

Takeo opened the packs of crab chips and strawberry biscuits. He placed them on the bench between the two of them and then proceeded to open a can of mango soda. He handed it to Nao, who took the cold, sparkling drink with a soft 'thank you.'

Side by side, they sat on the brown plastic bench, holding the sodas in their hands and watching the pond and its lazy ripples in front of them.

Nao took a sip of the sweet liquid, feeling the sugary taste spread on his tongue and the carbonic acid linger on his lips.

"I'm glad the exams are finally over," Takeo spoke into the light silence.

"Mm, me too," Nao replied.

"I think we might get the first results next week."

Nao could hardly suppress a sigh at that thought. He still felt jittery thinking about the outcome of his math exam.

"This is our last year of school," Takeo continued. "Next year, we'll already graduate. Do you know what you want to do after that?"

Nao shook his head. "No," he said, although he knew he was going to be shoved off to some third-class university.

"I don't mean university or something like that," Takeo suddenly said as if he'd read Nao's mind. "I mean what you want to do right after you have graduated. There is still some time before choosing a future path. What would you like to do in the time between that, when you are neither bound to school nor anywhere else?"

Nao's brain briefly short-circuited. His head went blank after being confronted with such an unexpected question. But even if he'd had time to think about it, he wouldn't have been able to answer it. So, he shrugged. "I...don't know."

Takeo took a sip of his soda before speaking. "Hm, I, for example, would like to travel. I've never left this prefecture and would really love to use that time to explore a bit. But I am honestly not really sure yet where I'd like to go first. There are so many cool places to see! Where'd you go?"

"If I could go anywhere...I think I'd go to Okinawa," Nao replied pensively while Takeo watched him intently. "Okinawa?" he asked, and Nao nodded. "I've never been there before, but I've seen pictures of it and thought that it looked pretty. Also, I would like to try shikuwasa."

"You like sour food?"

"Mm, I like sour and sweet food."

Takeo chuckled hearing those words. "What?" Nao asked, and Takeo just waved it off. "Nothing," he replied, yet had to hold back his grin. He thought it was a really cute answer coming from someone like Nao.

"Okinawa sounds nice," he then said. "Okay, then this will be my first destination."

Nao looked at him, surprised. "Just like that?"

"Just like that." Takeo nodded resolutely. "If you say you think it's pretty, then it surely is. And I've always liked warm places and the sea. So it sounds like the perfect place. If you want, you can join me."

Takeo let the last part sound like a joking remark, but Nao knew that he didn't just say it like that. He never did.

Running away from his family to a remote island sounded nice, really nice. But Nao knew that it was unrealistic. He smiled weakly. If the shackles of the world weren't so tight, he would have tried to get rid of them a long time ago. But they were still cutting into his ankles, bruising his bones and skin. Well…lately, though, the pain of them seemed to have eased a little.

"I would like to go there…" Nao just said and fidgeted with the can in his hands. "But what about you? You said you've never left the Ibaraki prefecture."

Takeo laughed bashfully. "That sounds pretty sad, right? Well, we just never had enough money to go on vacation and we also don't have any family outside to visit. That's why I'd really like to use the time after graduation to explore the country—to see a little bit of the world before I go to university and get a teaching license."

Takeo's eyes were sparkling as he talked about his future plans. Nao saw the soft blush of excitement blossoming on his cheeks, and he felt his own admiration growing. Takeo knew exactly what he wanted to do with his life. He had wishes and a destination. Something Nao had never had and therefore admired.

Absentmindedly, he wondered if he could ever feel such a yearning for something himself.

"But what about your family when you leave to travel?" The question left Nao's lips before he could stop it.

"I'm sorry," he apologised immediately. Perhaps this was too personal, potentially crossing one of the few borders they had left... Yet, Takeo just smiled amicably.

"Well, for the time being, my brother will take care of my mother. But after I study hard and get my teaching license, I'll save up a lot of money and get my mother into a good clinic. One that has a view onto the sea. I think she'd like that a lot.

"Also, when I earn my own money, I can finally pay my brother back for all the things he's done for me.

"I know it's a bit selfish wanting to travel and leave my family behind, but I would really like to experience a bit of the world before I am stuck at university. Even if it's just a sliver. That's better than never having left this place at all. I'd like to have at least seen a little bit before I grow up. That would already be a big part of my dream."

A part? "What else do you dream of?" Nao asked curiously.

"Oh, a lot!" Takeo exclaimed immediately. He straightened up and excitedly started counting all of them on his fingers. "Of course traveling and graduating. But I'd also like to try bungee jumping or sky diving. I've seen it on TV and thought it looked really fun! I would also like to fly in an airplane. Maybe even leave the continent if I get the chance! I've also thought learning an instrument could be fun. I might try that later on, too." He smiled sweetly. "What about you?"

"Me...? Uhm, there's not really anything I dream of."

"Really!?"

Nao nodded.

"Nothing?" Takeo asked again, and Nao shrugged helplessly. He suddenly felt a rush of embarrassment. After listening to someone talk about a life's worth of goals and passions, he felt like a fish stuck in a puddle. While the other drifted across the river with the possibility of the vast seas ahead, Nao was a small fish bobbing around in its little pond. The sea as far and unattainable as the sky. How could he admit this without feeling embarrassed?

He pressed his lips together and shook his head. "You ask such tricky questions! I have no goals. Maybe…maybe someday, though." He tried not to sound too bashful, but he was probably not very successful in doing so. Takeo gazed at him for a few seconds before saying, "You're right. It was indeed a tricky question. I didn't want to pry too much, I'm sorry."

"Don't feel sorry." Nao sighed. "You didn't pry. I just…have no answer to that question yet."

"And you do not have to. It's not like everything I plan out is written in stone either. I might change my opinion about them one day as well. Who knows, maybe in the end it's better not to focus on one thing too much and just embrace the possibility of the unknown. Has the world ever followed one's plans without twisting them?" Takeo gently bumped against him with his shoulder and smiled. "You might be onto something, Nao."

He leaned forward to catch the other's gaze and Nao snorted. "What are you trying to do?"

"I'm trying to cheer you up. Why? Doesn't it work?"

Always when I'm with you! Nao thought, but he coolly shook his head. "No."

Takeo's face fell, and Nao almost had to laugh out loud at the sudden change. He eventually took pity on him and said in a calm voice, "Maybe a little bit."

162

Takeo's face brightened again, though this time there was a teasing look to it. "You mean a little bit lot?"

"A little bit," Nao insisted.

Takeo beamed, nonetheless.

They spent the rest of the afternoon sitting on the bench, talking. It was easy. It was enriching. For those few hours, the world was peaceful, and Nao was happy. He could have stayed here for an eternity.

But as the sun slowly started to set in the distance and the breezy wind became somewhat chilly, they eventually decided to get up. They threw the empty snack packages and cans into the trash, and unhurriedly headed home. Takeo had insisted on accompanying Nao, so they wandered through the darkening streets.

The sunlight had already become a dark orange sliver at the bottom of the horizon as they arrived at the tall building. The street lamps sprang into life, and the bustling on the streets quieted down. It was a balmy summer evening; Nao and Takeo were right in the heart of it.

The two of them stopped in a side street next to the house. Almost in sync, they slowed their steps and came to a halt. Nao was playing with the fabric of the jacket he was still holding in his arms.

He held it up toward Takeo. "Here," he said and the other took it. "Thanks. Is your hair still wet?" Takeo asked.

Nao ran his fingers through the damp strands. "A little bit."

"Fortunately, it's not that cold today, or you might have caught a cold."

Nao shook his head. "I don't get sick that easily. And the fall wasn't that bad despite the fact that I snorted fish water."

Takeo laughed. "But in all honesty, I've never seen anyone snort fish water as gracefully as you did." He smiled cheekily as Nao pouted at him.

Takeo's eyes glided across Nao's face. The latter looked up at him with those deep brown eyes and softly furrowed brows. The damp black hair was still stuck to his forehead, and Takeo couldn't contain the urge and reached out with his hand. Tenderly, he wiped the strands out of the other's eyes. "You're the clumsy type, aren't you?" he said and smiled at Nao, who looked at him with wide eyes. Takeo pushed the wet strands behind his ear, feeling the silky hair beneath his fingertips.

What was he doing here? He looked at Nao, who was gawking at him with his round doe eyes. They held so much beauty the owner would never see. From the warm, brown irises, shining with so much mildness, to the long lashes, framing the soft ups and downs of his eyelids, his eyes resembled the placid mountain streams flowing through valleys and hills. He'd been enchanted by them the very first time he had seen him. Back then, when they were still strangers; but now he wanted them to be so much more.

Takeo swallowed thickly. *What was he doing here?* His heart hammered fervently against his ribs. They were so close. If he just leaned in a bit more he could...

Should he? Was it okay if he...?

He lowered his hand. Maybe it wasn't right. As much as his heart was beating right now and his palms were sweaty, he couldn't risk it. He didn't want to make Nao uncomfortable. No, even as much as he was tempted right now...he couldn't just succumb to his desires.

Takeo let his hand sink and gripped the jacket in his arms tightly. He probably shouldn't. It was best if he—

He felt Nao's lips pressing against his. Takeo's breath stopped. *W...what was happening?* But there was no doubt. Nao's lips were resting on his.

Takeo took a shaky breath and closed his eyes. Almost instinctively, he leaned forward into the kiss and placed a hand on the side of Nao's face. His fingers digging gently into his hair.

It didn't feel real. No, this was too good to be real. He must be dreaming.

With every fibre of his body, he took in Nao's warmth. He felt his quivering breath fanning his skin, the astronomically high pulse thrumming against the tips of his fingers.

Although maybe...this was real. Takeo changed his mind. Because even a dream could never be as enthralling as this.

Takeo melted into the kiss. He felt like a man who had tasted sugar for the first time in his life. The feeling was addictive, rich, moreish. Liquid honey surged through his veins, becoming sweeter and sweeter with every careful smacking of their lips. Was every kiss supposed to feel this way? Takeo dearly hoped so.

He could have continued this for much longer, until the sun had disappeared behind the horizon and stars speckled the vast sky. Takeo could lose himself in the feeling of Nao's lips —in fact, he had already done so—when the other pulled away at once.

The kiss broke off as suddenly as it had happened. Takeo opened his eyes, mind in a slight daze, and looked at the boy in front of him, who stared at him with eyes as wide as the moon. Nao had a hand clasped over his mouth. The sinking shock of what had just happened written all over his face.

Takeo was out of breath. His heart was hammering up to his throat. He should say something, shouldn't he? Even with his mind blank, he opened his mouth, but before he could utter anything at all, Nao had turned around and left.

Takeo watched the silhouette fading into the dark, and he remained with nothing but his wildly beating heart and a thousand questions.

Nao fell into his bed. He pulled the blanket over his head and dove into the dark security beneath it.

His face was all blushed and hot, and his hands shivered like crazy. He buried his face in his palms.

What had just happened!? What did he do!?

He couldn't explain it himself. He really couldn't. Had he been possessed or something? Had he gone mad? He must have lost his mind. It couldn't be explained any other way!

Nao's heart was skipping like mad. He could barely breathe. He had just...he had just kissed Takeo. The emphasis on *he;* Nao.

His mind had suddenly gone blank. He remembered Takeo wiping the hair from his eyes, his warm fingers grazing his forehead. He could see his gaze wandering across his face, felt his hand tuck the hair behind his ear. And then...then it had just happened.

Nao must have really lost his mind. Because never in a hundred thousand years would he have done something like that. No, never. This wasn't like him. But then again...he had done it.

He had once said that Takeo would make him lose his mind, but he didn't mean like *this*.

Shyly, he moved his fingers up to his lips, tracing the pink skin with the tips. They had kissed...

And it was his first kiss.

When he closed his eyes and cleared his mind, he could still feel the other's lips, his breath, the tender way he... Nao tensed his jaw, and a sound akin to a whimper left his mouth. Shaking his head like a lunatic, he rolled around, biting his fingernails. He had to focus!

So, three things were for sure.

First, he had just kissed Takeo Iwasaki. Second, it was his first kiss. And third…his heart was beating like crazy, which meant he had liked it, right?

Nao cupped his own face, feeling the burning skin against his palms.

It was crazy. He was crazy. Him liking that kiss was crazy. And Takeo for reciprocating it was also crazy.

Yes, Takeo had kissed him back. Nao couldn't believe it. Did that mean Takeo had also liked it? No, he couldn't have, could he?

Nao started tossing and turning in his bed. The feeling of the other's soft lips on his, the gentle hand playing with his hair…all of it kept replaying in his mind.

Possessed or not, mad or not, it had been an absolutely hauntingly beautiful and equally terrifying experience. But it was a mistake, wasn't it? He should feel bad about it, right?

As much as he wanted to, Nao couldn't feel any regret in that moment.

— Chapter 17 —

Yesterday, Nao had been filled with pure adrenaline after the kiss. Today, it had disappeared and he was left with the harsh reality of his actions.

He'd been bursting with butterflies the night before, but they grew into hornets the next morning.

He had made a grave mistake, right? Thoughts like these ate him up. *This was a mistake. But then why had it felt so natural?*

Absentmindedly, Nao poked with the spoon in his soup. He watched the bubbles of fat float on the surface and the thinly cut green onions stick to the ceramic bowl. There was a hole in his stomach dug by the hornets, and he was too distracted by his thoughts to lead the spoon to his mouth.

He had never been a big eater. Nao usually ate slowly, but to-day he seemed to have maxed it out.

"Don't play with your food! Sit up straight and eat like an adult," his father barked strictly, and Nao started at the sudden loudness. He straightened his back and tightened his grip on the spoon. "I'm sorry," he muttered and involuntarily downed a mouthful of the soup. The warm liquid ran down his throat like hot oil, and the hornets buzzed angrily in the pit of his stomach.

Racking his brain wouldn't matter anyway, Nao tried to con-clude. Takeo wouldn't want to see him anyway after what he had done, would he? After all, Nao had bolted right after realising what had happened. This was probably one of the most embar-rassing things one could do after a kiss… for both parties alike.

Nao's palms became all sweaty thinking about the next time he was going to see Takeo again. Desperately, he tried to push those thoughts away. At least he had the whole weekend left before he'd be confronted with the dire consequences of his actions.

As if the universe had heard him and decided to mock him once again, Mrs. Takahashi came into the room at once. She held the telephone in her hand and gazed nervously over to Nao. "There is someone on the phone for Mr. Nao."

The room couldn't go any quieter than this. His parents and brother looked in disbelief at Mrs. Takahashi, as if she had just announced that the prime minister of Japan was on the other line. However, considering the connections his family harboured, this was far more believable than a call directed at Nao.

He swallowed the soup and looked at his father, who slowly turned his head toward him. For a second, he just eyed his son. His gaze skimmed over his face as if he were trying to analyse his motives before he eventually pursed his lips.

"Go. But don't expect to finish your food when you come back."

Quickly, Nao stood up and took the telephone from Mrs. Takahashi. With the device in his hand, he hurried to his room, feeling the gazes of his family members stuck to his back like targets.

He closed the door behind him and leaned against the wood, nervously holding the phone up to his ear. "Hello?" he whispered.

"Hey, it's me." Takeo's voice resonated from the speaker and Nao's heart skipped a beat. "I hope it's okay that I called on this number. I didn't know how to reach you otherwise."

"I—…it's okay," Nao stammered, unsure how to breathe.

"I couldn't ask you yesterday because you left so suddenly." Nao tensed up. Takeo remembered what had happened the night before… Well, of course he did, but still, Nao had somehow hoped he might have forgotten about it. He had run away like a maniac directly after they had kissed. Even just the first incident was awkward enough, but bolting right afterward somehow made things even worse. Nao could slap himself silly for both.

He tightened his grip on the phone, his fingers digging into the plastic.

"I wanted to ask you," Takeo's voice rang out, "do you—"

"I didn't want to make you uncomfortable!" Nao blurted out, his heart pounding. "Yesterday... I don't know what that was... It wasn't intentional or anything like that... so I'm sorry if it made you uncomfortable."

For a second, it was dead silent on the other side of the phone. Nao closed his eyes, ready to hear the sound of the connection being broken. He waited for the crackling and static noises to turn into thick, irreversible silence, but to his surprise, it was Takeo's voice that continued first.

"I wanted to ask if you have time tomorrow."

"T-time? Tomorrow?" Nao parroted, dumbstruck.

"Yes," Takeo said. "I thought I could pick you up on the bike and we could ride to the sea... We can also do something different... But you don't have to if you don't want to."

Did he just ask him to meet again? Nao didn't believe his ears. But no, he had heard right. Takeo wanted to see him again.

Nao nodded slowly before realising Takeo couldn't see him over the phone. "Yes, okay," he breathed, hardly noticing the other's relieved sigh following it.

"I'll be by your house at four, okay?"

"Yes."

"Then... see you tomorrow."

"Yes, see you tomorrow."

The connection was cut off and Nao stood in his room with the phone still against his ear.

Silently, he slid down the door onto the ground, clutching the device tightly between his fingers.

He had kissed the guy he liked and now he had asked him to meet again… Was this reality?

Nao buried his red face in his hands, the cold plastic of the phone pressed against his hot cheek.

Nao didn't want to admit it but he could hardly sleep that night.

He felt like a dumb teenage boy whenever he noticed his heart pounding madly in his chest at the thought of seeing Takeo tomorrow. But then he remembered, he was a teenage boy and what he experienced was probably very normal.

His stomach felt all queasy during breakfast and lunch, and he spent way too long in front of his wardrobe choosing something to wear.

At last, Nao decided on a pair of shorts and a grey hoodie. Finally, it had become summer, and it was warm enough to wear airy clothes.

He briefly combed his hair with his fingers in front of the mirror, then rode the elevator down to the ground floor.

Takeo was already waiting for him when he stepped out of the main gate. He sat on his bicycle, dressed in a pair of black shorts and an oversized white shirt. His face lifted into a smile as soon as he spotted Nao. "There you are," he said. "Come on, let's go!"

Nao's mouth had gone all dry. He was puzzled how Takeo could be so casual. They had kissed just two days ago! But, on second thought, he was secretly grateful for it, as it made all of this a little less awkward.

Hesitantly, Nao sat on the bicycle behind Takeo. "Where are we going?" he asked.

"The beach again, if you're okay with that."

Nao nodded. "Yes."

"All right! Then hold on tight."

Like the last time they had taken the bike, Nao grabbed the sides of Takeo's shirt. Shyly, he held on to the fabric with his fingers, but Takeo turned his head to glance at him over his shoulder.

"It's okay, you can grab me tighter," he said easily. "I don't want you to fall off."

Nao was hesitant to move. He wasn't sure how to act, and so Takeo just gently gripped his wrists and wrapped them around his waist. "Like this," he said and then turned back around to grasp the handles of the bicycle.

Nao dearly hoped that Takeo couldn't feel his heartbeat through their clothes. They were so close to each other that he felt his body heat seep through the light fabric.

Nao squeezed his eyes shut as they started to move. The warm summer wind mussed his hair and he smelled the fresh breeze carrying the scent of grass and flowers. It had truly become summer.

They cycled across the city, through the packed streets, and farther to the outskirts.

Nao held tightly onto Takeo. He didn't really have another choice since the other's cycling skills were still as brisk as last time.

Beneath his arms, Nao could feel Takeo's body moving. He felt his legs pushing into the pedals and his ribcage rising and falling upon the movement.

On one hand, Nao felt a little embarrassed taking notice of this, but on the other, he quietly enjoyed it. From behind, he could watch Takeo's short hair get tussled by the wind, the hem of his shirt fluttering in the breeze.

Finally, they reached the edge of the beach. Even from far away, Nao could spot a ferris wheel in the distance. It stuck out like a skyscraper amidst the low buildings and scattered trees. As they came closer, Nao also spotted a small roller coaster as well as a colourful carousel. This definitely hadn't been there the last time they had visited.

In front of the trail leading down to the beach, they came to a halt. Nao loosened his arms around Takeo and jumped off the bicycle. He pointed at the ferris wheel, confused. "Is there a fair?" he asked.

Takeo leaned his bike against a fence. "Mm," he hummed with a proud smile.

"You knew about it?"

"Mm," he hummed again, still with the same cheekiness. "I thought it could be a fun visit since the weather has finally cleared up."

Nao huffed. That guy was really unbelievable. He had it all planned out.

Happily, Takeo cocked his head to the side. "Where do you want to go first? The fair or the beach?"

"The beach," Nao said, thus they moved down the sandy trail. Contrary to the last time, the sea was much calmer, nearly placid, in the way it swayed. Almost all of the clouds had vanished, and behind the few stray slivers gleamed the sun, tipping already slowly toward the horizon. Its light spread across the dark blue water, fragmenting and scattering into tender ripples and sparkles among the merry waves.

This time, there were a handful of people present at the beach. Presumably visitors who had also come to enjoy the fair.

Takeo bent down and untied his purple shoelaces. Nao watched him in confusion for a few seconds before asking, "What are you doing?"

"Taking off my shoes," Takeo said. "Last time, the water was too cold, but today the temperature is perfect for going in." He slid the old sneakers off and picked them up. "Come on, you too."

"Me?" Nao pointed at himself, and Takeo nodded. Nao regarded the soft-rippling water with a sidelong glance before hesitantly taking off his shoes and socks.

"Now let's go," Takeo said and headed toward the water. Tentatively, Nao followed him.

They placed their shoes close to the shore and then proceeded to walk into the sea. Almost immediately, a wave rolled toward them and engulfed their feet in a cold, wet hug. Nao flinched, feeling the cool water swallow his ankles and legs. "It's cold," he squeaked unintentionally high, and Takeo laughed. He walked deeper into the water until it reached all the way up to his knees.

He turned to Nao. "Come here. It gets warmer the longer you are in."

Slowly, Nao waded deeper into the ocean. He felt the water rising higher as his feet sank into the cold, soft sand beneath. The vast sea before them stretched out to the far corners of the horizon, seemingly filling the whole earth. The sun gleamed back at them, warm and dazzling.

Nao lifted a hand and held it above his eyes, watching the rays of light fall upon them. He closed his eyes, savouring the feeling of them on his face.

When he was suddenly shaken back to the present by a squeal next to him. Nao flinched and spun around just in time to see Takeo leap a meter backward.

"What is it?" Nao asked, and Takeo pointed at the water. "A-a jellyfish just touched me," he stuttered, and for the first time, Nao witnessed such a sound of distress in the other's usually calm voice.

"There are no poisonous jellyfish in this area," he replied calmly.

"I know. But, but I *hate* jellyfish!"

Nao looked around and found the white jellyfish head swimming in the water between them. It wasn't bigger than a saucer and floated leisurely among the waves, thoroughly minding its own business.

In disbelief, Nao looked at Takeo. "You're scared of that?" he asked incredulously, arching up a single eyebrow.

"Not scared... I just hate the look and feeling of them. They are...disgusting!"

Nao laughed. "You are for real disgusted by those little things?" He scooped up the jellyfish with his hand, holding the wobbly little creature in his palm. He gazed over at Takeo, who looked back at him skeptically, and then walked slowly over to him.

Takeo squeaked and immediately retreated several steps back. "Don't! I don't want to see that thing up close."

Nao laughed and released the animal back into the water, shooing it with his hands in the opposite direction of Takeo.

"I put it away," Nao said with a small giggle. "I didn't know this was all it takes. You stand head-on against a gang, but run away from a jellyfish."

Takeo pouted. His ears glowed bright red. "That's different," he argued. "They don't have tentacles and see-through bodies."

"I guess that's true. Don't worry, I put it away." He waded over to Takeo, who awkwardly scratched his ear. Nao could tell he was extremely embarrassed.

"You know...I really hate cows," he suddenly threw in to alleviate the mood. Thankfully, Takeo took the bait. "Cows?" he asked, and Nao nodded.

"I think they are really scary. When I was ten, my family visited a farm. Back then, I thought it was funny to sneak onto the field where they kept the farm animals. I just wanted to pet them, but one of the cows ended up chasing me instead. I haven't been on good terms with them ever since."

Takeo smiled faintly. "Is that true?"

"Unfortunately, yes."

His smile widened. "It's pretty odd to be scared of cows."

"Says the guy who ran away from a jellyfish."

"Fair enough." Takeo grinned. "But how did you escape from those cows?"

"Oh, that's…" Awkwardly, Nao scratched the back of his head. "The farmer actually had to save me. He pulled me out of the pen after I had been chased around for quite some time."

Takeo laughed heartily. "That sounds truly traumatising."

"I told you. We've been on bad terms ever since." He smiled. "But now, let's get out of the water before we get attacked by more jellyfish," Nao joked, and Takeo joined in. "Yes, I heard they are especially vicious here, just like the cows."

They headed out of the water. Neither of them had brought a towel to dry off their legs, so they picked up their shoes and walked barefoot in the sand.

Every now and then, a wave caught up to them and engulfed their feet in cool water.

As they walked side by side like that, Nao couldn't restrain himself and secretly glanced over at Takeo. The sunlight fell upon his face, throwing soft shadows and highlights across his tan skin.

Nao's eyes wandered slowly over his features, and as they finally stopped at his lips, he got all flustered. The memories flooded back into his mind—so violently that Nao had to avert his eyes. Unsure, he fumbled with his fingers.

Takeo hadn't spoken a word about it since it had happened. Nao didn't really know what to take from that. Maybe he just wanted to pretend like it hadn't happened. Maybe he was just uncomfortable because of it.

Nao fidgeted with his thumbnail. "Takeo...because of that thing two days ago..." he murmured anxiously. "I'm sorry. I didn't want to make things uncomfortable between us..."

Takeo suddenly stopped in his tracks. Surprised, Nao stopped as well.

He looked at Takeo, who gazed at him with drawn brows, a sudden gloom casting over his features. "Why are you sorry about it? Didn't you like it?"

"W-what?" Nao stammered, caught off-guard.

Takeo stared at him intently, his eyes fixing themselves on Nao's. "Did you like it or did you not?"

Nao gaped at him. Why was he suddenly so serious? He opened and closed his mouth, not sure how to act. He looked at Takeo, who basically skewered him with those intense eyes of his. For a moment, he could only stare into them, feeling as if they were piercing through his heart and mind, trying to stir up the truth.

Nao took a shaky breath. "I...did."

"Then don't be sorry about it. Because I liked it, too."

What? Nao gawked at the other, who had turned away from him. Even so, he could still see the flush of pink on his face.

Takeo coughed quietly and turned back around. His ears, cheeks, and nose all flushed. "If we're already on the topic... I'd like to ask you something." Flustered, he scratched his chin. "I'll just put it out there. I would like to go out with you."

— Chapter 18 —

Huh? Nao wondered whether he was hearing right.

"What do you mean?" he asked, slow-witted.

Takeo pursed his lips. "Like dating."

Nao stared at him in disbelief. "Dating? Like what?"

"Well… like…like lovers."

"L-lovers?"

"Yes." Takeo took a deep breath. "I like you, Nao. A lot. And I want to be with you. So if you want that too…then let's date."

Nao was in shock. Did Takeo really just ask him out? Nao's heart began pounding. He could feel it hammering against his ribs, his stomach flipping and turning.

His legs suddenly started feeling all weak. He couldn't tell whether it was because of excitement or fear.

All the logic and rationality inside him told him to run away, that this was a bad idea and he was a bad child if he consented to this. But his heart, on the other hand, was utterly and wholly convinced of the opposite. He was torn between the two sides of who he was and what he should be.

However, this was his chance to, for once, not run away. For the first time, he was given the opportunity to alter his life the way he wanted to. And Nao…he wanted to be with Takeo too.

He looked at Takeo, who watched him nervously. Then he spoke the words which, in retrospect, turned out to be the best decision of his life. "Okay."

Takeo's eyes widened. "Okay?" he asked. "Like yes?"

Nao nodded. "Yes."

Takeo's lips lifted into a joyous smile. His eyes began to sparkle like the sun on the ocean waves, and at once, he leapt forward and pulled Nao into his arms.

Nao's breath stopped as he was suddenly engulfed in the other's hug. He wasn't used to this much body contact, but after the first seconds of surprise, he relaxed and shyly wrapped his arms around the other as well. He clutched the fabric of Takeo's shirt, feeling his back beneath his hands.

Takeo had wrapped a strong arm around his waist, his right hand resting comfortingly on the back of Nao's head, sinking into the crown of soft hair.

Hugging felt unfamiliar to Nao, but somehow this felt safe.

He could sense tingles spreading throughout his body, a mixture of wild, novel sensations climbing up his spine, flushing through every nerve in his system, and making his chest feel incredibly warm. His heart fluttered incredulously.

They smiled timidly at each other once they broke apart.

"I promise you I'll be the best boyfriend!" Takeo exclaimed, and Nao felt his heart skip. "I may be inexperienced, but I'll try my best."

Nao stared shyly at the ground. "M-me too," he murmured, and Takeo smiled happily. His face was full of myriad emotions as if he couldn't decide what to do or say first in his excitement.

"Do you want to go visit the fair now?" he eventually chose to ask, his cheeks still flushed with a vibrant blush, and Nao nodded.

Together, they walked up to the promenade. They sat down on a flight of stairs that connected the beach to the promenade, and slid on their shoes.

Nao was still all shaky and flustered. Slowly but surely, the realisation of what just happened seeped into his mind, and his heart pounded wildly at the revelation. Was...was he truly dating Takeo? Did this mean he really had a boyfriend now? And didn't this also imply that this was a date?

His head was spinning like crazy.

They had reached the fair. Cheery tunes filled the buzzing atmosphere as families with their children sauntered about. The colours and smells were overwhelming. The sounds of music, laughter, and shouting from the rollercoasters were mingling with the crashing of waves, creating the perfect sound of summer. Pastel pink, blue, yellow, purple, and green stands were nestled in between the attractions and created a beautiful scene against the blue sky and soft yellow of the sun.

It was almost as full of life as Nao's heart right now, but only almost.

"What do you want to do?" Takeo asked and pulled Nao out of his train of thought.

"For now, just looking around, if that's okay with you." Takeo smiled and nodded.

They strolled about, looking at the stalls and attractions. There were countless food stands peppered all over the area. They sold everything from savoury, hearty foods to sweet and sugary snacks, though all of this was easily overshadowed by the abundance of rides available.

In Nao's eyes, one looked scarier than the next, but Takeo goggled at them with a shining gaze.

He stopped in front of a huge swing-like attraction. The large, circular middle part swung from left to right while spinning around itself simultaneously. The people riding it screamed loudly as the machine tossed them through the air.

It looks horrible, Nao thought.

"That looks fun," Takeo said.

Nao glanced at Takeo, who just gazed at him with excitement. Happily, he pointed at the ride. "Wanna try it out?" he asked.

Nao would rather die than go on that thing. He'd always had bad motion sickness and that beast looked like it was going to be his death wish. But looking upon Takeo's face, he could hardly decline. He gazed at him with such childlike joy and excitement that Nao couldn't bring himself to say no.

He wondered how Takeo always managed to tear down the walls of his stern refusal as if it were nothing, turning the mountains of harsh ice and frost into mere puddles. Somehow he could never decline him.

Nao sighed. "Okay."

He hated every single second as he was strapped into that monster. Takeo, beside him, wiggled excitedly with his legs.

"Is this really safe?" Nao asked, trying not to sound too nervous.

"Of course," Takeo replied, lighthearted. He glanced over at Nao. "Are you scared?"

Nao shook his head, but it didn't look very convincing. Takeo watched him in silence for a few seconds before he asked seriously, "Do you want me to hold your hand?"

Nao shook his head again. "No, I'm not scared," he repeated resolutely, but it was unclear whether he was trying to convince himself or Takeo with this statement.

"Okay," Takeo yielded, though it was evident that he did not really believe him.

After what felt like an eternity to Nao, the machine finally began moving. His stomach dropped to the ground instantly and his breath got caught in his throat. Nao's heart hammered inside his chest as if it were trying to run away, pounding against his ribs with panicked *thuds*. If Nao could only open his chest, he'd have let his heart and soul run free, dissociating himself from the present.

But his spirit was stuck to his body, and thus to this moment. As they started gathering more and more momentum, his world spun. Hot fear shot up his spine, and more or less unconsciously, he reached over and grabbed Takeo's hand.

He had his eyes shut tight and therefore couldn't see the other's reaction, but he felt Takeo's hand squeezing his reassuringly.

Nao didn't dare to open his eyes the entire time they got thrown around in the air. All he tried to focus on was the hand grounding him in reality. He must have squeezed it really hard, but the other didn't utter a single sound of complaint.

Finally, after what felt like hours to Nao, the ride stopped.

He almost fell out of his seat. He let go of Takeo's hand and staggered down the platform onto non-moving, solid ground. Nao gripped the handrail tightly, his legs wobbling like jelly beneath him.

Takeo, on the other hand, sauntered down the stairs with light, feathery steps. He looked even more stunning than before—his hair was ruffled by the wind, softly framing his bright eyes and red cheeks, which had blushed vibrantly from excitement.

Nao probably looked like he had crawled out of a sewer next to him—at least that's how he felt.

His stomach was twisting and churning as if someone had decided to dig a hole inside his guts. With shaking limbs, he bent over the railing, not entirely sure yet whether he'd throw up or not.

Takeo hurried to his side, gazing at him with furrowed brows. He looked deeply concerned. "Hey, are you all right?" he inquired softly.

Nao gripped the cold metal beneath his fingers. He had to take a few deep breaths before his body allowed him to answer. "…I think I might throw up."

Takeo's eyes bulged in shock. "What?" he exclaimed. Worried, he looked around. "W-wait here," he then said and suddenly disappeared into the crowd.

Even if Nao had wanted to leave, he wouldn't have been able to. He was at the full mercy of the iron bar holding him up.

Less than a minute later, Takeo reappeared at his side with a bottle of water. He uncapped it and extended it toward the wilted figure. "Here, drink," he said, and Nao reached for the water with shaking hands.

He leaned against the handrail and ingested a few sips. He was so focused on not throwing up that he didn't even notice the hand patting his back until he'd finished half of the bottle.

A little surprised, he looked at Takeo, who still gazed at him with a concerned look. "We wouldn't have gone on that ride if I'd known you were sensitive to motion sickness."

Nao tried to smile and his lips formed a weak curve. "Yeah, I didn't know it either," he said, even though he definitely did. Nao just didn't want Takeo to feel guilty for urging him to go on the ride with him.

"Let's sit down somewhere," Takeo suggested.

Nao agreed immediately. With his weak legs barely carrying him, he was glad to finally sit down.

They settled on a bench close to the pier. From here, they could look across the shore. The sea was still as lazy as before, and the waves crashed leisurely onto the sand. A few children ran around in the shallow water, shouting and laughing.

Nao was still holding onto the water bottle. The churning in his stomach had begun to cease a little after he had carefully ingested the water.

"Are you feeling better?" Takeo asked, and Nao nodded. "Yeah."

Takeo breathed a sigh of relief.

Nao fidgeted with the empty bottle in his hands. "It's a bit embarrassing to admit…but this was my first time on a ride."

Takeo looked at him, surprised. "Really?" he asked. "You haven't tried it before? Why?"

"Because I've always been too scared to go on one."

The other gazed at him, clearly baffled. "Then why did you do it today?"

He was silent for a while before murmuring a tentative reply, "Because I wanted to try it out with you." Embarrassed, Nao scratched the back of his head, and Takeo sighed softly. "You didn't have to do it just because I wanted to."

"It wasn't that bad," Nao replied dismissively, but Takeo raised his brows, and he remembered that a few minutes ago he had been dangerously close to vomiting all over the place.

Takeo sighed again and slid closer to Nao. Carefully, he placed a hand on the back of his head, stroking the mussed hair as he smiled at him. "Next time, tell me if you're scared, okay? It's not a shame to be afraid. I'll tell you too if I'm uncomfortable with something."

Waves of tingles surged down Nao's body from the place Takeo's hand rested on. He tried his best to keep his cool as he looked into the other's eyes. But they gazed at him with such fondness—Nao's chest immediately felt all warm and he nodded.

Takeo smiled comfortingly and lowered his hand again. Nao wouldn't have minded if it had stayed a little longer, though.

All of a sudden, Takeo jumped up. "Okay! You said you like sweet foods, right?" he asked, and Nao agreed, confused.

"Then wait here for a minute. We need something to get your energy back up." With these words, Takeo ran back into the fair. Nao watched as he swiftly merged with the crowd once again.

He had no idea what he was planning now, but he found out soon enough as Takeo suddenly returned with a stick of pink cotton candy. The soft-pink treat clung to the wooden stick like an altocumulus cloud caught in the early dusk. Proudly, Takeo presented his harvest to Nao. "I doubt it can get any sweeter than this," he boasted and sat back beside him. "This is basically pure sugar and sweetness. And maybe a bit of food dye."

Nao looked at him and the candy with wide eyes. "Did you just buy this?" he asked.

"Yes," Takeo confirmed cheerfully and plucked a piece from the treat. "Why? Are you still nauseous?" He looked suddenly very concerned, and Nao swiftly shook his head. After the initial surprise subsided, he smiled at Takeo and quickly grabbed a piece of the candy to hide his nervousness.

He stuffed it into his mouth, tasting the sweet sugar melting on his tongue, hoping the other wouldn't notice his reddening face that way.

But Takeo had watched him intently. He smiled with un-matched warmth. "You know, now that we are dating, I can finally say it out loud. You are really cute, Nao."

Nao felt his face heat up. *Why did he have to keep saying stuff like that!?*

He looked over with big eyes and gulped down the cotton candy.

"You really just say what you're thinking, don't you?"

"Mm, that's my way of flirting."

Nao huffed. Takeo was really something else. He looked over to him, seeing the confident grin on his face. Takeo had this natural charisma about him. He didn't really seem to care what other people thought of him, and Nao liked that.

Despite his nonchalance, he was still so soft and caring at the same time. It baffled Nao how a person could be so great, and how a great person like him was interested in an unworthy being like himself. But then again, Takeo didn't seem to see him like that. The way Takeo looked at him made Nao feel neither abnormal nor lacking, as he did with everyone else. He gazed at him with such thoughtfulness and care. He treated him with so much fondness Nao had never known before. With him, Nao felt whole. He felt wanted. And thus, he asked himself if this is what it felt like to be loved. If that was the case, he wished for Takeo to feel the same whenever he was with Nao.

He looked at the other, the corners of his mouth rising. "I like you too, Takeo."

Back at the beach, he hadn't said it out loud, but now he wanted his boyfriend to hear it too.

Takeo's eyes widened briefly and then immediately lifted into a smile. He blushed and turned away. "Now you're flirting too," he murmured, for once the shy one.

They shared the rest of the cotton candy and then strolled back to where they had left the bicycle.

It was already getting dark as they rode home amidst the thickening nightfall and cold wind. Nao had wrapped his arms tightly around Takeo's waist.

They arrived at his house long after the sun had set. Both of them got off the bike and eyed one another.

"I'll go in, then," Nao said, and Takeo nodded. "Yeah, I'll head home, too," he replied. It was about time for both of them to go home, yet neither moved. Hesitantly, they both gazed at each other.

Somehow, it didn't feel right to just leave. Nao's feet didn't seem to want to budge.

Takeo seemed to experience the same fascination.

For a few seconds, they looked at each other until Takeo finally spoke first. "Do you mind… Can I kiss you before I go?"

Nao's heartbeat accelerated. He stared at the boy whose ears had once again turned bright red. Nao hadn't said it out loud, but he thought Takeo was really cute as well.

He looked up into his gleaming eyes and nodded.

Nao was flustered when Takeo leaned forward and rested his hand on the side of his face, as though he was touching something incredibly precious, but he also delighted in the feeling of the warm palm against his cheek.

He closed his eyes and welcomed his boyfriend's lips brushing against his.

Takeo was warm and gentle. His touches always like a spring breeze; thoroughly sweet, unbelievably tender.

Nao rested his hand atop Takeo's, fingers sliding between his so perfectly as if he were mending an opening that had been empty for far too long. The soft skin of their fingers rubbed together, and Nao unconsciously sighed into the kiss.

Takeo felt secure. Whenever he was so close to him, Nao had the feeling that nothing in the world could harm him; he was safe.

Once their lips parted and their gazes met, Nao could hear his heartbeat rushing in his ears.

Slowly, Takeo withdrew his hand and left a cold spot on his cheek. His face was flushed—lips and cheeks as red as the blazing horizon. He cleared his throat, trying to sound stable, but his hoarse voice betrayed him. "I'll go home, then… I'll see you tomorrow."

Nao nodded. "See you tomorrow," he breathed.

It was squeezing his heart having to watch Takeo leave. He wanted to stay with him, keep him close, and maybe…repeat that kiss a few more times, but he was also painfully aware that both of them had to return home. So, he watched his boyfriend disappear into the night. Reluctance and heartache nagging inside his chest.

— Chapter 19 —

The papers in Nao's hands were all sweaty. He had tried to keep them dry and flat, but in his anxiousness, he'd clutched them too tightly with his sweaty palms.

He tried to smooth out the wrinkles, but the damage was done, and now he just had to present them with all of their flaws.

After a long wait and much hoping, they had finally received the results of the math exam.

Nao's grades had always been average. He wasn't terrible, though he wasn't outstanding either. But anything that wasn't outstanding in his family correlated automatically to terrible. It didn't matter whether Nao came in fifth, fourth, third, or second in his year. If he wasn't first, he had failed.

Over time, he had accepted being the flawed sprout of his family—a plant with malformed leaves, a cow with two heads, a flower without petals. He'd been born as a failure and therefore grew up living as the outcast. Lately, however, he had at least tried to up his academic results.

His grandfather had offered to take him out of this school for "problem cases" if he succeeded in improving his grades. But Nao didn't really care whether or not he got to transfer schools, to be honest.

No, there was a far more irksome reason he strived for change.

He had truly thought he'd gotten over the approval of his family. After all, he had never once been more than baggage to them. Yet, somehow, he still wished to be seen as something more than that.

It embarrassed him. He was annoyed by that feeble heart of his. He didn't want to look for the approval of someone who obviously never wanted to give it to him in the first place. But still, he found himself searching for it. In small actions and fleeting eye contact, he looked for something he knew didn't exist. It was his hunt for a white whale.

Maybe this was the curse of being his parents' child. No matter how they treated you, you still hoped for their approval. You searched for signs of acknowledgement in places where none existed.

It was similar to the relationship between a human and a god; they existed as the beings that created the flesh and shaped the soul. Everything one's body and soul consisted of grew forth from them. They were the first beings you saw when born into this world. And like a god, they looked upon you in your early years, guiding a naive soul through this world. They listened to one's words like prayers, punishing and rewarding like an almighty being.

So, wasn't it only natural to search for the acceptance of these creators?

Nao felt foolish. But as much as he wanted to, he couldn't stop himself from secretly hoping. In the end, he was their child, and it was only normal to want to be noticed by your gods.

Math had never been his strong suit. But he'd put so much time and effort into studying, and now he finally reaped the results of it. He might not have gotten a full score, but his grade had significantly improved since studying with Takeo. Seventy-five out of ninety points. It wasn't enough; he knew that. Therefore, he was still nervous as he approached his father in his home office that day.

Nao knocked on the door, and a few seconds later, he heard his father's deep voice telling him to enter.

Nao clutched the papers in his hands and walked in. His father sat at his desk, reading over a bunch of documents. Without lifting his head, he asked, "What is it?"

Carefully, Nao stepped forward, extending the hand with the exam papers. His father took a few seconds before looking up and taking them from his hands.

"What is that?" he asked, and Nao replied quietly, "The results of my math exam."

His father raised an eyebrow and looked over the sheets.

Nao's heart was hammering incessantly.

"I went up two grades," he said. "This was my weakest subject, so I think the other exams will turn out even better."

He was still studying the papers, skimming the page with dark eyes. His thick, dark eyebrows furrowed as he rubbed his temple with his long fingers. In moments like these, his father had always been hard to read. It was impossible to say whether he approved or was impressed by something, or if he absolutely despised what was lying in front of him.

To Nao, it had always felt like standing in the midst of a tiger's cage. You never knew whether it was going to jump at you the next second or turn around and let you live to see another day. It was impossible to tell—however, the gaze of it evaluating its prey was always the same.

"Sit down," his father suddenly spoke, pointing at the chair in front of the desk, and Nao sat.

"It's not that bad," he said, and Nao's breathing eased a bit. His father's deep-set eyes focused on him.

"It's not good, but it's improvement." He scanned his son's face. "Are you finally getting your head on straight?"

Nao didn't know what to reply and stayed silent. His gaze rested on him for a bit longer, and Nao struggled not to squirm in his seat beneath those pervasive eyes sizing him up. Eventually, his father averted his gaze with a shallow sigh.

"Your grandfather will be pleased to hear that you are at least trying to get back on track. If you keep this up, we'll start looking for an adequate university for you. We'll enrol you in a course even you should be able to pass—industrial engineering or economics. Not too shabby, and not too embarrassing either."

Nao stared at his lap and nodded, though his heart squeezed. He wanted to do neither of those things.

His father stood up and walked around the desk. All of a sudden, he laid a hand on his son's shoulder and Nao froze. "Who knows, after all, you might not end up as a dishwasher. You may even have inherited some good qualities from me." He looked pleased with himself at this thought. "Well, before being sure of that, we should see how you keep proving your worth. You can start this weekend during the banquet."

The banquet. Nao had totally forgotten about it. Since his father was the CEO of a big tech firm and his grandfather an ex-politician, they had harboured a lot of connections in their careers. Just last month, they had given the university they wanted Toyo to attend a generous donation. And as a token of gratitude, the university had invited them to their yearly charity event. It was a big attraction with many renowned alumni, politicians, and rich businessmen—all of whom hoped to send their children to that university as well. It was essentially an event where people either came to show off or suck up to others.

As a part of this family, whether wanted or not, Nao had to attend as well. Because something even worse than having to bring him along as a disappointment was having people notice that their family wasn't as perfect on the surface as they liked to portray themselves. For that reason, Nao had to accompany them and help uphold the shiny facade of the long-broken family name.

His father's hand around his shoulder tightened. "Take this seriously, Nao," he spoke, his voice as chilling as ice. "If you do well and manage to give a good impression at the banquet, we might even be able to enrol you in this university. Maybe then your grandfather will for once see you as his grandchild. Do you understand how important this is?" Nao felt the coldness of his father's palm sink through his shoulder. It seeped through his skin and paralysed his bones, like a snake dazing him with its venom.

Obediently, he nodded. "Yes."

"Do your best."

"Yes, father."

He withdrew his hand and Nao felt his chest lighten again.

His father sat back in his chair and then gestured for Nao to leave. Quickly, he grabbed his exam and left the office.

Nao was lost. He didn't want to go to university. He really didn't! …At least not yet.

He had no passions in his life, no perspective. It was odd. He knew that. But in his life, there'd barely been anything that had sparked something inside of him. Whether it was because of the way he was brought up, or something was just detrimentally wrong with him, he did not know. But one thing was for sure, he had no idea what he was supposed to do with his future—he was a leaf drifting aimlessly in the winds.

He envied people like Takeo who had a passion to pursue, an idea of what their life should look like—roots which reached deep into the earth, steadfast and unable to be moved, even in the most wicked storms. But Nao wasn't like them; they were completely different breeds. The only thing he was sure of was that he didn't want to follow the path his grandfather had carved out for him.

Something must be wrong with him, he believed. He was a lost cause.

Fortunately, Nao wasn't good at hiding his emotions when he was with Takeo. And so the latter pierced his facade in the blink of an eye, asking him what was racking his mind as they sat together in the study room.

They had met here to spend some time together. After the exam season was over, other students no longer had a reason to use this room, so they had claimed it for themselves once again.

Takeo eyed him with an attentive gaze. "What's wrong? Did your family say something about your math exam?"

"Yes, but that's not what I was thinking about."

"What is it then?"

Nao sighed. He leaned forward and rested his chin upon his palm. He felt embarrassed admitting his own shortcomings.

"…My father and grandfather want to send me to university after my graduation. It's something they've planned for a long time, since going to college and making a career is the only way to save face in my family… But I don't think I want to do that…" Nao clenched his jaw. "Honestly…I have no idea what I want to do. There's nothing I'm looking forward to… I know I sound dumb right now. Maybe just forget it."

"No," Takeo said quickly and leaned closer. "No, you don't sound dumb at all, Nao. Many people don't know yet what they want to do after graduation."

"Yes, but you know what you want to do! And so does my brother. And everyone expects me to do the same." Nao faced him with a frown. "I…I should either have my own plan for the future or follow my family's. But I want neither of those. In fact, I have no idea what I should do… My brother is smart and ambitious, you're athletic and a great teacher, so many people have talents and traits they can work with, but I…I have nothing. I'm not overly smart or athletic or passionate about something. I have no perspective or a plan. I have nothing… I am nothing."

Takeo grabbed his hands. It was so quick that Nao had no time to react; he could only look at the other with wide eyes.

Takeo stared at him with a piercing gaze, his brows furrowed in stubborn conviction. "You are *not* nothing, Nao," he said, his voice sounding unusually stern. "Never say something like that again!"

His hands squeezed Nao's tightly. "Even if you have no goal now, you have all the time to find one. Not knowing what you want to do does *not* make you nothing! It just makes you someone who's still finding out about themselves. This is not a race. You don't have to have a goal in front of you at all times. Just keep on striding forward, often that's enough. Live your life and try all the things out, and eventually you'll find something that will make you want to stay.

"And despite that, you have so many qualities! You are smart and ambitious. Just remember all those weeks you spent studying with me for the exam! You are also really brave, Nao. And in my eyes cute and funny as well. I can't believe you think you are none of the things I just listed!"

Takeo seemed genuinely upset, and it startled Nao. He stared at him with wide eyes, letting the words ruminate in his mind. Eventually, Nao tightened the grip around Takeo's hands.

He had forgotten. He wasn't alone anymore. He had his wonderful boyfriend, who, Nao knew, would be by his side no matter what.

Takeo had his back, no matter what the future would bring.

Nao's fear ceased a little, and gently, he smiled at him. "That got you really worked up."

Takeo still gazed at him with a deep frown. "Of course, if you talk yourself down like that."

Nao eyed his boyfriend's pouty face and squeezed his hands softly. He felt so immensely grateful for him in that moment. In his life, he had always been pulling blanks, but Takeo was the one-in-a-million jackpot ticket he had pulled.

"I'm sorry. I won't say stuff like that anymore."

Takeo nodded, pleased. "Good. And if someone tells you anything different, I'll pay them a visit and beat them up."

Nao huffed. There were a lot of people he had to beat up then, he thought, but didn't say it out loud. Instead, he leaned forward and kissed Takeo on the cheek.

It was a gesture very much out of character for Nao, but with Takeo, he discovered sides of himself he hadn't been aware of and learned to embrace them nonetheless.

As expected, Takeo was flustered by the sudden kiss. Surprised, he touched the side of his face, then blushed and smiled at Nao.

"I should threaten more often to beat up people if this is the reward I get," he chirped happily, and Nao scoffed. "Don't get cocky," he said, but Takeo's smile just widened.

"Oh yeah? Don't you have a few compliments for me too? What was that before? I'm athletic? A great teacher? Handsome? A perfect guy?"

"I never said the last two."

"Really? But I'd love to hear it." Takeo grinned cheekily, and Nao just pushed him away softly. "Maybe later."

— Chapter 20 —

The following days trickled past.

The big charity event was drawing closer with each fading day.

As the end of summer was approaching, the nights grew longer and the days shorter. This summer had felt like an eternity and a puff of breath at the same time. While there had only been a few true days of summer-like feeling, Nao had experienced so much warmth during these weeks. The person he had been before and the person he had become were two different people, yet Nao greeted the new version with welcoming curiosity.

Even though summer was slowly fleeting, he'd take all of the things he had learned and experienced with him into the colder seasons.

The sun was hanging low, and a lukewarm breeze drifted through the city. There were only two days left until the big banquet, and Nao couldn't think of anything he was less interested in. The fact that he had to accompany his family and make a good impression at the event hung over him like Damocles' sword.

He sighed inwardly just thinking about it, but then reminded himself that it was only one night. He could get through this! And maybe, the next day, he could meet up with Takeo.

Since exam season was over, they had much more time on their hands now. Nao's mood instantly lifted at the thought of going out with his boyfriend.

He was sauntering outside, swinging a plastic bag with snacks in his hand. Half an hour ago, he had left his family's apartment to go out and kill some time.

He'd overheard that his grandfather would come over today regarding the banquet, and Nao had taken the opportunity to sneak out and avoid them altogether.

He spent some time at the convenience store buying food and something to drink. He planned to stay away for the next two hours to make sure he wouldn't accidentally run into his grandfather after all. Fortunately, staying out wasn't much of a problem for Nao.

He sat down on a bench close to the park and opened a can of soda. He had bought enough snacks to make up for the dinner he missed that night.

Between the chips and biscuits peeked out a can of mango soda. Nao couldn't restrain himself upon seeing it in the refrigerator and had taken it with him to give to Takeo the next day. Well, provided that the latter would be at school tomorrow.

He took a sip of his soda. It was weird. Nao hadn't seen him after classes that day. It was unusual, and Nao had had a bad feeling about it all day. But he didn't want to let his thoughts spiral yet. Nao would just call him as soon as he got back home.

In silence, he drank his soda while watching the sun descend in the sky. It was barely eight in the evening, and the days had already grown significantly shorter.

He finished his drink and stood up. Nao felt bored and pondered whether he should take a walk in the park. He threw the empty can into the trash and then headed toward the walkway—when all of the hairs on his neck stood up at once.

Nao froze. Slowly, he turned around and looked at the bushes surrounding him, but nothing seemed out of place in the sparse patches of grass and dark green box trees.

Did he imagine it? Nao looked around with caution, but there was nothing to support his suspicions. He swallowed and continued his walk.

In the blink of an eye, all of his senses seemed to have heightened. He couldn't say for sure but he had the disquieting feeling that something was watching him.

His instincts in such cases were mostly accurate since he had been prey for most of his life. Like a bunny that sensed the hawk's eyes from miles above, he felt the impending danger sagging into the pit of his stomach.

He walked farther, and with each step, he became more and more confident that someone was indeed following him.

Nao clenched his jaw. He had a premonition of who it could be. But today he wouldn't make it that easy for him.

He might be prey, but he never gave up without taking at least one of his predators' eyes with him.

Nao stuffed his hands in his pockets and quickened his steps. He tried to throw off his follower somewhere among the narrow paths of the park.

Preferably, his shadow wouldn't be as familiar with this area as he was, but, as expected given Nao's luck, it seemed that they were. Even after taking a few random turns, he could still feel the foreboding presence looming somewhere behind him.

It seemed like Nao couldn't shake them off that easily, so he had only two options left: try to run away or face them.

He liked neither of these choices; therefore, he chose the one he was most confident in.

"Do you just want to keep following me or will you attack already?"

A quiet snicker echoed from the bushes. Nao turned around to where he felt the sound was coming from and saw a dark figure emerge from the shadows.

"You've got some nerve, kid," the man said as he looked at him with an ugly grin.

The man before him was tall and broad. He wore a black hoodie with the hood pulled deep into his face. Nao could hardly see anything beyond the bottom half of his head.

He felt his heart jump, but Nao tried not to let it show. "What do you want?" he demanded fearlessly. "Did Sho send you?"

The man snickered again. It sounded unpleasant and cold. "Someone bigger sent me."

Someone bigger? Nao had no idea what that creep meant. He frowned. "What do you mean?"

The stranger grinned widely. "Come with me and you'll find out."

"Why should I follow the person who crept up on me from the bushes like some perv?"

The grin, which already spread from one side of his square face to the other, stretched impossibly further. It looked uncanny. The corners of his mouth stretched so far out it was almost as if his skin could rip apart at any second.

"Because we got your friend," the stranger sneered.

Friend...? Nao turned white.

There was only one person he could mean.

His stomach dropped.

"I bet he's already desperately waiting for you," the man said, amused. "You might want to come with me now, don't you?"

Nao's mind was a mess. His thoughts were racing and tumbling over each other.

Did they really have Takeo!? It couldn't be, could it? The man had said he wasn't sent by Sho, but maybe that was just a fluke. Maybe Sho just wanted to lure him out with this lie...?

No, Sho would always proudly plaster his name on everything he did. He loved enticing fear in others with nothing but his name.

He was the type to even force his initials onto things he hadn't achieved himself. That bastard was shameless as hell, after all.

However, Nao couldn't confirm anything right now, and as he walked behind that man leading him to wherever this mysterious someone was, Nao felt like he was stepping across hot coals.

The stranger brought him to a desolate area. The sun had already vanished behind the horizon, and the wind grew frostier. The presence of humans became scarcer the farther they went. The houses and streets looked more and more dilapidated. Lit-up windows became soulless, empty window frames and front doors barred-up, broken shells. It appeared to be a housing area up for redevelopment, which meant that it was practically abandoned by this point. Nao was walking right into the lion's den.

They entered a smaller street, and Nao's biggest fear became reality right before his eyes—his gaze interlocked with Takeo's.

He kneeled on the ground. His clothes and hair were disheveled, and from a cut on his lip meandered a trickle of blood down his chin. Two huge men stood behind him like rabid guard dogs.

The moment Takeo spotted him, his eyes grew into two large circles.

He tried to stand up with his shaking legs. "Nao!" he shouted, pushing himself off the ground, but he was hit against the back of his head at the same time. He fell back onto his knees; a gurgling sound escaped his throat.

Nao's chest tightened in terror. "T-Takeo!" He wanted to storm forward, but a strong hand around his shoulder held him back.

He tried to fight it off, but the man who had led him here was overwhelmingly strong.

"What a heartwarming reunion," an unfamiliar voice chuckled.

Nao's eyes darted frantically around the alley until he found its owner emerging from the shadows.

The slim, tall figure cut through the darkness like a knife. He was young, maybe twenty or twenty-one, and looked upon Nao with a conceited gaze.

The man appeared scarily serene.

He had short, light hair with an undercut. It was dyed dirty blond, and the black roots were already peeking out beneath. His nose was straight and pointy, his lips thin and sharp. His left ear was adorned with three earrings: the first one on his earlobe and the third one on his auricle were connected by a thin golden chain dangling from his ear.

Nao had never seen him before, yet somehow he had a terrifying guess of who he could be.

The man's lips stretched into a wide smile and his whole face seemed to distort with it.

"You are Nao Miyamoto?" he asked, and Nao felt chills run down his spine.

His voice was cold and sharp like glass shards.

"Yes," Nao answered, suppressing the trembling agitation in his voice.

The stranger smiled with pleasure. "And your father is Tsuyoshi Miyamoto?"

What did this guy want from him!? "Yes," he answered again.

The man clapped his hands, satisfied. "Good. Then we have the right guy."

Nao was confused. Why had they been brought here? What did they want? Whatever it was, Nao knew it was dangerous, and he had to get himself and Takeo out of this situation as fast as possible. First, he should find out who and what they were dealing with before planning his next step. He gathered his breath and asked, "Who are you?"

The stranger's smile deepened menacingly as if he had just waited for this question. With swift steps, he walked over to

Takeo, crouched down, and wrapped his long arm around him. "Why don't you ask your friend? We had a good time catching up on a few things before you came."

Nao's eyes wandered to Takeo, who was as pale as a ghost. He looked shockingly small in the stranger's arm, as though he had crumpled into himself. His eyes were widened and unfocused, his chest heaving and sinking rapidly. It wasn't hard to see that Takeo was beside himself with fear.

Nao had never seen his boyfriend this terrified before, and it shot surges of pain and worry down his spine.

He didn't need Takeo's answer to confirm the identity of the man, though. The way the stranger spoke and moved, his arrogance and enjoyment of feasting on other's fear, it was all too familiar to Nao.

"You are Sho's older brother, aren't you?" he asked, and the man's grin grew even wider.

He let go off Takeo and stood up. "That's right."

So, this was Katsu Nishimura. The older brother of Sho Nishimura. The leader of the gang that had terrorised Takeo in middle school. He'd forced students to partake in his drug deals, harassed them if they refused, and broke Takeo's wrist and framed him for his crimes after Takeo had tried to take him down.

One only had to hear tales of his doings to deem him someone one would never want to cross paths with. Yet here they were—paths intertwined, locked in place.

However, Nao tried not to let himself get intimidated by that. With every ounce of courage he possessed, he straightened his shoulders and asked in a steady voice, "Are you here on your brother's behalf? Do you want to take revenge for him?"

To Nao's surprise, Katsu burst out laughing. "My brother!? That squirt?" He doubled over in laughter, clutching his stomach with his hand as if Nao had just said the funniest thing in the world. "Please," he said. "I don't care what that idiot does. It doesn't concern me in the slightest."

He waved him off, suddenly all calm again. "That small mind only focuses on revenge and pleasures. I, on the other hand, exclusively care about business." He solemnly laid a hand on his chest. "I'm a businessman. So the only things concerning me are how to grow and expand in my field of work.

"You see, I'm a fairly busy man. But still I came here today to see you." Katsu's eyes, gleaming with excitement, rested intently on Nao. "You're surely asking yourself why I let you and your friend be brought here. Well, to be frank, I have a deal for you."

The anxiety in Nao's stomach grew bigger. "…A deal?" he asked.

"Yes, a really good one at that." Katsu beamed. "Him," he pointed at Takeo, "for your labour." He turned back to Nao.

Nao didn't quite get what he meant, but Takeo started shouting before he could ask. "Nao, don't! Don't do it! You can't bargain with this assho—" One of Katsu's lackeys hit him across the head. Takeo seemed to have bitten his tongue upon the impact, fresh blood dripped out of his mouth, but it didn't stop him from screaming. "Don't— don't do it, Nao!"

Katsu sighed, irritated. He picked his ear with his pinky. "You still haven't learned how to shut up, have you?" He rolled his eyes and shot a sidelong glance at his subordinates.

One of them immediately produced a cloth from his pocket. While he held Takeo's head, the other forced the dirty piece of fabric between his teeth, tying it roughly together at the back of his head.

Hot fear seeped through Nao's veins. Takeo struggled. He tried to throw the men off, but they restrained him without mercy. They bent his head backward and stuffed the cloth deep into his mouth to finally shut him up.

Nao tried to run toward him once again, but the man behind him grasped his arms. "Stop!" Nao screamed and thrashed about wildly. "Stop it! Don't hurt him!"

Katsu snickered. "That depends on you," he retorted with an excited smile and nodded at his men, who, upon his gesture, brought a cinderblock. They grabbed Takeo's right arm and pressed it down onto the rough surface. With their thick, strong hands, they held him in place. No matter how hard Nao or Takeo struggled, they both had no chance against the men confining them.

Pure terror exploded in Nao's chest as he watched Katsu pick up a brick from the side of the road and approach Takeo with it. He stood in front of him, a wide smile was etched into his face as he eyed the outstretched arm like candy.

Nao could see the sheer thrill on Katsu's face as he glared down at his victim. His eyes sparkled excitedly, his ears turned red from adrenaline and pleasant anticipation, and his hands almost shook with unbridled glee.

He suddenly crouched down and stroked Takeo's hair with the gentleness of a mother comforting her crying child. Sneering, he gazed at him and spoke in a sweet, almost tender voice, "Don't be scared, Takeo. I know you probably remember my last visit, when I crushed your wrist, but today can be different. Just pray your friend won't do anything stupid."

Nao felt sick seeing this. It was like witnessing a swan covered in poisonous honey—the saccharine substance clung to its feathers, clumping them together, slowly destroying flesh and body. The harder it tried to escape, the stickier the poison became, staining every feather until the bird was incapable of flight, and eventually drowned in the deep waters below.

Nao knew he had to calm down to stop this. So, he forced himself to take in a deep breath before he stared straight into Katsu's bloodthirsty eyes. "What do you want!?" he barked. "What do you want from me?"

Katsu grinned. He playfully let his index finger run down the length of Takeo's arm, making him shudder instantly at the touch. The man's eyes locked onto Nao. "As I've already said, I have a deal for you.

"I know you'll attend a charity banquet with your family this weekend. And as chance would have it, I have a lot of customers attending the event as well.

"I'm quite the greedy man, you must know. If I see such an opportunity presenting itself in front of my eyes…" He raised the brick and hovered it over Takeo's arm, lifting and lowering it above the trembling fingers as if he were searching for the best angle. "I become like a child with candy. I can barely control myself." He looked at Nao and laughed. "So, how could I possibly let a chance like the banquet slip through my fingers? Unfortunately, the event's security is pretty high. And that's where I want you, Nao Miyamoto." The brick still in hand, he pointed at him. "I'll have you sell the goods for me. You'll easily get in and sell them to my customers."

Nao heard his heartbeat pounding in his ears. The tips of his fingers went numb. "You…you want me to sell your drugs?" he asked hesitantly.

Katsu nodded approvingly. "Exactly. You catch on fast," he praised.

"And since I know people don't like to go along with my plans that willingly, I brought your friend as collateral." He turned to Takeo. "If you follow my orders, I'll give him back to you in one piece. If you don't…" Katsu raised the brick above Takeo's hand again, gazing provokingly at Nao. "I will start by crushing his hand."

"No!" Nao exclaimed loudly. "No! Don't!" He wanted to storm forward and kick that bastard in his gruesome face, but forced himself to stay still.

Takeo let out a groan, and Nao looked over to see him stare back at him with wide eyes.

He shook his head with force, and Nao knew exactly what Takeo tried to tell him; he pleaded with him not to take the deal. Through his eyes, Nao could read with certainty that Takeo would rather endure this punishment than see him make a deal with the devil.

This idiot, Nao thought.

Katsu's smile deepened. "So what will it be? Become my humble pawn or watch your friend get every single bone in his hand crushed. I honestly like both options, but I think there's one you'd prefer more."

"I will do it!" Nao exclaimed. "I will! But let him go." He couldn't let Takeo get hurt. Never. He could *never* let something like this happen to him again. Agitated, he tried to ignore the panicked look Takeo was throwing at him.

Katsu grinned smugly, finally lowering the hand with the brick. "Wise choice, kid," he said. "You are smarter than my brother told me." He placed the stone back on the ground.

"Tomorrow you'll come to the address I give you and then you'll receive the rest of your orders. But I warn you," Katsu's eyes pierced him, "If you try anything funny or dare to snitch on me, I'll pay this rat a visit and torture him in your stead. So think twice before you try something stupid."

Katsu turned around and grabbed a fistful of Takeo's hair. In one swift motion, he yanked his head back, exposing the latter's bare throat. He stretched his neck until Takeo's head touched his back and the tendons ached. From high above, he glared at Takeo as he grunted in pain.

"The same goes for you," Katsu whispered menacingly. "Don't think I have forgotten your foul play from back then. I was merciful with you then, but if you should ever try to trick me again, I will not hesitate to find you and end this. You know the Naka River, right? If you don't behave, I'll make sure you spend the rest of your days on the ground of it."

He let go of his hair and Takeo's head snapped forward again. He panted frantically.

Katsu turned around and smoothly wiped a strand of blond hair out of his eyes. "And you," he said to Nao. "My men will see you tomorrow. Don't even think of contacting your friend before you finish the job. You'll only see him after your task is done. Do you understand?"

Nao clenched his jaw. "Yes."

Anxiously, he looked at Takeo, who gazed back at him with dark eyes. Nao could see the unhidden disappointment pooling inside them. But whatever Takeo might be thinking, Nao could have never let him get hurt. He would rather risk himself trying to solve this situation before he let Takeo go through any of this madness again.

Takeo had always tried to protect him. Now it was Nao's turn.

— Chapter 21 —

Nao had almost forgotten that romance wasn't the original genre of his life. As much as he had wanted to forget reality, the past weeks weren't what his life actually looked like.

His reality was much scarier and bleaker. Takeo had let him forget about it for a short while, but now life had caught up to them. It was again surviving rather than living.

Nao's heart was already pounding like crazy as he sat in the car with his family. He bounced agitatedly with his foot and stared out of the window, watching the cars and buildings pass by as they made their way to the charity event.

It was still early in the evening. The banquet was yet to start.

Nao sat in the backseat next to his little brother. The car was rocking across the uneven street and the silence inside was deafeningly thick. He squirmed nervously in his seat.

Since the beginning of the evening, Nao's dress shirt seemed to be too tight, the suit jacket was cutting into his armpits, and his necktie felt as if it were strangling him.

With jittery hands, he fidgeted with the tie clip between his fingers. They hadn't even arrived yet, but Nao already felt like all eyes were stuck to him.

Coming from the small pocket inside his suit, he could feel the pressure of the small plastic bags against his chest. He tried to ignore it, but they seemed to be piercing right through his heart. Nao would be glad when he had finally sold them all off.

The image of Katsu holding the brick above Takeo's hand was stuck to his inner eye like a film. It was the looming threat of what was going to happen if he failed here. So there was only one option for Nao. He had to succeed.

Anxiously, he bounced with his foot and stared out of the window. He wondered if Takeo was doing well right now. Nao crossed his fingers. *He had to succeed.*

His adrenaline started pumping as the car drove into the parking lot. The underground garage was already packed as they arrived.

It truly was a big event. Nao was flabbergasted at the number of men and women in suits and dresses making their way outside to enter the main hall.

Even his family barely managed to find their grandparents in the bustling crowd.

His grandfather greeted them with large strides and a confident smile. He looked powerful with his grey, slicked-back hair, neat black suit, and shiny leather dress shoes. He still wore the mightiness of a politician like back in his active days. Nao guessed it was a trait one could never unlearn.

With attentive eyes, he examined every member of his family, then bent down to straighten Toyo's lopsided bowtie. He smiled warmly at his grandchild and stood back up. "You all look dashing." He beamed. "It's great to see the Miyamoto family all presented together. This is an event of utmost importance, so make sure to show only your best tonight."

"Of course, father." Tsuyoshi Miyamoto smiled and laid a hand on his youngest son's and wife's shoulders. "We know this is important for Toyo's future. We are prepared. Shall we go in, then?"

His grandfather nodded, and as a group they started moving.

Nao fumbled with the collar of his shirt as he followed behind the rest. He loosened his tie a little when he suddenly felt a hand closing around his shoulder. Startled, he looked up to see his grandfather's smiling face. He didn't say a word, nor did he change his facial expression, but he didn't need to. Nao understood what he told him, nonetheless. *No mistakes today.*

It was a message as clear as day. For a few seconds, they looked into each other's eyes, then his grandfather let go of him. He retracted his hand and followed the rest of their family.

Nao stayed in the back. The pressure of the pocket had suddenly increased twice as much.

The hall where the event was being held was breathtakingly huge. The arched ceiling was so high one could barely see the intricate drawings and ornaments carved upon it.

The room was filled with dozens of round white tables and chairs. On the north side stood a wide stage which hovered a few meters above the ground. Thick, red curtains were drawn to each side of the platform, bound by heavy, golden cords. Big spotlights hung suspended in the air and illuminated the great hall.

It was a truly impressive sight. Nao had never been to an event this huge before. But what stumped him more was the amount of security they had to pass through on the way.

There were different checkpoints where they had to present their invitations and IDs. It was much more secure than Nao had expected, and he understood why Katsu had wanted an outsider to do the job. It was much easier to threaten him than to conduct a plan himself and get past all the security.

Nervously, he fumbled with the lapels of his jacket.

His family was guided to one of the tables reserved in their name. A few other people sat with them. Nao didn't recognise them, but he guessed they must have been pretty high-profile too, considering they were also invited to the event.

It puzzled Nao, knowing that there was a considerable number of guests who were also Katsu's customers. He hadn't expected his influence to have already reached so far.

Nao inhaled deeply and unconsciously shook his head. He had to keep his eyes open for the customers to approach him. His hands started trembling at the thought.

"Are you perhaps Ikuto Miyamoto?" one of the people they sat with asked.

Nao's grandfather smiled politely. "That's right. And you are?"

They shook hands. "Ah, it's my pleasure! I'm Sero Tashima. And these are my wife Akiko and my son Mizuki Tashima. We are honoured to have been invited to such a high-class event and to have the chance to meet esteemed guests like you."

"Oh, it is my pleasure," Ikuto Miyamoto replied with a cordial smile. "Does your son also wish to attend this university?"

"That's right. We hope our Mizuki can enrol here next year," Sero Tashima said and his eyes fell upon Nao and Toyo. "I suspect it's the same with your grandsons?"

"We have high hopes for our youngest, Toyo. He is the one with great potential." He gestured at the boy. "Introduce yourself."

Surprised, Toyo looked up and immediately leapt to his feet to bow to the guests. "It's an honour to meet you! I'm Toyo Miyamoto," he introduced himself and remained in a deep bow before sitting back down.

Sero Tashima laughed warmly. "You didn't have to stand up, kid," he said. "What a well-mannered child." He looked at his own son. "Come on, Mizuki. Your turn."

Mizuki, an annoyed-looking teen around Nao's age, looked up. Without standing up or holding eye contact, he briefly inclined his head and mumbled a half-hearted introduction. "Mizuki Tashima. Nice to meet you."

His grandfather smiled at the Tashimas, nonetheless. "The name Sero Tashima seems quite familiar. Where do I know you from?"

The man smiled. "Oh, I'm the head of the local hospital. It's been in our family's care for generations. I recently took over after my father went into retirement."

"Ah, yes, I remember your father. Great man. We used to go sailing together back in the old days. I'm glad to hear that he went into his well-deserved retirement."

Sero Tashima nodded in agreement. "He was a great doctor and boss. I have my hands full trying to fill his shoes." He laughed. "After me, it's my son's turn to take over the hospital."

"The medical faculty here is famous for its successful graduates. Once accepted, there's no doubt about their outstanding capabilities."

"In our family, it's tradition for the oldest son to attend this university. Our Mizuki is still a bit overwhelmed by the shoes he's trying to fill. But I'm sure he'll fit in just fine. What about your grandson? What course does he want to enrol in?"

"Toyo is also applying to the medical faculty. He's recently been shortlisted for the sponsorship program."

Nao was sick of listening to them showing off their achievements and sweet-talking each other with empty courtesies. He barely managed to stop himself from sighing out loud and instead just turned away. He averted his gaze when he suddenly made eye contact with Mizuki Tashima. Nao had noticed that the other had been looking at him for quite some time, but now that their gazes finally interlocked, he immediately knew why.

Mizuki's eyes kept darting downward to Nao's tie, and Nao understood.

Nervously, he grabbed the tie clip. This was one of the items he had received from Katsu's subordinates the day before. A small golden tie clip in the form of a moth. Unassuming yet unique. It was the sign identifying him as the seller to Katsu's customers.

Nao swallowed. So Mizuki Tashima was his first buyer? He felt a bead of sweat forming in the crease between his brows.

Quietly, he coughed and rose to his feet. "I'll quickly go to the restroom." Everyone at the table turned their heads toward him, and his grandfather's smile cracked ever so slightly. "Be quick. The opening speech will commence soon," he chided.

Nao nodded and swiftly walked away.

Shivering, he clasped his hand over the left side of his jacket as he searched for the restroom. He wanted to get this over with as quickly as possible! Mizuki was one of the seven customers he had been assigned to. The faster he could get this job done, the better.

His nerves on the edge, Nao waited in the restroom. Fortunately, since the event hadn't even officially started yet, he was the only soul around.

Arms crossed, Nao leaned against one of the sinks, looking up when someone opened the door.

Mizuki Tashima walked in.

He was a teenage boy around Nao's age and height. But that's where the similarities already ended. Mizuki seemed to have been born with a sour face. His lips were naturally pursed, his eyebrows drawn in a slight frown. Shoulder-length, black hair fell down the sides of his face and wispy bangs covered his left eye. He looked at Nao with an arrogant gaze, scrutinising him with a barely concealed smugness.

"You were sent by Katsu?" he asked, and Nao nodded.

"W-which colour?"

Mizuki rummaged in his pocket. "Purple."

Nao opened his jacket and the inner pocket. Inside were multiple small plastic bags filled with colourful pills. All of them had small markings in different colours on them. They helped him differentiate which goods belonged to which customer.

Nao took out the one with the purple dot and handed it to Mizuki, who gave him a bundle of money in exchange.

Nao grabbed it and quickly counted the notes. Then, he shoved them in his suit. "Good, that's it."

Mizuki stuffed the pills into his pants pocket and nodded.

Nao turned around to briskly leave but Mizuki's sneering stopped him. "Hey man, try to cool down. Everyone can see it's your first time doing this. So don't get us busted with your nervousness."

Nao took a deep breath. Mizuki was right. He had to keep a cool head to finish this. He couldn't mess this up!

Fortunately, the first deal of the evening was done. Only six more to go. Hands shaking and heart thrumming, he returned to his family.

It felt like someone had substituted Nao's chair with a plate of hot coals. He kept squirming, receiving occasional chiding glances from his grandfather, which prompted him to stay still.

He sat through the opening ceremony speech thanking all the high-profile guests for coming and also reminding them to donate to their charity. It was boring, but Nao tried his best to get through it while appearing as interested as possible. After the speech, they opened the buffet, and one after the other they were allowed to fill their plates with delectable food. It was there that Nao found the next customer.

A man in his thirties pierced him with his eyes, and shortly after they exchanged goods and money in the corner next to the stage.

Barely half an hour later, he finished the third deal with a young woman at the back of the hall.

The pressing weight in Nao's chest slowly lifted. As the left side of his suit jacket was getting lighter, the right side grew incessantly heavier. Soon this would all be over. Nao's heart fluttered in relief as he thought of Takeo. He just had to wait a bit more and then this would all be done.

With a boost of confidence, Nao looked around the crowd to find his last four buyers.

The tables had been moved to the sides and the center of the hall turned into a spacious dance floor. The lights were changed to red and blue, plunging the hall into a deep purple. Dozens of pairs took the initiative to enter the floor, dancing what appeared to be a modern waltz.

He was waiting at the edge of the crowd, keeping a lookout for the customers, when he was startled by a sudden crash and shout.

Nao spun around, just in time to see a tray with champagne glasses shattering on the ground. The glasses broke and golden liquid spilled from between the shards. Next to them sat a boy. With furrowed brows and livid eyes, which looked nothing less than murderous, he glowered at the waiter. "What the hell!" he shouted, and Nao instantly recognised him as Mizuki. "Watch where you're going!" he exclaimed furiously, and the waiter bowed abjectly. "I'm sorry. I'm sorry, sir," he stuttered and reached out to help Mizuki off the floor, but the latter simply pushed his arm away. "Don't touch me, moron," he grunted and got up on his own.

The commotion had drawn quite the attention. With wide, curious eyes, the guests watched the angry Mizuki dust off his pants.

He scoffed and glared at the waiter. "Incompetent idiot," he said loud enough for everyone to hear, then spun around to strut away.

The waiter bowed meekly and apologised over and over to the other guests for causing such a tumult before he knelt down and began picking up the glass shards.

It was then that the worst thing possible happened. The man picked up a small plastic bag with a purple dot on it. He jumped up immediately and chased after the retreating Mizuki. "Sir! You dropped something." But the moment he said this, he took a closer look at the pills in his hand.

Nao's heart dropped, and Mizuki's seemed to as well. He whipped around, so fast that his clothes flared with the movement, and stared with wild eyes at the pills.

If he'd been smarter, he might have been able to turn this around. He could have come up with a lie or an excuse, turning the entire situation around with a few well-chosen words; but that was not who Mizuki was. Instead, he looked at his father who had also been summoned by the loud commotion and started shouting. "It's not as it seems! T-that's not mine!"

Mizuki frantically looked around until he found Nao in the crowd. "I-it's his! He gave this to me!"

The people around them turned to Nao, among them also his own family.

"It's his! He forced me to take it! He's the dealer!"

Nao stared at them. His chest clenched.

"He's the dealer! It's him!"

— Chapter 22 —

The air in the car was as thick and stifling as water. Nao could have been dunked into the ocean and it wouldn't have made any difference to how this car ride felt.

He sat with his brother in the backseat. In the front, next to the chauffeur, sat his grandfather. He hadn't said a single word since telling them to get in the car.

Nao had no idea what was happening to him. His parents and grandmother had been left behind, and Ikuto Miyamoto only took his two grandchildren with him.

But whatever was about to happen now, Nao didn't dare to speak.

His grandfather had only barely managed to stop the security from calling the police.

After Mizuki's accusations, everything had tumbled over. It was so chaotic that Nao could hardly recall what had happened. He only knew that his grandfather had taken them with him.

Why he had also brought Toyo with them, he didn't know either.

His little brother sat on the other side of the car. Nao cast a brief glance over and saw him chewing nervously on his fingernails.

He averted his gaze again and stared out of the window into the all-devouring darkness.

After about twenty excruciatingly endless minutes, the car finally began to slow down. Nao's whole body went as taut as a bowstring. Where had they arrived?

His grandfather turned around in the front seat, and without meeting their eyes, he spat out a curt demand. "Get out."

Nao unfastened the seatbelt with trembling hands and climbed out of the car. He looked around and realised that they were in front of his grandparents' house.

It was a mighty building; the four walls rose imposingly into the night. There was a large foreyard, which was filled with tall birch trees and a deep pond. A path of white stone tiles led to the entrance, ground lights illuminated the pathway up to the door.

Hesitantly, Nao stared at the entrance. He didn't want to go into the house. He couldn't! Every instinct inside him screamed at him to run away—to flee. He was scared out of his wits; limbs shaking, head swimming. But he had already been caught. Running away was like thrashing in quicksand. As futile as it was fatal.

Wordlessly, he and his brother followed their grandfather inside. They headed into the living room, where Ikuto Miyamoto eventually stopped and turned around.

In silence, he unbuttoned his jacket, loop by loop, without giving his grandsons so much as a single glance. Leisurely, he pulled out each arm, first the right, then the left. He folded the fabric in half, giving it a firm stroke to smooth out the wrinkles before laying it over the backrest of a chair. Finally, his gaze moved toward Nao. His eyes were as unfathomable and dark as a lake at night.

"Take off your jacket," he spoke, voice cold and rigid like ice.

Nao looked at him, confused. "What—"

"TAKE OFF YOUR JACKET!"

Nao and his brother both started, and quickly Nao slid it off. His grandfather yanked the fabric from his hands and shook it in the air. A clattering downpour of pills and money descended upon the floor.

With eyes too blazing to be called icy, and yet too frosty to be called fiery, he stared at the evidence in front of him.

The eyes climbed up Nao's face, scrutinising and burning every inch they touched. "I thought you couldn't fall any deeper," he said, his voice drenched in pure disgust and condemnation, dripping like acid. "How is it possible that something like you emerged from my genes?"

He threw the jacket to the ground and walked up to his grandchild. Nao was frozen in fear.

Without lifting his eyes off him, the man continued, "Toyo, you have to look very closely now. I will show you what happens if you misbehave like your brother."

His glare pierced his oldest grandchild like a spear. "Kneel down, Nao."

Nao looked at his grandfather with wide eyes, and the latter merely repeated his words.

"Kneel down."

Very slowly, Nao followed his order. He sank to the ground, his knees touching the cold wooden floor. His heartbeat hammered inside his ears.

His grandfather walked around him until he stood behind his grandson. Nao could hear something rustling before his dress shirt was pulled up. He felt the cold air hit his bare back as the skin was exposed. The hem of the shirt was yanked up to his shoulders.

Nao forgot how to breathe. "Grandfather, I—"

"Shut up!" he barked. "Don't come grovelling to me now. You have left me no choice, Nao."

He heard the sound of a belt being unbuckled.

"Good behaviour deserves to be rewarded. Bad behaviour needs to be punished."

Nao had already understood what was going to happen by now. But still, even expecting it wasn't enough to brace himself for the pain that was about to be unleashed on him as the belt hit his back.

It was the sheer pain of leather cutting into his skin. Nao whimpered. Tears shot into his eyes.

Immediately, he was hit a second time. And a third.

It hurt! It hurt so much! His muscles spasmed and he fell forward, holding himself up on his hands. Right now, he couldn't even punch back, as he did with those gang bastards. He was forced to endure the pain. To sit through this punishment. However, it wasn't the worst part of it all. Even as he was in pain—on his knees, being whipped like an animal—his thoughts only fled to Takeo.

He had failed. He had failed his mission to protect Takeo.

Nao's heart clenched. What was going to happen to him now? It was surely going to be worse than what Nao was experiencing right now.

He dug his fingers into the hardwood floor, nails scratching against the lacquer. What should he do? How could he protect him from Katsu? His thoughts were frantically racing while he was hit a fourth and fifth time.

He tried to keep his grunts of pain as silent as possible. They shouldn't know how much it hurt.

Nao had his jaw clenched, his tongue pressed against the roof of his mouth. He was still thinking about the consequences of his failure for Takeo when the lashing suddenly stopped.

For a second, Nao hoped it might be over, but then he heard his grandfather's booming voice. "Toyo! Don't look away! You have to learn from this."

Nao glanced up and spotted his little brother at the back of the room. He stood there, shaking, his hands covering the pale face. He had tears running down his cheeks as he sobbed and whimpered quietly into his palms. "Grandfather, p-please stop…" he stuttered. "Please, t-this isn't necessary."

"NOT NECESSARY!?" their grandfather bellowed, and Toyo flinched. He had never been screamed at like that in his life. "Who do you think you are!? Didn't you see what your brother was doing at the event? This isn't something to be taken lightly. His actions could ruin your chances of getting accepted at that university! It could jeopardise your whole future! Our whole plan! If anything, you should be begging me to punish him more!"

Toyo sobbed and glanced over at his brother. Their gazes met and Toyo's face distorted in anguish. New tears poured from his eyes as he whimpered.

"Get a hold of yourself and act like a man, Toyo," their grandfather said before lifting the belt again and bringing it down for the sixth time.

His back burned so much, it was difficult to form any thoughts. Every time something sprouted in his mind, it was immediately cut down by the pain devouring Nao's whole being. His breathing was heavy, the vision in front of his eyes becoming gradually blurry. He wanted to throw up from the shock. He wanted to pass out. But he tried to keep himself together as best as he could.

He still had to find a way to prevent Katsu from going after him and Takeo.

Nao knew he shouldn't snitch, but what if this was their only way out of this shitty situation?

He may have been delusional from all the pain, but in that moment, he believed his grandfather might be of help to them. He was, after all, an ex-politician. He still had a lot of connections and influence behind the scenes, and maybe, just maybe he could stop Katsu's gang if he told him the truth. It was better than nothing, and Nao was desperate with fear.

The belt cut him a seventh and eighth time before he finally turned around. Nao looked over his shoulder, and even though it felt like his skin was being ripped apart from this simple movement, he stared into his grandfather's eyes with all the poise and will he could muster in that moment.

"Those weren't my drugs. I was set up for this," he forced out between gritted teeth.

Ikuto Miyamoto's eyes narrowed and he raised his arm for the ninth hit, but Nao quickly continued. "I was forced to do this by a local gang. Their leader, Katsu Nishimura, blackmailed me and a classmate into doing this. I only did it because he threatened to beat us if we don't listen to him."

The hand with the belt sank slowly. His grandfather's eyes observed him skeptically.

"It's even worse when you're lying," he spoke coldly.

"But I'm not," Nao assured him quickly. "It's the truth, I swear! He's known for making other people do the dirty work for him."

His grandfather frowned, and Nao could see him pondering behind those dark eyes of his.

"He approached me and a classmate, Takeo Iwasaki, and threatened us to do this. I didn't know what else to do."

Ikuto Miyamoto walked to the table and finally laid down the belt. Nao felt a breath of relief pass his lips.

The man grabbed his chin and seemed deep in thought. "Katsu Nishimura you said?" he asked, and Nao nodded fervently.

His fear eased the tiniest bit. If there was one thing more important to their grandfather than success, it was their reputation. To him, the family name was everything. What was attached to their name was their reality. And having a gang leader blackmail one of his grandchildren into selling drugs was definitely one way of dragging their reputation through the mud. How dare a lowly criminal like that mess with the Miyamoto family!? That's what he was probably thinking right now.

His grandfather's pride was like glass: sharp enough to cut your hand if you dare to touch it, but just as easy to break.

After a minute of silent contemplation, his grandfather turned back around. "I will look into what you told me," he concluded, and Nao sighed in relief. "Now leave. My chauffeur will bring you home."

Nao barely made it up to the apartment. He dragged himself like a man who had been stabbed and left to die. Pain bled out of his wounds and seeped into his body like blood spilling out of stab wounds. Only now, as the adrenaline was slowly fading away, did he really feel the agony of his bruises set in.

In the bathroom mirror, he saw eight large welts swelling on his back. They were growing with each minute and throbbed so intensely that Nao could feel it reverberating in his teeth. He could hardly lie down in his bed.

Despite the pain and ache tearing at every single one of his nerves, he somehow managed to take off his shirt. The fabric had become a bunch of needles, scratching at his terribly raw and sensitive skin. He had no choice but to rest on his stomach—the blanket pulled up to his waist, his back bare and untouched.

Nao hugged the pillow under his head and stared at the wall.

His body felt ten times heavier than usual. He was so tired and exhausted, every ounce of vitality seemed to have been drained out of him. Nao just wanted to fall asleep and escape this perpetual nightmare, but the throbbing and aching of his back anchored him to the present.

If he were only able to move his body! Then he would be running to Takeo's house right this instant. He wanted to see him, or at least hear his voice. Anything that would help him find out if he was okay.

But neither of those things was possible right now. Nao couldn't move and was therefore forced to live with the uncertainty of it. It nearly killed him!

In the past, Nao had never been scared of his bullies. After all, they might have been ruthless and thirsty for blood, but in the end, they were just pathetic beings who felt powerful upon stepping on bugs.

Those had been mere idiots who leeched off weaker beings to feel some kind of self-accomplishment.

But Katsu was a different breed. Although he was also a predator feeding off the weaker ones, it wasn't solely for pleasure or fun. He wasn't like others; bears and hawks—mindlessly chasing their prey, trying to tear it to bits and pieces like beasts. No, Katsu was much more like a spider; building his net, waiting for his victim to present itself, and methodically trapping it beneath his fangs, devouring it slowly and lusciously, like he had all the time in the world. He was aware of how to use his advantages and he knew how to wait and linger.

Everything about this intimidated Nao far more than any of his other bullies had. He had come across this person who scared him almost as much as his father. And knowing that Takeo was at this spider's mercy terrified him even more.

Nao desperately wished to be able to do anything at all, but, to his own horror, he could only rely on his grandfather's twisted sense of pride right now. Nao was solely able to hope that he and his connections could get them out of this situation somehow.

It was hard to accept, but due to him being confined to his bed for now, he had no other choice at that moment.

Nao was falling deeper and deeper into the spiral of self-deprecation when he was startled by the sound of a quiet knock at his door.

He tensed up but didn't answer. Whoever it was, he was not in the condition to deal with them right now.

Patiently, he waited for the person to leave, but to his surprise, there was a second knock, followed by a voice. "Nao," they whispered quietly. "Are you awake?"

It was his little brother. Nao was puzzled, yet he didn't reply. Instead, he waited for the other to leave on his own. The moment he realised there was no answer coming back, he'd surely retreat. At least, that's what Nao believed—until he heard the delicate creak of the door handle being pushed down.

His breath hitched in surprise, and quickly he closed his eyes.

In the thick silence, he listened to Toyo's soft footsteps approaching him. His walk was quiet and gentle so as not to rouse him.

Still, those were unmistakably his little brother's steps. One might confuse them with the steps of a child, as light and feathery as they were, but Nao would recognise the sound of them anywhere at any time. He was intimately familiar with them from all the times Toyo had tried to silently disappear when Nao and their parents were fighting, leaving Nao with the faint bitterness of pointless loneliness on his tongue.

He heard the rustling of clothes close to him, followed by a soft *thud* on his bedside table, as if something had been set down there. He sensed a mild waft of chamomile filling his nose.

For a second, there was only silence and the breathing of the two young boys. Then the footsteps disappeared into the distance again. The door was closed and Toyo had left.

Nao opened his eyes and managed to make out the shape of a mug on his bedside table amidst the blurry darkness. The balmy scent of chamomile now filled up his entire room. Next to the mug lay a blister of pain medication.

Surprised, he stared at the tea and medication.

His little brother had brought these for him…

Nao felt a surge of puzzlement taking over his body. A flicker of thankfulness twinged at his heart, but even more than that he just felt baffled.

He hadn't known he and his brother were close like that.

— Chapter 23 —

Somehow Nao had managed to fall asleep later that night. In a constant haze between horrible pain and terrible nightmares, he made it through the night.

Though his sleep was more like a punishment and not in the slightest bit restful, it seemed to have been a deep slumber, none-theless. He first roused at noon when muted noises pierced through his veil of sleep.

All groggy, eyes puffy and swollen, he tried to sit up. At once, a stinging pain electrified his body and punched the air out of his lungs. Nao trembled, cold sweat clinging to his skin, and it took him a few laboured breaths before he was able to fully raise his torso.

Last night he had taken the pain meds Toyo had given him, but they seemed to have gradually worn off. With a shaky hand, Nao reached for the blister and washed down the medication along with the last sips of chamomile tea.

Waiting for the pills to do their magic, he sat on his bed and tried to decipher the noises coming from outside his room.

He perked up his ears and caught the deep, pervasive voice of his father. He seemed upset about something. Well, that meant it was probably about Nao.

The counterpart to his father's angry shouts was the thin yet equally strong voice of his mother. They seemed to fervently discuss something, and Nao wondered whether he should wait until they had both left. But then a third voice struck him. It hit his heart like lightning—worse than any of the belt-lashes could have.

His grandfather. He was here as well.

Without thinking twice, Nao jumped out of his bed and leapt for the door. But his body was nothing more than mud in comparison to his determination of steel. Almost immediately, he dropped to his knees, an agonised yelp passing between clenched teeth. He writhed in pain, feeling like the skin on his back was being split apart once again. This damned weak body! Yet he refused to concede to this bastard of water and dirt. He wouldn't let something petty like this stop him!

Gritting his teeth, Nao stood up and yanked open the door. He found his parents and grandfather in the living room. He headed toward them with shaky yet determined steps.

"Grandfather," Nao croaked, his voice still weak from sleep.

The three of them turned their heads to him. Nao was quite the peculiar sight: disheveled bed-hair, worn-out pyjama pants, naked from the waist up. If it weren't for the back full of red, angry bruises, he would have surely made a comical picture.

Nao pierced his grandfather with his gaze, brows pinched tightly. "Did you stop Katsu Nishimura?"

Ikuto Miyamoto scrutinised his grandson with narrowed eyes. The corner of his lip lifted in disgust, but he chose to answer anyway. "I sent someone to sort this out. He won't bother you from now on."

Nao breathed a sigh of relief. His grandfather's connections had worked! Even a ruthless maniac like Katsu couldn't compete with the power of a renowned ex-politician.

"So, my classmate and I are safe?" he asked hopefully.

"I said he won't bother *you* anymore."

"B-but what about Takeo Iwasaki…"

"I have no idea who that is. But even if I did, why should I help some classmate of yours? I only helped you out in the first place because you still carry the family name."

"But…but…"

"Don't bother me, Nao," his grandfather cut him off strictly, his patience already stretched a little too far by his grandson. "Leave me and your parents alone. We still have a lot to sort out because of you." With a gesture, like someone swatting away a mosquito, he told him to leave. Nao knew it was definite; if he kept talking now, he would just be squashed beneath his palm like the bug he was in his eyes.

Nao's heart faltered. His legs suddenly felt all weak, and he almost dropped to the ground right then and there. Only with his utmost strength did he manage to carry himself back to his room and sit on the bed.

He couldn't believe it. He didn't want to believe it.

All of this—all this talking and bargaining with his grandfather—was for nothing if Takeo wasn't safe.

Katsu couldn't hurt him anymore, but he could very well hurt Takeo. And he was going to. Nao was certain of that.

No, no, no, no, no, no, no, no, no, no, no, NO, NO, NO, NO.

Nao buried his face in his hands. He had trouble breathing.

Katsu would hurt Takeo because of *his* failure. He was going to suffer because of *him*! His chest ached. He couldn't let that happen.

Nao jumped up, ignoring the searing pain spreading across his back. He grabbed a shirt from his wardrobe and pulled it over his head. The fabric touching his back felt like someone rubbing burning hot sandpaper against it. But he did not let that stop him. He had to see him. Whatever it took.

Nao left the apartment.

He took the first bus that would bring him to the neighbourhood Takeo lived in.

He sat on hot coals the entire ride while the bus carried him farther and farther out of the city.

Takeo lived pretty far outside. It was a desolate area with scarce housing and fields as far as the eye could see.

The sun stood high in the sky as he stepped off the bus. The air was mild and smelled of grass and fresh earth. Somewhere in the distance, Nao could hear the faint sound of a tractor driving across the fields.

Nao had Takeo's address, but he had never actually been to this area before, meaning he was going in practically blind. It took some time before he found the street scribbled down in his notes.

Finally, though, he found himself in front of a small, one-story house.

It was an old, run-down building with a crooked roof and flaking paint. The front yard was overgrown with grass and weeds. A small path of chipped stone tiles wound its way to the door.

At first, Nao felt his chest lighten with relief, but that feeling swiftly turned into bone-chilling anxiousness.

The moment he saw the kicked-in front door, he knew he had come too late. Katsu had already claimed his prize.

Nao's heart quivered in fear.

He decided not to go through the front door in case Katsu's men were still around. Instead, Nao circled the house to see if he could get a grasp of the situation at hand.

Cautiously, he entered the yard and took a turn around the building. All of the windows had been smashed in. Piles of glass shards and splinters of wood lay scattered all over the garden. The twinkling shards stuck out between the stalks of grass like claws waiting to pierce the inattentive. It was a scene of utter destruction, and yet, surprisingly, there was no one present. What must have been a battlefield of slaughter shortly before had turned into an empty ghost town.

Growing more and more agitated, Nao began peeking through the windows. And eventually, amidst all of the chaos and fear, he found the familiar frame of a person sitting on the ground.

Nao's breathing hitched immediately.

"Takeo!" he shouted, and the person looked up.

"Nao!" they exclaimed.

Nao's heart twisted in agony upon seeing his boyfriend's appearance. The latter had been beaten to a pulp.

It wasn't much different from his state after the attack in the alley. His face was littered with cuts and bruises. The bottom lip was split open, and tracks of dried blood crusted the wounded skin. His right eye was swollen, the brown iris swallowed by a ring of blood; the part of the eyeball that should have been white was now red. His clothes were partially torn as well. Nao could see deep bruises blooming on his arms and chest.

Nao wanted to scream at this sight. He wanted to shout and rip that bastard Katsu apart.

Why, why, *why* did he fail? How could he have let this happen!? Nao was distraught, hurt, and ashamed seeing the consequences of his incapability.

If he had just been more capable, more careful, if he had just been…*better*, then it might not have come this far. But he wasn't, and instead he had brought this upon the only person by his side. How could he even face him with such shame?

Despite all of it, however, Takeo had the audacity to actually gaze at *him* with a worried look. "What are you doing here?" he asked.

"I came looking for you."

Nao reached through the broken window and opened the empty frame. Fortunately, the window was low enough for him to climb through it without much effort.

As he stood in front of Takeo, the guilt and shame became only more unbearable, causing his chest to clench and his lungs to squeeze. Takeo looked so small and vulnerable. And it was all because of him…

"I'm sorry," Nao pressed out. He couldn't look him in the eyes. "I'm sorry. This is all my fault. This only happened because I failed the job. I'm so sorry, Takeo. I'm so sorry. I should have done better! I'm sorry!"

Takeo grabbed his arms and forced him to look up.

"Stop apologising. This isn't your fault!" He gently squeezed his arms, and Nao struggled to hold his gaze. "I know you did everything you could. And even if you had done everything to Katsu's liking, he still would have found a way to screw me over. It was never about the drugs, anyway. He could have very well done the job himself; he just wants to see other people struggle. He loves to see them dance for him. Don't take it to heart. None of this is your fault, okay?"

Takeo's eyes gazed at him warmly—and it puzzled Nao how he could still be so gentle and comforting when it was *he* who should be comforted instead. Nao didn't deserve this.

Takeo tried to smile, which seemed to bring him a lot of pain. But he smiled at him nonetheless. So lovingly, in fact, it felt like a jab to Nao's heart. How could he be so kind when the world had fucked him over so bad?

Takeo saw Nao's pinched brows and drooping lips, and immediately tried to lift them with his words. "It really is okay," he assured him, and leaned forward to hug him.

There was only one problem. Nao's back was littered with an abundance of fresh bruises, hardly any older than Takeo's. As Takeo's arms enveloped him and pulled him close, he unknowingly squeezed them—and pain was ignited in them once more.

Nao instantly tensed and winced, the burning sensation flared up once again and licked greedily at his wounds. He couldn't suppress the sound of pain that escaped his lips, and surprised, Takeo let go of him. "Are you okay?" he asked, clearly alarmed, yet Nao just nodded and turned his head in an attempt to conceal his pale face. "Yes, I'm okay," he quickly retorted.

He wouldn't have to tell Takeo about his bruises. There were more pressing matters at hand and he didn't want to add any more worries to Takeo's own. He wouldn't pour fire into the pit he had dug. So to ease the tension, he sat on the bed and had Takeo follow his lead.

Nao took a closer look around the room once they were seated, and only now did he truly notice how chaotic it was. Just like the entrance, the door had been kicked down. All contents had been thrown off the shelves and into the middle of the room, where they appeared to have been stomped on by a horde of elephants.

The wardrobe and desk had been smashed into tiny pieces, lying scattered across the ground. In one of the corners, Nao spotted a few trash bags that had been torn apart, their contents seeping all over the floor.

As he looked at Takeo, he saw little remnants of food and unknown fluids stuck in his hair, and he promptly understood that they must have hit him with those trash bags.

"Where's your family?" Nao asked, on the verge of collapsing all over again.

"My brother is at the police station to file a report. He was also present when those gang bastards showed up this morning. He got a good beating as well, but thankfully my mother wasn't home at the time." He tried to flash him an encouraging smile, though it was hardly recognisable through the swollen flesh.

"But what about you? You should be careful as well, Nao. What if they seek you out next?"

Nao averted his eyes, the guilt squeezing his heart. He was the one who messed up, and yet he had protection.

Mortified, he stared at his lap. "Katsu won't come for me... My grandfather used a few of his old connections to keep him away."

He heard Takeo let out a sigh of relief. He rested his hand on Nao's thigh; it was warm and comforting. "I'm glad," he said. "I'm relieved you're safe."

Nao spun around to glare at him. "How can you say that?" he shouted, exasperated. "It's not fair! It shouldn't be just me! You are the one who should be protected!"

Takeo should scream at him! He should hit him if necessary! It was what Nao deserved, after all! But somehow, he still dared to gaze at him with the same softness Nao had grown used to. The gaze in Takeo's eyes as he looked at him was no different from the day he had confessed to him at the beach. The brightness, the gentleness; it could not be concealed, even through wounds and agony.

"This is not a matter of being fair or not," Takeo continued calmly. "I want you to be safe, just as much as you want me to be. And knowing you are gives me so much relief."

Nao glowered at Takeo. He knew that the latter one hundred percent meant what he had said, but Nao wasn't blind. He could see the faint tremble of Takeo's hands, hear the minute quiver in his voice. No matter how heroic Takeo liked to act, his fear was still obvious.

Angered, Nao pressed his lips together. "When will Katsu's gang come back?"

Takeo pondered. "Maybe next week. As compensation for the lost money and drugs, they took everything valuable they could find with them. It wasn't much to begin with, but they will probably come back soon and search for more."

Takeo tried to laugh but it failed horribly. "Well, if they don't find anything, they might just beat me again. I think blood is also some kind of compensation for those sick bastards."

He smiled with his terrifyingly distorted face, but the fear was written all over it nonetheless.

Nao wanted to punch him. "Stop acting," he forced out. He couldn't take this false act of bravery anymore. "Only a few days ago you told me that it's okay to be scared. So don't go back on your word now. You try to act like everything's fine. But it's not!"

Takeo's smile faltered, and he lowered his head. "You're right," he breathed. "It's not fine…"

He pressed his lips together as he stared at his lap, fumbling with the torn fabric of his shirt. "I didn't want to worry you…but…I'm scared, Nao… I'm scared of them." His voice began to shake, and Nao saw a veil of tears forming in his eyes. They threatened to fall any second, held back only by a last sliver of resistance—a final, desperate try to keep it together.

It broke Nao's heart.

Takeo hemmed and hawed, but at last, he couldn't hold the agony and fear in his heart any longer.

"I don't know what I'm supposed to do anymore… I tried so hard to survive back then in middle school, but now…it's just the same. I don't know what to do anymore…"

The tears finally spilled over and ran down his bruised cheeks, leaving wet tracks in between blood and dirt. Takeo's hands began trembling.

Slowly, he lifted his head and looked at Nao. His gentle face was twisted in fear, the corners of his mouth quivered. He gazed helplessly at his boyfriend, eyes filled with so much unspoken terror. "I'm scared, Nao…" he choked out. "I'm…scared…"

It was so utterly devastating, so utterly raw.

Before Nao could think about what he was doing, his hands snapped forward and cupped Takeo's face. He could feel the warm, moist skin beneath his palms. "This time let me promise you something, Takeo," he said earnestly, staring right into his teary eyes. "I promise you, we'll take those bastards down. No matter what it takes. I'll get rid of them. I will never let them hurt you again."

I'll keep you safe.

— Chapter 24 —

That night, Nao lay wide awake.

As the moon wandered across the sky and the sun was slowly drawing closer, he tried to figure out how to finally put an end to this carnage.

He thought long and hard, racking his brain for what felt like hours on end. It took him longer than he wanted to admit, but Nao eventually found it. When he did, he almost laughed out loud. It had been in plain sight all along, hadn't it? Takeo had already given him the answer weeks beforehand.

As it finally clicked in his head, Nao remembered a small detail Takeo had told him about once. What might have been a pebble of information then could turn into the boulder capable of crushing their enemies. If it really was true, who knew, it may be the opportunity they had been desperately searching for.

He immediately shared his thoughts with Takeo the next day— thus, they took the following days to plan out their next steps. However, for their plan to work, they had to leave the city for a few days.

They were still two minors with barely any money at their disposal. They could compile all of their savings, but it would still be insufficient.

Nao felt bad when he secretly plundered his little brother's savings. He promised himself that he would pay Toyo back. Right now, he needed that money desperately, though.

Nao tried to pack his belongings as inconspicuously as possible. Although he'd only be away over the weekend, he still didn't want to alert his family by accident. They would certainly never let him go; not since the catastrophic incident during the charity banquet.

Nao stashed a few of his clothes in a bag and hid it beneath his bed.

He and Takeo were about to depart really soon. Nao was anxious whether everything would work out like they had planned, but in the end, it just had to. There was no other chance. This was their best shot.

Back that night, when he had lain awake, his thoughts all over the place, Nao remembered a certain thing Takeo had told him when he had shared the story of his middle school days.

Back then, he and a few friends tried to report Katsu to the police by secretly filming his criminal activities and taking testimonies from the victims. They were busted due to someone snitching on them, and the footage was destroyed. Yet in the same breath, Takeo had also mentioned Hana. She was an old friend who had recorded the videos for them. At that time, she claimed that there was only one version of the videotape, which had undoubtedly been destroyed. But Takeo never believed that story.

He claimed: the Hana he knew would've always had a back-up copy, and he was sure she only denied it because she was too scared of the perpetrators.

If that footage still existed somewhere, if Hana had really copied the tape and just kept it to herself, then maybe, years after it had happened, she might be willing to hand it over to them.

It was their best chance. And Nao strongly believed in the existence of that copy. He just had to.

According to Takeo, Hana and her mother moved away after all of the drama with the gang and the police. They hoped for a new start and fled from the chaos which had taken over their lives.

Takeo had lost all contact with her after she was gone, but he still had an old address for the place she and her mother had moved into back then.

It was an unreliable piece of information since no one could tell them if she still lived there, yet it was Takeo's and Nao's best chance.

They were desperate, and so were their methods.

Over the following week, they carefully planned this trip. It was a risky adventure with no guarantee of success, but they had to try nonetheless.

The weekend was drawing closer, and with every passing night, their hearts grew tenser. It was nerve-wracking. But at least they had each other. Together it felt only half as intimidating. And bit by bit, they prepared themselves for their trip to Tokyo.

Friday, 4am; it was the night of Nao's and Takeo's departure.

Nao was already wide awake. The bag with his belongings waited at the end of his bed, ready to be taken along.

Agitated, he peered at the clock on his bedside table.

It was four thirty. Time to leave.

Nervous but also weirdly excited, he got up and grabbed the bag.

As quietly as possible, he slid into his slippers and opened the door.

The hallway was shrouded in deep darkness, so thick he could barely see his own hand before his eyes. Through the thickness of the night, he made his way to the bathroom.

He simply had to grab his toothbrush before he was ready to leave. He didn't want to raise any unnecessary suspicions by having his toothbrush suddenly go missing, so he had left it untouched until now. No one would probably have noticed it in the first place, but Nao still tried to be as careful as possible. There was no place for missteps.

With the footfalls of a ghost, which he had learned to master early in his childhood, he tiptoed down the hallway.

Tonelessly, he pushed down the handle of the bathroom door and almost shut it just as quickly again. His heart performed a startled somersault.

Someone was already inside!

The orange lights blinded Nao, who had gotten used to the darkness, and he squinted his eyes involuntarily. It took a few seconds before his pupils adapted to the sudden shift and he was able to recognise the crouching figure in front of the toilet.

A small body sat on their knees by the bowl and retched. Nao stared at the person with wide eyes.

The figure was throwing up, laboured breaths forced their way out of convulsing lungs as chunks of barely digested food splashed into the water beneath.

The person shivered, and with a body quivering like autumn leaves in the wind, they sat up, wiping vomit from the corners of their mouth.

"…Toyo?" Nao asked, startling as the boy turned around. His face was incredibly pale and the eyes sunken in. He blinked passively at his older brother. The boy's eyes were glassy, and there was a thin layer of sweat glistening on his white forehead. He looked clammy and frigid, as if his body had been bathed in frost, cold permeating from his every pore.

Nao was too shocked to speak. "…Are you sick?" he eventually managed to ask after a couple of stifling seconds.

Toyo wiped his mouth, then reached out to flush the toilet. The water gurgled loudly as the vomit was sucked down the pipes.

He sniffled, and then replied calmly, "No, it's nothing."

Silently, Nao closed the door behind him and came closer. "Don't you have a test tomorrow?"

Toyo's lip twitched yet he held his brother's gaze. "Yes," he said quietly. "I just felt a little nauseous, but I'll go back to bed now." He leaned over the rim of the toilet seat and used it as leverage to push himself up. Staggering slightly, he came to his feet.

"What are you doing here?" he then asked all of a sudden, glancing at the bag in Nao's hand.

"Uh…" Nao stammered and hid it behind his back, but it was obviously too late. Frantically, he thought of a lie he could feed Toyo when the latter spoke up first.

"You're going somewhere, aren't you?" he asked.

Nao looked at him with big eyes. Well, Toyo was smart, of course he'd figure it out.

"That's why you took the money from my desk, right?"

Nao gritted his teeth. "Listen, I will pay you back. I needed that money really urgently. And I'll only be gone for a few days. You can tell our parents I am back on Sunday."

Toyo nodded. "It's okay. I will do that."

Nao exhaled, relieved. With a swift motion, he grabbed the toothbrush off the shelf and stuffed it into his bag. "I'll go now."

Toyo nodded silently, and Nao turned around to head back outside when he was halted by his brother's thin voice calling him. "Nao," he said quietly, and he turned back around. With his jaw hesitantly clenching and unclenching, Toyo gazed at his older brother. After a spell, he finally said, "Be careful, okay?"

Surprised, Nao stared back, then nodded.

And he left.

Nao and Takeo met up at the train station. It was around five thirty when the train rolled into the station. On the far horizon, a sliver of slightly paler blue was already emerging from below.

Their mission was risky and maybe even a little reckless. On top of that, there was the constant possibility that all of this might not even work out! But even with those prospects looming over their heads, Nao felt a treacherous surge of excitement seize his heart.

The train cabin was almost empty as they entered. Only a few other people sat scattered across the rows of seats.

Nao and Takeo must have been quite the peculiar sight for the other passengers. They were two minors, taking the train at five in the morning to the capital. How often did one stumble upon this?

Well, whatever those people might be thinking, to Nao, this actually felt like a long-awaited adventure.

For the first time in his life, he dared do something so "foolish."

Even though he was the black sheep of his family, held up as the example of what *not* to do, he had always tried to play by their rules, nonetheless. He'd never wanted to be the black sheep; he had wished to be praised and adored, just like any child. But as it turned out, he was just exceptionally bad at fulfilling those expectations. No matter what he did, he'd always stuck out like a sore thumb. He could kneel on the ground and not speak for three days, and somehow he would still manage to offend someone.

Nao was a born disappointment, the curse his family had been burdened with. As often as this fact had distraught him in the past, right now, he felt like he had been finally freed from this weight holding him down. He'd been the unruly kid his whole life, so what if he finally started acting like it? His family's opinion of him was written in stone anyway; no matter how he bent and yielded, they would never reconsider him as anything else. At least now, he could freely follow his own desires and run away with the only person whose opinion of him truly mattered. It might only be for a few days, but it still felt like an act of rebellion. A first step toward self-liberation. The world was so much bigger than his cage. And he finally ventured into it.

Takeo was the same side of the same coin. Having never once left the prefecture and wishing for a life outside of what he knew, he was also taking a step outside his eternal confines. This trip was so much more than a simple mission. It was their first steps into a new future.

As the train rushed across the tracks, through cities and landscapes, neighbourhoods and fields, both of them felt such excitement.

Their eyes met, and they didn't even have to say anything. Naturally, their faces just lifted into smiles.

They arrived in Tokyo at noon.

Both of them were immediately overwhelmed by the flood of input that washed over them like waves devouring the land.

Their hometown wasn't that small to begin with. It still had a population in the six digits, but it paled in comparison to the capital. Here, every square meter seemed to be plastered with some kind of sign, ad, picture, or commercial.

Nao's eyes didn't know what to focus on first. It was a challenge to get through the crowd and find the way out of the station.

It felt like they had become ants which had fallen into a busy beehive. Fortunately, they had each other, and by holding the other's hand, they managed to stay together until they ventured off to a calmer area. A little way off from the center, the currents were much more tranquil, the waves almost placid.

They caught their breaths.

"It's scary out there," Takeo laughed.

Nao nodded. "I thought we were about to be swept away by the crowd."

Takeo rolled back the sleeve of his button-up and glanced at his wristwatch. "We should try and find somewhere to stay for the night before it gets dark."

He was right. They had come all the way here, yet they had no place to sleep. Like almost every aspect of this trip, it was a feat they had to conquer spontaneously.

"I think we should go to a less crowded area and try looking for some hostels there," Nao proposed, and Takeo agreed. "Yeah, that's probably best. Do you want to go sightseeing after we find a place to stay? We agreed to look for Hana tomorrow, so we can use the rest of the day to explore the city, right?" Takeo's eyes sparkled as he spoke these words and simultaneously eased Nao's tense heart. He broke into an unconscious smile.

"If we're lucky enough to actually find something, we can do that," he yielded, and Takeo nodded excitedly.

They moved farther out of the center and deeper into the side streets and alleys.

They were still youngsters, so it wasn't exactly easy to find a place that would let them stay anyway. The moment most of the hostels wanted to see their IDs or credit card, they had to bolt.

It felt like an eternity. They continued walking from one building to the next. Nao's feet ached after having circled the area for more than four hours. The bag's shoulder strap was cutting violently into his shoulder, and his stomach began acting up, grumbling woefully with hunger.

Nao almost feared that they would have to sleep on the streets tonight when, at some run-down, dodgy place, they actually managed to get a room.

The hostel was sketchy and definitely not completely law-abiding if they let two minors stay over the weekend, with no proper identification whatsoever... But they had a roof over their heads, and that was everything they could have hoped for.

The room they stayed in was just as run-down and scruffy as the lobby.

It was a small, squarish place with two single beds and an adjacent shoe-box-sized bathroom. The wallpaper was damp and already peeling off the walls. On the opposite side of the room were two small windows facing a grey brick wall. The entire floor was covered in a musty green carpet, and Nao was convinced that somewhere in those green clumps of fabric, there must be living cockroaches or bugs.

The entire room gave off a stench of old mattresses, must, and black mould.

It was disgusting, without question, but Nao and Takeo were just glad to have finally found something.

Nao threw his bag onto the bed by the door, thus Takeo took the bed next to the windows.

Nao fell onto the thin mattress, feeling the springs beneath poking his behind. Well, whatever, he could finally sit. His legs were thankful, nevertheless.

He sighed, thoroughly exhausted, and put up his feet.

Takeo followed suit. "We might contract some diseases staying here, but I couldn't be happier to finally sit."

Nao smiled, and commented, "I hope I got all of my vaccinations."

Takeo looked up from his bed, suddenly a mischievous glint in his eyes. "I think even vaccines won't work against the organisms living in these mattresses. They might have evolved beyond those known to humankind."

"No doubt. Then we should pray to the ghosts of the rats and cockroaches that have died in this carpet and hope they'll spare us."

Takeo laughed loudly.

It might have been a horrible place to stay, but it didn't feel horrible at all with Takeo by his side.

They spent a few more minutes on the beds, resting their travel-worn feet. But eventually, they were forced to get up and search for a place to eat. They were incredibly tired, yet hunger was pulling them out of their beds.

The sky was already darkening outside. They had spent so much time searching for a hostel that all of the daylight had slipped between their fingers, leaving only evening to commence.

The streets were still crowded and bustling with life, and Nao figured it would never be any different in Tokyo. Here, night was just an imaginary concept.

Both of them were awestruck as they walked through the city overflowing and bursting with vitality.

The view was astonishing. So many different kinds of people filled the broad streets; young and old, teenagers and adults, students and businessmen. The ads all over the buildings and streets were flashing in vibrant colours, one more captivating than the other.

All of this was a feast for the senses. From the jumping colours and patterns of lights, to the sounds of chatting, laughing, and music, all the way to the diverse scents wafting from food stalls and restaurants.

Nao had to suppress his laughter when he looked at Takeo. The latter looked so excited, like a puppy that had been taken to the big city for the first time. The colourful lights reflected in his dilated pupils.

"Any idea where we could eat?" Nao asked his boyfriend, who simply shrugged.

"No. Let's just follow our noses?" he suggested, and since Nao didn't have a better idea, he just went along with Takeo. Together, they sauntered through the crowd.

In a smaller street, which, despite its narrowness, was still overflowing with countless people, they found a food stall selling ramen. They had been drawn by the rich and savoury smell of broth and noodles.

Both of them ordered a bowl, and it turned out to be just as delicious as it smelled. Side by side, they sat at the long table next to the stall and hungrily devoured their ramen as the crowd streamed past them.

The noodles were thick and chewy and the broth the perfect balance of salty and sweet. Perhaps it was because both of them had been starving or because they were just so happy to be here with each other, but this ramen tasted like the finest dish in the world. It filled their empty bellies with contentment.

"Nao," Takeo suddenly called him, and he looked up. Takeo was smiling as he leaned forward and picked something off Nao's face.

Nao froze instinctively as Takeo's fingers grazed his cheek, but when he pulled back, he saw him pinching a piece of noodle between them. It must have been stuck to Nao's face.

Nao was embarrassed and quickly snatched the noodle out of Takeo's hand. He devoured it in one bite, as if trying to get rid of the evidence.

Takeo burst out laughing and almost fell off the chair as he doubled over.

"What are you laughing at…" Nao asked awkwardly, and Takeo waved it off.

"Nothing. It's just cute," he said, and Nao felt his cheeks heat up. "Well, you have also something on your face," he retorted sternly, and Takeo's laughter stopped instantly. "Really?" he asked and began patting his face.

Nao broke into a smile and shook his head. "No, I'm just kidding."

Takeo stopped touching his cheek and jokingly glared at him. "Not fair."

Nao shrugged nonchalantly and stirred the broth in his bowl. Suddenly, his face grew even hotter, and hoarsely he said, "B-but there's really something on your face…"

"What?"

As quick as lightning, Nao lunged forward and pressed a kiss to the side of Takeo's mouth. It was supposed to hit the center of his lips, but in his nervousness, he missed his target and unintentionally placed a quick peck on the corner of Takeo's mouth instead. Nao was burning up with bashfulness as the other gawked at him with round eyes. Takeo recovered much faster than his boyfriend, though.

"Hm, thank you. But I think I might have something on the other side as well." Brazenly, he pointed at the other corner of his mouth, and Nao wanted to smack that smug grin off his face. "You can take care of that yourself," he simply retorted and turned around.

Takeo pouted, but swiftly decided on an appropriate counter-attack. He leaned forward and pressed a kiss to his boyfriend's cheek. Nao's heart jolted. He refused to look at the other as he almost melted on the spot.

They leisurely finished the rest of the ramen and spent the remainder of the night strolling around the city.

They looked at different stores and attractions, and saw the illuminated Tokyo Tower in the distance. It felt much more like a vacation than a mission.

The two of them enjoyed their time thoroughly, even though Nao had to drag Takeo away from every gaming store they passed.

Tonight they blended in perfectly with the other people. For once, they were just two young boys that had fun together. No worries, no threats, no fear attached.

And suddenly, Nao thought that this could be the future he envisioned. He'd always been unsure of it and had never dared to glance past what was directly in front of him. The future had been a scary blank space for him, and therefore he'd never dreamed of what it could look like. But tonight, as he and Takeo were just two lovestruck teenagers, he believed that this could be a future worth pursuing. Maybe it wasn't a dark place, after all. Maybe there was something great waiting in front of him.

Nao was ready to believe in it.

Late after midnight, they returned to the hostel. Comfortably tired from the day, they fell into their beds and almost immediately passed out.

Today had been a long, eventful day. Tomorrow they were going to find Hana, to finally lay the groundwork for a hopeful future to come.

— Chapter 25 —

Nao woke up and was at a loss.

The mattress felt unfamiliar, the pillow smelled different, and as he opened his eyes, he was met with an unknown place instead of his familiar bedroom.

For a moment, his mind was running wild before the memories of the past twenty-four hours rushed back into his consciousness.

He was in Tokyo!

And if this was real, then when he turned around, there must be…

Nao sat up and whipped his head around to face the bed on his left. Wrapped in the old, musty blanket, he could make out the long body of a person.

Takeo was still fast asleep. One of his legs was sticking out from beneath the blanket and dangled over the edge of the bed. Half of his head was nuzzled into the thin pillow while his black hair was wildly spread out across it. Nao's heart bloomed and he suppressed a chuckle. *Cute*, he thought.

Quietly, so as not to wake him up, he slid off the bed and tip-toed into the bathroom. He used the toilet and brushed his teeth. With clumsy fingers, he tried to comb his hair, but it still looked like a mess even after his half-hearted attempt. He let it go and left the bathroom again. When he stepped out, he was immediately greeted with a half-awake Takeo.

He sat on his bed and tiredly rubbed his face. "Morning," he mumbled drowsily, his voice still croaky from sleep.

"Did I wake you?" Nao asked, and Takeo looked up through his fingers. He shook his head. "No."

Nao nodded, relieved, and grabbed his bag to pull out something to wear. They'd been so tired and exhausted yesterday that they'd immediately fallen asleep, the thought of changing their clothes not even close to crossing their minds.

He sat back on the bed, taking on the task of organising his belongings.

"Did you sleep well?" Takeo suddenly piped up from behind. His sleep-addled brain seemed to slowly clear up. When Nao turned around, he was already sitting on the edge of the mattress, his hair successfully tamed with a few practiced strokes.

"I passed out pretty quickly. I don't think I even dreamed anything."

Takeo nodded. "Yeah, same here. How late is it anyway?" Before Nao had time to search for a clock, Takeo answered the question himself by glancing at the watch on his wrist. "It's already eleven. We've totally overslept, ha ha. We should start getting ready. We still gotta catch the train."

Nao was already on it. He had succeeded in organising his clothes, which had gotten all messed up in the bag, and took off the shirt he'd been sleeping in.

He didn't think much before doing it; it was just the familiar muscle memory of quickly changing one's clothes—off and on. Yet, the moment the shirt was over his head, he realised he had completely overlooked one crucial detail. His back! He still carried the bruises from his grandfather's belt all over his body.

It'd been a week since then, and the wounds had changed from deep purple and red to vibrant blue and green.

The moment his skin was exposed, the realisation shot back into his head, but it was already too late.

Nao's luck was truly horrible. Takeo sat—of course!—right behind him, and—of course!—he immediately noticed the morbid shapes of hydrangeas and roses blooming vividly across his boyfriend's back.

"What is that?" he asked, his voice suddenly as cold and hard as ice.

"Nothing important." Nao quickly dismissed it and hastily reached for a shirt to pull over his head, but Takeo was faster. All of a sudden, he stood beside him and restrained his arm in a gentle yet unyielding grip. Nao looked up.

Takeo gazed at him with shockingly serious eyes. His expression had gone blank, as always when he was angered by something. Although his anger wasn't directed at Nao, but at whoever was responsible for what had happened to him.

For a moment, they looked each other in the eye. Takeo's gaze was intense yet soft. He might've been angry on the surface, but beneath his gaze, Nao could see the imminent sadness and helplessness.

He sighed. "It isn't as bad as it looks, okay? This happened after the charity event when I was busted with the drugs. My grandfather got a little angry and then…this happened. But it barely hurts anymore."

Nao carefully brushed off Takeo's arm and pulled the shirt over his head, covering up the ugly memories.

He wanted to move on, but Takeo was still looking at him with this strange gaze. Nao sighed once more and stared at him in earnest. "You don't have to keep looking at me like that. It really isn't as bad as you think."

Takeo pressed his lips together. "I'm sorry."

"What are you sorry for?"

"I'm sorry I wasn't there when he hurt you."

His words drove a sting into Nao's heart. He let his eyes wander across Takeo's face, which was still battered from the last attack. There were still green and yellow patches on his jaw, and running from his eye to his ear, he could clearly make out the pink scar. Nao's chest clenched.

"I could say the same to you."

Hesitantly, he raised his hand and placed it on the side of Takeo's face. His thumb stroked gently across the bumpy scar. "But neither of us can change this anymore. So we should just focus on what we can achieve in the future."

Takeo's lips started quivering as though he was about to cry. Suddenly, he leapt forward and hugged Nao. His arms were gentle and careful not to press on his back, yet they still held him incredibly tight. He buried his face deep in the crook of Nao's neck, and the latter could feel warm breath fanning his skin.

Naturally, Nao wrapped his arms around him as well.

"Do you think this will ever end?" Takeo asked quietly.

Nao felt his lips brush against his neck as he spoke. He stroked his back comfortingly. "Of course it will," he answered just as quietly. "All things end. And soon we will look back on all of this as the past."

For an indefinite while, it was silent between the two. They shared the hug and each other's presence, neither of them wanting to let go first.

It was almost as if they were shielding each other from the frightening world that lay outside of these four walls. As if their mortal bodies out of blood and flesh could hold off even the most wicked horrors from each other. It didn't matter whether it was actually possible or not. All that mattered was that it felt like it was. In their tight embrace, even a weak body could become an armour impenetrable to the nightmares of the world.

Eventually, though, they had to let one another go.

"We should leave now," Nao said, and Takeo nodded reluctantly. "Mm…you're right."

They caught the train just in time. Hana's old neighbourhood turned out to be an exceptionally beautiful and serene area.

Rows upon rows of small square houses were lined up beneath telephone poles. It was a lively and flourishing neighbourhood, almost like those out of a picture book. White curtains swayed in the mild breeze, pots of flowers and homegrown vegetables adorned the many window sills, and colourful bicycles were neatly parked in front of the houses. A few adults were outside, working in their front yards to garden and groom the abundant plants.

Nao and Takeo approached a house nestled comfortably in between two other residential buildings.

They walked up the small staircase to the entrance and rang the bell. A pleasant three-time chime resonated through the inside.

For a second, it was silent, and Nao feared that they might've pursued a false lead, but then they heard steps emerging from inside. Softly and quietly, they approached the door.

In the entrance, the face of a young woman appeared. She was pretty. Chestnut brown hair fell in loose waves over her shoulders, and her slim face was framed by feathery bangs. The girl had big, shining eyes and delicately arched brows, which complemented them perfectly. She was rather short and petite in stature.

Despite her slim appearance, however, Nao could see the undeniable protrusion of muscles on her lean arms. She was shorter than both of them, but even so, Nao didn't doubt that she could still take on the two of them in an arm wrestling match if she wanted to.

He had no idea whether the person they were facing was really the Hana they were searching for, but when he saw her eyes widening incredulously the moment she looked at Takeo, he knew they had definitely found her.

Her eyes grew big and her jaw dropped. It seemed like she wanted to say something, but no words left her lips.

For a spell, Hana und Takeo just stared at each other—until Takeo spoke first.

"Hi," he said lightheartedly, and Nao asked himself if he was for real. A single "Hi" after seeing each other for the first time in three years? He doubted this was an appropriate way of greeting someone after such a long period of time.

Hana probably felt the same. She still gaped at them blankly and appeared to be completely at a loss. Then, without warning, she decided to slam the door shut.

It was so fast that Nao could barely process what was happening, yet Takeo seemed to have expected it. He blocked the door with his leg and looked at her through the crack.

"Hana, I know it's been a while, but I need to talk to you."

Angrily, Hana pressed her lips together. "I don't know why we would need to talk!" she countered curtly and tried to close the door once again, but Takeo blocked the attempt successfully.

"Come on. It's pretty rude to kick someone out like this. Let's just have a talk and then we'll leave."

She narrowed her eyes and warily scrutinised the two boys in front of her. Her gaze wandered across Takeo's face and then jumped to Nao. Full of suspicion, she scanned the stranger. "Who's that?" she asked.

"My boyfriend," Takeo replied easily, and her eyes snapped back to him.

For a second, she observed both of them, and they could see the gears turning in her mind. Then she suddenly backed up and reluctantly opened the door. "Okay, come in," she muttered in defeat. "I'll give you one chance!"

Takeo smiled happily. "Thanks."

They walked in, sliding off their shoes at the entrance before following Hana into the house.

Just like the neighbourhood, the interior was pretty and well-designed. Everything was clean and tidy. The air smelled of sandalwood and fresh cotton, and Nao could hear the faint rumbling of a washing machine.

He glanced at the framed pictures on the wall while they walked down the hallway. All of them were photos of Hana and someone he assumed to be her mother.

It pictured them from early childhood up until what seemed to be the present. In most photographs they were hugging each other and smiling brightly at the camera.

They must be really close, Nao thought absentmindedly.

They entered the living room, which was decorated just as simply as the rest of the house, with a small ground-level table, pillows on the floor around it, and a modest balcony facing the street outside.

Hana sat down on one of the pillows and crossed her arms. Takeo and Nao followed her lead while she glowered at them like a general before an enemy's interrogation.

It definitely felt like an interrogation when she opened her mouth and immediately demanded, "So, what's so important that you come all the way to Tokyo to talk to me?"

Takeo and Nao exchanged a quick glance before Takeo took the initiative to answer. "I think you can already guess why I came here," he said, and Hana's mouth twitched.

"Forget it! I have already told you that there's nothing like a copy of that tape. It was all destroyed back then."

"Hana... We've known each other since elementary school. And if there's one thing I know about you it's that you are the most meticulous person in existence. You always wrote two versions of your assignments in case one got lost, you helped organise the library in our old school and operated as the recorder in the school officials' meetings because others were too "incompetent" and "foolish" to do it right. You honestly expect me to believe that you never made a copy of the tape that could have freed us from the tyranny of that gang!?"

"It's not my problem whether you decide to believe me or not. I don't have it! Accept it and let it go. I don't have anything to do with this anymore."

"Hana!"

"Leave it, Takeo!"

They glared at each other. It was almost as if there were two continental plates clashing with each other, and Nao sat in the middle of the epicenter. He felt the suffocating pressure of the two plates squashing him, and at last, he couldn't take it anymore.

"I know you didn't leave your hometown on good terms and want to forget all of what happened there," Nao diplomatically intervened. "But we wouldn't have come here if it weren't so urgent. Katsu Nishimura is still running free. He's still harassing people and he blackmails Takeo and me. This tape is our only chance to put an end to this. It would really change everything if you could give us that footage."

Hana looked at Nao. She stared at him so intensely that Nao almost started squirming beneath her glare. He tried reading her expression, but it was impossible to decipher.

All of a sudden, she narrowed her eyes and stood up. With a stern glare, she propped her hands on her hips and gazed at the two from above.

"I might think about it if we go out and you buy me lunch."

Dumbstruck, Takeo gaped at her. "You want us…to buy you food?"

Hana nodded unapologetically. "I'm hungry and I can't think with an empty stomach. I also know you won't leave me alone, so I can just as well take advantage of the situation."

Takeo scoffed incredulously and rose to his feet. "I didn't know you started ripping people off."

"Only if they get on my nerves."

Takeo rolled his eyes and Hana smiled complacently.

The three of them left the house and walked downtown to a more commercial area. Numerous small shops sprouted from the ground and there was a significant increase in the number of people passing them by.

Hana led them to an unassuming restaurant in the heart of the shopping district. It was small but packed.

There was a long counter at which customers could order or sit as well as a bunch of red leather benches along the window facade.

They settled onto one of the benches. Takeo and Nao sat next to each other, with Hana across from them.

When Hana had said she was hungry, she definitely had not exaggerated. While Nao and Takeo barely ate anything, focusing on only a cup of soda and a bowl of fries each, Hana devoured a whole burger meal: a burger the size of her face, a huge bowl of fries, and a large chocolate milkshake.

Delighted, she dug into the food and ate as if she had three stomachs.

"Food tastes so much better if someone else is paying for it," she exclaimed with a cheeky grin.

Takeo just looked at her grimly as he heard those words. He stirred the drink with his straw. The ice swirled inside the glass, making faint clanking sounds as it hit the rim.

"You haven't changed one bit since I last saw you," he suddenly piped up, and Hana lifted her gaze off the plate. For a second, she glanced at Takeo in surprise, a speck of ketchup stuck to the corner of her mouth.

"Shall I take this as a compliment or an insult?" she asked.

Takeo shrugged. "Probably a compliment." He smiled wryly. "It's been so long. Everything happened so fast back then, I couldn't even properly say goodbye."

Hana took one of the napkins, wiped her mouth, and then looked up and smiled as well. "Yeah, it was unfortunate. But my mother and I wanted to start a new life as fast as possible."

"And did you get the new life you wished for?"

Hana nodded slowly. "Yes. It wasn't easy, though. Rumours follow you wherever you go, but it was the right decision. I transferred to a new school here in Tokyo. I thought it'd be difficult to find connections, but the people at school were surprisingly nice. You know how I always said I wanted to attend a school in a big city because of all the various opportunities and club activities? Well, I've joined the photography club and the judo club."

"Judo? That's new. You didn't do this when we were in middle school."

"Yeah, after everything that's happened, my mother wanted me to be able to defend myself. So I've been training ever since. What about you? Are you still playing baseball?"

Takeo made a sound of assent. "The school I've been transferred to also has a baseball team, so I've been training there for the past three years. Although the team is not as good as the old one, it's still fun to play."

Hana took a sip of her milkshake and poked the thick liquid absentmindedly with her straw. "How has it been for you, though...?" she inquired slowly. "How have things been after I left?"

Takeo's lips curved into a crooked smile. He averted his eyes. "…Complicated," he eventually said after a few seconds of silence. "I wouldn't have come all the way here if it had been easy, would I?"

Silently, Hana set the cup back on the table. She didn't look Takeo in the eyes. Instead, she glowered at her plate. "I don't want to imagine how the last three years must have been for you…"

For a moment, a heavy silence settled between the two. It was a space filled with the regrets of the past. And nothing weighed heavier than the silence of countless paths one could have tread instead.

Then, all of a sudden, Takeo piped up as he looked over at Nao, who had followed their conversation in silence until now.

"But I got to meet Nao," Takeo said and his face beamed with the purity and happiness of these words. "Everything has become so much brighter with him."

Nao stared at him with big eyes while Takeo gazed back at him with a look full of affection. It was one of those intense gazes Nao had been receiving from Takeo a lot these days. They were so full of emotion, filled so plenteously with sentiments, and cutting so deep into his flesh that it left Nao drowning in his own blood. It made him feel warm and breathless. He was bleeding out, but who cared if this was the way he went out.

Nao's heart was still processing the surge of emotions flushing through its veins when Hana spoke up.

"Nao, we haven't really introduced ourselves yet. It's probably a little too late now, but nice to meet you, anyway."

Nao tried to calm his breathing. His chest and heart were filled with warmth and chaos. He did his best to swallow those feelings down, and with as much composure as he could muster, he reciprocated Hana's gaze.

"Likewise," he said.

Hana glanced over at Takeo. "It's so unfair! How did you manage to get a boyfriend before me?"

Takeo shrugged nonchalantly. "Maybe if you were a bit nicer and didn't force others to buy your food—"

"Hey, I see an opportunity, I take it," Hana countered quickly and looked at Takeo through narrowed eyes.

Takeo just laughed. "Whatever. Just finish the food I paid for till I get back from the restroom." With these words, he stood up and walked off, leaving Hana and Nao by themselves.

Hana sighed and crossed her arms in front of her chest. "He hasn't really changed either," she mumbled to herself and looked at Nao. "What about you?" Curiously, she tilted her head to the side. "How did you two meet?"

"Ah... We're in the same class," Nao answered a little shyly.

Her lips lifted into a soft smile. "Takeo might be a bit hard-headed sometimes, but he's a good guy. Although you surely must have noticed that as well."

Nao nodded. Takeo truly had a talent for running head-first into danger. But he always did it with other people's wellbeing in mind.

Thus, Nao took a deep breath and looked at Hana. "That's why I need your help. I know it's a lot to ask from you, but you've seen the bruises on his face, haven't you? Those bruises... They're Katsu's doing. And it will only get worse if we don't do something."

Hana eyed Nao with a stern gaze. A deep frown grew on her face, and her eyes darkened as severely as storm clouds drifting in front of the sun. "But what about me?" she suddenly asked. Nao looked at her, dumbfounded. "I was also used and harassed by them. I barely managed to escape and build a new life. Why should I risk my safety for him? Just because we were once friends in the past?"

Nao clenched his jaw. Of course, she wasn't wrong... She had also been a victim that managed to escape after many hardships. She spoke the truth anyone who had survived Katsu would speak. How could Nao demand of her to dive back into her worst nightmares?

Hana was so desperate to keep the life she had built out of blood and ruins...and yet, Nao was just as desperate, maybe even more than her.

"He's in this predicament because of me, and I will do anything to get him out of there! I know it's not fair to ask this much of you, but please, help me save him."

A mountain of silence fell between the two. It was too big to conquer, and so they could only stare at each other in pressing stillness. Both of them were caught up in their own sorrowful despair.

Hana's brows furrowed deeper as she clenched and unclenched her jaw. "I..." she finally tried to speak, yet stopped herself again.

Nao stared at her intensely. "Please."

Hana opened her mouth to say something, but whatever it was, Nao would never find out. In that moment, Takeo came back from the restroom and slumped onto the seat beside his boyfriend. "Hey, you still haven't finished your food," he commented lightheartedly, unaware of the mile-high mountain spreading between the other two.

Hana averted her eyes and turned to Takeo. She looked at him with a crooked smile. "I'm not really hungry anymore. Sorry."

Takeo sighed. "Then don't order that much next time if you can't finish it. Let's go."

The three of them stood up and left the restaurant. Nao tried to continuously make eye contact with Hana, but she avoided his gaze like a disease.

They walked down the shopping street back to Hana's house. When they turned into the street leading back home, she suddenly stopped in her tracks. Surprised, Nao and Takeo came to a halt as well.

With a deep frown, Hana looked at the two. Her hands were clenched into fists and she pressed her lips together until they were nothing but a thin line. For a moment, Nao wondered if she wanted to punch them and test out a few of her judo moves on them—but unexpectedly, she began to speak.

"...I will give you the copy," she said, and it sounded like she had trouble bringing those words out of her mouth. Her face was pale and her eyes glassy, but the words rang out loud and clear. "I will have to search for it first, though. Since our house is too small and we couldn't store all of our stuff there after moving, it's probably crammed in a box in some storeroom in a warehouse. But...I will look for it."

Both of them stared at her with wide eyes. Especially Takeo, who hadn't heard anything of the conversation between the two, was flabbergasted at this sudden change of mind. Although, just as quickly, his surprised expression turned into a big smile. "Thank you!" he exclaimed, grabbing Hana by both of her shoulders. "Thank you!"

"I still have to look for it first," she reminded him. "But I will contact you when I find it." Her eyes darted over to Nao, who glanced back at her gratefully.

Hana cleared her throat and brushed Takeo's hands off. "Well, but you owe me after this."

Takeo huffed and smiled. "You're still not done with ripping me off?"

Hana jokingly glared at him and Takeo laughed. "Yeah, okay, I owe you."

With significantly lighter steps, they brought Hana back to her house. When they were only a few meters from the entrance, Hana leaned closer to Takeo and spoke so quietly that Nao behind them couldn't catch it.

"You got yourself a good boyfriend there," she whispered and Takeo smiled, whispering back, "The best."

— Chapter 26 —

After bringing Hana back home, Nao and Takeo continued to saunter through the city.

Hana had promised to look into the warehouse as soon as possible. Though Nao and Takeo would depart from Tokyo the next day, they had exchanged numbers, so she could contact them as soon as she found it.

Their hearts felt a lot lighter now that they knew there was this beacon of hope gleaming above the abyss. It was unfortunate that they still had to wait before they could actually grasp it, but now there was the promise of hope—a light in the long, narrow tunnel in front of them.

It was already late in the afternoon when they set off from Hana's place. Tomorrow, they would already have to take the train home, leaving Tokyo behind.

It was unlucky that their trip was so short-lived. Both of them seemed to feel the same way, since Takeo turned to Nao as soon as they reached the train station, and asked, "I don't really feel like going back to the hostel already. How about we explore the city a little more?"

Elated, Nao nodded, and they boarded the train carrying them to the heart of the capital.

"Do you have an idea of what you want to do on our last evening here?" Takeo inquired curiously as they sat next to each other in the cabin. The scenery of the city flitted past them outside the windows. The sky grew darker with each passing minute, and slowly the lights of street lamps and homes alike sprang into life, splattered and dispersed across the scenery like a swarm of fireflies among a jumble of trees.

"I don't know," Nao answered truthfully, and Takeo pursed his lips pensively.

"Then let me phrase it differently," he continued. "Is there something you've always wanted to do that we can try out tonight?"

Nao gazed out of the window and pondered for a bit before looking back at Takeo. "I've always wanted to visit an aquarium," he replied, and Takeo's lips lifted into a smile.

"Okay, then let's do that."

At the next train station, they studied the map of the city for a bit until they found the sign marking an aquarium. They instantly boarded the next train, and when they arrived at their destination, the sky had already grown black and specks of stars had blossomed in the darkness.

Nao had never been to an aquarium for two simple reasons. First, there was nothing like that in their hometown. Second, even if there had been one nearby, Nao's parents would have never visited it with him anyway. So, he was really excited to finally fulfil an old childhood wish of his tonight.

The two of them entered the aquarium, and it was like stepping into another world—as though with one step, they had entered the deep depths of the ocean.

Engulfed in the immersive blue world, Nao and Takeo stared in awe at the water, which seemed to surround them on all sides. From the ground up to the high arched ceiling, the world of teal and navy enclosed them. Behind the pristine glass swam countless sea creatures—from tiny fish to huge stingrays. It was even more beautiful and exciting than Nao had expected.

Side by side, they walked among the crowd and admired the view of this alien world in which nothing but blue and serenity existed.

"A sunfish!" Nao exclaimed as one of those huge beings swam past them. Nao remembered seeing a picture of one in a textbook back in elementary school. He had always found them funny-looking, but seeing one up close now and in its full size, he was totally impressed.

Takeo chuckled beside him. "They look really cool," he agreed, and Nao nodded excitedly.

Together, they watched the sunfish swim past and disappear back into the depths of the water.

As they walked farther, Nao suddenly felt something warm grazing his hand. He didn't have to look to know that it was Takeo's hand. Carefully, as if he wanted to give Nao the option to pull away, their fingers brushed against each other. Softly and almost timidly, they grazed his, and Nao felt tingles running down his spine. His heart skipped a beat, but he didn't pull away, and so Takeo's hand slowly engulfed his.

His fingers slipped between his own, and Nao could feel Takeo's warm palm gently moulding against his.

They didn't talk, nor did they take their eyes off the fish. Hand in hand, they continued their stroll through the aquarium.

It felt so natural and organic, as if Nao had held Takeo's hand a thousand times already.

The pace of their footsteps aligned, and they walked so close to each other that their shoulders kept occasionally brushing against one another.

It was simply perfect—watching the array of iridescent fish swarms float past them like slivers of silk, feeling the warmth of each other's skin seeping into their own. Takeo's hand grounded Nao so deeply in the moment that even the fury of a storm couldn't break them apart. Like two cliffs, unwavering and stead-fast in the midst of a raging ocean.

Nao couldn't fall if he was close to Takeo. And neither would Takeo.

They continued to stroll leisurely through the aquarium. Curiously, they walked from tank to tank filled with all of the diverse species. Nao had to laugh when he saw Takeo's displeased face as they walked past the jellyfish. Needless to say, they didn't spend much time there and instead went over to the stingrays.

They spent a few hours at the aquarium, and when they arrived back at the hostel, deep in the night, both of them felt content and drowsy.

Tired out, Takeo fell into his bed, and so Nao was the first one to use the bathroom.

He brushed his teeth and changed his clothes. Once he was finished, Nao collapsed onto the bed and Takeo dragged himself into the bathroom.

Comfortably exhausted, he lay on the thin mattress and looked up at the shabby ceiling. Through the windows fell faint rays of light, shrouding the room in a soft, dim glow.

Drowsily, Nao rested an arm over his eyes. Tomorrow, they would already have to leave.

He felt deep disappointment at that thought. He wished to stay with Takeo in Tokyo a little longer. As a matter of fact, he would have liked to stay with Takeo anywhere, regardless of place or time. Anywhere would be enough as long as they could just escape their lives for a little longer.

Nao was so deep in thought he barely noticed Takeo coming out of the bathroom and sitting on the neighbouring bed. He could hear the springs creak quietly as he lay down.

Silently, Nao lifted his arm and peered over. He could make out Takeo's frame against the dim light outside.

Unsure, Nao bit his tongue before whispering the next words very tentatively.

"Do you…do you want to come over?"

Takeo turned around, and though he wasn't able to see his expression in the darkness, Nao could still make out his nod.

Shyly, Nao scooted over as Takeo grabbed his pillow and climbed next to him into the bed.

Nao's heartbeat accelerated, his pulse thrumming in every single tip of his fingers, as the weight on the mattress shifted and the warmth of the other body slowly engulfed his.

They both lay on their sides, face to face. Now that he was so close to him, Nao could finally see his face clearly, and through the twilight, he noticed the soft look on Takeo's face as he gazed at him—his eyes were soft and gleaming, his lips curved upward, tender and delicate.

The feeble rays of light seeping through the old glass refracted and dispersed. The fragments fell across Takeo's face and grazed him like a veil made of light.

In the half-dark, his eyes sparkled as bright as stars in the night sky. They were pools of deep darkness, with stars speckled across their immeasurable vastness. Nao almost believed he could count the constellations inside them.

For a moment, they admired each other in silence. Takeo's eyes lingered on him, like an echo drifting from the top of a mountain—ceaseless, loath to part. It seemed as though he was taking all the time in the world to count the stars and constellations in Nao's eyes as well.

After a while, Nao whispered into the quiet. Looking at Takeo's face through the dense twilight reminded him of a conversation they'd had a while back.

"Do you remember back in that alley, when you said you think you were a murderer in your past life? I said I believe it could be the same for me. If that really were the case, then why do you think we crossed paths in this life?"

"Oh, that's a difficult question... Who knows the reasons of the universe for doing things the way it does?" After pondering it for a bit, Takeo added, "I would like to tell you, but I don't think I can."

Nao let his eyes wander across his face. "I don't know the answer either, but if we were really bad people...I'd like to think that maybe this is our chance to start over; to lay a better foundation for the next life... If you could find out who you were in your past life, would you do it?"

Confident, Takeo shook his head. "No," he replied. "I wouldn't want to know what I did or who I was."

"Why?"

"Because...if I really were a bad person in my past life, then I might deserve all of this. What if I really murdered people, or exploited, or raped them? If that's who I were, then I shouldn't fight this, right? It means I deserve all of this. That this is really justice."

Nao looked deep into his eyes. "We don't know if any of this is true. We don't even know if there really is such a thing as a past life or a next life. But what I know for sure is that the *you* right here doesn't deserve any of this. You're so kind and just, Takeo. You genuinely want to save people. You endanger yourself to protect them, even if they didn't ask for your help. This sometimes might be wrong, but it is also brave.

"In this life, you don't deserve any of this. And I'm willing to go above and beyond to show you this! I don't care if I go against some kind of karma or universal justice. I would take on god if that's what I need to do."

Stubborn like a child, Nao stared at Takeo, who just looked back at him with wide eyes.

His eyes were round, his mouth slightly agape in surprise or shock. Nao couldn't really tell, but before he could ruminate on it, Takeo suddenly broke into a beaming smile, his eyes burned with what could only be described as a declaration of love. He spoke with a soft laugh, "You really are amazing, Nao."

He extended his hand to tenderly rest it on the side of Nao's face, cradling his cheek in his warm palm. "Whatever the universe's reason may be, I'm glad to have met you in this life. You are truly the best thing to ever happen to me."

Nao smiled back. His heart was filled to the brim with the love and adoration conveyed in these simple words. He took a deep breath and let his heart respond in kind. "I feel the same. You're the best thing in my life."

Takeo smiled and leaned forward to kiss him.

Nao felt his boyfriend's lips crash into his, and he instinctively leaned deeper in, reciprocating the kiss with the same fervour.

Takeo's hand at the side of his face dug gently into his hair as he slid closer.

Nao took all of his warmth and presence in. Gladly, he drowned in the kiss and reached out to rest his hand on the back of Takeo's head.

Their exchange was warm, it was tender, and yet there was this unyielding need simmering beneath the surface. In every touch, in every breath, there was an urge to be closer, a need to take what was so readily in front of them. Like blossoms devouring the sun's warmth to nourish, like butterflies hungrily tasting a flower's nectar.

There was so much greed—greed for closeness, for acknowledgement, greed for love. Both of them were so ready to give what the other needed and take in return.

Neither time nor place mattered anymore. Suddenly, the only important things in the world were these two in that room together, Takeo's soft hair between his fingers, and their lips melting into one another.

Takeo's hand slid from Nao's face down to his waist and pulled him even closer.

— Chapter 27 —

It was around nine in the morning and faint rays of sunlight slanted through the windows.

Both of them packed their bags, throwing their clothes and belongings inside.

Nao pulled the zipper close and heaved the handle over his shoulder. He looked over at Takeo, who was already waiting for him at the door. As their gazes intertwined, Nao couldn't help but blush. He knew it was stupid, but thinking about last night…he felt a little shy. Two red circles adorned his face as he let the memories flow through his mind.

It had been perfect, and Nao didn't regret it in the slightest, but who could have predicted that he'd lose his virginity in a shabby hostel somewhere in the backstreets of Tokyo.

Takeo surely hadn't expected his first time to happen in a place like that either.

Well, however, it wasn't like either of them was regretting this turn of events.

"Are you ready?" Takeo asked, and Nao nodded. "Yeah," he said and quickly followed Takeo out of the room.

As they rode the elevator down to the ground floor, Nao felt Takeo grasp his hand and give it a gentle squeeze. Nao looked up and smiled at him.

When the elevator doors opened, they let go and walked to the counter to return the keys.

The train ride back to the Ibaraki Prefecture was calm. Surprisingly, there weren't many people in the cabin, and peacefully, the train rolled across green fields and languid cities.

They arrived back in their hometown late in the afternoon.

It felt like the gates of the cage had been opened and closed again. The lock had been placed in front of the door once more, but this time it was different.

They'd had a taste of freedom. It was sweet and ended with a bitter aftertaste, following the imminent return to old confines. But this didn't mean that they could never taste it again. After all, the horizon was only the border until one crossed it. Behind lay whole new lands the eye hadn't been able to see thus far—and on those lands grew novel fruits, offering a multitude of flavours one had yet to try. The old bitterness could be forgotten, as new sweetness was to come.

Though their mouths were filled with a sour taste as they arrived at the train station and had to bid farewell to each other, the promise of fertile lands eased their worries a tiny bit.

Nao and Takeo didn't want to let go of each other yet. As much as both of them were aware of the fact that they had to keep going on with this reality for a little longer, it was hard to accept.

"Hana said she will call us as soon as she finds the copy," Takeo said. "And after she mailed it to me, we'll bring it to the police."

Nao nodded confidently. "Then Katsu will be done for." Nao looked deep into his boyfriend's eyes. "It will work out. It has to work out."

Takeo nodded reassuringly. "It will."

He leaned forward and kissed Nao. It was brief but sweet. If they hadn't been in a semi public place, Nao would have thrown his arms around Takeo's neck and kissed him deeply, not letting him go anywhere. But they were still at the train station, and therefore he held himself back, even though it was as impossible as breathing under water.

"We should go now," Takeo said. "We'll see each other at school tomorrow."

Nao sighed, but reluctantly agreed. Takeo turned around to leave, though he immediately spun back around and grabbed Nao's hand. The tips of his fingers dug into his skin. It was gentle but also urgent.

"Will you be okay?" he asked with a deep frown.

Nao knew that he was referring to his family. Both of them had just disappeared without a word over the weekend. Just like frost in winter, there was bound to be trouble.

"I could ask you the same," Nao replied calmly.

Takeo pressed his lips together, and with a worried look, he stared at his boyfriend before very reluctantly letting go of him. "Just call me if anything happens, okay?"

Nao nodded. "I will."

Slowly and painfully, they parted ways.

Nao recognised the familiar weight settling inside his chest once he stood in front of the apartment.

He tilted his head back and looked up the tall building. Then, with a deep sigh, he gathered his strength and forced himself to keep moving inside. The elevator brought him up without mercy or regret.

Once at the top, he opened the door and stepped into the warm apartment. It smelled of cleaning products and bitter perfume.

With his head held low and his hands stuffed inside his pockets, he headed toward his room, but, of course, never made it there.

"Nao." The voice of his father pierced the walls and Nao's skull. "Come here."

He did as he was told.

With heavy steps, he dragged himself into the living room where his parents were already waiting. They looked at him with scornful eyes.

Before any of them could say anything, a door in the hallway was opened and a person ran toward them. Out of the corner of his eye, Nao recognised his brother, who must have heard that he had finally come back home.

Their father simply ignored the newcomer and stood up from the armchair he'd been sitting in until now. Steps sturdier than a boulder, he walked toward Nao. His eyes piercing him like a thousand arrows.

Father and son glared at each other; neither of them made a sound. Until, suddenly, his father raised his hand and slapped Nao across the face.

Nao's head was whipped to the side and he immediately felt the unpleasant stinging sensation blazing across his left cheek.

"Who do you think you are?" his father growled, every word was pressed out between gritted teeth, as if he could just barely restrain himself from hitting him again.

"You ungrateful, rotten dog!"

Nao looked at him emptily.

"What do you have to say to defend yourself, huh!? What made you think you could just run away!?"

"I had something important to do," Nao responded flatly.

His father took a deep breath, his son's disrespect sagging into the pit of his stomach like a stone. Heavily, his chest heaved and fell as his hand formed into a shaking fist. His teeth were bared like those of a wild beast.

"What would be so important to do for a wimp like you!?" he screamed. "What makes you think you can treat your parents this way!? Talking back! Running away! Selling drugs! How can a child be so disrespectful!" His voice blared through the apartment like dynamite in a mine.

"I've raised you! I've fed you! I've given you a bed to sleep! Why can't you be like other children!? Why can't you be grateful!?" Every word was spit in his face.

"Grateful for what?" Nao mustered his courage and asked. He clenched his jaw and glared back at his father. "What...what should I be grateful for?"

For a second, it was dead silent in the room. The world seemed to have temporarily held its breath and stopped. But then, in the blink of an eye, he was hit in the face with a fist.

Nao lost his balance upon the impact and fell backward onto the ground. He slumped back-first onto the carpeted floor. Startled, he pressed a hand to his bleeding nose.

Through his eyelashes, he looked up at the person towering above him, glowering down at him like an insect in the dirt.

"I see. I have been too soft on you," the voice, cold and empty, echoed down to him. "Shall I teach you how to respect one's parents?"

His father was about to bend down and grab his son when Toyo suddenly screamed.

"P...please stop!" he exclaimed and leapt in front of his brother, panting frantically as he faced his father. "F-father p-please... I...I-I..."

Both Nao and their father stared at Toyo's back and front with bulging eyes.

Toyo...was standing up for him...?

Humans liked to say that things like miracles existed, but this was one Nao would have never expected to see. And neither had their father.

With widened eyes, he looked at his younger son. For a moment, speechless, he eyed him as if there were a stranger in front of him. And then, his face darkened just as quickly.

"Get out of the way," he barked strictly, but Toyo shook his head.

He took a shaky breath and tried to carefully form his words. "F-father, I don't think…this is the…this is the right thing to do…"

Stripped of any logical explanation for his favourite child's behaviour, he looked at Nao. His eyes pierced him with so much fury that it sent chills down Nao's spine.

"Did you do that?" he asked. His voice as cutting as a blade. "Did you manipulate him to act this way?"

Nao was too shocked to answer, but Toyo took over for him.

"He didn't do anything… I just don't think…that hurting him is the right answer," Toyo stammered. His words trembled like his breath, and from behind, Nao could see his legs shaking like leaves in the wind. However, despite all that, he stood in front of his brother like a tree. Swaying and shaking in the face of the hurricane, but nevertheless holding on.

"Did you spend too much time with your brother that he gave you such rotten ideas? Move to the side, Toyo! We'll talk later."

His father reached out to grab him by his arm, but Toyo dodged it.

"Father…please. Let's just all talk about it…"

The hurricane raged and turned around to his wife. "Kaori!" he shouted. "Take Toyo to his room!"

Their mother, who, as always, had just passively watched all of this going on, came forward and gently touched her son's shoulders. "Come, Toyo. This is none of your business," she said, but Toyo brushed her off.

"No! No!" he shouted, his voice growing more and more desperate.

With tears in his eyes, he stared at his father.

"I…I will go if you don't hurt Nao and just talk to him…please…then I will go…"

Their father's eyes narrowed drastically. He gritted his teeth and reached out to seize Toyo by the collar of his shirt. "Who do you think you are to order me around!? Did you catch a disease from that dirty dog on the ground? Will you also turn into a useless, homosexual disgrace!?"

Tears spilled from Toyo's eyes as his father screamed at him. He was out of words and full of fear. Terrified, Toyo hid his face behind his hands and started sobbing.

"Now you dare whimper like a mutt!?" the man bellowed and pulled his son closer, yet stopped when he suddenly felt a hand resting on the side of his arm.

He turned around and looked at his wife, who gently shook her head. "Not Toyo," she said, and surprised, as if he had just now realised that he was shouting at his golden child, he let go of him and took a step back.

With his nostrils flaring and his fists shaking in anger, Tsuyoshi Miyamoto looked at his two sons. One on the ground with a bloody nose, the other standing in front of him, trembling and sobbing.

His dark eyes fixated on Nao, and with a hard voice, he spoke, "This is not over yet. I'll talk to your grandfather about what kind of punishment will be appropriate for your foul behaviour."

He took a deep breath as he tried to calm himself down, and then added, "Now leave! I dare you to show either of your faces again today."

Nao needed a moment before he could free himself from his petrification. Slowly, he rose to his feet.

He tried his best to seem steady and not reveal the quivering legs barely holding him up.

Without uttering a word, he grabbed Toyo by his arm and dragged him out of the living room.

In the hallway, he let go of him, convinced that he'd now be able to find his room alone, and left for his own.

Nao stilled the bleeding of his nose with a few tissues and then sat on his bed, exhausted.

His heart was still racing wildly, and he couldn't believe that today he had stood up against his father. It wasn't something he usually had the guts to do, and it rattled him to the core. But what had shocked him even more was the sight of his little brother coming to his aid.

There was no reason for him to do so. He was the blessed child. The hope and treasure of the family. He never rubbed anyone up the wrong way, nor did he break any rules. Who could be a better embodiment of the perfect child than him?

And yet, today, he had stood in front of and shielded his worthless brother, who never missed an opportunity to offend their family.

Why should he have stooped so low? Why should a deity protect a sinner?

Nao couldn't make any sense of it, no matter how much he thought about it.

He lay in his bed for a long time. The sun was slowly but inevitably setting outside while the light of the day dwindled by the second. All the while, he could hear his brother's sobs coming from the other side of the wall.

He was crying for a very long time, and Nao asked himself why he had even done something as stupid as standing up for him when he couldn't handle it.

A few times Nao debated whether he should go over to his room and look after him, but he quickly shook those thoughts off. They had never been close enough to take care of a relationship like that. And even if he were to go, he honestly had no idea what he should say to his brother.

He came to the conclusion that it was best not to interfere with him.

After a while, Nao became drowsy. His stomach grumbled with hunger, but he didn't dare to leave his room and get something to eat from the kitchen. When his father had warned them not to show their faces again today, he had really meant it. And Nao was neither dumb nor brave enough to defy his command.

Eventually, he fell asleep despite the persistent growling of his belly. It wasn't until late into the night that he got shaken awake by a timid hand on his shoulder.

In utter surprise, his eyes snapped open and he sat up, only to nearly clash heads with the person above him. The other could dodge just in time, and with a surprised pant, he jumped back.

In the shadows shrouding his room, Nao quickly searched for the intruder. With his eyes squinted, he could make out a petite stature in the dark. "Toyo?" he asked sleepily.

The person moved toward him again, and their voice, soft and thin, rang through the silence, much like the twitter of a sparrow. "I'm sorry. I didn't want to scare you."

Drowsily, Nao reached for the lamp on his bedside table and pressed the switch. A dim, orange light illuminated the small room. In the soft glow, his brother's features finally became visible, and Nao immediately noticed his swollen and red eyes.

With a sigh, he rubbed his face and then swung his legs over the edge of the bed to sit up properly.

"What are you doing here?" he asked.

Toyo fidgeted with his hands, and then sat on the ground in front of his brother, as if he didn't dare to sit on the bed next to him.

His gaze directed to the ground, he spoke very quietly after a long period of stifling silence. "How...how do you do it?" he breathed timidly.

"What do you mean?" Nao asked, not entirely sure whether he was still asleep or not.

Toyo fumbled with his hands a little harder. "How do you manage all of this? How can you endure it?"

Confused, Nao blinked a few times. "Do you mean our parents?" he asked after a while.

Toyo nodded quietly.

Nao was thoroughly confused. He had no idea what had gotten into his brother and why he was behaving this way. To be so vulnerable and attentive in front of each other was something they had never done. Not to mention that this was probably one of the longest conversations they'd had in years.

Nao sighed. "Look... I'm thankful for what you did for me today, but you should never do anything reckless like it again. It's not worth it and it will only cause you more trouble to suddenly get involved in this. It's disadvantageous for both of us."

As if he didn't want to hear any of this, Toyo started shaking his head. He still wasn't looking at his brother and instead stared intensely at the ground.

"Nao..." he pressed out quietly. "Do you...do you know why I was in the bathroom throwing up a few days ago?"

Puzzled, Nao looked at his younger brother and then shook his head.

Toyo took a shaky breath and clutched his own trembling hands. "During exams...I can't help but throw up every night because I am so scared of what happens if I fail."

He dug his hands into the fabric of his pants.

"What will happen to me if I can't keep up with the expectations? What will I become if I can't bring the achievements I used to? What is my worth then…?" His thin, gentle voice broke during the last sentence, his knuckles all white from clutching his pants so desperately. "How can I endure this? I don't know…how to deal with my life right now…but I also don't know how I can if I'm not perfect anymore… Nao… How do you survive?"

Nao stared at his little brother, robbed of words. There he sat. So small and vulnerable in front of him. He had never seen his perfect shell crack so drastically. Before him was just a little boy, scared sick by how the world worked.

For the first time, Nao felt like he was looking at a person, his little brother, rather than a deity he was forced to compete with.

Automatically, he slid off his bed and sat on the ground in front of him. He looked at the boy with drawn brows. "I don't know how I get through it either…" he answered truthfully.

Lately, he had Takeo, who made all of this a lot easier and bearable, but for most of his life, he had been alone with this sense of helplessness too. And in those many years, he had also just barely hung on.

Nao had always clung and clawed to life, even if he didn't know where it led him. But in all those years, he'd never noticed that his little brother could possibly feel the same.

He was the fragmented vase and his brother the one embellished with gold. How could he have known that while one of them had to deal with the problem of being cracked and useless, the other had to hide its cracks in fear of being thrown out as well.

"I just…never wanted to give up, I guess," Nao said a little helplessly. "But why do you even ask me? I've never achieved anything. In our family, I'm nothing but a worthless nobody."

Toyo lifted his round eyes off the ground and directed them straight at his brother.

"You're my big brother, which means I will always look up to you."

It was spoken with such truthfulness and sincerity that Nao was taken aback for a moment. Yes, they were brothers by blood, but that Toyo would also see him as a brother figure...he never would have expected it.

Suddenly, Nao felt a huge amount of guilt twinging at his heart.

Full of his own struggle, he had completely overlooked that there was someone else who might have wanted to depend on him. Someone who needed the same help that he had yearned to receive in his childhood too.

In hindsight, Toyo might not be that different from him. He suffered differently from Nao, but he suffered nonetheless. Nao had never expected for the blessed child to feel like it was cursed as well.

With pinched brows, he looked at his little brother. Like a sparrow whose wings had been clipped, he sat in front of him. His shoulders were slouched, the black hair falling ruffled in front of his reddened eyes. Right now, he was nothing more than a child, and Nao's heart stung with the realisation of that.

If he had lifted his eyes from his own problems a little more, he might have been able to notice Toyo's too.

Maybe then, he could have been a better big brother to him as well.

"Toyo," Nao spoke, his voice thin and soft like the other's.

The boy looked up, and upon seeing his round-eyed gaze, Nao had to avert his own in shame.

"I'm sorry I haven't noticed any of this earlier..." he whispered. "I thought you enjoyed all of this. I believed...you liked how your life went. I'm sorry I've never noticed how much it tormented you..."

Toyo rubbed his swollen eyes with his thin fingers. He still kept his gaze on his brother.

"Don't apologise," he responded, surprisingly strong in tone. "How could you have noticed, with the way they treated you? I think I would have resented myself too if I were in your position.

"I'm sorry I've never had the courage to stand up for you until now…"

Finally, Nao lifted his gaze as well and looked back at his brother. He wanted to say he had never resented him…but that would have been a lie. Of course Nao had been envious of his brother… And after years of feeling like this, he might have also unconsciously resented him without actively acknowledging it.

Nao felt his heart brim more and more with the feelings of guilt and shame born from his own behaviour. He clenched his jaw.

"Don't apologise to me either… And also, you shouldn't try to stand up for me again. I appreciate it, but it will only cause you more trouble in the long run."

Taken aback, Toyo blinked at him. "But…but I want to do it!"

His older brother slowly shook his head. "That's…brave of you, but it'll just bring more harm. Don't throw away your chances for me."

"Are you sure…?"

Nao nodded reassuringly. "I am. And regarding you and me… Why don't we try to start anew? Let's try…to not be strangers anymore…"

Toyo's thin lips lifted into a shy smile. His eyes turned into little crescents as his pink cheeks pushed them up when he smiled.

"I'd like that," he said. "Let's not be strangers anymore."

Nao's lips twitched upward as well. His younger brother smiled at him, and for the first time, it felt neither taunting nor distant. This time, it carried the sentiment of a child's laughter; innocent and pure.

Maybe Toyo had always smiled at him like that, and Nao had just never acknowledged it. Whatever it was in the end, Nao had made up his mind to become a better older brother for him.

All of a sudden, Toyo blinked at him and cocked his head to the side. "Let me ask you something… The important thing you left the city for, did it go well?"

Nao nodded. "Mm, it did."

Toyo smiled, delighted. "I'm happy to hear that. I hope it'll work out, whatever it is."

Nao pressed his lips together. He hoped so too.

— Chapter 28 —

Monday came, and Tuesday passed.

Finally, Nao saw Takeo at school again. Hana hadn't yet gotten back to them and they grew more and more agitated by the day. It was only a matter of time until Katsu would come back to collect his debt in the form of cruel violence.

Nao tried to be optimistic, but it was difficult considering the stakes they were gambling with.

His only ray of light was Takeo, with whom he met up in the study room every day after class.

His heart was tumultuous, but the moment he saw his boyfriend, it calmed down.

When they'd met on Monday, the day after returning from their little adventure, Nao had told Takeo about his conversation with his little brother—though he deliberately left out the part of his father beating him up.

It freed him, having someone to finally speak his thoughts to. Initially, Nao had never seen the benefit in sharing his heart with someone else. In the end, one's problems still stayed the same, no matter if you were to voice them aloud or not. Ultimately, everyone lived and died alone.

But now that he had someone he could open his heart to, he realised that, even though every soul was originally alone in this world, the mere existence of someone's presence could be enough to make one believe that those universal laws could be bent.

Suddenly, one's life was intertwined with that of another; and with it were the depths of their hearts.

Takeo had also told him about his situation at home. It seemed that his brother had also been incensed by his sudden disappearance, but due to the investigation tied to the attack of Katsu's gang on their house, Takeo's brother had too much on his own plate to care about punishing him for his little weekend-trip.

On Tuesday, Nao inquired again whether he had heard anything about Hana and the copy of that tape, but Takeo denied it. Nao couldn't understand what was taking so long! What was so hard about searching a warehouse when another person's life was at stake!?

Nao tried to swallow down the impending helplessness and agitation, but it was barely concealable.

Takeo squeezed his hand reassuringly. "It's only been three days," he said, as though he had read his thoughts.

Nao's lip twitched. "Three days is plenty of time," he countered grimly. "Maybe we should just call her over and over again until she finally sends it over."

"Give her time," Takeo said and smiled at him comfortingly, his eyes forming soft crescents.

Nao sighed and lowered his head. "She might have time, but we don't..." he muttered quietly beneath his breath. Unsure whether Takeo had heard it, the latter just kept talking.

"But it was nice seeing her again. It'd been such a long time, and everything ended so abruptly back then that it was truly an unworthy parting of ways. And though the reasons we went to Tokyo weren't cheerful, I really enjoyed our trip there." He sighed deeply. "It already feels so nostalgic. I'd like to go back!"

Nao could understand him all too well. He was already yearning for that feeling of freedom they had experienced there.

Far away from the grasps of his family, Nao had seen a future worth fighting for. Out there was still a future untainted by anyone else. He could build a life he wanted to live, with whoever he wanted to share it with.

292

Automatically, his eyes fixated on Takeo.

Some while ago, Takeo had said he wanted to travel the country after their graduation. Back then, he had also half-jokingly half-seriously asked whether Nao wanted to join him.

Nao hadn't seen it as a realistic option. How could he leave a place he had only ever known as his past, present, and future?

But this time, Takeo had shown him something he hadn't known before.

The strength to trust in and achieve your goals on your own.

Takeo was filled with the confidence and motivation given to him by his unyielding passion. He had never given up on himself, even after being wronged over and over again, degraded to this hellhole of a school.

How could Nao keep accepting his own misery if there was someone right beside him pushing against fate head-on?

Thus, he could see it. A future.

An apartment, a job, and university. Every morning when the warm rays of sun peeked through the window, drawing soft shadows and highlights across the wall and furniture, the two of them would get up, not afraid of what the day would bring, but rather excited for it.

They'd eat breakfast at the small table in the kitchen, the four walls surrounding them comfortably, snuggling them close and showing them just how beautiful an ordinary life could be. They'd get dressed and ready for work or university, prepared to grab the day by all of its opportunities instead of running away from them.

And in the evening when the sun was heading to bed, moon and stars growing more prominent and more beautiful in the sky, they'd chat about their day. The ups and downs. The happy things and the sad things. And hence, all of the sad things would not feel as bad anymore. Once spoken within the four walls of a home, the heaviness of them would subside. In the end, all that remained were the comforting words of a lover, the arms that shielded one from everything bad, and the sweet, sweet feeling of not having to endure this world alone. No matter how sappy or cheesy it might sound, Nao craved it. He craved it like sugar on a diet, like water in a drought. He'd never thought he could yearn for something like this; even imagining it seemed like an absolute impossibility. But now he could see it. He could feel it. The urge to love and be loved—unconditionally, purely.

His heart welled with so many emotions. It was almost too much. He wanted to grab Takeo by the shoulders and never let him go. Because right in front of him was that future he had just imagined.

Nao looked at him—his eyes were filled with so many profound feelings, barely containable in a single person's heart.

His lips must have unconsciously curved into a smile because Takeo suddenly cocked his head to the side in playful curiosity.

"Why are you smiling?" he asked, and at once broke out into a wide grin as if he'd just had an epiphany. "Because you looked at me and realised how lucky you are to have such a handsome boyfriend?" Cheekily, he pushed his hair back and leaned closer to Nao. "Want to take a closer look?"

"Dream on. I thought about lunch later."

"Then take a good look at me now." He smirked and leaned even closer.

Nao cupped his face and looked deeply into those bright eyes. He tilted his own head to the side and commented nonchalantly, "Indeed. Very handsome."

Takeo's grin grew even wider.

Nao couldn't hear it, but Takeo's heart was dancing excitedly inside his chest.

Clearing his throat and trying to compose himself, Takeo took a good look at Nao too and replied just as smoothly, "The one in front of me is not bad either."

"Just 'not bad either'?" Nao asked a little taken aback.

Takeo smiled, amused. "Do you want me to tell you that you're handsome too?"

Shyly, Nao averted his eyes. "No…"

Takeo chuckled, and then with every other word, he planted a sweet peck across his boyfriend's face. "Good. Because even a word like beautiful wouldn't do you justice."

Immediately, Nao's whole face was burning red, and embarrassed, he covered it with his hands. "Stop that," he choked out, and Takeo laughed. "What? Kissing you? I thought you liked that when we slept with each—"

He couldn't finish his sentence as he was rather roughly shut up by Nao's hands covering his mouth.

"You're really out for blood today, aren't you?" Nao exclaimed loudly, and Takeo just laughed behind his hands. Gently, he grabbed his wrists and pulled them down.

"I'll stop," he chuckled heartily. "I'll stop. Just don't smother me, please."

Embarrassed, Nao withdrew his hands and coughed quietly. Thinking about their night together in the hostel made his cheeks flush in equal parts of excitement and shyness.

"Whatever." Nao cleared his throat. "I would like it if we went on another trip together once we graduate…provided you'd like that too."

Takeo smiled brightly. "I'd love to," he chimed immediately. "You know I want to travel the country anyway. It'll be even better if you tag along."

Nao nodded. "Good."

Suddenly, Takeo sighed deeply, propping his chin on his hand. "Unfortunately, there's still over a whole semester until our graduation. I don't know if I can wait that long."

He exhaled theatrically and Nao snorted. "You'll get over it," he jibed, and Takeo directed his gaze at him. With sparkling eyes, Takeo observed him, already making up his mind for the next tease.

"Soon the summer holidays will start, and then we won't get to see each other at school every day. Are you sure you'll be able to survive that long without seeing your stunning boyfriend's face every day?"

Nao huffed an amused laugh. He leaned forward and rested a hand on Takeo's cheek; his skin felt soft and warm beneath the tips of his fingers. "You're right. How will I be able to survive without seeing this brazen face teasing me every day? I might even forget what you look like."

"That'd be really tragic," Takeo murmured and scooted closer to fill the gap between them.

At once, he sealed Nao's lips with his.

Nao's heart thumped gleefully in his chest. His torso was filled with a wave of warmth and he could feel the tips of his fingers tingling with excitement.

In moments like these, his mind seemed to be only capable of thinking about the person in front of him. His body and mind screamed *Takeo* over and over again.

Even without voicing it, Nao knew that he could never forget this gentle, fair face of his boyfriend. From those striking, deep brown eyes, his sharp, full eyebrows, long, straight nose, to his curved lips—it was a face that expressed nothing but comfort and security to Nao.

He could recognise this person in an ocean of imposters, because no matter how many, no one could ever come even close to the way it made Nao's heart cheer in happiness when he laid his gaze upon this person. Like an enchantment that only existed between the two of them.

As their lips parted and Takeo leaned back, his eyes grazing Nao ever so delicately, it was obvious that both of them shared that same sentiment.

Their farewell was accompanied by the usual heartache. It always felt a little tragic to their hearts when they had to split up to head home for the day.

Nao sighed deeply without realising it as he turned around to walk home.

He was glad that they had at least the study room in which they could meet without anyone interfering. What had once started as a room simply for teaching and studying was now a secret little shelter for both of them.

If only Hana could call them and tell them she'd found the tape—then Nao would be able to finally relax...

Tuesday, the third day after their departure from Tokyo, ended, and Wednesday dawned.

It was a leisurely day with nothing much going on. The situation at Nao's home had temporarily calmed down as well. He left for school early in the morning.

Eyelids drooping, he tried to listen to the lesson. When his class finally ended, he was elated to meet with Takeo again at their usual place.

It had become a habit, and almost automatically, Nao packed his bag, ready to venture up to the third floor. Yet, as he was just about to leave, Takeo intercepted him.

With an apologetic expression, he smiled at him. "I have to cancel our date. I've got something important to take care of at home. I'm really, very sorry!"

Nao looked at Takeo with widened eyes. "Is everything okay with your family?"

Takeo quickly waved his hand, flashing him a bashful smile. "Yeah, it's nothing big. My brother asked me to help him out with the police report he's filed. Nothing major. He just wants to take me with him to the station to give a statement."

"Okay, then I guess we'll see each other tomorrow?"

Takeo nodded confidently. "Yeah. Again, I'm really sorry I have to run off so suddenly. I'll make it up to you."

Nao smiled gently and shook his head. "What's there to make up for? It's good if you help out your brother with the report. Just...don't downplay what happened because Katsu has us by our necks. Maybe the police can be of help with this."

Takeo nodded. "I won't." He smiled weakly and turned around to leave. In the last second, Nao reached for his hand and effectively stopped him from moving. Startled, Takeo spun back around.

"Call me when you're back home and tell me how it went, okay?"

Almost relieved, Takeo flashed him another smile, nodded again, and then left. Nao watched him disappear through the door. After he had left, Nao looked down at his own hand. He could still feel the sensation of the other's skin brushing against his. But weirdly enough, Takeo's palm had been covered in cold sweat.

With furrowed brows, Nao glanced at his own. Was he that nervous because of the statement...?

Well, Takeo would tell him how it had turned out once he was finished.

Nao tried to shake the other thoughts off and finished packing his bag. Roughly, he shoved in his books and papers, and then heaved the handle over his shoulder. When he turned around to leave, something suddenly sprang into the corner of his eye.

At the back of the classroom, on top of Takeo's desk, lay a lone bag. Alone and forgotten by its owner, it sat on the wooden surface, waiting to be picked up.

He must have forgotten it in his hurry.

On impulse, Nao grabbed it and decided to run after Takeo to give it back to him.

There were most certainly important belongings like his student ID and keys inside, so Nao should act quickly. Fortunately, it had only been a few minutes since the other had left, so he couldn't have come far.

With both bags on his back, Nao ran out of the school.

He squeezed his way through the mob of students who were also trying to leave. Once Nao had exited the school grounds, he ran north, the direction Takeo usually took to walk back home.

Nao kept his eyes wide open to spot the familiar frame of his boyfriend, yet strangely enough, he seemed to have been swallowed by the ground.

Dumbfounded, Nao tightened his grip around the bag. Where was he? He couldn't have come that far, right? There had only been a few minutes' difference between their departures.

He looked around the empty street, puzzled.

Should he continue following Takeo's way home in the hope of maybe running into him or just leave it? Nao could also bring the bag back to the classroom, in case Takeo returned to collect it once he noticed it had been left behind.

It was probably smarter than taking it home with him.

Once he had made up his mind, Nao turned back around to head to the school. Though this was the moment, his core was shaken and his heart seized by indescribable fear as an eerily familiar voice drifted toward his ears.

At once, all the hairs on Nao's neck stood up and he felt chills run down his spine.

He hadn't heard this voice often, yet the impression it had made on him was inevitable. Just like footprints on cement, it had left an eternal scar on the ground—one to never fade, to always remind the builder of their deeds.

But it couldn't be that person, could it…?

His heart torn between agitation and curiosity, Nao decided to look into it.

He walked toward the sound. All of Nao's reflexes and instincts were on high alert, stretched taut like a bow before its imminent release, and even though he didn't want to accept it, he knew from experience that his hunches were mostly correct.

Very quietly, Nao followed the voice coaxing him to investigate. It led him into a smaller side street, and as he turned around the corner, he was greeted with the sight he had feared the most since that horrifying night in the alley.

His eyes fell upon Katsu Nishimura.

Beside him stood a few of his lackeys, and in the middle of them was…*Takeo*.

Instantly, Nao's breath hitched and his heart shook.

Takeo didn't seem hurt yet. He stood next to Katsu, his eyes narrowed and brows furrowed.

Nao's lips trembled, yet he exclaimed a very strong and clear, "Takeo."

The latter turned around, and as his eyes locked onto his boyfriend, they widened in shock.

"Nao," he breathed, his voice feeble and agitated.

Nao's eyes flickered between the two boys. "What's going on here?" he asked.

Katsu's sharp face lifted into a smile, and with an arm slung around Takeo's shoulders, he jeered at the newcomer. "Well,

well, well, this makes things a bit more complicated," he said, but didn't sound worried in the least.

At first, Nao didn't understand, but then it suddenly clicked.

His hands tightened into fists. "Let him go! I was the one who lost your drugs, so why don't you take me instead?"

Katsu snorted dryly. "What's this sudden chivalry? Did you watch too many movies, brat? The world doesn't work that way. And this isn't about the drug deal anymore. Both of you have managed to piss me off even more than that!"

The grip around Takeo's shoulders tightened, his fingers dug into the fabric of his sweater jacket and further into the skin beneath. Nao's gaze flickered to Takeo, who looked at him with an unmoving face. It was drained of all colour, shimmering almost grey.

Nao gritted his teeth. *This idiot! This idiot! This idiot!* He was never going to the police station with his brother! It had only been a cover-up to throw Nao off.

He didn't know how, but somehow Katsu must have contacted him in the last twenty-four hours and threatened him into meeting them here.

And knowing Takeo, he would have never told Nao about it, because he knew there was no way Nao would ever let him go alone.

That idiot just wanted to shoulder all the burden himself!

He had wanted to protect Nao.

But Nao wanted nothing more than to strangle him for it in that moment.

He took a trembling breath. "What…do you mean?" he asked.

"What I mean!?" Katsu exclaimed loudly, his eyes sparking with flames and frenzy. "You seriously thought I wouldn't find out!?" He pointed at Nao with his free hand. "You thought I wouldn't find out about you two dirty rats traveling to Tokyo looking for the copy of that tape!?"

Nao's heart dropped hearing his spewed words.

"Do you think I'd be stupid enough not to notice you two sneaking around!? You must be dumber than I thought!" Katsu laughed mirthlessly. "I warned you not to deceive me! Especially this one right here!" He pulled Takeo closer. "This is his second time trying to rat me out! The first time I only broke his wrist as a warning, but today I won't be as gracious. Not even ten broken bones will be enough to make up for this dumbass's stupidity."

Katsu sneered at Nao. "Do you wonder why you've never received that tape? It's because I paid a visit to that bitch myself and destroyed it personally." He laughed loudly. "It's been quite a while since I beat up a woman, but it's almost as fun as beating men."

Nao's heart trembled wildly. His legs felt like they were about to break away beneath him, but there was no way he could just bend right here.

With knitted brows, he stared at Katsu. "Okay…then you caught us trying to deceive you. But instead of revenge, why don't you let us work even harder? I can work for you again! I can make even more deals! Just leave him alone and I'll become your pawn."

Katsu grinned, amused, his eyes glinting with malice. After a dry snort, he retorted, "Nice effort. I like your desperation. But I have no intention of clashing with your stupid-ass grandfather again. You're lucky to have such an influential family or I would've taken you with me as well! Also, this brat has already betrayed me twice! I am kind enough to believe in second chances, but this dumbass was stupid enough to squander both of his. A rat is a rat. No matter how often you train them, they'll eventually try to bite off your finger. Before that happens, I'll rather drown that rat myself."

Nao felt his heart ache in fear and frustration. With all of these pent-up emotions, he turned to his boyfriend. "Takeo! You can't do this!" he shouted at him. "I know you didn't tell me about this because you didn't want to pull me in further. But that's not fair of you! Your responsibilities are mine too! Don't try to act tough because you can!"

Upon Nao's fervent speech, Takeo clenched his fists. He pressed his lips together, and with a soft, yet determined gaze, he looked at him; the spark of a reassuring smile was hidden inside his eyes. "It's fine, Nao. I'll be okay."

Nao was speechless. Who was he to spew such nonsensical words!?

He wanted to storm forward, he wanted to rip Takeo away from Katsu and tell him how he should finally stop with this charade of the fearless warrior!

Why did Takeo always have to play the hero? Why did he always want to shoulder the burden alone? Why did he have to be such an idiotic, hardheaded, selfless person?

Nao was about to punch those answers out of him when he felt someone roughly grabbing his arm. He turned around and behind him stood one of Katsu's lackeys, confining him in an iron grip.

Nao wanted to tear himself free, but it was like fighting against a mountain.

"What are we going to do with him?" the lackey asked Katsu, who just dismissively waved his hand.

"We can't take him along with us because of his damn grandfather, but he'll only cause trouble if we let him run free. Just give him a good knock-out until we're finished with our business."

Nao struggled. He wanted to break free, he wanted to scream. With feverish eyes, he glared at Takeo, who gazed back at him, his own eyes filled with the utmost pain.

It was unbearable for Takeo to see his boyfriend being treated this way, but in his mind, this was still a better option than having him in Katsu's close proximity as well.

If this was what it took to keep him safe, then it had to be.

Takeo wanted to take care of this himself, so the two of them could live their happy ending together.

Nao yanked and tore, but he could not free himself before being struck down by a heavy blow against the back of his head.

It was an almost instant knock-out.

His legs faltered beneath him like those of a paper doll. Within the blink of an eye, the world had gone black and his consciousness slipped away.

The next time Nao opened his eyes, he looked at the reddish sky above him. Dark clouds passed by and a flock of birds traveled through the heavens.

His body felt fuzzy and the back of his head was aching faintly. His eyelids were heavy and kept drooping down, his lashes fanning his cheeks lightly. The edge of his vision was blurred, his mind still painfully slow. It felt like his brain had been transformed into a puzzle he needed to solve first before he could recall what had happened to him.

It took a long while before his mind slowly cleared up and the fog in his head lifted.

The feeling in his limbs returned bit by bit, and at once, the memories flooded back. So sudden, it felt as though he were hit against the head all over again.

Startled, Nao sat up, but groaned almost immediately. His head began throbbing violently and the world spun. He held his head with both hands as he waited for his view to steady.

Very slowly, the carousel stopped, yet the dull pounding in his skull persisted.

Nao looked up with a groan and tried to comprehend his situation.

He sat in a bush at the side of a street—discarded like trash. The sun had already set behind the horizon and all that was left was a bloodied sky, tainted by its final reach for freedom.

How long had he been out cold? Judging by the dying day, it must have been at least a couple of hours.

Aching all over, Nao tried to stand up. That was when he noticed he was still holding on to something with his right hand. He looked down and found Takeo's forgotten bag on his lap.

Nao's chest clenched in fear.

They had taken him… They had taken him away.

— Chapter 29 —

Nao ran home like a maniac.

The moment the doors of the elevator opened, he dashed forward and ripped the telephone from the counter. With shaking fingers, he dialled Hana's number.

The phone rang and rang, excruciatingly slowly. With every unanswered ring, Nao's anxiety grew deeper and deeper.

He dug his nails so forcefully into the cold plastic that it felt like they could break off.

Finally, someone answered the call. Nao sucked in a relieved breath, only to be shattered by the connection being broken off.

The person on the other side had hung up.

For a second, Nao stared aghast at the phone, then instantly dialled the same number again.

It rang and rang again, and when the call was finally taken anew, it was just as quickly cut off again.

In his panic, Nao repeated this over and over. He called and called, dialled and dialled. But the person on the other side of the line hung up on his calls every single time.

Obviously, Hana did not want to talk to him.

Did this mean that what Katsu had said was the truth? Had she really been beaten up and threatened by him again? Had their last line of hope truly snapped?

Nao dropped to the ground. He still held on to the phone with both hands as though his life depended on it. After a second of trying to gather his thoughts, he called again. But this time it was not Hana's number.

With stiff and numb fingers, he entered Takeo's number into the device.

Who knew, maybe he was already back at home. Maybe Katsu had let him go! Or he could have escaped his cruel claws! Maybe…maybe it was just a big misunderstanding!? Nao clung to delusional hopes like that.

He pressed the receiver against his ear as the connection was built up. His breath was growing ragged, his heart thumped in pure fear, and his limbs had lost all feeling in them.

Yet, with all of his remaining strength, he pricked up his ears and listened intently to the phone ringing.

It went on for a long time.

Like an eternity, the hollow ringing echoed inside his skull—a desperate scream in the desert, which could only resonate across the vast sand dunes and never found a living being to hear it.

He waited and waited. Nao couldn't bring himself to break the connection. Not if his despairing calls could be answered at any moment, extinguishing the wildfires of panic ravaging his heart with a single voice. But it didn't matter. No one granted him release… His pleas stayed unanswered.

Was it because they didn't hear the phone? Or was no one at home? Maybe the phone had just been placed in an unusual spot and no one could find it to pick up?

Maybe if he tried once more, Takeo would pick up!

So, Nao called again. Just like with Hana, he didn't stop. Over and over again his fingers entered the number into the phone— relentless and perpetual, like a mantra made to give him hope.

He was let down every time.

No one was there to pick up. His anxiety couldn't be tamed; instead, it just flared up higher.

Calling didn't help in any way. So maybe Nao should just see for himself.

Staggering, he rose to his feet and placed the phone back on the table.

He had to make sure with his own two eyes.

He was about to dash forward when he remembered that it was already late evening, and no buses ran this late to the desolate neighbourhood where Takeo lived.

He gritted his teeth. Then he had to walk. That was also okay! He just had to find out where he was!

Mind set, Nao headed toward the door when he was stopped by a voice booming from the other side of the apartment.

"What's all this noise!?" they screamed, and Nao flinched instinctively.

He turned his head to see his father stalking out of the living room. "Did *you* just keep making all those calls!?" he bellowed, and Nao stared at him.

Then he took a deep breath, gathered his courage, and continued with his stubborn walk to the door.

"Where do you think you're going!?" his father shouted and seized his son's arm. His fingers dug so violently into Nao's flesh that he could feel the blood circulation stagnate. Nao clenched his jaw and shook him off.

"I have something important to do," he retorted, surprisingly calm yet strong in tone.

His father, disturbed by his son's unusual demeanour, stepped forward and grabbed him once again.

"You're talking about your cryptic important business again?" he chided. "Who do you think you are? The president or something!?" Roughly, he yanked Nao back. "Do you think I'm stupid!? I won't let you run rampant again! You only want to go out to deal some more or run away again! Just because I've been too soft on you until now doesn't mean I'll let you have your way now. Go back to your room and don't dare set another foot outside today!"

Nao gritted his teeth with such force it felt like they could be ground to ashes. With all of this pent-up anger and frustration bundled up, he spun around and glowered at his father.

For a split second, the latter appeared to be taken aback by his son's deathly glare; only to become even more enraged afterward by his blunt audacity to stare at his own parent like that.

In the blink of an eye, veins bulged on his forehead and his hand cut even deeper into his son's skin. "You ungrateful brat!" he pressed out between gritted teeth and then yanked him along.

In three big steps, they had reached Nao's bedroom. He ripped open the door, he flung his son inside and shut the door.

Nao slumped to the ground, hands and knees chafing against the floor. He instantly jumped up again and ran to the door, but his father was already blocking the exit.

Furiously, Nao threw himself against the door. He crashed into the piece of wood, yet it hardly moved more than a few millimeters. His father, holding the other side, was just too strong for Nao.

Full of frustration, Nao screamed and shook the handle. It didn't budge.

"Let me out!" he screamed, but his father didn't move. Instead, he called out for Nao's mother.

"Kaori!" he exclaimed, and after a few seconds, there was a clear voice answering him.

"What is it?" she asked.

"Bring me the key to this door!" Tsuyoshi Miyamoto shouted and Nao could have exploded in pure rage.

He crashed into the door again. He tried pushing down the handle, he kicked the wood, but it all amounted to nothing.

He was just physically too weak to break through.

Realising his body's defeat in a situation like this, his frustration and agitation grew even bigger.

He had been too powerless to retrieve Takeo from Katsu's clutches when he'd been right in front of him. And now he was too weak to simply break out of this room and find him.

Why couldn't he help him…? Why was he always too powerless or too weak?

Nao had always known that he was a failure…but why now? Why couldn't he just succeed this once? He just wanted to save the person he loved… Was this too much to ask for…?

Tears of anger brimmed in his eyes, and with both fists, Nao started banging on the door. "Let me out!" he screamed in raw desperation—his chest aflame, his vocal cords taut. "Let me out! Let me out! Let me out! I have to find him!"

He repeated those pleas over and over again. His banging didn't stop and soon his fists were numb and swollen.

He bellowed in anger, but his father didn't spare him a single reaction. With a clanking noise, he heard the door being locked from the other side, and Nao knew that he would never let him go.

He slid along the door onto the ground. He drew his legs close to his chest and buried his head between his knees.

He was stuck.

For a fleeting second, he wondered if Toyo could retrieve the key and get him out. But just as quickly, Nao realised that his father would never leave the key so easily accessible. Especially now that Toyo was acting so out of the usual, he would not just let it out unguarded.

No, if Nao didn't suddenly grow stronger, there was no way he could get out of here.

He clasped his arms over his head, pushing it deeper between his legs.

He was such a failure…such a failure and so useless…

Nightfall came, and the darkness crawled by excruciatingly slowly. Nao stayed crouched on the ground the entire night.

A few times, he must have nodded off; the weight of his weary body pulled his head to the side. It startled him, and he quickly shot up again, rebalancing himself.

Despite those mere seconds, he didn't sleep at all. His mind was too tumultuous for that. Like a hornet's nest buzzing manically inside his head.

Sleep was for those at peace or seeking refuge. Nao, though, was preparing a cruel war and running away was unthinkable.

From his shelter by the door, he watched the dark sky slowly lighten. Grey rays of feeble light slanted through the window and a sky filled with a turmoil of grey clouds announced the new day.

Nao watched the previous day fade into nothingness.

Following the rising sun, he could make out the sounds of living inside the apartment. His parents must have woken up by now, and soon Toyo should get ready for school, which meant they should also unlock his door very soon. In the end, even worse than him acting up or selling illegal substances was the very idea of him missing a single day of school.

And Nao should be proven right. After a while of this daily commotion bustling outside, he heard a key being pushed into the lock and turned around.

The door opened with a creak and the other person was greeted by the sight of Nao sitting on the ground, shoulders slumped forward, hair and clothes disheveled.

Tonelessly, Nao lifted his head and locked eyes with his father. He observed his son quietly for a few seconds before speaking.

"Did you finally calm down?" he asked.

Nao didn't respond.

His father scoffed, annoyed, and turned around. While walking away, he just let out a dismissive, "Get ready for school. Don't even think about coming too late."

In his confinement, Nao had had a lot of time to think about his next steps.

His limbs stiff and numb, he rose to his feet. He had been locked up and slumped against the door for the last ten hours.

He was hungry and thirsty, and he needed to use the restroom, but none of that was the top priority in his mind right now.

Nao simply changed his clothes, took his bag and left for school.

He had failed yesterday. But he had not given up. He would not rest until he knew Takeo was safe.

He entered the school, looking for his boyfriend. When he couldn't find him there, he immediately whirled around and left.

Nao took the next bus to the desolate neighbourhood outside the city.

Since he'd been here before, he found Takeo's house fairly easily this time. The doors and windows had been repaired after his last visit.

The small front yard was lit up by a pleasant three-tone chime as Nao rang the doorbell.

A few seconds later, the door was opened by a tall man. He looked strikingly similar to Takeo, and Nao was immediately aware that this must be his older brother Mamoru.

Except for the eyes and jaw, both of them looked shockingly alike. Contrary to Takeo, Mamoru had thin, slanted eyes like a fox as well as a protruding jaw. He was also broader and more muscular than his little brother.

The man observed the boy in front of him with narrowed eyes.

"Who are you?" Mamoru asked, his voice was deep and smooth.

Nao didn't have time for such formalities, though. He'd rather just plunge directly to the point.

"Is Takeo here?" he asked bluntly.

The man was a bit taken aback by this strange student's sudden question, yet answered after a moment of unsure hesitation nonetheless.

"No, he's not. Are you his classmate? Do you know where he has been overnight?"

The words struck immediate fear into Nao's heart. "He hasn't come home since yesterday…?"

Mamoru shook his head. "He didn't. And I can't reach him. You must be a classmate of his, right? Do you know where he went?"

Nao's mouth had gone dry during Mamoru's reply. He could feel all of the blood leaving his face. As pale as a ghost and unable to speak, Nao shook his head.

Takeo had been missing since Katsu had taken him with them…

Not even his brother had had any contact with him since then. Nao's heart lurched in fear. He could feel his knees weaken as this nightmare became tangible reality.

With all of his might, Nao swallowed the lump in his throat and forced his numb, lifeless lips into motion.

"We have to go to the police immediately," he said with grave seriousness.

If anyone else had stepped up to his door and randomly told him to report his brother missing, Mamoru would have probably thought they were crazy—but upon seeing this person's eerie graveness and adamant conviction, he couldn't help but put some trust into their words.

"I guess this means you haven't seen him either…" Mamoru replied.

"Something really bad happened. But we have no time to talk about it now. I'll tell you on the way to the police station."

Mamoru pressed his lips together, and after another moment of careful consideration, he decided to believe this strange classmate for now.

"Wait here for a second. I have to take care of someone. We can leave afterward."

Nao understood immediately. He assumed it was about their mother, who presumably wasn't in a condition to care for herself.

Mamoru vanished back inside, and after about ten minutes, they finally headed out.

They took the next bus to the closest police station.

Nao was so caught up in his fear that he didn't even grasp the peculiarity of the situation. Having never met his boyfriend's brother face to face before, here they were, sharing a double seat on a bus on their way to the city. If his mind hadn't been so completely consumed by worry and fear, he might have even laughed out loud. But this wasn't a laughing matter right now.

Something must have happened to Takeo. Either he was still held captive by Katsu, or he was too injured to come back home. Whatever it was, it had to be horrible.

Nao swore to himself that if he ever came face to face with Katsu again, he would repay that bastard tenfold!

During their ride, Nao quickly briefed Mamoru on what had happened. Mamoru's face grew paler and paler with every word. In the end, he could only blankly stare out of the window.

He clutched the fabric of his jacket, knuckles turning white.

"This is really bad…" he said, his voice hollow.

Nao nodded, feeling just as dejected.

They sat in silence for a while until Mamoru suddenly turned toward him. A little hesitantly, he asked, "Are you…by chance Nao Miyamoto?"

Nao was startled. How did he know his name? He looked at the other with wide eyes, yet still nodded. "Yes…"

Mamoru managed a small smile. "Takeo often mentioned that name at home. And since you came to our house to tell me about the situation, I assumed it might be you…"

"Oh," Nao stammered, taken aback by the revelation that Takeo talked about him at home. He was pensive for a few seconds but ultimately couldn't withhold the question. "What…what did he say about me?"

Mamoru huffed an amused laugh. "Don't worry, he only spoke exceptionally well of you. He said you two have spent a lot of time together and he laughs a lot when he's with you. I've noticed this as well. Since he started mentioning you, he seemed much happier than before." Mamoru's smile broadened. "You two must be really close friends."

Nao coughed awkwardly at the last comment. "…Yeah." Quickly, he tried to control his facial expression, then added a little shyly, "I can only speak highly of him as well. He has a good heart and great ambitions."

Mamoru laughed again, though this time it sounded a bit dry. "He definitely has a good heart, but he still causes a lot of trouble. Last week, he just vanished over the weekend! I only found a note from him on the kitchen table saying he has important things to take care of. I promise he'll be the reason I go bald! He only means to do good, but still manages to stir up a lot of trouble along the way."

Unfortunately, Nao couldn't argue with that. Takeo had a talent for throwing himself into danger; just like Nao.

He sighed internally.

After about twenty minutes, they finally arrived in the city.

The unlikely pair walked into the police station.

One thing must be made clear: Mamoru didn't fumble with important matters. The moment they stood in front of the counter, he immediately ordered, with unmatched poise and confidence, that they speak to the next available police officer to file a report. Even Nao was taken aback by his nonchalant adamancy. It reminded him a little of Takeo.

After a brief waiting period, they were gestured to an officer's desk. Both Mamoru and Nao sat before him and looked expectantly at the middle-aged man.

He gazed at the two with bored indifference and then asked very groggily, "How can I help you?"

"I want to report a missing person," Mamoru replied immediately. "He is presumably the victim of a violent crime."

Still, with the same apathy, the police officer nodded. He started typing on his keyboard, his fingers pecking the keys with a tired heaviness.

"Please state your name and relation to the person you want to report."

"Mamoru Iwasaki. I'm his brother and legal guardian."

The officer's fingers moved across the keyboard and he looked at Nao. "And you?"

Nao pressed his lips together, then replied confidently, "Nao Miyamoto. I'm his boyfriend."

The man's fingers froze above the keys. For a few seconds, he was torn out of his apathy and seemed shaken. Then, as though nothing had happened, his hands descended again and Nao saw him type the word "Acquaintance" into the report.

Nao's fists clenched, but he remained quiet. Though he didn't look up, he could still feel Mamoru's widened eyes staring at him from the side. A few things suddenly seemed to click in his mind, yet he decided to keep his mouth shut for now.

The police officer sighed exhaustedly. "Then please state the missing person's name, age, and the time of their disappearance."

"Takeo Iwasaki. He's seventeen years old and has been missing since yesterday afternoon," Mamoru complied calmly.

The officer's hands froze again, and with a pointed glance, he looked up. "So it hasn't even been twenty-four hours?" The obvious nitpicking in his tone couldn't be ignored.

Immediately, Mamoru's brows furrowed and he stared at the man with narrowed eyes. "That's right. But I am led to believe that he has become a gang's target. In fact, the boy beside me has seen him being taken away by them." His voice was still calm, but nevertheless strong and sharp at the same time. "What was that gang leader's name again?"

"Katsu Nishimura," Nao answered promptly.

Mamoru nodded strongly. "See. I want you to instantly look for my brother and that Katsu guy!"

The officer sighed. "You can tell me what you've witnessed. But according to the data on my computer, Takeo Iwasaki has been previously charged with cases of drug possession and violent assault on classmates. Which leads *me* to believe that he might not be a victim but rather the offender."

Nao's heart blazed in fury. His fists clenched even tighter, and he wanted to jump up and scream at that nonsense-spewing man—but to his own surprise, Mamoru was faster.

He leapt up so swiftly that his chair was pushed backward with an ear-deafening screech as the legs scratched against the linoleum floor. With an outstretched finger, he pointed furiously at the man in front of him. "First, none of that bullshit is true. Second, even if it were, it has nothing to do with this case! My brother has been abducted by some lowlife criminals, he is still a minor and a victim in this case, so if that badge on your chest isn't just some cheap accessory, then it is *your* fucking job to find him!"

The officer was startled by the sudden accusations. With widened eyes, he stared at the fuming man. Nao could see a film of sweat building between his thinning strands of hair.

Quickly, he tried to recompose himself and gestured for the other to sit back down.

"Please calm down, Mr. Iwasaki," he said. "This is still a police station. Please refrain from making a scene."

Mamoru took a heavy breath. His hands were twisted into fists, veins were popping on the back of his hands, and his face was reddened from anger. Nao could basically hear him grinding his teeth, but after a few seconds, he sat back down nevertheless.

The officer took a tissue and started dabbing his forehead with a stressed sigh. "Your brother's background is rather…risky, and it hasn't even been twenty-four hours yet. So if he does not show up until the end of the day, I suggest you come back and submit an official report. Until then, I ask you to stay calm and not act hastily."

Mamoru's hands were shaking. Nao expected him to jump up in another fit of rage, but surprisingly, he just scoffed and rose calmly to his feet. "For your own wellbeing, I hope he'll resurface unharmed," Mamoru pressed out between closed teeth.

"Watch what you say. This could very well be seen as threatening a police officer, Mr. Iwasaki."

"If that's what it takes to get your asses to work."

Before the officer could mutter a single word in return, Mamoru had already turned around and left. Nao got up as well and followed the other outside without sparing the officer so much as a second glance.

He found Mamoru leaning against a handrail outside the station. The latter was breathing heavily, his face still flushed in anger.

Nao tensed his jaw and walked up to him. "What are we going to do now?" he asked.

Mamoru looked at him, his brows furrowed deeply. "I guess we have no other option but to wait till the end of the day... Maybe he will really show up by then."

"But...but..." Nao stammered angrily. "Katsu is not someone to joke with! I'm not sure what he did to him...but knowing him, it has to be really bad!"

Mamoru stared bleakly at the sky. For a moment, he watched an airplane fly in and out of the thick blanket of clouds, then sighed. His gaze fell back on the boy, although now it was laced with traces of dejected softness and pitying empathy. "Nao," he said, his voice deep. "I can see you worry about Takeo just as much as I do. If I could, I would force those lazy pigs to immediately send out twenty troops to search for Takeo and that Katsu guy, and make them work until they either find them or pass out from exhaustion... But as you grow older, you realise that sometimes there are situations where your hands are tied.

"As long as the police won't cooperate, there's nothing we can do. We'll have to wait until the others start moving first."

Nao could feel his hands shake. It wasn't from fear, however, but from anger.

"That's bullshit!" he exclaimed.

Mamoru looked at him with a pained smile, which infuriated Nao even more. "What do you want to do, Nao?" he asked sympathetically. "Find him yourself? Search every single house in the city until you find him?"

Nao clenched his fists. "If that's what I need to do."

Mamoru laughed dryly. He reached out and gently patted his shoulder. "You're obviously still a child. And surprisingly similar to Takeo at that; always reaching for the stars." Suddenly,

Mamoru's smile faded as if he'd just remembered something, and he gaped at Nao with comically wide eyes.

"What you said inside...about you and Takeo...is that true?"

Nao nodded confidently and Mamoru's expression grew even more baffled.

He took his hand off Nao's shoulder and seemed deep in thought. It was a while before he spoke again. "I...I didn't know Takeo is...is..."

...*gay*, Nao completed the sentence in his head. Thus, he prepared himself to defend Takeo with his whole heart, but to his surprise, Mamoru just started to laugh quietly.

He slapped his forehead with his palm and looked at Nao with a smile. "No wonder he always seemed so excited when he talked about you. I'm really an idiot for not noticing. Ha ha..."

Mamoru observed Nao in silence, then broke into a warm smile. "Let's grab something to eat as soon as Takeo is back, all right? All three of us. Once this situation is over, I'd really like to get to know you better."

It was spoken with such sincerity that Nao was deeply startled. He looked at Takeo's brother with wide eyes, not having expected such a pleasant reaction. Somehow he managed to nod. "Okay..."

Mamoru nodded back. "But first...let's focus on how to bring Takeo back."

— Chapter 30 —

Nao was inevitably losing his mind.

With both feet firmly on the ground, a pen clutched tightly in his hand, and his gaze unfocused as he stared at the teacher and the board in front of him, he let the lesson flow past him.

He pressed the pen firmly between his fingers, the inside of his hand already aching from the metal digging into his skin; Nao barely noticed it.

It was Friday: the third day after Takeo's disappearance. Yet there was still no trace of him.

The same day Nao and Mamoru had visited the police station, Mamoru had gone back there again in the evening. As Takeo still hadn't shown up and the twenty-four hour mark had passed, he filed an official missing person report.

It was easy to tell that none of the police officers took the case seriously. For them, the data on their computer spoke louder than words. Takeo was a juvenile offender in their database. Who knew why he really might have disappeared? Probably to scheme more crimes and harass innocent people. This was the person they pictured in their minds.

Trash, far away from redemption.

Nao started shaking in anger just thinking about it.

Those disgusting pigs! Takeo was in danger. He had been abducted by some sadist and no one had seen a trace of him ever since.

These thoughts thrashed wildly in Nao's mind. He clutched the pen even harder until it drew blood. A drop of crimson swelled in his palm and dripped onto the surface of the desk. He didn't even feel the pain. How could he? How could he care about something so trivial when he didn't know what was happening to his boyfriend right now?

In fact, how could he just sit here in school, listening to the teacher and writing down notes, while Takeo's desk had been empty for two days?

How could he just live his life, calling Mamoru several times a day, asking for news that never came?

Was he really that powerless?

Nao's chest heaved and fell heavily.

Mamoru had told him over and over again that their hands were tied. They couldn't do anything. They could only wait for the police to find him. But this was the other problem. They didn't care about Takeo! They saw him as nothing but a criminal who had run away to pursue illegal activities. How could Nao put Takeo's safety in hands like these?

How could he stay still when they only wanted to find him to prove that he was the horrible person in their minds?

The real offender was still out there and not even on their radar. That lunatic Katsu Nishimura was as free as a bird and as invisible as a ghost. He was smart enough to never get caught, and pushed other people before the executioner in his stead. This was what he had done to Takeo. Put all the blame on him, taint him with his dirty hands and bloodied conscience, and afterward live with the purity of a white vest.

He was a snake coaxing his prey while simultaneously wrapping himself around their necks. And yet, in the eye of the law, he was but a harmless caterpillar.

Except for his victims, no one knew what dark evil was slumbering inside that cocoon. His venomous fangs always ready to dart out and drag his next prey with him.

Nao ground his teeth.

Katsu was out there. Free and joyous. Plus, he was probably the only person who knew of Takeo's whereabouts.

He was the criminal who had kidnapped him, and yet the police didn't even notice him.

How could Nao trust them when he knew who the offender was but no one listened to him!?

Mamoru kept saying their hands were tied, but how could Nao possibly just sit here and wait for all of this to play into Katsu's hands?

No, he couldn't let this happen. He couldn't let Katsu win again as he always did.

Nao was the only person who truly knew what had caused Takeo's disappearance. And that cause ran free until someone would finally stop him.

If the police didn't do it, then Nao had no choice but to act on his own.

His hands weren't tied—in fact, they were reaching for Katsu's throat.

He would find him. He would kill him. He would bring Takeo back.

The fury was boiling up in Nao's chest. His heart was tightly engulfed by pure wrath, its flames devouring him more and more with each passing second. Soon, there'd be nothing but hellfire left inside his chest.

But it was good this way. He needed hellfire to incinerate a demon.

Without any other thought than revenge in his mind, Nao rose to his feet. The rest of the class looked at him with wide eyes. But he didn't spare them a single glance.

Tonelessly, he turned around and walked toward the door. He could hear his teacher calling after him with irritated confusion.

"Miyamoto. Miyamoto! Where are you going? Class isn't over yet!"

That voice didn't even pass through the sea of flames enclosing his brain. There was only the deeply ingrained desire to find Takeo. Nothing else could pierce his mind right now.

Nao left the classroom and headed down the hallways toward the exit. But he didn't leave the school grounds. He just changed buildings instead.

As he walked across the empty courtyard, his eyes fell upon a pile of bricks that lay there for some construction work in the school yard.

Blood cold as ice, he grabbed one of the heavy bricks and entered the adjacent building.

He knew exactly where he was going.

With steps as heavy and crushing as an avalanche, he headed along the empty corridor. He walked upstairs, stalked down the hall and opened the door.

The gazes of twenty students flickered up to him. Eyes wide and tainted with surprise at the sudden guest, they stared at him. The teacher had also temporarily stopped talking to look at the new student. After a moment of silence, she inquired what he was doing here.

Nao didn't hear her.

He went straight for the person sitting in the middle of the classroom.

They didn't even know what was happening to them when they had already been thrown off the chair by a heavy fist.

The students screamed and jumped up from their seats, staring at the violent entrance in shock.

"Who are you? What are you doing?" the teacher screamed in terror, but Nao didn't respond.

He only had eyes for the person sitting on the ground in front of him.

Their eyes were round in shock, their face blanched, and the hands shook in fear.

Calmly, Nao crouched down in front of him, holding the brick firmly in his fist.

"Where's your brother?" he asked.

"W-what?" Sho stammered meekly.

"Where's your brother?" Nao repeated.

"I…I don't know," Sho stuttered, his lips quivering.

Nao seized him by his collar and threw his fist in his face. There was a loud crack and Nao felt something bend beneath his knuckles. As he retracted his fist, there was a gush of blood rushing out of Sho's nose, running down his mouth and chin.

It seemed that he had broken his nose with a clean punch, and Nao felt a twinge of satisfaction at the realisation.

Sho's gruesome face couldn't become uglier anyway. If anything at all, Nao had only done him a favour by having his face match his soul. Ugly and wretched.

He grabbed his collar and pulled Sho close, staring right into those frightened, pain-stricken eyes gawking at him.

"I don't believe you. You know where he is." Nao gritted his teeth. "Tell me."

Sho took a jagged breath. He opened his lips like a fish, inhaling and exhaling through his mouth as blood was still gushing out of his nostrils and dripping into his throat, tainting his teeth and tongue deep red.

"Why…why the hell should I tell you? You…you loser!"

He could barely finish his sentence before he received another punch. And after that a second and immediately a third one.

Blood gurgled out of him. He could hardly choke out any noises of pain before they were cut off by new ones.

Deep, jagged grunts crawled from the depths of his throat, like a swine during slaughter.

Nao didn't stop. He landed his fist in his face over and over; the blade stabbing the pig again and again.

The classroom had gone dead silent. Except for the gruesome sounds of skin and bones cracking and animalistic grunts, there was nothing, not even the sound of breathing. No one dared to make a single noise in the face of the maniac slaughtering a student.

After a while, Nao stilled. His knuckles were bruised and bloody from the continuous beating.

He took a deep breath, inhaling the air thick with the scent of blood and sweat.

"Where is he?" he panted, piercing Sho with his glare. "Where is your damn brother!?"

Sho coughed. Blood splattered across his front and he had trouble catching his breath. His pupils shook in terror as they fixated on Nao.

Finally, it seemed like the pig accepted its role. For once, it saw it was not the butcher but the flesh.

"I...I..." Sho breathed, trembling.

Nao looked at him intently. "Yes?"

"He's...he's..."

After a while of more stuttering, he finally spilled the address.

Nao nodded, satisfied. He let go of Sho's collar and the latter immediately let out a sigh of relief as he believed this madness was finally over. But it wouldn't be that easy for him.

Nao didn't forget what kind of anguish Sho had inflicted on him, Takeo, and others. His constant beatings, derogatory insults, relentless harassment, and the sick joy he felt along with it.

Nao didn't forget a single punch this bastard had thrown at them, every single insult he had spat. And now he was already whining solely because of a few punches when his victims had to tolerate much worse than that!?

He deserved more pain than this, didn't he?

Calmly, Nao grabbed the brick he had put down. He gripped Sho's right arm, almost tranquilly, and pressed it down onto the ground.

Sho's breath hitched. He tried crawling away, but his attacker held him firmly in place. Like a fish on land, he wiggled and tried to extract himself from Nao's clutches.

"What…what are you doing, Miyamoto? I told you what you wanted to know! Isn't that enough… Do you…do you want me to apologise? If that's what you want…then I'm sorry… I'm sorry… I really didn't mean it back then… It-it was just silly jokes… I'm sorry…"

Nao nearly burst into laughter. Suddenly, the big Sho turned into a small, pathetic shrimp in the face of being the inferior one for once.

Nao huffed. As if anything of what that bastard said could hold an ounce of truth.

He pinned his arm to the ground and raised the brick into the air.

Nao glanced at Sho, who gaped at him with horror-filled eyes. "Think of me the next time you try to hurt someone with this hand." He swung the brick downward.

Sho broke into a sharp, bloodcurdling scream. A few of the students, who were watching them in shock, also screamed as the brick smashed his hand.

The pig on the slaughtering block writhed in pain. Its limbs curled inward, its muscles spasmed, and its face distorted in anguish.

Nao didn't care. He just wanted this bastard to never touch another human being again.

He hit it again, and again, and again. With every hit, the pig and the audience were screaming. The choir of pain and terror was almost too gruesome. If Nao had been in his right mind, he would have clasped his ears to avoid having to listen to these sounds of horror that would certainly haunt every human being to ever hear it. But as his mind was ragged by fear, anger and desperation, he didn't realise any of this.

He could only think about the pain this lunatic had inflicted on him and Takeo.

It felt like an eternity, but eventually there was nothing left to smash. On the ground, somehow still connected to the wrist, was a puddle of bones and flesh.

Finally, Nao straightened up and wiped the sweat off his forehead.

Sho was weeping in pain. His face was torn in agony and thick tears rolled down his bloody face. Feeble whimpers and sobs crawled out of his throat, and he didn't even have the strength left to sit back up.

Like a shrimp, he lay on the floor—just as unthreatening, just as powerless.

With heavy breaths, Nao stood up. He held the blood-coated brick in his hand, his own front and face were peppered with the splatters of Sho's blood.

In exhaustion, he staggered a bit. He exhaled deeply and looked around to see twenty frightened faces staring at him.

He didn't care.

As if controlled by some external force, he just turned around and left.

Leaving all of the mess he had made behind, he was now heading toward the address Sho had given him.

Nao panted heavily.

Next up was Katsu.

— Chapter 31 —

Nao reached his destination in less than thirty minutes.

He arrived at an old, desolate building which appeared to have once been some kind of small warehouse.

The streets were littered with trash, the crumbling walls had been vandalised with graffiti, and all of the metallic doors were covered in a crust of brown rust.

This was Katsu's hideout.

As expected, it was an area devoid of people. Nao thought this was perfect.

Whatever was about to happen, it was probably best if there were no witnesses around.

Nao went inside; the brick, clutched tightly in his fist, was now coloured crimson.

He entered a large hall. The overhead windows were cracked and grey rays of sunlight slanted through the dirty glass. Rubble and stones were strewn everywhere; with every step, Nao stirred up clouds of dust.

A few men stood at the side of the hall, watching Nao with grim faces, but none of them made a move to stop him, so he just went on.

Nao crossed the hall, and through an uneven hole in the wall, which seemed to once have held a door, he reached the next room. It was a hall nearly as large as the one before.

But instead of another passage leading to the next room at the end, there was a big stone slab flat on the ground. It was about a meter in height and almost looked like some kind of stage. On top of it stood a seat made of cartons and stones. Even though it was built from rubble and trash, it still had a dignified, reverent aura. Almost like a throne.

And on top of that throne sat a young man. One leg crossed above the other and his chin propped up on his hand, as though deeply bored, he gazed at the boy entering his kingdom.

Wearing his blond hair like a crown, he looked down at the pawn approaching him with relentless strides.

Just like in the room before, there were henchmen standing on each side of the hall, glaring at the intruder with dark stares. Yet they didn't move a single millimeter as Nao approached Katsu.

He halted a few meters in front of him.

Through his lashes, he glowered up at him.

"Where is he?" Nao asked. His voice echoed across the big hall. It bounced from stone to stone; metallic and hard.

Katsu eyed the intruder for a few seconds and suddenly broke into a wide smile. "Miyamoto, my friend!" he exclaimed excitedly, his eyes glinting with sick anticipation. "I already expected you. It took you longer to get to me than I thought. But I can tell from the blood on your clothes that you used some fun techniques to find me," he chuckled, amused.

Nao gripped the blood-coated brick in his hand harder. "It's the blood of your brother."

Katsu's maniacal smile grew even wider. "Really? I could've expected that moron wouldn't even be able to fight you off. What a disappointment." He kept chuckling.

"You're here to look for your friend, am I right? So sad you couldn't join us a few days ago."

Nao's breath hitched. He ground his teeth. "Where is he?" he asked again. "What have you done to him?"

Katsu shrugged dismissively. "That's a business secret. I can't tell you, sorry."

Finally, Nao snapped and ran forward, grabbing Katsu by the collar of his shirt. Menacingly, he raised the brick above his head. In an instant, all of the henchmen in the hall tried to move and seize the intruder, but Katsu stopped them with a wave of his hand.

"Don't bother." He grinned. "This is just about to get fun."

Nao glowered at the man beneath him. The hellfire in his chest was flaring up and engulfed him wholly.

"Where is he!?" he screamed. "Where is Takeo!?"

Katsu didn't answer. He just kept staring at his attacker with those sick eyes of his, grinning and jeering.

Nao took a few heavy breaths, then let the brick fall out of his hand. With bare fists, he started bashing Katsu's face just as he had done with his brother. Yet it was different this time.

With every punch, Katsu just let out laughter. As his head was whipped from side to side and blood gushed out of his nose, he laughed. A cold, maniacal, *relishing* laugh.

His dark eyes glinted excitedly, like black holes revelling in sucking in any of these punches.

Even as his nose bled and tainted his teeth red, he didn't take his eyes off Nao. As though he wholeheartedly enjoyed watching him like this.

It infuriated Nao more and more. He wanted this bastard to stop smiling! He wanted him to weep and surrender.

Nao thrashed this lunatic with everything he had. *Die. Die. Die,* he repeated in his mind, but it had no effect.

Katsu just kept grinning at him, the blood on his face was making it even harder to not feel taunted by him.

After about ten hits, Nao stopped. He breathed heavily, his forehead was covered in sweat. Furiously, he glowered at his opponent. He grabbed Katsu's collar with both hands and started shaking him. "Where is he!? Where is he!? Tell me! Finally tell me, you psycho!"

Katsu snickered. Blood and saliva ran out of the corners of his mouth.

"I don't know," he said, grinning mockingly. "Wherever the current takes him, I guess."

"What does that mean!?!?"

Katsu shrugged again.

Nao was close to losing his mind. Maybe he already had. He only felt his deeply ingrained love for Takeo in his heart, along with the subsequent fear of losing him. The only one who had ever loved him, and the only one he truly loved.

His lips started trembling in despair. "What did you do to him?"

Katsu's mouth grew once again into a wide grin. "Takeo got what he deserved. He had to pay for his sins."

"HE IS INNOCENT! HE DOESN'T DESERVE ANY OF THIS!"

Katsu chuckled. "For you, maybe. But he tried to destroy my life's work twice. So I had no choice but to punish him. I wish you could've been there when he screamed in pain and tears ran down that pathetic face of his."

Nao punched him again. This time it was with such strength that Katsu was thrown off his throne.

He slumped to the ground, holding his nose with his hand, and started to laugh yet again. His whole body shook with the force of it.

Thrilled, he looked up at Nao. "But why are you only punching me, by the way? Isn't your family just as guilty?"

Nao furrowed his brows. "What do you mean?"

Katsu sat up, smiling at him with his blood-red teeth.

"Well, the only reason I didn't take you with me to punish you back then was because of your grandfather. I wasn't allowed to touch you. But Takeo, on the other hand, was free meat. Tell me, why were you under his protection, but not he? To be brutally honest with you, I would've been powerless if Takeo had been put under his protection as well.

"We wouldn't be in this situation right now if that had been the case. But look at us. You take your anger out on me when your grandfather is just as guilty as me."

Nao froze. With his fist ready to throw another punch, he stared at man on the ground.

He wasn't completely wrong. Nao had told his grandfather that both he and Takeo were victims of blackmail, but he had decided to only defend Nao. It was the same with his father. If he hadn't locked Nao in his room that night, he might have been able to find Takeo before he vanished to who knew where.

Those two, his grandfather and father, were not much better than Katsu. They might not have played an active role in how all of this had played out, but nevertheless, they were still the force in Nao's life that had always screwed him over.

Sho, Katsu, his family; weren't they all just part of his misery?

Katsu seemed to sense his internal struggle and snickered excitedly. "See? See!? I will never tell you what happened to Takeo. But maybe you can ask your granddaddy to find him for you." He cackled. "After all, he's just as ruthless and calculating as me."

"Sh…shut up!" Nao pressed out between gritted teeth. "Shut up!"

Katsu burst into loud laughter once again as he watched Nao turn around and leave, heavy silence burdening his every step. Nao exited the building, those crazed laughs haunting him all the way.

Katsu would never talk—he enjoyed Nao's despair far too much. Nao realised this now. As long as he could make other people suffer, Katsu would accept his own suffering as well.

It was just too thrilling for him to see someone be unwound bit by bit, until flesh and bones were bare and raw, worn down by despair and fear, ready to be devoured by merciless teeth. It was a spectacle for a predator like him, and as long as he viewed the other as entertainment, there was no chance to get him to concede. It was thus a hopeless feat.

Until he could find another method to get Katsu to talk, Nao had to try something else. And unfortunately, Katsu was right.

If there was one person who had the connections to find Takeo, it was his grandfather.

He was one of the reasons why all of this had spiralled so irrevocably out of control, and now he owed Nao for the trouble he had caused.

There was nothing in this world Nao feared more than the thought of losing Takeo, not even his grandfather or father. Now he would make them obey him, whatever it took.

Nao knew exactly where to find them.

Every Friday, those two lunched together in one of the fancy restaurants his family liked to visit. It was already noon, and Nao figured he'd find his grandfather and father at their favourite lunch spot.

With the blood-crusted brick in hand, Nao entered the tall building. He took the elevator up to the restaurant. As the doors slid apart, he was greeted with the view of a waitress behind a counter, ready to greet the next guest. Her delicate face was already lifted into a pretty smile, her eyes formed into welcoming crescents. But as soon as she saw the figure of a savage young boy appear in the doorway, face and school uniform splattered with blood, her face swiftly blanched. Aghast, she stared at the stranger. And shock turned into fear as her eyes fell on the brick tainted with blood in his hand.

Nao didn't spare her a single glance. With the adamancy of a soldier before battle, he walked past her. When she watched the horrifying student stain the clean and pristine ambience, something inside her seemed to click. Despite her initial fear, she followed after him.

"Sir, excuse me, sir!" she exclaimed meekly. "Sir, you, you can't just enter. Please, stop."

As if Nao would listen to her. Unyielding, he continued his search throughout the restaurant. He started tearing open doors, checking if his grandfather and father were inside. The moment the doors were yanked open and the ice-cold face of the bloodied student appeared, the guests either screamed in shock or just stared at him, paralysed.

The waitress stopped her futile pursuit after a while and went back to call for backup. Nao didn't care. He only saw his family's faces in front of him, like targets on a firing range.

And finally, as he opened a door close to the end of the hall, he found himself face to face with those two disgustingly similar faces.

With widened eyes, his grandfather and father stared at him as they suddenly saw their grandchild and son in the doorway. This wild, dirty boy stood out so violently against the elegance of the restaurant, it almost looked like someone had spawned him there. As if he were a glitch in their ignorant reality.

For a few seconds, the three of them stared at each other. Two pairs of eyes in utter disbelief, the third pair blazing with cold hate.

After a moment of silence, Nao finally began moving. He stalked forward, and with a swing of his arm, he threw the brick onto the glass table in the middle of the room.

With an ear-splitting, gruesome sound, the table broke into thousands of pieces of sharp, cold glass.

Twinkling shards scattered all over the floor, food was spilled, and plates broke into large pieces of porcelain. It looked like a field of frosty snow where a battle between two vicious armies had taken place. Blood and corpses were strewn across the cold landscape.

Nao panted heavily, and with crazed eyes, he looked up. He had never seen the expressions on either of his victims' faces. It was pure shock mingled with a hint of fear.

It satisfied Nao deep within his soul.

He reached out and grabbed his grandfather by his collar. He clutched the fabric with both hands and pulled him up. Relentless and unyielding, he stared straight into his steel-hard eyes, witnessing them waver for the first time in his life.

"It's your fault! You're the reason they took him with them!" Nao growled, holding his grandfather so tight his knuckles turned white.

"What are you talking about?" Ikuto Miyamoto asked. It was apparent that he tried to keep his cool. His voice was as firm and cold as always, but the expression on his face couldn't lie. The shock was clearly written all over it. His eyes were round, the pupils shrunken to the heads of needles, his mouth twisted in discomfort.

He took a few heavy breaths.

"Nao. Whatever it is, let me go and talk to me like a person. You will regret—"

Ikuto Miyamoto was shut up by a fist knocking his head to the side.

Nao's knuckles burned, his shoulder ached, and his heart felt like it was going to jump out of his chest, yet he felt strangely good. Seeing the swelling emerge on his grandfather's face and watching his eyes dart frantically around gave him courage.

Behind him, his father had risen in shock. He tried to move forward to seize his son, but Nao had expected it. With fiery viciousness, he whirled around and screamed, "SIT BACK DOWN!"

Nao had never spoken like that, and he had never shown such fiery emotion before. It was like seeing a whole new person in front of them, and it was precisely this shock that actually persuaded Tsuyoshi Miyamoto to slowly sink back down. His face pale and lips tight, he stared at his son, who, in this moment, looked nothing like the silent, brooding boy he had raised.

Well, that wasn't entirely true. The truth was that the one he saw before him was the result of his upbringing. Full of hatred and despair, eaten alive by hellfire and ice, he was unleashing all those years of suffering. Nao had felt everything. Their hate, disgust, resentment, indifference, frustration, anger, rage, disappointment; all of the feelings they had directed at him.

And he had always swallowed them down.

It'd been okay, because what did Nao have to prove? He didn't believe in himself either, he had no goal or ambition he could chase to prove them wrong. He was nothing and he had learned to live like nothing. There was not a thing worth fighting for in his life anyway.

But that had changed. Now this person had appeared in his life, someone who looked at him with sincere fondness, devotion, affection, admiration, and, most of all, love in their eyes. For this person, he was *something*. He felt *something*.

Suddenly, there was someone worth going on for. Worth dreaming for.

And at once, everything he had swallowed down in those years was churning in his stomach like fire. Nao still couldn't believe in himself, but he believed in his future. He believed in Takeo.

They were a purpose worth fighting for, a dream worth breaking for.

Nao would do anything, *anything*, to keep them together.

He glowered at his grandfather, whose face was swelling up. "Takeo Iwasaki," he said. "Find him! It's your fault he went missing! So pay off your debt and *find him!*"

"Takeo Iwasaki…? Who…is that?"

Nao punched him again. "YOU DON'T EVEN REMEMBER HIS NAME!?" he screamed.

His grandfather grunted in pain, cupping his aching cheek with one hand. "How can I remember such an unimportant nuisance's name?"

This was too much. Nao burst.

He grabbed his grandfather's thinning hair and yanked his head down against the armrest of his chair. With a loud, uncanny *thud*, his skull hit the metal, and as his head resurfaced, there was a thin stream of blood trickling from his forehead.

"*HE IS THE BOY I LOVE!*" Nao screamed with his whole chest. He wanted to throw another punch, but his wrist was caught in the air. When he turned around, he saw his father's eyes glowering at him. "Stop it," Tsuyoshi Miyamoto said.

Nao tried to wrestle himself free from his grip. When he noticed it was pointless, he threw his other fist in his father's stomach. Reflexively, he released him, and Nao immediately spun back around to his grandfather.

He grabbed him again and started shaking his petrified body. "You have to find him! You have to find him! Give him back to me! Give him back to me!" he bellowed and screamed. His throat burned like it was about to be torn apart from the strain, and his lungs felt as though they were going to collapse.

Still, Nao would have continued this for as long as it took.

He wanted Takeo. He wanted him back. He had been missing for three days, and there was nothing he yearned for more than to finally have him in his arms again.

Nao would have fought anyone to achieve his goal, take on and destroy everyone who dared block his path—yet he still couldn't keep up with the security men pressing him to the ground.

Two of them had entered the room and taken him down in an instant. They seized him and wrestled him to the ground, pinning both of his arms behind his back.

Nao screamed and fought like his life depended on it, but he was nevertheless far inferior in strength.

As he was taken away, both his father and grandfather looked at him like they had never seen such a ferocious beast before.

They were right. Nao was a beast. But he had only become like this because he believed this was the sole way he could save the only being he loved.

The cold of the floor seeped through Nao's clothes.

His joints hurt and his body shivered. He could grab one of the rubber mats or a thin, old blanket to ease his struggles, but no matter how much he wanted to, he couldn't move.

With his legs drawn to his chest and his arms wrapped around his knees, he sat in the small holding cell at the local police station. He leaned against a pile of green rubber mats and stared apathetically at the grey, cold stone tiles.

Outside the cell were a bunch of police officers running around and chatting. He could've watched them through the bars of the cell, but Nao had no interest in doing so.

He just cowered on the ground and waited for time to pass by.

After the security guards had restrained him, the restaurant called the police, and thus Nao had been brought here.

It had been many, many hours since his arrest and yet no one had come to pick him up. Nao wasn't surprised. In fact, he was sure that his father had asked the police station to keep him locked up as long as possible. They surely didn't want to see his face right now, and Nao didn't want to see theirs either.

An hour after being arrested, a police officer asked him if he wanted to make a call, but Nao declined. Who should he call anyway? His family was glad to have this maniac locked up!

Despite what everyone would tell him, Nao didn't regret what he had done. He had always been the one to receive, now, for once, he had been the one to give.

He didn't regret it. And he would do it again if it meant finally getting Takeo back.

As Nao had expected, they kept him for a long time. Night fell and he was still in the cell.

The police officers gave him something to eat and to drink and let him out to use the restroom.

He eyed his own gory face in the mirror. Splatters of blood were still all over his face, and a pair of hollow, weary eyes gawked back at him in the reflection.

He was neither shocked nor aghast by his own reflection. Just empty.

Nao washed his face in the small sink. He rubbed the blood off his skin.

His knuckles were bruised from all the strain they had taken that day. Layers of different blood had piled up on the thin skin, and beneath all of them was his own. The skin had ripped open and left him with bruised hands. He barely felt the pain.

When he was brought back to the cell, he neither ate nor drank. He sank back against the wall and watched the clock turn.

The night passed and morning dawned. Around seven, new officers bustled in, and with every passing clock hand, the station grew more and more crowded.

Even though he could watch the flow of time, it still felt like he had lost all sense of it. As the morning passed slowly, it was like time had moved too fast and not at all.

Was it already the fourth day after Takeo's disappearance? Hadn't he just kissed and held him four days ago and talked about a future that both of them wanted to make come true?

It felt as though with every minute Takeo was drifting further away from him, but also as if his lips and hands had never left his.

Who knew, maybe the police had already found a new trace of him? Maybe he was already back home with his brother? Nao pondered whether he should ask an officer to let him make a call. Then he could call Mamoru and ask him himself.

But just as Nao made up his mind, a shadow appeared outside the iron bars.

Slowly, Nao lifted his head and met the eyes of the familiar person.

The wounds from yesterday's mayhem were still very apparent on his face. The left side was swollen and blue, on his forehead was a band-aid covering a bloody bruise. Yet his eyes had returned to their old superiority and coldness.

With obvious disgust, Ikuto Miyamoto scrutinised his grandson.

"I have always expected you would end up in one of these one day," he said, his voice thick with repulsion and discontent.

Nao didn't reply. He just stared squarely back, as though he was looking at a block of stone.

"This time you will have to stand up for your actions. You just got sued for mutilating a student's hand at school."

"He deserved it," Nao replied quietly.

"And you deserve this too." Ikuto Miyamoto pulled a picture from the inside of his jacket. "Takeo Iwasaki was found last night...or rather what is left of him."

Instantly, Nao tried to jump up. But due to his prolonged time on the ground, his joints had become stiff, and his muscles had fallen asleep. He fell forward onto the cold floor before arduously managing to crawl up with his hands and knees. He ran toward the bars and stared at his grandfather with huge eyes. "What do you mean!?"

Wordlessly, he gave him the picture. Nao yanked it out of his hand and looked at it.

It was the image of a riverside, grass and stones enclosing a shore where dark water rolled onto the land. Between the river and the stones lay two items washed up by the current.

One was a grey sweater jacket, crumpled and drenched; the other was a single shoe, a sneaker with purple shoelaces.

For a while, Nao stared at the picture, then looked back up at his grandfather, his brows furrowed. "This doesn't mean anything!"

"They did a DNA test with the DNA remnants found on the clothing and matched it to Takeo Iwasaki. His brother also confirmed that both of these items belonged to him and were worn the last time he had seen him."

"But...but...it still doesn't mean anything! He might have just lost them."

"They didn't find a body, but this boy will be pronounced dead very soon. Since he has been missing and comes from a difficult background, the police will sign it off as suicide."

"What!? No! NO! Katsu...Katsu hurt him! I-it was Katsu's fault!"

"Who cares," Ikuto Miyamoto countered bluntly. "Takeo Iwasaki is a criminal with a very bleak record. He's small fry from a poor family. No one cares to investigate him. The faster the case can be closed, the better."

"No! No! No! NO! NO!" Nao shook his head violently. "He is not dead! He did not commit suicide! Katsu has him somewhere locked up! Or he is very badly hurt!"

Nao didn't want to believe it. He couldn't believe it. Katsu wouldn't have... he wouldn't have...

Suddenly, Nao remembered what he had said to him yesterday when he had asked him about Takeo's whereabouts.

I don't know. Wherever the current takes him, I guess.

No, no, no, no, no, no, no, no, no, no, no, no, no, no, no, no, no, no, no, no, no, no, no, no, no, no, no, no, no, no, no, no, no, no, no, no, no, no, no, no, no, no, no, no, no, no, no, no, no, no, no, no, no, no, no, no, no, no, no, no, no, no, no, no, no, no, no, no, no, no, no, no, no, no, no, no, no, no, no, no, no, no, no, no no, no, no, no, no, no, no, no, no, no, no, no, no, no, no, no, no, no, no, no, no, no, no, no, no, no, no, no, no, no, no, no, no, no, no, no, no, no, no, no, no, no, no, no, no, no, no, no, no, no, no.

Nao fell to the ground. He clutched his head, shaking it like a madman. "No! No! No! No!" he screamed. "That's not it! This is not real!"

His grandfather watched him with displeased eyes. "Think whatever you want, but Takeo Iwasaki is a dead man." He crossed his arms. "Get a grip on yourself. Your so called "love" is over. I hope you can now finally forget about this perverted affection of yours and start living properly."

Nao sat on the ground. His world was spinning. It was falling apart and he was falling with it.

Takeo was not dead. He wasn't dead. He couldn't be dead. Takeo was alive. He was still there.

His grandfather scoffed. He regarded him with a loathing gaze, and said, "I'll get you out once you have calmed down." before walking off.

Nao was left alone. Not only here. It felt like he had been left all alone in this world.

It was not true! It was not true! *It was not fucking true!*

He started rocking back and forth, clutching his head and whimpering.

It was not true! It was not true! It was not true.

— Chapter 32 —

They say grief comes in five stages.

For Nao, it was just one.

Denial.

He tried to tell the world the truth. He tried to make himself heard and have the real offender pay.

But very soon, he had to realise that this wasn't about true or false. They just didn't care.

Nao could have come bursting in with a handwritten confession from the true offender, and even then, it was not clear whether they would have listened to him.

For the police, for everyone else, the case was closed.

Takeo Iwasaki was pronounced dead, even with his body never found. They said it must still be drifting out there somewhere. The currents in the river that claimed his body were too fierce, and it was likely his remains would forever be lost in them. Forever torn between the currents, forever freezing in the opaque dark, until there would be no remains left.

Nao still didn't believe it. He just couldn't believe it.

If he did, then he had to forcibly accept it. And acceptance meant it became reality.

And he could not bear a reality in which Takeo was no more.

It would mean that he really was left all alone in this world. That between all those stars in the sky, the only one that mattered was gone.

After that fateful day, when Nao had lost his mind, he was now met with the consequences.

The case of him mutilating another student's hand to the point where it could not be fully reconstructed was seen as especially grave. Almost instantly, he was expelled from school. Which was a real achievement, considering most students attending it were previous offenders that had been kicked out from other schools before. Being expelled from a school that normally took in unwanted trash was a truly remarkable feat in itself.

Hence, Nao was sued by the Nishimura family. They sued him for grievous bodily harm.

Honestly, Nao didn't really care. The opposite: when he saw Sho's battered face and his heavily bandaged hand, he just thought how unfortunate it was that he didn't get to ruin his left hand as well.

Since he had no plan of denying his actions or showing remorse, he was close to receiving time in juvenile detention. It was only because of his grandfather's pulling of a few strings behind the scenes that Nao didn't. Of course, someone carrying the name of the Miyamoto family couldn't be sent to jail! What a disgrace that would be...

Instead, Nao was penalised with probation, a hefty fine, and anger management training.

After getting expelled and punished by the law, no other school wanted to take him in.

For a while, there was a lot of discussion in his family about what to do with him now—he was a dog that had bitten a child, and now they had to decide whether it was worth saving or not.

Nao didn't know either whether he should be saved or euthanised. He didn't really care, to be honest. Since all of it had taken place, he pretty much lived like a dead dog anyway.

Eventually, they forged a decision, and thus Nao was home-schooled for his last year of high school.

From Monday to Friday, he was taught at home. On Thursdays and Saturdays, he was sent to a therapist for the court-mandated anger management training.

It was just as boring as it was useless.

The therapist asked him why he had decided to hurt his schoolmate's hand.

And Nao firmly replied that he deserved it.

She then asked what made him deserve it.

And Nao responded that he had hurt so many people with this hand it was only fair to inflict the same pain on him.

She asked why Nao thought he was eligible to decide another person's punishment and not the law.

And Nao replied that if the law were eligible itself, they wouldn't have come into this situation at all, because then the true offenders would have been caught a long, long time ago before any of it could have escalated like this.

Nao was treated for anger issues, but since all of it had happened, he didn't feel any anger at all.

He just felt hollowed out.

His heart had been torn out, and along with it his ability to fight.

There was one time when the sadness and hollowness had swallowed him up. His limbs and torso had been scraped clean and someone had poured all of the misery and despair of the world into him. He was a walking mould of anguish.

Back then, not long after the news, Nao had ventured to the beach he and Takeo had visited before.

The waves were towering up; walls of water clashed and shattered into each other, as if they were just as upset as Nao about the state of the world.

He looked across the turbulent sea, tears falling down his face. And he couldn't take it anymore.

Nao's heart was breaking anew every second and his soul felt like it had been ripped apart in a futile attempt to reach Takeo's soul with a piece of his. But it only showed him that he was really left all alone in this frightening world.

All his sadness and despair welled up inside of him, and with a tear-stricken throat, he screamed, "TAKEO! …I…I HATE YOU! I HATE YOU! I HATE YOU! How… HOW COULD YOU DO THIS TO ME!? HOW COULD YOU LEAVE ME!" The tears streamed down his ashen face. "WHY DID YOU LOVE ME ONLY TO LEAVE ME! HOW COULD YOU DO THIS!? THIS IS NOT FAIR! …YOU'RE SO CRUEL! DO YOU HEAR THIS!? YOU ARE SO CRUEL!"

Sobs shook his body and his legs went weak.

He fell to his knees, feeling the cold, wet sand beneath his hands. The taste of his own tears and snot mixed in his mouth as he was shaken by cries.

His weeping was carried across the ocean. The waves temporarily calmed down, and in gentle thrusts, they rolled onto the beach. It was almost as if they tried to comfort the bawling boy.

But there was nothing in this world that could have eased his pain.

Takeo was gone. The light had left his life.

What was left of Nao was less than a shadow.

As he kneeled before the vast sea, the waves listening to his grief and the wind caressing his face, he realised that Takeo really was gone. And no matter how much he had dreamed and talked of the future, with his vibrant eyes beaming and his soft lips smiling, it had become nothing more than an imagination. A future that would never be lived by the boy who had been so excited for it.

Nao clutched the cold sand with his fists. "Takeo… You…you haven't even traveled the country yet! We haven't been to Okinawa yet! Did you just forget about that!? Did you leave your dreams behind?" Nao wildly shook his head. "Why? Why? Why did you have to leave me!? Why am I all alone again…?"

That day, he had asked the sea a lot of questions. But no one answered them for him.

Nao had to leave with his heart even emptier than before and a soul incomplete.

Somehow life still progressed. The sun still rose and sank, and weeks and months went past.

How Nao proceeded to live, he didn't know either.

He lived. Yet he didn't.

He ate. He drank. He slept. He moved. But it was merely more than automatic motions.

There was no purpose behind his movements. No particular reason.

He moved because that was what a body did. If it hadn't been for this body and its deeply rooted desire to survive, he wouldn't have moved at all.

He might have become a statue—stiff and cold like stone. Curled up on the ground until his last breath had been taken. But somehow he still kept on living.

He didn't know how and why. But he guessed there was still some part of him that didn't want to die.

Thus, his existence in this world continued as half.

Half a will to live. Half a soul.

It was worse than anything he had ever endured before in his life.

Like a heavy breath, winter came. The year was irrevocably and irresistibly coming to an end.

Nao was still being homeschooled and his therapy sessions had finally been concluded. All while the world outside was growing darker and colder.

The first snowfall arrived and smothered the earth in a blanket of cold, thick snow.

The weather only worsened his condition. On one deep December night, he had broken down in the snow. His muscles stopped moving, and like a puppet, he fell into the dense, icy frost. Yet he had no intention of getting up again.

While lying there, snowflakes flurrying through the air and kissing the earth, the snow was seeping through his clothes and the cold gnawed at his skin. He stared up into the dark sky while slowly letting himself be buried beneath a new layer of ice.

He became one with the earth and was gradually losing himself in the night. When all of a sudden there was the crunching of hurried footsteps trudging through the snow. The sound of them echoed in the hollow night and was muffled by the frost.

Hurried, they came closer, and at once, there was the silhouette of a person outlined against the black of the sky above Nao. A boy wrapped in a thick winter jacket, warm boots, and a blue beanie looked down at him. He stared with furrowed brows and sorrow-filled eyes. His cheeks and nose were all pink from the cold.

"Nao! What are you doing here?" the boy asked, his thin voice thick with worry. "I've seen you from across the street. Why are you lying in the snow? You're going to freeze!"

He held a winter jacket in his arms. But when Nao didn't answer or make any motion to get up, he placed the jacket over his unmoving body. Toyo wrapped his brother in, and then sat next to him in the snow. He sighed and a cloud of white smoke left his mouth.

"If you won't come in, I'll just sit next to you," he said, drawing his legs to his chest and gazing into the dark.

For a while, they sat in silence. Snow was still falling around them. All sounds were muffled by the thick, unrelenting ice, and so the night was eerily quiet. One could hear every breath in the atmosphere and every swaying branch of the bleak trees.

Toyo started trembling. He was obviously freezing, but he stayed alongside his brother.

After a while, he spoke first. "Aren't…aren't you getting cold? You've been out here for a while. What if you get sick?" His words were spoken with so much sorrow and compassion, yet Nao didn't answer. He was still staring at the dark sky, snowflakes flurrying in and out of his vision.

Toyo didn't give up, however. With a voice as soft as the fresh snow and as good-hearted as a child, he continued. Every word was spoken with much sincerity.

"It's really difficult…isn't it? You must be suffering a lot…" He took a silent breath. "I have never talked to him…but he must have been a really good person. For a brief while, I could see that you were happier. You seemed a lot lighter and much more at ease. It felt like I could suddenly see the true version of you— not the one our family made of you, but the one you truly are. I'm sure it must have been because of him… You liked him a lot, didn't you?"

"I love him."

The words hung in the air like heavy rain clouds. As soon as Nao spoke them, they wafted in the air above them and pushed down.

Toyo gazed into the night sky. "I'm sorry that it ended this way. But please, take care of yourself as well. Here's still someone who cares about you."

With these words, silence fell between them once again. Nao let himself be buried by the winter snow and Toyo stayed beside him. He didn't leave his side the whole night.

Ultimately, the year came to an end.

Just like that, 19 turned into 20.

The twenty-first century.

People were exhilarated about it. A new millennium.

They called it a new start—a book full of unwritten pages and new hopes. But for Nao, it was the end of that book. The pages were written, the ink set. No matter how often he tried to turn over the last page, the ending never changed.

And it always hurt the same.

The sun still rose, just as it still sank. The circle of day and night continued, and so did life.

But even so, Nao couldn't stop.

All the time, he asked himself what it would have been like.

Us in the twenty-first century.

Nao Miyamoto died four years later. During a car ride with a fellow university student, the driver lost control of the vehicle due to excessive rain and darkness.

Subsequently, the car crashed into the guardrail—everyone inside died instantly. The ambulance couldn't arrive in time.

It was a futile and pointless death. Just like the life Nao had lived after losing the love of his life.

It could hardly have been called a life anyway. Beneath the clutches of his family and his past, he had lived senselessly from day to day. Following orders he didn't care about.

His life had been miserable since those fateful days four years ago. And as his heart had been torn out, he could never get over what had happened. He had never fallen in love again, he had never kissed anyone again, and he had never slept with anyone again.

He lived day to day, thinking about the one he had lost.

After Nao's death, his family arranged a small memorial service. His body was incinerated and his ashes laid to rest. He received flowers, but none of them were signed with his grandparents' names. They didn't show up to his funeral either.

It must sound like a tragic life and a tragic death; which in itself was the truth.

But maybe it was a blessing in disguise. Because who knows, he might reunite with his love in their next lives. After all, their souls never stopped searching for one another.

The End